PRAISE FOR MATT DUNN

'Funny, warm, honest . . .'

—Jenny Colgan

'Matt Dunn is officially funny.'

—Jojo Moyes

'Matt Dunn's writing makes you laugh out loud.'

—Sophie Kinsella

'Wonderful . . . Will make every lunch break feel like a mini-break with your favourite friends.'

—Chrissie Manby

'This is Matt Dunn at the top of his game. Funny, poignant, and big-hearted . . .'

—Mike Gayle

'Sharp and witty . . . I loved it.'

—Milly Johnson

THEN I MET YOU

ALSO BY MATT DUNN

Best Man
The Ex-Boyfriend's Handbook
From Here to Paternity
Ex-Girlfriends United
The Good Bride Guide
The Accidental Proposal
A Day at the Office
What Might Have Been
Home
A Christmas Day at the Office
13 Dates
At the Wedding

THEN I MET Y⦿U

MATT DUNN

LAKE UNION
PUBLISHING

Text copyright © 2019 by Matt Dunn

Published by Lake Union Publishing, Seattle

www.apub.com

Amazon, the Amazon logo, and Lake Union Publishing are trademarks of Amazon.com, Inc., or its affiliates.

ISBN-13: 9781477823453
ISBN-10: 147782345X

Cover design by Ghost Design

Printed in the United States of America

To Sanj.
Too Soon.

Chapter 1

Simon Martin stood in the middle of Primark and frowned at his phone. 'What do you mean, "what are you wearing"?' he said, exasperated. 'What's *that* got to do with anything?'

'Just, you know . . .' On the other end of the line, Will hesitated, and Simon rolled his eyes. Will was his best friend, but sometimes he could be a little . . . well, 'superficial' often summed him up. Though, right now, 'weird' was perhaps a bit more appropriate. 'Your clothes?'

'Huh?'

'Because the restaurant's quite cool.'

'Cool,' Simon said, tensing up a little at the mention of the c-word, though mainly because it didn't apply to him. He'd been to a few 'cool' places with Will before, back when they'd shared a flat in London – typically dimly lit establishments that made you sit on uncomfortable wooden benches while you squinted at menus that never seemed to feature the pound sign or more than one figure after the decimal point, as if you were supposed to regard '16.5' for a burger as some sort of secret code for quality, rather than being pretentious . . . not to mention ridiculously expensive. 'It's a street food restaurant. And in Margate. How "cool" can it be?'

'Even so, it's street food, not roadkill. So make a bit of an effort.'

Simon checked his watch. He had half an hour before he was due to meet Will for lunch – not quite long enough to go home and change . . . Then again, he *was* in Primark. He could probably *buy* 'cool' and still have change from a twenty-pound note. Though given how busy it was, being half past twelve on a Saturday, and with the queue for the changing rooms stretching almost to the door, perhaps going home was the better option.

'I'm sure it's hardly The Ritz.'

'Maybe not. But I'm reviewing it for the *Gazette*. Which means I can't turn up with someone who looks like . . .'

Will's voice trailed off, and Simon found himself bristling a little. 'Someone who looks like *what*, exactly?'

'Like they don't care,' Will said, and Simon sighed. It wasn't that he didn't care. It was quite the opposite, actually. Why did Will find that so hard to understand?

'Will, I . . . I just . . .' Simon stopped talking. He knew precisely why Will found it so hard to understand. Because Simon found it so hard to tell him.

'Si, I just want you to be happy. After all, it's been, what . . . ?'

'Two years,' said Simon, quietly.

'Exactly!' said Will.

'Well, not *exactly* two years . . .'

'That's not what I meant, and you know it.'

Simon stood to one side to let a shop assistant carrying a huge armful of jumpers past, then moved back sharply as her equally laden colleague came at him from the opposite direction. 'Will, I appreciate you tiptoeing around this, but can't we just have a nice lunch without the constant undertone of me needing to – what was it – "get back in the saddle"?'

'Of *course* we can,' said Will, sounding sympathetic. 'No worries. I won't even mention it.'

'Good. Thanks.'

'Although . . .'

'Although?'

'You kind of *do* need to.'

Simon could hear the italics, and he sighed even louder. 'And I will, Will. When I'm ready.'

'Great. And, um, when is that going to be?'

'Soon. I promise.'

'Brilliant!' Will hesitated, then took a deep breath, and Simon braced himself for what he suspected was imminent. 'Because Alice isn't coming back, you know?'

At the sound of his ex-girlfriend's name, Simon winced. 'I know, Will. I just . . .'

'So you need to move on, buddy.'

'I *have* moved on.'

'You've moved house. That's not the same thing.'

'It's . . . a start.'

'And you're not getting any younger.'

'I'm thirty-one. That's hardly old.'

'You want kids, right?'

Will sounded like he was in danger of getting on a roll, and while Simon appreciated where it was coming from, this wasn't a conversation he wanted to have right now. Or any time, for that matter. But especially not in the middle of Primark.

'You'll have to at least buy me lunch first,' he said, trying to deflect his friend with a joke, and Will laughed.

'Good one!' he said, then his voice took on a serious tone again. 'All I'm saying is, if you do want them, first of all you've got to meet someone, then after a while you move in together, after that you get married . . . These things all take time. And if you aren't doing anything about the first one, simply because you're holding on to something that . . .'

'Okay, okay.' Simon anxiously ran his free hand through his hair. 'Jeans and a sweatshirt, to answer your original question,' he said, in an attempt to change the subject.

'Smart ones?'

Simon looked down at his outfit, suspecting Will might look down *on* it. Not exactly dad jeans, but not quite Will's turned-up-at-the-ankle, skinny-fit selvedge denim either, and an old, dark grey sweatshirt that had possibly begun life as a black one – Simon couldn't remember. 'Smart-ish.'

'Fine,' said Will, though the tone of his voice suggested it wasn't. 'And don't be late.'

'I never am!'

'Because the restaurant gets busy. What with it being new, and Saturday lunchtime.'

'Haven't you booked?'

'You can't. But I'll meet you on the long table in front of the food truck.'

'There's a *food truck*?'

'At the opposite end to the entrance. You can't miss it, on account of it being, you know, a truck. And if you're there first, grab the seat in the middle.'

Simon let out a short laugh. 'Yes, sir!' he said. Will had asked him to lunch a week ago, and for some reason had been calling him almost every day since then to confirm. 'Is Jess coming?'

'Jess?'

'Your new girlfriend? The one you met at work? The one you keep telling me is "the one"?'

He could almost hear the cogs turning in Will's head. 'Why would she be coming?'

'Just a wild stab in the dark, but because she's your girlfriend?' said Simon. 'Not to mention the "the one" bit.'

'Oh. Of course. Ha ha. No – no women allowed! Just you and me, matey. Simon and Will. Will and Simon. Buds. Amigos.'

'You're scaring me now.'

'Plus, I never said she was "the one".'

'Oh no. Sorry. What was it? "The *current* one"?'

'Something like that,' said Will. 'Besides, she's working.'

'On a *Saturday*?'

'The *Gazette* won't write itself,' said Will, evasively. 'So – one p.m.?'

'Fine, for the millionth time. Did you want me to pick you up?'

'No!' said Will, quickly. 'You're all right.'

If only, thought Simon, as he said goodbye and ended the call.

The worst thing about it all was that Simon knew his friend was right. Alice was gone. He *did* need to move on. The trouble was, he didn't want to. Certainly not yet, anyway. And besides, he didn't have the faintest idea *how*.

He checked his watch again, then resumed his search for a coat – though so far everything he'd tried on had been too similar to the ones the hip young men who frequented the coffee shop he worked at wore: either so tight-fitting it was surprising they could even breathe, or parkas so thick and with so much fur round the hood they were more suited for a polar expedition than for the Margate seafront. On Simon, quite frankly, they looked ridiculous.

On the other hand, he couldn't quite bring himself to cross the retail park and look for something perhaps more appropriate in Marks & Spencer, fearing it was a short step from there to wearing shoes that fastened with Velcro or trousers with an elasticated waistband. But that was the trouble with being thirty-one, in that awkward 'middle' age before you were *actually* middle-aged. You didn't quite know where you belonged. A feeling Simon had had for a long time. And especially since Alice.

Disheartened, he began making his way towards the exit, then hesitated. Hanging on the end of a rail of yellow Hawaiian shirts so brightly coloured he was sure the positioning of a rack of sunglasses next to them was no accident was exactly the kind of coat he was looking for: a puffer jacket, like the black Superdry one Will owned but in navy blue, and not *so* puffy that he'd look like the Michelin Man. *And* it looked suspiciously like it might be his size. It appeared to be the last one left too, unless some other shopper had found it somewhere else in the store, brought it over to try on in front of the mirror, then – too lazy to take it back to wherever its hanger was – had simply dumped it here.

Congratulating himself on his good luck, he squeezed past a couple trying on sunglasses in front of the mirror, retrieved the coat from the end of the rail and slipped it on, pleased to find it an almost perfect fit. Between them, the couple were blocking the mirror, so he fought his way across the store until he found another one, then admired his reflection, turning one way and then the other, more than happy with his opportune find. *This* would do, and what was more – though even thinking the word left a slightly unpleasant taste in his mouth – it was almost *cool*. Simon could turn up at the restaurant in this, and Will would have no complaints. And although it might be a little warm to wear during the meal, it was all about first impressions, wasn't it? As long as it wasn't too expensive . . .

Simon almost laughed. This was Primark, and even though his job as a barista wasn't the highest-paid in the world, nothing in here was expensive. Or perhaps this didn't even cost anything *at all*, he thought, as he tried – and failed – to find a price tag.

Still wearing the coat, he strode across to where the shop assistant who'd passed him earlier was arranging the jumpers into a neat pile – a pointless task, Simon was sure, given how the shop's clientele seemed to have turned every other display into something resembling a jumble sale – and tapped her on the shoulder.

'Can you tell me how much this is, please?'

The assistant glanced down at Simon's empty hands, then frowned. 'What?'

'I said, can you tell me how much this is?'

'How much *what* is?'

'This coat.'

'Which coat?'

'This one.' Simon smoothed down the coat's front. 'I can't seem to find a price tag.'

'Right.' The assistant reached into her back pocket and produced what looked like a rubber-clad mobile phone. 'Can I see the label?'

'There isn't one. That's why I'm asking.'

'I mean the one inside. There's a bar code. I can scan it, and—'

'Oi!'

Simon almost jumped out of his skin. From the other side of the store, a man was storming towards him, his face like thunder, closely followed by an equally angry-looking woman.

'That's my coat!' The man was glaring at him, and Simon took a step backwards, nearly impaling himself on the clothes rack behind him.

'What do you mean?'

'You thick or something? That coat. It's mine. Not sure I can make it any clearer.'

The man was clearly livid, so Simon was careful not to make any sudden movements. They occasionally got bolshy customers in the coffee shop, and he knew a calm response could defuse the situation.

'I didn't see you trying it on.'

The man's eyes were bulging. 'You're the one who's bloody well trying it on, mate!'

'Listen. There's obviously been some misunderstanding here. And I'm sure they've got more of them in stock.' He turned to the shop assistant, who was looking like she'd rather go back to stacking jumpers. 'Haven't you?'

'Um . . .'

'And you're the one who's misunderstanding,' spat the man. 'That's actually *my coat*.'

'*Your* coat?'

'Took it off when I was trying some sunglasses on, didn't I?'

'What?' said Simon, again, though he was tempted to add the word 'for'.

The man was making a beckoning gesture with his hand. 'Give,' he said, though Simon was reluctant to concede just yet. The coat did fit him extremely well, and was particularly warm. Though that might not have been the only reason he was sweating right now.

'Can you, you know, *prove it*?' he asked tentatively, and the man rolled his eyes.

'It's a bloody Nike,' he said, pronouncing the make as a rhyme with 'Mike' rather than 'Mikey', and Simon was tempted to correct him – surely if it *were* his coat then he'd be able to say the name of the brand correctly. He wondered whether mentioning that he had a degree in linguistics might swing the argument his way, but decided he was more worried about the man's fist swinging towards his face.

'And?' said Simon, just as he stuck his hands defiantly into the coat's pockets, only to find what appeared to be a set of keys in one, and what felt suspiciously like a wallet in the other.

The shop assistant had raised a hand. 'We, um, don't sell Nike,' she said, and Simon's face turned a bright shade of red.

'O-kay,' he said, reluctantly slipping the coat off, and the man snatched it back from him.

'Bloody thief,' he said, and Simon's jaw dropped open.

'I'm not . . . I mean, I didn't . . .' he stammered, and the man gave him a smug smile.

'Prove it!' he said.

'Well, because . . .' He looked anxiously at the man's female companion, then at the shop assistant, both of whom seemed to be keen to hear his defence. 'Because I asked how much it was. And last I heard, thieves weren't interested in paying for things. They'd prefer to, um, *steal* them. Because that's what they, you know, do.'

The man was glaring at the shop assistant now, as if she were Simon's accomplice. 'Did he?'

'He did,' she said. 'But like I told him, we don't sell, you know . . .'

'Nike,' said Simon, taking care to overemphasise the second syllable. 'Right. Well . . .'

The man had pulled his coat back on – it didn't fit him quite as well as it had Simon, and he considered pointing that out, then decided there probably wasn't an upside to that particular conversational route. 'Sorry?' he ventured, and the man's expression softened.

'Forget it,' he said. 'Easily done, I suppose.'

As the couple headed off in the opposite direction, Simon breathed a sigh of relief and hurried out of the shop. Things like this had never happened when Alice was around – and even if they had, the two of them would probably have laughed about it. Since she'd gone, he hadn't had much to laugh about. At all.

He made a mental note not to tell Will the story later. No doubt he'd make some well-meaning but clumsy attempt to turn it into a metaphor to do with women, and Simon could only imagine where Will's 'trying on someone else's coat' analogy might lead. Probably to Simon getting punched on the nose by a jealous boyfriend. As, he suspected, had often happened to his friend.

No, he decided, this would join the ever-increasing list of things he definitely wouldn't tell Will – a list headed by how he really felt about what had happened two years ago with Alice. He'd put this incident behind him. Learn from it and move on, just like the therapist he'd been seeing back in London had advised him to do with the 'Alice' chapter of his life.

With a rueful smile, he made his way through the car park and located his car. He'd been careful to memorise *exactly* where he'd parked it, keen to avoid a repeat of the previous weekend's incident, when he'd spent ten frustrating minutes trying to get into a silver Ford Focus that had been parked three cars along from *his* silver Ford Focus, until the angry owner had appeared and proceeded to point out the error of his ways in no uncertain terms. *Forget it. Easily done*, the man had told him once they'd both realised what had happened, just like the coat owner in Primark – though Simon was beginning to worry he did that kind of thing a lot more easily than others seemed to.

Then again, maybe life just had it in for him. What happened with Alice would seem to have confirmed that.

And as for forgetting *her*?

That wasn't easily done at all.

Chapter 2

Lisa Harrod was walking purposefully past Margate clock tower, though as she neared the bus stop, where the number 52 was idling with its doors open, she had to fight the urge to break into a run and jump on. Why on earth had she agreed to this? Who even went on blind dates nowadays? What if (she narrowed her eyes as she tried to remember . . . *Simon*, that was it) Simon turned out to be a nutter, or a serial killer, or still lived at home with his mum – or, even worse than all of those, was shorter than her?

Though she knew the answer to that first question. Her dating history had been going from bad to worse, especially since Chris – her latest in a string of unsuitable boyfriends – had dumped her a couple of months ago, after the best part of a year together. What was worse, it had come out of the blue, when he'd suddenly told her he 'just wanted to have some fun', and 'wasn't ready for anything serious', which had come as a shock to Lisa, because according to the song, it was *girls* who just wanted to have fun, and being together for a year *was* serious, surely?

They'd been a *couple*. Done everything that couples did. Together. At least, when he hadn't been at the pub with his mates, or out playing five-a-side football on a Wednesday evening, or for his pub team every Sunday morning, a bored Lisa often waiting dutifully for him to finish (something that also applied to their sex life, she'd reminded herself, in an attempt to make herself feel better). But despite his apparent enthusiasm for their cosy little twosome (and her continued attempts to please him), she'd found herself single.

Again.

When eventually she'd stopped crying and started to think about it, Lisa had realised their relationship stopped being fun a while back and, since 'fun' was the opposite of 'serious', she could perhaps see Chris's point. And when she'd thought about it some more (at a yoga retreat, of all things, in Cancún, which she'd booked herself into after googling 'spiritual holidays' one tearful – and drunken – night), Lisa had recognised that despite her best efforts to make them happy, *all* of her boyfriends had ended up dumping her. Something she'd only truly grasped on the last day, when she'd burst into tears in the middle of performing a particularly sweaty-palmed, arm-shaking, hamstring-twanging downward dog.

Her instructor (an impossibly lithe, ridiculously tanned Australian, who she'd have gone out with like a shot if he'd asked her . . . and if he hadn't liked boys just as much as she did) had taken her to one side, sat her down, and given her a piece of relationship advice that, upon returning to a damp and dismal Margate, she'd resolved to follow: *find out what makes* you *happy*.

Something else he'd told her had resonated, too: that she might have to get out of her comfort zone (one that, if Lisa was being honest, had never felt particularly comfortable) to do that. And while Margate seafront was still very much within her comfort zone – given that she'd lived in the town all her life – what she was doing there *wasn't*. Because she was about to meet up with someone she'd never met before, on the recommendation of her best friend Jess – someone whose success rate in matchmaking (judging by the 'Blind Date' column she wrote every week for the *Gazette*, at least) wasn't exactly stellar.

But while – according to Jess – the paper often mismatched the people who wrote in and applied to go on these blind dates for entertainment value (because people apparently love reading about things that make them feel better about their own failing relationships), every now and again they liked to put two people together who might be perfect for each other. Simon had been single for two years, had a 'respectable' job (though Jess wouldn't say what it was, not wanting to ruin the 'surprise element') and was her age, so Jess had thought he might be ideal, and while the old Lisa might have dismissed someone like Simon simply for being single (let alone single for two years) – just like she'd never buy a bottle of wine from the supermarket if it was dusty – she'd thought about it, and realised that was perhaps a little short-sighted. Besides, *she* was single, and there was nothing wrong with her, except for the fact that she was . . . 'attracted to the wrong sort of men', she decided to go with.

In any case, the picky approach had gotten her nowhere so far, so – and she had her recent spiritual awakening in Cancún to thank for this – putting her choice in the hands of fate (or, at least, the *Gazette*) might actually work out okay. Especially since the people who wrote in – *because* they'd written in – were looking for something serious. Lisa hoped.

She stood back as a frazzled-looking woman her age with three under-fives in tow struggled to manhandle a pushchair off the bus.

'You couldn't just . . . ?'

Lisa suddenly realised that the woman – awkwardly holding one child in the crook of her arm as she attempted to extricate the push-chair from where one of its wheels appeared to be jammed in the door mechanism – was speaking to her.

'Of course!' she said, though with a little more enthusiasm than she felt. The child – and Lisa couldn't work out if it was a boy or a girl – was happily chewing on half a breadstick, the mushy remnants of the other half smeared around its mouth, and she was a little wary that her pristine white top might not come out of the encounter unscathed. She hesitated, wondering where best to grip, and quickly decided on under the arms, then winced at the weight.

'Thanks,' said the woman, as the child – evidently anxious about being passed to a stranger – produced a wail of eardrum-shattering proportions, and Lisa couldn't help but wince a second time.

'I'm sorry,' she said, assuming it was something she was doing wrong. 'I don't really know how—'

'You don't have kids?' said the woman, though almost with a jealous tone, and Lisa shook her head.

'No,' she said, quickly adding, 'I do want them, though,' then just as quickly wondering what it was that drove her to feel she had to always admit that. There was more to life than being a parent, surely? Besides, she had a long way to go before she was anywhere near that. Having a *boyfriend* would be a start.

'Want one of mine?'

'Ha!' said Lisa, though, judging by the woman's expression, if she'd had to bet on it she wouldn't have been confident that had been a joke.

As the woman finally freed the pushchair and the bus doors hissed shut behind her, Lisa regarded her charge with something between fascination and horror. She was aware she was expected to say something along the lines of 'he's gorgeous' (or 'she's gorgeous') at this point, but she was still unsure of the child's gender, and asking 'What's *its* name?' wasn't on – so she addressed the child directly.

'Hello, gorgeous,' she said, keeping a safe enough distance to avoid getting a breadstick in her eye. 'What's your name?'

'This is Addison,' said the woman, as she shepherded the rest of her family away from the kerb, leaving Lisa none the wiser.

'Right. Hello, Addison,' Lisa said. When the child just looked blankly at her, she repeated it in a slightly more babyish voice (in the same vein as her dad on their regular family holidays to France, speaking English with a French accent in the hope he'd be understood a little better), though the child didn't seem to notice. 'And how old is . . .' She ended her sentence there, still unsure which pronoun to use.

'He's eight months.'

'He!' said Lisa, a little too quickly, then she said 'he' again, trying to make it sound like a laugh, not quite knowing what else to do. She was still keeping the child at arm's length, mainly to preserve the cleanliness of her top, and her shoulder muscles were tiring under the effort. 'You're a big boy, aren't you, Addison?'

Fortunately, the woman took the hint. 'Shall I . . . ?' she said, holding her arms out, so Lisa gladly passed the baby back to her.

'Bye, Addison,' she said. The child offered her the remains of his breadstick and, not wanting to offend him – something Lisa only appreciated later was hardly an issue – she took it with a cheery, 'Thank you!'

The woman nodded her gratitude, then headed off in the opposite direction, and Lisa wondered where her husband was – something she'd recently begun to suspect her mother often wondered about *her*, which was another reason she was about to do what she was about to do. Not only that, but Lisa was also well aware that, at thirty-one, she'd reached the point in life where some of her friends were getting pregnant – on purpose – and she didn't want to be left behind. *Or* on the shelf.

She hurriedly found a tissue in her handbag and wiped the soggy bread-and-saliva combination from her fingers, then she resumed her journey towards the new street food restaurant on the seafront she and Simon were meeting at (called, imaginatively, 'Seafront Street Food'). As she hurried along the pavement, her phone rang, and Lisa's first thought was that – knowing her luck – it was Jess calling to tell her Simon was going to be a no-show. But then she caught herself. Those kinds of negative thoughts weren't doing her any good, as her yoga teacher had reminded her, while forcing her into yet another excruciating position – though none had been quite as excruciating as she feared today's lunch might be. Hurriedly, she took the call.

'Everything okay?' she asked, tentatively. 'Because I'm still going through with it, if that's why you're calling.'

'That's *exactly* why I'm calling. And I'm pleased to hear it.' Jess let out a short, tinkling laugh, and Lisa did the same in response, though perhaps with a little less tinkle and a touch more nervousness. She'd often wished she could be more like her best friend, but then again she supposed it was easy to be happy-go-lucky and super-confident if you looked like Jess did. Though while Lisa wasn't quite as stunningly pretty, didn't have quite the same, gym-honed figure (and didn't dress to show her body off as well – or as much – as Jess did), she wasn't a bad package. She paid attention to her appearance. Kept herself fit, thanks to the three-times-a-week spinning classes she attended at her local gym. And she didn't eat *that* much chocolate, except on weekends. Or special occasions. Or when she was feeling low. Which, in the later stages of her relationship with Chris, and up until Cancún, had been most days.

'In fact . . .' Lisa checked the time on the clock tower. 'I'm even a little early.'

'God, don't be, whatever you do!'

'What?' Lisa slowed her pace a little. 'Why not?'

'Well, it shows that you're . . . I mean, you don't want him to think you might be . . . you know . . .'

'Desperate?'

'Exactly.'

'I'm going on a *blind date*, Jess.'

'That's not desperate.'

'Isn't it?'

'Of course not. The people who write in . . . it's because they want a relationship. They're fed up with all the game-playing that goes on out there. And, personally, I think it's exciting. Seizing the day. Being impulsive. Trusting in fate. Letting the universe give you a helping hand, while taking control of your life. And definitely something the newly enlightened Lisa would do.'

16

'Maybe.'

'*Maybe?*'

'I'm not so sure I—'

'What happened to all this "I am the architect of my own destiny" stuff you learned in Cancún?'

'I still believe that. Of course I do. But . . .' Lisa sighed loudly. 'It's the truth, though, isn't it? Otherwise why on earth would I be resorting to a . . .' She lowered her voice, aware the pavement was busy, full of people on their way to the amusements, or to Dreamland, the funfair that drew a fair percentage of the day trippers down from London, or perhaps just off to meet a loved one, a possibility she knew should stiffen her resolve. '. . . *blind date*. Besides, being early is just polite.'

'Yeah, but what if Simon's not going to be there . . .'

'Why wouldn't he be?' said Lisa, anxiously.

'. . . *on time*, I meant!' Jess laughed again. 'He'll probably be expecting you to be late, so he might have allowed an extra half an hour or so, which means you'll be sitting there like the third book in a three-for-two deal.'

'I don't even know what that means, and I work in publishing, so . . .'

Jess did the tinkling laugh thing a third time, so loudly that a man walking in the opposite direction looked over at Lisa and widened his eyes. She shut him down with a glare. 'The one that nobody really wants,' said Jess. 'There's always a bigger pile of them left, next to the . . . you know . . .'

'Popular ones? Thanks very much!'

'Gawd. Sorry, Lise. That's not how I—'

'That's okay. Maybe I'll open with that. See whether he – *Simon* – finds it funny.'

'He's bound to. I'm sure he's got a great sense of humour.'

'You'll be telling me he's got a good personality next.'

'He has! Apparently.'

'Well, that's something I sup—' Lisa narrowed her eyes. 'Hang on. Back up a moment. "I'm sure"? And, "apparently"? I thought you'd met him?'

'Well, not "met" in the traditional sense, maybe.'

'What on earth does *that* mean?'

'Normally, I'd interview them first, but . . .'

'*Jess* . . .'

'I've seen a photo.'

'Right.'

Jess had gone quiet, so Lisa glared at her phone, then put it back to her ear. 'And?'

'He's . . .'

'Jess!'

'I'm teasing you. He looks nice.'

'*Nice*,' said Lisa, any remnants of her enthusiasm draining out of her.

'At least, he does in his photo.'

'A recent photo?'

'It's hard to tell. In any case, some people aren't that photogenic. And beauty comes from within, remember?' The tinkling laugh again. 'Besides, when you've gone for looks in the past, how has that worked out for you?'

Lisa felt her heart begin to sink. 'Give it to me straight, Jess. On a scale of one to ten – where "ten" is that guy in the white Speedos from the Dolce & Gabbana advert – where exactly does Simon sit?'

'Depends who "one" is.'

'*Jess!*'

'Relax. Like I said, he's nice-looking.'

'No you didn't. You said he looks nice. There's a difference.'

'Okay, okay. He's nice-looking *and* he looks nice. But just in case you're not attracted to him, if you want me to call you mid-date, pretend there's some emergency at home, I'm quite happy to—'

'I couldn't!'

Lisa could almost hear Jess frown. 'Why not?'

'That would be rude.'

'Even so.'

'Plus, I'm quite capable of ending the date if I'm not interested, thanks.'

'Fine.'

'Even if I don't fancy him, we're adults. We can just have a pleasant lunch. Laugh about the whole set-up.'

'Sure.'

'And if all that happens is I make a new friend, that's good too,' said Lisa, a little worried she was sounding like she was trying to convince herself.

'Great.'

'Exactly.'

'Well then.'

There was a pause, and then Lisa puffed air out of her cheeks. 'But would you? Say, one-thirtyish?'

'Of course! But make sure you answer. Just so I know you're okay.'

Lisa felt a strange, panicky feeling beginning to develop in her chest. 'Why wouldn't I be okay?'

'I didn't mean it like—'

'You do hear these stories, don't you? Something slipped in your drink, the next thing you know, you're waking up in some strange—'

'Babe – relax! He's not like that.'

'Not like that,' said Lisa, flatly. 'This man you've *never met?*'

Jess did the tinkling laugh thing one more time, though Lisa was beginning to find it annoying. She'd almost reached her destination – the freshly painted food court in a former factory next to the old British Home Stores building across the road – and now wasn't the time to be taking dating advice. Particularly not from someone who only had to flutter her eyelashes to get the attention of every man in the room.

'Do you really think I'd set you up with someone who'd do such a thing?'

'No, but . . .'

'No buts! You're a gorgeous, strong, funny, independent woman. Simon's going to fall in love with you the moment he sees you. I know it.'

'I wish *I* did.'

'He will! You mark my words.'

'Three out of ten,' said Lisa, though she feared she was being generous.

'That's my girl! Well, you have fun now.'

Lisa smiled grimly. 'I'll try.'

'And don't do anything I wouldn't do,' Jess added, and Lisa raised both eyebrows. Knowing Jess, that pretty much gave her carte blanche.

She marched towards the crossing, then hesitated at the kerb. The green man had begun flashing, and while normally she'd have stayed where she was, she was a different person now. Ready to take risks – or, at least, stop being so cautious. Stop falling at the feet of every man she'd ever known. In fact, she'd make them fall at *her* feet, for a change. And this blind date was about to be the start of that.

'Well, as lovely as this little chat has been . . .' she said to her friend, then without even glancing left *or* right, Lisa took a deep breath, stepped purposefully off the pavement and into the road.

And right into the path of a fast-approaching, silver Ford Focus.

Chapter 3

Simon slammed on his brakes, just in time to avoid running over the girl who'd stepped out into the road in front of him. Okay, so maybe he'd been in a bit of a hurry, and perhaps he hadn't slowed down as much as he should have given the flashing amber light, but he didn't want to be late for Will, plus the crossing was clear, which meant he had priority, *and* she hadn't even looked when she'd stepped off the kerb. Worse than that, she'd been glued to her phone – probably talking to her boyfriend, he supposed – and completely unaware of her surroundings.

He hurriedly put the car into neutral, pulled on the handbrake and waited for his heartrate to return to something approaching normal. Simon wasn't the biggest fan of mobiles. They banned you from using the things when driving for a reason, and he'd often thought they should be outlawed in other places too – at the cinema, on the train, at supermarket checkouts (something he found particularly rude) and on dates – a girl he'd gone out for a drink with once in the time Before Alice had taken seven (he'd counted them) calls during the hour and a half they'd spent together, each one preceded with an 'I've got to take this', though every time the content of the call had demonstrated that, actually, she didn't.

He mentally added 'crossing the road' to his list, and widened his eyes at the girl in a 'no harm done' kind of way. She was pretty – once you got past the scowl she was currently giving him – and she was dressed to make the best of herself, if a little conservatively, rather than how most of the girls dressed around here, as if they were off to an Ibiza club rather than a Margate pub, with so much flesh on display (whatever the weather) that Will would often break off mid-conversation with him to stare, as if nowadays staring was an accepted way to express interest. No, this was definitely the kind of girl he'd find attractive, if he were ever back in that mode – not that he'd be able to get up the courage to speak to her. Though the fact that she'd marched round to the driver's-side window and was currently rapping her knuckles against it seemed to suggest that wasn't a problem *she* had.

'*What do you think you're playing at?*'

The girl sounded as angry as she looked, and, for a second, Simon regretted winding down his window so quickly.

'Pardon?'

'You could have killed me!'

'Doubtful.'

'You *could!*'

'I was doing less than twenty miles per hour.'

'And your point is?'

'Well, that most traffic fatalities occur at a speed greater than that, and . . .' Simon stopped talking, not keen to go down that particular conversational road. Besides, despite her question, the girl's expression suggested she wasn't interested in whatever point he'd been about to make. 'Anyway, technically it would have been suicide.'

'What?'

He nodded in the direction of the lights. 'Your cross . . .'

'Of course I'm bloody cross, given how you nearly—'

'. . . of the road. It would have been suicide, given that you, you know . . .' He indicated the bonnet of his car. 'Stepped out in front of me.'

'Hel-lo!' The girl was giving him a look – one usually accompanied by the word 'duh!' 'The little green man?'

'What do aliens have to do with anything?'

'No. *That* green man,' the girl said, as if addressing a five-year-old, pointing at the crossing light.

'I, um, think you'll find it's red.'

'It is *now*. It was green then.'

'But it was flashing.'

'When?'

'When you started to cross.'

'And?'

The girl was showing no sign of backing down, and Simon surreptitiously glanced at the clock on his dashboard. He had five minutes to find a parking spot, then he had to grab a table as per Will's instructions before the place got too busy, and right now he wasn't that confident about managing either of those two things.

'Well . . .' he began. The girl was standing, glaring aggressively at him, her hands on her hips, and Simon swallowed hard. 'Technically, you're not supposed to. Cross. If it's flashing.'

'I'm sorry. I didn't realise I was speaking to the person who wrote the Highway Code.'

She'd folded her arms now, and was showing no sign of moving despite the fact they were blocking the road, and Simon was beginning to wonder why on earth he hadn't just apologised and gone on his way.

'No, I just . . . Rules are important in a civilised society. That's all.'

'So is not running people over.'

'Which is why I hit the brakes.'

The girl was looking at him like she'd like to do some hitting and breaking herself, and Simon edged his finger towards the 'window up' button. Then a loud honking alerted him to the fact that the driver in the car behind was getting impatient, and even though he might not have written it, he liked to follow the Highway Code to the letter.

'Yes, well, I'd love to stay and chat, but . . .' He jerked a thumb back over his shoulder to indicate the vehicle behind him (though the girl had already silenced the driver's horn-tooting with a glare), then put his own car in gear.

'Just watch where you're going in future.'

'You too,' said Simon, as pleasantly as he could muster. Which, when he played it back in his head as he drove off down the road, wasn't as pleasant as it might have been.

He made his way along the seafront, gripping the steering wheel a little too tightly. Girls like that always scared him a little. *Every* girl scared him a little. Sometimes a lot. Especially since Alice. Which, Simon knew, was one of the reasons he was still single. One of the *many* reasons. Though not the main one.

He sighed through his nose and concentrated on trying to find a parking spot. Parking near the seafront was always a nightmare, but he'd driven in anyway, partly because, if he drove, he wouldn't drink, and if he didn't drink, he wouldn't get too emotional when Will gave him the usual pep talk, or insisted they went and spoke to a couple of girls because one of them had allegedly been giving Simon 'the eye'. Though it usually turned out to be of the 'evil' variety.

Taking the next turn on the right, he headed up the High Street and, as if by some miracle, spotted a space, so he quickly (but not *too* quickly) parallel-parked, debated briefly whether to wear his coat or leave it in the car, then quickly decided on the latter (despite his earlier Primark incident, Simon doubted anyone would try to steal *his*). Finally, he checked he hadn't left any valuables on display (not that he really had any valuables), double-checked exactly where he was leaving it, and locked the car. His hands were shaking – adrenaline after the almost accident, probably, rather than the freshness of the day – so he stuffed them into his pockets and did his best to put the near miss behind him. *That* was something he'd tell Will about, if Will brought up the subject of him meeting women. How he'd run into one just now. Nearly.

With a half-smile, he filed the joke away for later, and began walking towards the seafront.

Chapter 4

Lisa watched the car accelerate away, trying her best to be Zen about what had just happened, which really just consisted of her resisting the temptation to give the driver the finger as he went. This wasn't the ideal start to her blind date – turning up flustered from nearly having been hit by a car on the way to the venue. Maybe it was a sign. Though of what, she didn't like to think.

She crossed the road, careful to ensure the green man *was* illuminated this time and looking left and right anyway – just in case the Focus had circled the roundabout by the clock tower and was coming back for another go on the other side of the road – then headed into the restaurant. Her heart was pounding, perhaps an after-effect from almost being run over, though it was more likely nervousness about her upcoming date. Something confirmed by a sudden, desperate need for a wee.

She checked her watch: just enough time to head to the toilets, adjust her make-up, find the seat where she and Simon were due to meet – if he wasn't there already – and then . . . well, like Jess said, that was assuming Simon was on time and not expecting her to be late. But that was what other women were like. How they behaved. Not how *she* was. Punctuality was a virtue, in Lisa's book. And, in fact, not even that; it was a basic human requirement, or at least it should be. She had friends who were constantly late – Jess was one of the worst – and Lisa often lectured them about how rude it was, that they regarded their time as more valuable than hers. And though they all denied it – Jess in particular – she suspected that, actually, they *did*.

Besides, Simon being on time would show her if he was keen or not. If he wanted to make a good first impression. If he was a decent human being. And after Chris – who she'd half expected was about to present her with a ring, but in the end hadn't even *called* – Lisa was desperate to meet one of those.

A sign above her head was pointing towards the toilets, so Lisa followed the direction of the arrow, then blanched when she saw the size of the queue. Why was it always like this, a ten-minute wait to use 'her' loo, when you could always walk straight into the men's?

Anxiously she checked the time again, then joined the back of the queue as she weighed up her options. Wait in line here, and she was sure to be late – and Simon might think she was one of *those* women, or even that she wasn't going to turn up, and he might leave, and neither of those outcomes was what she wanted. Or she could head straight for the table and hope the feeling would pass, though if it didn't . . . Best-case scenario would involve her sitting there uneasily until there was a suitable pause in the conversation; worst-case might mean . . .

Lisa didn't want to think about that. Even if Simon *did* have the 'great' sense of humour Jess had promised, her bladder might not find it so funny.

She could just push to the front of the queue, she supposed, explain she was late for a blind date, and appeal to the spirit of sisterhood, hoping they'd let her go first, though by the way the girls ahead of her were hopping anxiously from one foot to the other, she didn't fancy her chances. Alternatively she could just stroll confidently into the men's, avert her eyes, pray there was a cubicle free, do what she had to, and be sitting at the table on time.

The line wasn't moving, and Lisa realised there was nothing for it. Besides, her retreat in Cancún had taught her that life was all about new experiences. And while maybe this wasn't the kind of new experience her instructors had been referring to, it would have to do.

Her head held high, and careful not to meet anyone's eye, she slipped out of line and walked purposefully towards the gents. A man was just coming out through the door, so she nodded a quick thanks as – though looking a little bewildered – he held it open for her and she nipped through. Then she hesitated in the doorway, doing her best not to gag. *This* was why there was never a queue – the place was *disgusting*.

The door swung shut behind her – it was one of those bi-directional ones – and hit her heavily on the backside, catapulting her into the middle of the white-tiled room. To her right, three men were stood at the five urinals, evenly spaced at every other one, while a fourth man hovered behind them, waiting for one to be free, as if acting on some unwritten understanding that he couldn't use any adjacently occupied one.

Holding her breath, she marched confidently past them, ignoring their suddenly panicked expressions when they caught sight of her in the mirror above the urinals (and what was the point of *that*, Lisa wondered – to prevent someone sneaking up on them, like the mirrors they had at cashpoints?) and strode into the nearest cubicle. Then, horrified, she strode straight out again. 'Don't you guys ever *flush*?' she said to herself, making her way into the adjacent stall and pulling the handle without daring to look in the pan.

Doing her best to breathe through her mouth, she locked the door behind her, grabbed a handful of toilet paper, gave the seat a thorough wipe, grabbed some *more* toilet paper to fashion a layer to put down on the seat, slid her jeans below her knees (careful not to let them touch the floor) and, with a silent sigh of relief, sat down. As she studied the graffiti on the wall to her left (a surprisingly detailed drawing of what she'd first thought was a woman playing the clarinet until she remembered where she was), a commotion outside was followed by a loud knock on her cubicle door.

'Occupied,' said Lisa, firmly, then she lowered her voice an octave or two. 'I mean, *occupied*.'

'Security,' said an *actual* male voice from the other side of the door. 'Could you come out of there, please, miss?'

'What do you mean, "miss"?' she said, doing her best to mimic the same gruff tone.

'Just come out, will you?'

Quickly, Lisa pulled her jeans back up, flushed the toilet, then worried that by flushing it, she'd already given the game away.

'What for?'

'This is the gents.'

Lisa cracked the door open to see a bald, heavily muscled, stern-looking security guard glowering at her – the kind you'd imagine might graduate top of his class from security guard school on appearance alone. 'So?'

'And you're not.'

'Fair point, and, can I just say, well spotted, but there was a queue for the ladies and I was desperate . . .'

'Even so.'

She glanced around the room. It had suddenly emptied, as if the fire alarm had gone off and everyone but Lisa had heard it. 'It's not as if I *saw* anything.'

'Did you want me to call the police?'

'The *police*? Is this against the law, then? Because I can't recall the last time I saw someone in court for using the toilet.'

'The *wrong* toilet.'

The security guard had folded his arms, revealing biceps the size of her head, and Lisa suspected the game was up. She stalked past the sinks, wondering whether stopping and washing her hands would be pushing it.

'Hey,' she said as the security guard took her gently but firmly by the arm and escorted her back out. 'I might be transitioning, for all you know.'

'Are you?'

'No, but—'

'Well, if you could transition yourself into the ladies next time.'

'Okay, okay,' she said, then she realised the man was steering her towards the exit. 'What's going on?'

'I think you should go.'

She shook the man's hand off, and rubbed the spot on her arm where he'd been holding on to her. 'That's what I was trying to do. But like I said, there was a queue for the ladies, and—'

'Outside, please.'

Lisa glanced helplessly back towards where she was supposed to be meeting Simon. Surely her chances weren't going to be scuppered before the date had even begun? But what to do? She could cry, she supposed, but she'd spent ages putting on her mascara, and that wasn't how she wanted Simon to see her – or to be featured in the *Gazette* when the photographer turned up later.

'Listen,' she said, an idea suddenly coming to her. 'I'll level with you. I'm actually here on a blind date. That's why I had to use the gents. Because I was worried I'd be late, and Simon – that's my date – might have thought I'd stood him up. And you men are always complaining that women are late all the time, so I thought . . .'

Lisa stopped talking. The man had folded his arms again. His biceps really were scarily large. 'That's a lovely story,' he said. 'But what does it have to do with me?'

'Well . . .' Lisa peered at his name tag. 'Michael. Can I call you Michael? The thing is,' she continued, without waiting for his permission, 'this particular blind date is for a feature in the local paper. The *Gazette*. Perhaps you've heard of it?'

'So?'

'So I'm going to be interviewed afterwards. In the paper. The local paper. That everyone here in Margate reads. And when they ask me about where we ate, I can either tell them that we had a lovely meal, and how the staff were all so friendly, which means loads of people will read that and think, "Hey, perhaps we should give Seafront Street Food a try", or . . .'

Michael's eyes flicked across to a man in a shirt and tie who was watching them from an office in the corner. 'Or . . . ?' he said, nervously.

'*Or* I could tell them that the date never happened, and the reason it never happened was because the restaurant's' – she cleared her throat – '*facilities* weren't up to scratch, and when I pointed this out I was roughly frogmarched outside.' She rubbed her arm again for good measure, then realised she was rubbing the wrong arm, although Michael didn't seem to notice her mistake. 'And by an overly efficient security guard called . . .' She peered closely at his name tag again. '. . . *Michael*. I mean, what with you being a *new* restaurant, looking to develop a good reputation, I can't imagine that kind of publicity is the sort of thing you want.'

Lisa did her best to look more confident than she felt, then folded *her* arms, hoping her nerve was stronger than his, even though her biceps plainly weren't. Then, after another anxious glance towards the man who was evidently his superior, Michael stood to one side. 'Fine,' he mumbled. 'But keep out of the gents in future. Please.'

'My pleasure!' said Lisa, smiling sweetly, then making herself scarce before he could change his mind.

She pushed her way back through the groups of diners, grateful security wasn't escorting her off the premises – after all, how would *that* have looked? Still, it could have been worse. Simon might have decided he'd needed the gents at the same time, and *that* would have made for an interesting lunch.

For a second, she froze. Maybe he *had* been one of those men at the urinals, nervously emptying his bladder before meeting her. Perhaps he'd been the one who'd given her a strange look as he held the door open. And if he was, when he saw her appear at the table he was sure to make a run for it. If he recognised her . . .

Lisa told herself to relax. The men at the urinals had been more concerned with making sure she had nothing to look at, rather than looking at her. And even if he had been one of them, it would be an amusing incident for the 'Any awkward moments?' section of the questionnaire she and Simon would have to do for the paper after their date.

She checked her watch again – two minutes to one – and took a couple of breaths to calm herself down, a feeling of excitement replacing her earlier nerves. This could be *it*. Finally, she might be about to meet the man of her dreams, instead of something out of her nightmares, as most of her exes had turned out to be.

Excitedly, she checked her make-up in the selfie camera on her phone, then made her way to the rendezvous point, fixed a hopeful smile on her face and sat herself down to wait.

Chapter 5

Simon hurried towards the restaurant, wondering whether he'd beat Will to the table, hoping he hadn't been delayed too much by the incident with the girl at the crossing. Then, as if on cue, and just as he caught sight of the venue, his phone rang: Will – to find out where he was, probably. With a defeated sigh, he answered the call.

'Maaaaate!' said Will, before Simon had a chance to say anything.

'Maaate,' Simon parroted back, sounding a little too much like a bleating sheep for his liking. Will was always like this: gregarious, upbeat, confident. Pretty much the opposite of Simon, in fact – so much so that he sometimes wondered why the two of them were such good friends. Some variant on the old 'opposites attract' idea, perhaps, though it wasn't something he really wanted to analyse. Simon had done too much analysing recently. And he wasn't sure it had got him anywhere.

'You there yet?'

'Almost. You?'

'I'd hardly be calling to ask if you were if *I* was, would I?'

Simon rolled his eyes. 'I'll be there in two.'

'Excellent.'

'And you?'

'Yeah,' said Will, cagily. 'About that.'

Simon reduced his walking speed from 'hurry' to 'stroll'. 'What "about that"?'

'I'm not coming.'

'What?' Simon stopped in his tracks. 'Why?'

'Because I never was.'

'I don't—'

'But you should go. Have to go, in fact.'

'What for? And why?'

'Because you're meeting someone.'

'Pardon?'

'Someone . . . *female*!'

Will had given that last word the same amount of emphasis a magician might pull a rabbit out of a hat with, and Simon felt his insides clench. 'Will . . .'

'Relax.' Will laughed. 'She's attractive.'

'That's not the point. And I'm turning right round and heading back to my car.'

'You can't!'

'Why ever not?'

'You don't want to stand her up, do you?'

'What do you mean, "stand her up"? It's not a *date*.'

'Um, it is, actually. At least, *she* thinks it is.'

'Will,' said Simon, calmly – a lot more calmly than he felt. 'What have you done?'

'Just call me Cupid.'

'*Stupid*, more like.'

His friend paused, and then: 'You know that "Blind Date" feature Jess does for the *Gazette*?'

'What about it?' said Simon, even though to his immediate horror, he could probably guess.

'I'm sure I've shown it to you? The one where single people write in, and she matches them up, and the paper pays for them to go on a—'

'I didn't write in.'

'As far as your date's concerned, you did.'

'So I'm not going.'

'Like I said, you have to.'

'I don't.'

'You do,' said Will patiently.

'I *don't!*' Simon said, again. As much as he wanted Will to understand how losing Alice made him feel, right now arguing like a five-year-old was a lot more appealing than getting into the *actual* reason.

'You do,' insisted Will. 'And I'll tell you why. One, because you don't want to leave some poor girl sitting there like a lemon. Two, because if you don't, then Jess won't have a piece to write for next week's paper, and that'll be your fault . . .'

'*Your* fault, actually.'

'And three – and understand I'm only saying this for your own good – you need to get out more. Get back in the—'

'If you say the word "saddle", I'm going to—'

'Trust me, you *do!*'

'*Trust you?*' said Simon, incredulously, though he knew he shouldn't be angry at his friend. After all, Will didn't know how he really felt after what had happened with Alice – though probably because Simon hadn't told him. *Couldn't*, in fact. Will might even have assumed – because Simon never spoke about Alice – that he was over her, and ready to move on. But the truth was, Simon couldn't talk about her because he wasn't over her. And he certainly wasn't ready to move on.

'Yeah, I know how that sounds. But, despite my best efforts, you're hardly going to go up to someone at a bar and ask them out, and I don't see you as a Tinder kind of guy, so this is the best way. The only way.'

'To what?'

'Break your duck.'

'I don't *have* a duck,' said Simon, though he feared that was because it was more of a chicken. 'And even if I did, I might not want to break it.'

'Yeah, but don't you think you kind of *need* to?' Will paused, perhaps to let what he'd just said sink in, though before Simon could reply he launched into the next part of his spiel. 'Lisa's your age, and—'

'*Lisa?*'

'The girl you're meeting? She's Jess's best friend. And Jess isn't going to be best friends with just anyone.'

'And yet she goes out with you.'

'Ha ha. Good one. Joking aside, though, Lisa's apparently had a bit of a . . .' Will hesitated. '. . . chequered dating history.'

'What do you mean by that?'

'Just that she could do with meeting someone decent.'

'So I'm doing this for *her?*'

'It doesn't really matter why you're doing it, as long as you do it.' Will laughed nervously. 'Seriously, mate, you need to go. And you need to get a move on, because otherwise you're going to be late, and she might leave.'

Simon sighed. Right now, Lisa leaving was the most appealing option, even though he suspected – no, *knew* – that Will was probably right. Plus he liked Jess, and didn't want to let her down – or, perversely, stand Lisa up. And maybe, just maybe, if he went this one time, and the date was the disaster it was sure to be, Will might realise he was a lost cause. It would certainly be easier than flat out telling him.

'Fine!' he said, reluctantly resuming his walk towards the venue. 'I'll stay for one drink, and—'

'Hopefully you'll be staying for more than that. Assuming Lisa wants to. It's a date, after all.'

'For her, maybe. And correct me if I'm wrong, but a date's normally one drink. "Let's go for a drink . . ." That's what you say, isn't it?'

'Not at lunchtime. A lunchtime date involves, well, *lunch*.'

'You'll be telling me I have to talk to her next.'

'Funny man!' said Will. 'Keep that level of humour up, and Lisa will be eating out of the palm of your hand.'

'Don't they have plates at this place, then?'

'My *sides!*' said Will. 'And listen, I'm sorry about the deception, but it was the only way I could think of to get you back out there.'

'Hence your "What are you wearing?" question earlier.'

'Yeah. Let's just hope jeans and a sweatshirt is smart enough.'

'It's not an interview.'

'You clearly haven't been on a date in a long—' Will cut the sentence off abruptly. 'Sorry, Si. And you're right. As long as you've got a clean pair of underpants on.'

'I don't *need* a clean pair of underpants!' Two girls who'd just passed Simon on the pavement overheard him and started giggling, so he lowered his voice. 'No, hang on, that came out wrong. By that I mean I'm not going to, you know' – he lowered his voice a little further – '*sleep with her.*'

'You should be so lucky!' said Will. 'And you're sure about that, are you?'

'Yes, I'm sure!'

'Fair enough – if you're that confident that you can afford to turn down sex after two years, good for you. But if it was me . . .'

'Well, it isn't!' Simon snapped. 'And what I meant was, I'm sure it won't come to that. Besides, who sleeps with someone on a first date, let alone a *blind* one?'

Will was silent for a moment, which Simon knew was an answer of sorts.

'Whatever,' Will said. 'Anyway, I won't keep you. Just wanted to give you a heads-up, and wish you good luck.'

'Thanks,' said Simon, as if the words 'a' and 'lot' followed it.

'Right. Well. Give me a call later. Let me know how you got on.'

'Sure.'

Simon had reached the food court's entrance now, and he glanced up at the sign above the way in, just to make doubly sure he'd got the right place. In truth, he suspected he probably wouldn't have to call at all. Lisa was bound to report back to Jess, so Will would probably know how well the date had gone long before Simon did.

'Great,' said Will. 'So, have fun. Or try to, at least. And keep your receipts. The paper is picking up the tab.'

'I should hope so! And, um . . .' Simon coughed awkwardly. 'What have you told her about me, exactly?'

'Not much. Just that you'd written in and—'

'But I didn't!'

'Don't tell her that, whatever you do! And listen – she doesn't know your life story or anything. Which should give you something to talk about.' Will hesitated. 'And on that note, just, you know, try to keep things . . . upbeat.'

'Upbeat.'

'Yeah. And Simon—'

'Bye, Will.'

Simon stabbed the 'End call' button on his mobile, then he glanced at his watch, double-checked it against the time on his phone, wondered whether he had time to visit the gents (he'd gone before he left his flat, but felt a slight urge to go again – anxiety, probably – which, after a moment's consideration, he thought he could ignore). Besides – not that he'd ever timed himself – it was already two minutes to one, and he wasn't sure two minutes was long enough to find the bathrooms, check his reflection in the mirror, then find his way back, particularly if there was a queue, or he had some sort of accident with the hand dryer, or, even worse, some drunk guy at the adjacent urinal accidentally peed on his shoes, as had happened the last time he'd been out in Margate.

With a final deep breath, he made his way through the door, wincing a little at the cacophony of noise that hit him, and peered around the venue. To his horror, it looked just as 'cool' as Will had described: a series of brightly varnished wooden tables in the middle of a cavernous ex-industrial space, with a number of different food vendors operating out of various customised caravans and contraptions stationed around the outside. At the far end, a food truck was parked – an old Volkswagen camper van that had been converted into a mobile kitchen – with a sign above the side window that read GOURMET SCOTCH EGGS. Beneath the sign, a man dressed in what appeared to be the de rigueur black chef's outfit was staring, a little bored, at the centre of the room.

Simon hesitated, wondering whether he should call Will back to find out what Lisa looked like – not so he'd know if she was attractive or not, but so he could actually spot her in the crowd. Then again, Will had been very specific as to where to sit, so Simon shifted his focus to the table in front of the van where he'd been due to meet his friend, then nervously made his way across the room. The place was packed – couples, mostly, plus what he guessed must be a few out-on-the-pull gatherings, judging by the various groups of men (outnumbered by the empty beer bottles on their tables) and women (except the bottles were labelled *Prosecco*), and Simon began to feel even more anxious. This was what people his age did at the weekend: came out to places like this; mixed, flirted, chatted up; ate hipster food and drank copious amounts of super-expensive micro-brewed craft beer and fizzy Italian wine. This was how young couples entertained themselves, entertained each other, and how single people behaved nowadays – or rather how *young* single people behaved. After Alice, he'd moved here partly to get away from all that – to a Londoner like himself, Margate had always been a place to be visited on a day trip, for the beach and the funfair rather than its social scene, but since its recent trendification (if that was a word) Simon had sensed that things were changing. And quicker than he liked.

Emerging from the other side of a group of giggling girls he'd just self-consciously excuse-me'd his way through, he located the rendezvous point Will had told him to aim for, where he supposed Lisa should be sitting, waiting. At the far end of the table, two women were sharing a plate of something Simon couldn't identify that *did* actually look like roadkill, while in the middle a girl was sitting, her back to him, alternately checking her watch and drumming her fingernails on the table.

He assumed neither of the women in the couple was Lisa – unless she'd brought backup, something that would definitely have encouraged Simon to make a run for it – so the girl on her own must be his date. She certainly looked like she was waiting for someone, and – Simon noticed, to his relief – she wasn't glued to a mobile phone like everyone else always seemed to be, whether on the bus, on the beach, in the park he often ran round after work, at a bar, or – five minutes ago – stepping off a kerb.

Simon took another deep breath, wondering what that strange thumping noise was, then he realised it was his own heartbeat. He cursed Will as he exhaled and made his way to where the girl was sitting, and then – conscious he was about to step off a metaphorical kerb himself – he coughed politely.

As the girl looked round, her face fell so quickly Simon suddenly, *desperately* wanted to be anywhere else but here.

Chapter 6

'Well, if it isn't Lewis Hamilton.'

'Pardon?'

'Come back for a second go, have you?' Lisa jabbed a thumb at the food truck. 'You could try to get that thing started, and I'll make a run for it, if you like? Or are you thinking about stoning me to death with an order of gourmet Scotch eggs?'

Lisa had instantly recognised the driver of the car that had nearly run her down, though she wasn't sure he'd recognised her given the strange, almost disappointed look on his face. But while she'd presumed he'd either come over to apologise for nearly killing her earlier or to continue his lecture about the finer points of the Highway Code, a man hanging around her while she was waiting for Simon was the last thing she wanted. She sighed, smiled up at him and relaxed her tone.

'Here's an idea – let's just say we were both in the wrong place at the wrong time, and let that be the end of it, shall we?'

'But . . .' The man swallowed, so loudly the two women at the end of the table looked up at the noise. 'I've only just got here.'

'And it was very nice of you to come. But it's probably best if we just go our separate ways and don't give each other another thought. And by "we" . . . seeing as I'm already sitting here . . .'

She said that last sentence with as much finality as she could muster, and it seemed to do the trick, because the man stared at her for a moment or two longer, opened his mouth as if to say something, then obviously thought better of it, because he turned around a hundred and eighty degrees and headed smartly back into the crowd.

With a satisfied sigh, Lisa watched him go, quickly checked her phone for messages, then scanned the room anxiously. Simon was in danger of being late. And while she'd already decided she'd give him fifteen minutes' grace, she'd been stood up before, and the last time had been in a restaurant full of couples. She'd gamely stayed and eaten dinner on her own, but it wasn't an experience she wanted to repeat, even at lunchtime in an anonymous venue like this.

She tried to ignore the sudden sinking feeling in her stomach. Maybe Simon had already turned up, taken one look at her, decided she wasn't his type and fled. Perhaps he *had* been in the toilet when she'd gone in there. But surely not. Or rather, hopefully not. How would *that* look in next week's paper? Margate was a small town. You didn't want to get yourself a reputation. Of any kind.

She checked her make-up for the umpteenth time with her phone's selfie camera, then looked up to find the man from the car had sat down opposite her, and her jaw dropped. Nearly running her over was one thing, but potentially ruining her date . . .

'I'm sorry,' she said, politely but firmly. 'But I'm meeting someone here, so . . .'

'So am I,' said the man.

'Right, well, small world and all that, but do you have to meet them *right* here?'

'Kind of.'

Lisa narrowed her eyes at him. 'It's a big table. Perhaps you could wait a little further along?'

'Fine,' he said, wearily, then he hoisted himself up from the bench, and shimmied along a yard or so. 'Far enough?' he asked, half sitting, half standing, as if reluctant to sit down again without her approval.

'Actually . . .' Lisa stopped short of saying 'no'. A group of rowdy girls – probably on a hen weekend given the matching bright pink T-shirts with *Final Fling Before the Ring* printed on the front – had just sat down at the far end, and to ask him to move any further would mean he'd be joining them. Given how raucously they were all laughing (and how drunk they already appeared to be), Lisa didn't think he'd fancy that. Or perhaps even get out alive. 'Sure,' she said.

The man lowered himself back down on to the bench. 'Thank you,' he said, and Lisa shrugged.

'It's a free country.'

'Right,' he said, in a tone that suggested he doubted that. Then he leaned across the table towards her. 'Can I ask you something?'

'Like I said, it's a free country.'

'Are you always this . . . confrontational?'

'I'm not confrontational.'

'I thought you were going to grab me by the lapels and haul me out through my car window earlier.'

Lisa almost smiled. It was exactly how she'd felt. Though perhaps not quite in line with her new Zen approach to everything. 'You nearly ran me over!'

'Well, the way I see it, you virtually threw yourself in front of my car. You should thank me for stopping in time.'

'*Thank* you?'

'You're welcome!'

'No, that wasn't . . .' Lisa stopped talking. The man was smiling, and not in a 'gotcha!' way, but almost apologetically, as if acknowledging how poor his attempt at humour had been, and she couldn't help but soften her expression a little.

He blushed, almost like he was embarrassed by the success of his own joke, then peered around the room, and she took the opportunity to check him out. Not bad-looking, she supposed, as hit-and-run drivers went, perhaps in need of a haircut; in decent shape, tall and well proportioned, built like a runner rather than the kind of man she was normally attracted to, who spent more time in front of the mirror at the gym than Lisa did in front of the one in her bathroom; and dressed . . . well, 'dressed' just about summed it up. Under normal circumstances, she might not have given him a second look. But, as she'd had to remind herself a little too frequently today – these weren't normal circumstances.

In any case, she was here on a date, and being seen talking to another man when Simon turned up – *if* Simon turned up – probably wouldn't get them off to the greatest of starts. Besides, he'd said he was meeting someone too – probably a woman, given the way he was peering nervously around the venue – and what were the chances that neither of their dates turned up?

She checked her watch again, a little more anxiously, and noticed the man was looking at her – maybe even about to say something. Then a thought occurred to her. *Surely not*, she thought, before realising she'd actually said it out loud.

'"Surely not" what?' said the man.

'I'm sorry. I wasn't talking to . . .' Lisa narrowed her eyes at him. 'What did you say your name was?'

'I didn't,' said the man. 'But since you ask, it's Simon.'

'Oh *no*!' Lisa clapped her hand to her mouth. 'Not "oh no" in the sense that you're, you know . . .' She indicated the two of them and made a pained face, then sighed apologetically. 'I'm . . .'

'Lisa?' said Simon, miserably. And with about as much enthusiasm as she probably deserved.

Chapter 7

Simon couldn't believe his luck – or rather, his lack of it. If Will was going to set him up, why oh why couldn't he at least have done it as part of some relaxed foursome with him and Jess, rather than what was sure to be an extremely uncomfortable blind date – *and* one that was going to be featured in the local paper?

Now, not only was he supposed to spend the next hour or so on a date he hadn't wanted to go on in the first place – hadn't even known he was going on, in fact – but he was also supposed to spend it with someone who quite clearly hated him on sight (something not at all helped by the fact that, in her eyes at least, he'd started the date off by nearly running her over). And when he'd first appeared, she'd seemingly rejected him from the get-go. He'd have walked away at that point if he hadn't promised Will he'd see it through. A promise he was already wishing he hadn't made.

He sat there awkwardly, wondering whether Lisa might move along her bench to sit opposite him, and when she didn't he slid across the required yard or so, just as she decided she would after all – as if the two of them were taking part in some rehearsed comedy routine. He waited a few seconds, just to see whether she'd slide back to sit opposite him, and then decided for safety's sake, he'd better ask.

'Did you want me to . . . ?' He indicated the space he'd been occupying a moment ago, and Lisa sighed.

'Be my guest,' she said, so Simon allowed himself to relax a little. 'Be my guest' was a little warmer than 'it's a free country', and, like a drowning man reaching for a lifebelt, he'd grab on with both hands to any glimmer of hope right now that the next however-long-it-was-going-to-be wouldn't be as excruciating as he feared.

Desperate for an icebreaker, he thought back to what Will had mentioned earlier, about utilising his sense of humour. 'Well, this'll be a funny how-we-met story to tell the grandkids,' he said, and when Lisa couldn't quite seem to hide her horror he had to physically stop himself from facepalming. If he *had* been looking for a girlfriend, coming out with statements like that probably wouldn't help his single status.

'Sorry,' he said, as Lisa gave him a look to suggest statements like that might not be the only thing. 'I'm just a little nervous. I've never been on a blind date before, and this one's going to be in the local paper, which makes it doubly important that I don't embarrass myself. Or embarrass you! Ha ha. If I haven't already.' He waited for Lisa to contradict him, and when she didn't he decided – mindful of Will's *other* advice – to stop talking, conscious he'd been doing almost all of it, then regarded Lisa shyly across the table. She was attractive, there was no doubt of that – Will had got that part right, at least – so as to why she was single . . . Will had mentioned something about a 'chequered dating history', which might just be down to her as much as any of her exes. He started fearing the worst, then told himself not to be ridiculous. Everyone made dating mistakes along the way. Some people just hadn't met the right partner yet. And some people had, but – as he well knew – for reasons beyond their control, it didn't work out. If he and Lisa did get together . . . well, like he'd just blurted out, at least they'd have a story.

Simon caught himself. He wasn't here to 'get together' with anyone. He was here – if Will was to be believed – because he had to be, because he *needed* to be, to get some practice, get rid of any 'ring rust', and because he'd promised Will he'd go through with it, so as not to leave Lisa in the lurch, and so Jess would have something to write about . . .

A lot of reasons. None of them romantic.

'Anyway,' he said. 'Like I mentioned, I'm Simon. Martin.'

'Which is it?'

'Huh?'

'Simon or Martin?'

'No, Martin's my surname. Confusing I know, when you have a surname that sounds like a . . . you know, first one.'

'Right.'

He held a hand out across the table, and Lisa regarded it suspiciously for a little longer than he was comfortable with, and he was just considering whether he should withdraw it – *and* withdraw gracefully from the date – when she shook it, replying with a curt 'Lisa. Lisa Harrod.'

'Like the shop?'

'That's Harrods.'

'I know. Obviously. But "Harrod" is still *like* the shop. If it isn't *exactly* the shop.'

'Right,' said Lisa, again.

'Anyway. Nice to meet you,' he said, and then, conscious he'd been holding on to her hand for a second or two longer than perhaps was acceptable, he let it go. 'And just to double-check, you're here for the *Gazette* blind date thing, yes?'

Lisa smiled as she nodded, though in the way you might at a stupid person. 'What are the chances of me not turning up, and there being another girl called Lisa here at exactly the same table at exactly the right time, do you think?'

Simon answered with a lopsided grin as he wondered whether he should try to work out the odds – then, conscious he possibly looked a little unnerving, he cleared his throat and stared at her for a moment, wondering where to go from here, what to say next.

'Have you been here before?' he said, aware that was only a slight step up from the oh-so-lame 'Do you come here often?'

Lisa shook her head. 'It's only just opened. So no.'

She flashed him a brief, almost apologetic smile, perhaps to say sorry for the terseness of her reply, and, for the first time, it occurred to Simon that she was possibly as nervous as he was. 'Oh. Right. Of course. Silly question,' he said, wondering why Lisa was peering over his shoulder, in the manner of someone chatting to you at a party while looking round for someone more interesting. He swivelled round in his seat, and spotted the bar located next to the food truck.

'Should we get a drink?' she said, and Simon spun back round so fast he almost gave himself whiplash.

'Great idea!' he said, perhaps a little too enthusiastically. He was a little surprised at the feeling of elation that swept through him at the fact that Lisa was prepared to stay – at least for one drink. Then he feared she might think his eagerness was because he had a drinking problem, so he reined himself in a bit. 'What would you like?'

'No, that's okay . . .'

Lisa was already halfway out of her seat, and Simon began to panic. He was a gentleman, and a gentleman bought (or in this case 'fetched', seeing as the *Gazette* was paying) the drinks. The first ones, at least. But while he had territorial advantage – the bar was behind him, and Lisa would have to circumnavigate the long table to get there – his date looked very determined.

'You can get the next round,' he suggested quickly, and Lisa gave him a look, as if doubting there'd *be* a next round, and, again, he felt uncomfortable. 'I didn't mean to be presumptuous,' he said. 'I just wanted to get you a drink, that's all. If you don't want to stay after that, then you can just give me the money for this one and . . .' As Lisa's eyes widened, he wanted to facepalm again – so this time, he did. 'Of course you don't have to give me the money. Seeing as the *Gazette* are picking up the tab.' He exhaled loudly. 'I bet you didn't think you'd be meeting *this* much of a smooth operator, did you?'

'No,' said Lisa, flatly. 'I didn't.'

Simon smiled awkwardly. He knew he could take that one of two ways.

'So what do you want?' she asked, and Simon's mind went blank. His first thought was 'not to be here', but he was pretty sure that wouldn't go down well. 'To drink?' she continued, as if reading his mind, so Simon thought quickly.

'Well, I'm driving,' he said, miming steering a car through a gentle chicane, then he realised that reminding Lisa about him behind the wheel wasn't the smartest of moves given their first encounter. 'So I'd better have something, you know . . .'

'Soft?' said Lisa, in a manner that suggested that was what she thought of him.

'Yes, please,' he said, then it registered that she was probably expecting him to pick something. But what to choose? After all, there weren't many drinks you could order that made you sound both manly *and* a responsible road user. Unless . . .

'I'll take an alcohol-free beer, if they have one, please.'

'Coming right up,' said Lisa, picking up her things – all of her things, Simon noticed – and making her way towards the bar.

He sat there, not daring to watch her, drumming his fingers on the table, half hoping she was making her way towards the exit instead, then he almost jumped out of his skin when his phone rang.

Will. Again.

'Maaaate!'

'What do you want?' Simon said, curtly.

'Can you talk?'

'You mean generally, as in a life skill, or right now?'

Will laughed – a little excessively, Simon felt. 'Just checking in!'

'Checking up, more like. Don't worry. I'm here.'

'Is Lisa?'

'Not right at this minute, no.'

'What? She should be . . .'

Simon almost smiled at the panic in Will's voice. 'Don't worry. She's gone to get the drinks.'

'Shouldn't you be doing that?'

'I offered. But she insisted. Plus it's 2019. In case it's passed you by, women have the vote now. They can even *drive*.'

'Right. Good. So how's it going?'

'Let's just say it's early days.'

'That good, eh?' Will let out another, shorter laugh. 'Well, it's a first date, so . . .'

Simon took a couple of breaths. 'It's not a *first* date, Will. It's a blind date. One date. A first date would suggest there's going to be a second, and I can already tell you there won't be.'

'Okay. But technically it's your first date since Alice, so . . .'

'*Will!*'

'All I'm saying is, it's understandable you might be a bit rusty. Don't expect it to be all plain sailing. And make sure you're interesting.'

'Interesting,' said Simon, flatly.

'You do know the best way to be interesting?'

'Um . . .'

'Be interested in *her!*'

'I get it, Will.'

'Excellent. Now promise me you'll see it through. To the end.'

Simon was pretty sure the word 'bitter' would slot neatly in between those last two words. Though given how things had gone so far, at least the end would no doubt be soon. 'Fine,' he said, eventually. 'I promise.'

'Great.' Simon could hear the relief in Will's voice. 'You won't regret it.'

'I already do,' he said, then he glanced over his shoulder. There was still no sign of Lisa, but Will didn't need to know that. 'Listen, Lisa's on her way back to the table, so I should really—'

'Okay, okay.' Will cleared his throat awkwardly. 'Just remember what I said. You need to see this through, buddy. I know it's tough, but today's an important step towards getting over the fact that Alice, you know . . .'

'*Died*, Will,' said Simon, quietly. 'The word you're looking for is "died".'

'I know, mate. I just—'

'Bye, Will.'

Simon ended the call, then shook his head as he slipped his phone away. Will was right – of course he was. Today *was* an important step. Every day was, in a way.

But Simon already knew that getting over losing Alice would take an awful lot more than this.

Chapter 8

Lisa glanced back at the table as she pushed her way towards the bar, and tried not to read anything into her feeling of indifference when she couldn't spot Simon through the crowd. Maybe he'd made a run for it. Decided that he didn't fancy her, or that she'd been a little too – what was it? – *confrontational* for his liking. In her defence, he *had* nearly run her over. Plus she'd been on edge. Truth was, she still was. But that was no surprise. The stakes were high, after all, and she couldn't – *wouldn't* – allow herself to fall into another 'Chris' situation. No, she'd keep her defences up, and she wouldn't be dropping them for Simon – or anyone – any time soon.

For a moment, it occurred to her to sneak out, and end this farce before it became even more of a disaster than it already was. But that would be rude, not to mention the fact that Jess would never forgive her. And the thought of the look on Simon's face when she didn't return to the table . . . she'd be devastated if someone did that to her, and, if she was being honest, she probably didn't have it in her to do it to someone else. And – since Cancún – Lisa believed too much in karma to risk it.

From what she could already tell, she and Simon were more than likely incompatible. Had nothing in common. Wouldn't get on. Although maybe that was her problem. Perhaps she needed someone to *force* her out of her comfort zone. Make her try something different. Like Jess convincing her to go on today's blind date.

She still didn't know why she'd agreed, though she suspected the bottle and a half of wine she'd drunk before Jess had tentatively suggested it might have had something to do with her saying yes. But over the course of her week at the retreat, Lisa had learned that in order to move on, she needed to make some changes. To live her life differently. Say goodbye to the loser men she usually found herself attracted to (and found herself bending over backwards trying to please). And how better to do that than leave her choice of partner up to fate?

And while 'fate' was actually her best friend picking from all the single, eligible men who wrote into the paper every week, desperate to meet 'the one', she was still leaving *something* to chance.

With Jess all coupled up with Will now, Lisa knew it wasn't fair to expect her best friend to be there for her in the same way she had been when Chris dumped her. Jess had been amazing. And so Lisa owed it to her to – in the words of another of the spiritual gurus in Cancún – 'stop being a drain, and start being a radiator'.

She moved through the crowd until she was sure Simon wouldn't be able to see her, pulled her phone out of her bag and dialled Jess's number. Perhaps not surprisingly, and probably because she was waiting to call Lisa as arranged, Jess picked up before the second ring.

'Well?' Jess's voice was heavy with expectation, and while Lisa didn't want to disappoint her, she feared her own voice would give everything away.

'What do you mean, "well"?'

'As in "is it going . . ."?'

Lisa thought for a moment. 'It's . . . *he*'s not what I expected.'

Jess let out her trademark tinkling laugh. 'Well, you expected it was going to be a disaster, so that's a good thing, surely!'

'Ha ha. And I didn't expect it was going to be a disaster. The hand of fate and all that . . .' Though she feared the hand of fate was actually about to slap her. 'He seems nice enough, I suppose.'

'"Nice enough"?'

'Yes. Though I'm not sure how much we've got in common. Why's he been single for so long?'

Jess hesitated. 'Perhaps you better ask him that,' she said, followed by: 'Actually, don't.'

'What?' said Lisa, suddenly alarmed. 'Why not?'

'It's not exactly a first-date question, is it? Effectively asking someone what's wrong with them? Maybe he's just been . . . picky.' She let the sentence hang, and Lisa tried to ignore the accusation. 'Anyway. Could you see yourself shagging him?'

'*Jess!*'

'I'm sorry, but the physical side is important. If I didn't fancy Will, then there's no way we'd be doing it as much as we are. And *because* we're doing it so much, we're—'

'Too much information, Jess.'

'I'm just saying.'

'Well, don't!'

'But are you attracted to him?'

Lisa stepped out from where she'd been sheltering behind a group of older women, and glanced back towards their section of the table, where Simon seemed to be in the middle of an animated phone call. 'He's not bad-looking, I suppose. A bit like that guy who plays Thor's brother in the *Avengers*. Although a value-brand version.'

'Loki?'

'Yeah,' Lisa said, taking a sudden sidestep to avoid running into the security guard who'd almost thrown her out earlier. 'Not at all up himself. Which I suppose makes a nice change from Chris.'

'Not "low key"!' Jess sniggered. 'His name . . . Thor's brother. It's Loki.'

'Jess, you've lost me,' said Lisa, then realised she was in danger of actually getting lost. She got her bearings, and pushed her way towards the bar.

'So, what are you doing now?'

'Getting the drinks.'

'Shouldn't he be doing that?'

'Two words: Drink. Spiked.'

'Simon's hardly likely to—'

'And you know this because you've met him *how* many times?'

'Okay, okay.' Jess was laughing again, and Lisa couldn't help but join in.

'Listen, I ought to go. Simon's guarding our seats and . . .'

'Ooh. Sounds manly!'

Lisa laughed again. 'Leave him alone. He's nervous, which says something.'

'"Nervous", "nice" . . . I don't know why you haven't jumped him already.'

'Jess!' Lisa took her phone away from her face and glared at it, then put it back to her ear. 'Anyway, I just wanted to report back, to tell you that you don't need to call, and . . . that's it, really.'

'Well, stop wasting your time talking to me, then! But, Lise . . .'

'What?'

'See it through, won't you? Give him a proper chance. You never know . . .'

Lisa sighed. Experience had taught her that was the problem. You never knew. Or not until it was too late, at least. But Jess was probably right. Simon deserved a chance.

'Fine.'

'Plus if it doesn't work out, there'll be hundreds of men who read about you in the paper and are bound to be interested.'

'That happens, does it?'

'Of course!' said Jess. 'Especially after I've written you up as the catch of the century. *And* when they see your photo.'

Jess had begun wolf-whistling, so with a 'Later, babe' Lisa ended the call and made her way to the bar – a long, silver caravan, open along one side and with AIRSTREAM written on the end – then elbowed her way to the front. Miraculously, she managed to catch the eye of the barman on her first attempt.

'What can I get you?'

'An alcohol-free beer, please.'

'Really?'

'Yes, really.'

'Only it tastes like shit.'

Lisa did a double take. 'Are you supposed to say things like that?'

The man nodded briefly. 'Just being honest. And it's not like I work on commission.'

'Fair enough,' said Lisa. 'But it's not for me.' She aimed a thumb back over her shoulder in response to the barman's raised eyebrow. 'It's for the nervous-looking guy at the long table.'

He peered over her shoulder. 'He looks like he could do with a fully leaded one.'

'He's driving.'

'Is he driving you?'

'I've seen him behind the wheel. So no.'

'Then what's the problem?'

Lisa smiled politely. 'Best not,' she said. 'Oh, and a glass of white wine.'

The barman grinned back at her as he retrieved a bottle of beer from the fridge behind the bar. 'Small or large?'

'You don't do extra-large, by any chance?'

He shook his head. 'Sorry. I can do you two instead?'

Lisa thought for a moment. Two might work – she could chug down the first one here to settle her nerves – though Simon might see her, and then what would he think?

'I'll stick with the one – and small, please. Don't want to make the wrong impression. And it'll be quicker to finish.'

'Suit yourself.' The barman poured her wine, then slid the drinks across the bar towards her. 'Nine fifty, please.'

'Thanks,' said Lisa, pressing her bank card against the terminal and then pocketing the receipt. Jess had told her to keep a record of everything she spent, though at this rate, this would be it.

Clearing her way with a series of loud ''scuse me's, she carried the drinks back to the table, sat down, and deposited Simon's beer in front of him.

'Alcohol-free, as requested.'

'Thanks.' Simon clinked his bottle gently against her glass, took a swig, then tried unsuccessfully not to make a face. Lisa smiled. 'Something funny?' he said.

'The barman said it'd taste like . . . not that nice.'

'It's fine,' said Simon. 'Everything okay?'

'Why wouldn't it be?'

'You were gone a while, that's all.'

'Sorry. I was speaking to Jess.'

Simon looked around, suddenly panicked. 'Jess?'

'From the *Gazette*.'

'She's here?'

'On the phone.'

'Ah. Of course.' Simon relaxed a little. 'About?'

'What do you think?' said Lisa, and Simon blushed.

'One of *those* calls, eh?'

'One of *what* calls?'

'Those prearranged ones. You know, you get a friend to phone you half an hour into the date to see if you need rescuing, she pretends there's some emergency, you make your excuses and go, and I never see you again.'

'It's not been half an hour yet,' said Lisa, then she felt bad when Simon's face fell. 'I phoned her, actually.'

'To tell her to call? Or not to call?'

'We'll just have to wait and see, won't we?' Lisa met his gaze for a moment or two, then she laughed. 'Relax. She won't be calling. Unless of course she has some *genuine* emergency.'

'So I got the thumbs up?'

Simon was looking surprised, and Lisa didn't know what to feel about that. 'I came back, didn't I?'

'So I see,' he said, and, though she might be imagining it, Lisa thought he sounded disappointed.

'Right,' she said, wondering where to go from here – though to her shame, her first thought was 'home'. She'd told herself that going through with today's date would be an experience, and her Cancún week had taught her life was all about experiences, good *and* bad – though she *had* hoped the majority of them would be good. While it was early days, Lisa already wasn't sure about this one.

She gulped down a mouthful of wine, wondering what on earth she'd got herself into, and whether to just be honest, cut her losses and leave. She should find Simon's nervousness sweet, she supposed, and while every survey she'd ever read in the glossy magazines she occasionally bought told her that confidence was the most attractive feature a man could have, she'd been out with enough arrogant men to know confidence was a continuum, and she'd actually prefer someone at the lower end of the scale. Though perhaps not off the bottom of it, like Simon seemed to be.

And while he perhaps wasn't the kind of man she'd notice if she saw him out in the street (though it was lucky he'd seen *her* on the street earlier, otherwise their date might have begun with an ambulance ride to A&E), what was it everyone always said? Never judge a book by its cover? But Lisa worked in publishing as a book jacket designer, and therefore knew the hours and hours of effort that went into getting a cover right, so she wasn't sure that was the best of sayings. Nor was the 'plenty of fish in the sea' one that Jess often tried to console her with whenever she'd been unceremoniously dumped. Because what there was *also* plenty of in the sea was rubbish, just floating around, waiting to surprise you with an unexpected, unpleasant encounter. That was something she'd discovered on her daily dips in the Caribbean – and something her dating history had taught her time and time again.

But Cancún had taught her a few more important things. About herself, mainly, and how she needed to *be* herself in relationships, rather than trying to be whoever any future ex-boyfriend might want. She knew she had to become a bit more flexible too – and not in an after-a-week-of-yoga way, but in terms of the kind of men she dated. Men who didn't try to mould her into their idea of the perfect girlfriend, because they already thought she was.

On occasion, Chris had suggested she wore a shorter skirt, or a more low-cut top, or hint that the burger she'd ordered might be a 'little fatty' – and to her shame, she'd gone along with it, much like she had when it came to his choice of where to go on holiday, or what film to watch.

Now Lisa could see the 'little fatty' comment had been directed at her rather than her choice of meal, and though back then she'd convinced herself that making Chris happy would make her happy, there was no way she was going to put herself in that kind of situation again. And that was why she was here. Doing her best to go for what *she* wanted.

She took another sip of wine, and glanced up furtively from her glass. Simon was sitting quietly on the other side of the table, seemingly fascinated by what was written on the label on his bottle of lager, and while Lisa knew she could ask him about it in an attempt to kick-start the conversation, it was the contents of his head, rather than his beer bottle, that she was interested in.

So – batting down the urge to just get up and go – she peered around the venue, took a deep breath, tried not to make her exhale sound like a sigh, and smiled as pleasantly as she could.

Chapter 9

'So, what do you do?'

Simon looked up with a start, then – pleased he had something to contribute – nodded at the crowd of people waiting in front of the nearest food stall. He walked past this building most days on his way to work, so he'd followed the refurbishment with interest. He'd even checked out its history. It had been a disused factory before it was sold and turned into a food court – the latest phase of Margate's regeneration scheme that had begun with the opening of the new gallery some ten or so years ago. He'd visited the town a few years back, and he'd nervously locked his car doors when he'd driven along the seafront, but now? The area had certainly moved on. Unlike – if you listened to Will – Simon.

'Well, from what I can work out, you have a look around, decide what you want – there's Vietnamese, and pizza, and burgers, and Italian, and even gourmet Scotch eggs, whatever they are. Then you have to queue up, order what you want, and pay – obviously. Then you find a seat and, well, *eat*. Though it's pretty busy, and we've already got a seat, so maybe it's best if you go and have a look around while I mind the table, then I can go and get the food, and . . .' An amused-looking Lisa was regarding him quizzically, and he found himself blushing. 'What?'

'For a *job*?'

He reddened even more, then let out a short laugh – it was progress, as far as he was concerned, that he could see the funny side to his awkwardness. And a sign that he was relaxing a little.

'I'm a barista.'

'Really?' Lisa's expression was hard to read.

'Yes, really,' he said, wondering why anyone would question that, unless she thought that making coffee for other people somehow wasn't a worthy career. Or a worthy career for someone she was considering dating, at least.

'I'm sorry. It's just . . . you don't seem the type.'

Simon reached for his drink, then put it straight back down again. 'I'm not sure how to take that.'

'Well, I thought you had to train for *years*. And unless you've had major work done – and if you have, can I have the name of your plastic surgeon? – you don't seem that old.'

'You don't have to train for that long. I did a weekend course.'

'*One weekend?*'

He leaned in conspiratorially. 'Between you and me, it's not that complicated. Once you learn the basics.'

'Right,' said Lisa, though she didn't sound convinced. 'And do you have to wear one of those wigs?'

'What wigs?'

'Those white ones.'

'To make *coffee*?'

Simon sat there patiently as Lisa's face went through a series of expression changes, then she burst out laughing so loudly that the group of girls at the far end of the table stopped drinking whatever their garish pink cocktails were and stared at her.

'I'm sorry,' she said, eventually. 'I thought you said . . .' She started laughing again, so hard that tears were streaming down her cheeks, so

Simon passed her a serviette from the dispenser in the middle of the table.

Still, he reminded himself, girls were supposed to like men with a good sense of humour, and Lisa was obviously having a good laugh right now. Hopefully not at his expense.

'Said what?' he said, once he was sure her shoulders had stopped heaving.

'*Barrister*,' she gasped, dabbing at her eyes with the serviette. 'Like a lawyer. But with one of those . . .' Lisa began miming wearing a hairpiece, then stopped abruptly, as if she'd thought better of it. Perhaps because Simon obviously wasn't sharing her amusement.

'I know what a barrister is,' he said, curtly. 'But no. Sorry to disappoint. I'm a—'

'*Barista*. I get it now.' Lisa dabbed at her eyes again, then did that fanning-her-face-with-her-hands thing that women always did to stop themselves either crying or laughing. 'Sorry. It's a little loud in here.'

'No problem,' said Simon, though he suspected it might actually be a major problem from Lisa's point of view. For a moment or two, she had believed he was some kind of high-flying-lawyer type. How could she not be disappointed to hear that, actually, he made coffee for a living?

'So you . . . I mean, do you . . . ?'

'Yeah,' said Simon, not sure what he was agreeing to, but he nodded enthusiastically anyway. 'There are so many elements that go into a good cup of coffee, so many factors you have to get just right. It's kind of an art *and* a science. I mean, not rocket science, exactly, but . . .' He stopped talking – worried he sounded like he was bigging up what he did, perhaps as some sort of overreaction to Lisa's earlier mistake – and checked to see if her eyes were glazing over, then worried she'd think he was looking at her a bit too intensely, so changed his focus to his beer. 'Yes, I enjoy it,' he said, picking at the label on the bottle with his fingernail.

'Great.'

Simon glanced up at her, assuming she was being sarcastic, but to Lisa's credit, she seemed genuinely pleased that he liked what he did.

'Plus, everyone loves coffee,' he added.

'Um . . .'

'Um?'

Lisa took a sip of her wine. 'I don't.'

'*What?*'

'Always been more of a tea girl.'

'How much more of a tea girl?'

'About a hundred per cent.' Lisa pursed her lips. 'Sorry. I always have a cup or two at breakfast, at least.'

'Good to know. Not that I'm expecting to be making you – ahem – breakfast . . .' Simon stared down at the table, wondering how long it was going to take him to get over this bumbling awkwardness. He took a moment to compose himself, then looked up at Lisa. 'Anyway. The tea thing. Not to worry. People are different. It's what makes the world go round. Well, technically that's the rotation from when it was formed, and the lack of forces to stop it, even though the moon's doing its best to put the brakes on, but you see what I . . .' His voice trailed off. Lisa now looked like she was doing her best to stifle a yawn, and a change of subject seemed sensible. But before he could think of which of his library of facts to bore her with next, she smiled.

'Okay. For a non-coffee-drinker like me, if I was to go to Costa, what should I get?'

'Out of there as quickly as possible!'

She looked at him blankly for a moment, then cracked a smile. 'Sorry if my mentioning of a hugely successful coffee chain offends your sensibilities.'

'No, their coffee's not bad. It's just . . .' Simon hesitated, wondering how best to get across the difference between what they did and what *he* did, and Lisa raised both eyebrows.

'What?'

'Well, there's coffee, and there's coffee . . .' He hastily replayed the memory of the last time he'd checked out the menu there. 'But "Double Chocolate Cookie Mocha" is another thing. Another thing *entirely*.'

'So should I stick to their tea?'

'Um . . .'

'What's that supposed to mean?'

'Nothing. Except that you're in a coffee shop. And you've ordered tea. That's like going into Burger King and ordering a pizza.'

'You're just a coffee snob.'

'Not at all! Well, maybe a little. Though "snob" is a little harsh.'

'Sorry. Should I have said "stickler"?'

'It's like anything in life. You've just got to know the rules.'

'There are rules?'

Simon nodded enthusiastically, pleased Lisa seemed to have hit upon his specialist subject. Since losing Alice, it had been the rituals – the routines – that kept him sane, and his attention to detail when making coffee was one of the best. His job was fortunate in that respect – he was able to lose himself in a process he knew so well.

'There are *always* rules,' he said, deciding not to refer to Lisa's road-crossing earlier.

'I might regret asking this question, but . . . such as?'

'You're sure you want me to . . . ?' Lisa was looking interested, or at least doing a good job of pretending to be, so Simon sat up straighter. 'When and where to drink what, for example. Cappuccino's Italian, right? But you'd never see an Italian order one in the evening, and especially not after dinner.'

'What would they have? Expresso?'

'It's, um, *es*presso. With an "s", not an "x". And, yes. If you order a cappuccino after a meal in an Italian restaurant, the owner's going to think you haven't enjoyed your food, because if you've still got space for a large cup of milky, frothed coffee, the food can't have been that good.'

'But *espresso*,' said Lisa, making an effort to pronounce it correctly. 'After dinner, at night . . . ?'

'What about it?'

'Hello? Caffeine?'

'Aha.'

'What's "aha"? Apart from an eighties Norwegian pop group.'

Confused, Simon stared at her, then rolled his eyes when he finally got the joke. 'Well, caffeine actually raises the levels of acid in your stomach, aiding digestion. Plus the way espresso is made, with an extraction time of around twenty seconds, it means there's not too much caffeine. And it's a relatively short drink, so . . .' He stopped talking, and rolled his eyes at himself this time. 'Sorry. That must have been especially fascinating to someone who doesn't even like it.'

'No, it was . . .' Lisa looked like she was struggling to find the appropriate word, then evidently decided to stop looking for it. 'You certainly know your stuff.'

'Only if we're talking about coffee.'

She smiled, though the rest of her face didn't seem to follow through, and Simon tried desperately to think of something else to say.

'Who'd come on a blind date, eh?' he said, after a silence so long and awkward anyone watching might have thought they'd just had an argument, and Lisa nodded.

'Not me!' she said. 'At least, you're my first.'

'You've never done this before?'

'I haven't had to.'

'Right.' Simon shifted uncomfortably in his seat, wondering not for the first time how to process something Lisa had said.

'Oh god! Sorry – I didn't mean it like *that*. But – and don't laugh – my horoscope said something about not being afraid to take a few risks, so . . .'

'Your *horoscope*?'

'You don't believe in astrology?'

Simon let out a short laugh, then feared it might have sounded a little rude. 'Personally, no. Though I fully accept that some people might.'

'That's big of you,' said Lisa, though Simon could tell she was being sarcastic. 'What star sign are you?'

'I'm not sure.' He thought for a moment. 'Velociraptor?'

'That one doesn't exist!'

'It might as well be one, though, given that *none of them do*!'

Lisa gave him a look – one he was becoming familiar with. 'When's your birthday?'

'First of March.'

'A Pisces!'

'I'll take your word on that.'

'You should – that's a good one. Sensitive and reserved. A good listener, and a good friend.'

'Well, that's me all right. Maybe there's something to it after all?'

Lisa shot him another, slightly less kind look. 'I'm a Virgo,' she said, and Simon sniggered.

'How old are you?' said Lisa, sounding annoyed, and Simon assumed it wasn't really a question he was meant to answer.

'And are they, what is it, *compatible*?'

'Funnily enough, yes. Despite being opposite each other on the zodiac chart.'

'Right. Well, that's . . .'

'Isn't it?'

As Lisa sipped her wine, Simon sat there for a moment or two, wondering what they should talk about next and then remembering Will's advice about asking Lisa questions, but as hard as he tried he couldn't think of a single thing to say. Besides, given their obvious incompatibility (something that proved him right about astrology), he realised he wasn't actually all that interested in her answers.

'Maybe the *Gazette* should make you fill in some sort of form or something,' said Lisa, after a moment or two more.

'Form?'

'Beforehand.' Lisa smiled, in the manner of a primary school teacher explaining something to one of her pupils. 'Questions. To see if you're compatible. Ensure you've got something in common. Or, at least, give you something to talk about.'

'What, like "What's your favourite colour?"'

'Why not? Or whether you prefer dogs to cats, or *EastEnders* to *Coronation Street*. It'd save a lot of time, and stop you making a . . .' Lisa cleared her throat, then took a large glug of wine. 'Mistake.'

Simon laughed politely, though in truth he was horrified. He'd been struggling to work out why on earth someone like Lisa would have had, in Will's words, a 'chequered dating history', but right now he was beginning to understand why. Even *he* knew that relationships weren't just based on a series of shared ideas and likes and identical interests, or even a corresponding lack of bad habits: he and Alice had been so, so different – and that had been half the fun. If Lisa was simply looking for someone who ticked all her boxes, then she was going to be looking for a long, long time.

He picked up his beer and took a swig, and tried not to make a face – the warmer it got, the worse it tasted. Normal beer wasn't his favourite, and this wasn't even as 'nice' as that, nor did it have any of the benefits.

'Do you really feel that's the best way to find out all about someone?'

Lisa was looking at him the way you might regard a drunk on a bus. 'Why wouldn't it be? Cutting to the chase and all that.'

'Well, because . . .' Simon took a deep breath, fearing he was about to go seriously off-piste – and not only because this was hardly his area of expertise, but also because he was worried he'd forgotten how to ski. 'Surely it's more useful to give a Q&A like that to someone *after* you've split up with them? Almost like an exit interview? You know, to find out where you'd been going wrong.'

'Where *I'd* been going wrong?'

'No – not in terms of anyone's fault. Rather in terms of the sort of person you were seeing. How well you got on. Which isn't the same as compatibility. Besides, don't you think that successful relationships aren't necessarily – *shouldn't be* – things that work on paper? Sometimes the best ones don't.'

'The problem with that, though,' said Lisa levelly. 'Is that – no offence – most men are liars. They'll say anything to get what they want. And then say something completely different afterwards.'

'Such as?' said Simon, though he suspected he'd made a mistake as soon as he asked the question, because Lisa's eyes flashed angrily.

'I love you,' she said, quietly.

For a second, Simon considered making a joke, saying 'I love you too' or something similar, hoping he might score at least half a point like he had done with his 'You're welcome' quip earlier, but Lisa wasn't looking like she'd find anything funny right now.

'I'm sorry,' he said. 'If, you know, that's happened. To you. It's a horrible thing to' – he cleared his throat awkwardly – 'be on the receiving end of. But most people have probably said that at some point in their lives and . . .' He swallowed hard, a task made harder by the fact that his mouth had suddenly gone dry. '. . . not meant it.'

'Have *you*?'

'Possibly. I mean, I can't think of a specific time, but I'm sure . . .'

Lisa folded her arms. 'And what circumstances could there possibly be to justify saying something like that?'

'You might not want to hurt someone's feelings.'

'But it *would* hurt their feelings. If they ever found out.'

'How would they find out?'

'Because if you tell someone you love them, then you split up with them soon afterwards, then when I . . . I mean, when *that person* thinks back to that conversation, she – I mean, *they* – will realise the person had been lying to them, and be even more hurt.'

'They might not have been lying. At the time.'

'Yeah, right!' said Lisa.

'All I'm saying is, sometimes, perhaps a little *white* lie—'

'Is still a lie!'

Simon found himself wishing he'd ordered a normal beer. 'Not . . . always.'

'What is it then?'

'It might be, er, postponing the truth.'

'So you're saying honesty isn't always the best policy?'

He hesitated, wondering whether Lisa was trying to catch him out. 'Maybe. Sometimes. If it comes from a good place.'

'If *what* comes from a good place?'

'Um . . . *dis*honesty.'

At this, Lisa sat back in her seat and linked her arms behind her head in an 'I win' way, and Simon found it difficult to disagree with her. Besides, she was looking like she couldn't be bothered to argue any more, so he smiled as pleasantly as he could.

'Okay, okay,' Simon said, noticing Lisa had almost finished her drink. Then he realised the conversation ball was firmly in his court. 'Nice place, isn't it?'

'It is.' She gazed around the venue. 'If you'd asked me five years ago whether I'd ever be eating at a street food restaurant in Margate, I'd have thought you were having a laugh. But now? Just shows you anything's possible, I suppose.'

She sounded hopeful, as if the fact that somewhere like Margate could change for the better meant there was no reason why she couldn't too, and to his surprise, Simon found himself admiring her for that. 'You a local, are you?'

Lisa nodded. 'Margate born and bred. And lived here all my life.'

'Right,' said Simon. 'That's . . .'

'Choose your next word very carefully!'

'Nice,' he said, as neutrally as he could.

'I'm guessing you're not from here?'

'London. I moved down after . . .' He caught himself. Now wasn't the right time to get into his life story – not that he was planning to at *any* time. 'After my friend Will did,' he said, instead.

'*Will?*'

Simon nodded, wondering why Lisa was frowning, then to his horror he remembered Will had told him he was supposed to have written in to the paper. He fixed his gaze on a spot in front of him on the table and soldiered on, hoping Lisa hadn't smelled a rat. 'Anyway, Will used to be my flatmate – in London – and he moved down here to work at the *Gazette*, and I'd already decided I wanted to move out of London. Too many' – he stopped short of saying 'memories' – 'people. So I fancied a change of scene, then this job came up at Wholly Ground, the new coffee place in the Old Town. Funny story – they were going to call it "Grinder" but . . .' He felt himself blushing at the prospect of explaining why a similar name to an app for hook-ups maybe hadn't been the best idea, and decided against it. 'They didn't, in the end. Anyway, Will was forever banging on about how Margate's the new Shoreditch-on-Sea, which it isn't, because the old Shoreditch isn't on the sea, despite having the word "shore" in it – it isn't even on the river – so technically you should say it's the new Shoreditch *but* on sea . . .' He paused for breath, sure Lisa's eyes had glazed over this time but not wanting to look up for confirmation, still trying desperately to cover his slip-up. 'Anyway, the job's good. We roast our own artisan blend. Import the beans and everything. Which makes it a bit more interesting.'

'Let me stop you there,' said Lisa, in a tone that suggested making coffee – or, indeed, anything that was coming out of Simon's mouth right now – wasn't interesting at all. 'You're a friend of *Will's*?'

'That's right.'

'Jess's *boyfriend* Will?'

Simon nodded nervously. 'That's the one. He's the one who told me I should, you know . . .' He made a face, trying to represent the 'gawd, isn't this embarrassing, but there you have it' aspect every blind date must surely come with, and crossed his fingers under the table. '. . . write in.'

Lisa was regarding him with narrowed eyes, her expression hard to read. 'Listen,' she said eventually, then she reached across the table and patted Simon's hand. 'I think it's obvious what's happening here. Don't you?'

'Um . . .'

Simon realised he must have been looking like it wasn't obvious at all, because Lisa decided to soldier on. 'You like coffee, I like tea?' she said, by way of an explanation. 'I suppose it's the risk you take, isn't it, when you go on a blind date?'

'Er, what is?'

'That you don't get on. That you're not compatible. Haven't got anything in common.'

'I suppose.'

'We've quite clearly got different views about everything, from road safety to our favourite hot beverage, and, who knows, the perfect partner for each of us might be just around the corner. So we could sit here, make small talk, be polite, both of us just waiting until the other one decides they've had enough, or . . .'

Lisa was nodding encouragingly at him, as if expecting him to complete her sentence, but given how things had gone so far, Simon didn't dare.

'Or we can just call it a day now,' she continued, when he was silent. 'Cut our losses. Onwards and upwards, that sort of thing!'

'Right,' said Simon. 'Although technically there haven't *been* any losses. Seeing as the *Gazette* are paying.'

'You know what I mean,' said Lisa, impatiently. 'So. Shall we?'

'I do,' he said. 'So let's.'

And though he knew he perhaps shouldn't be, Simon had never been more relieved about anything in his entire life.

Chapter 10

Lisa fished around inside her handbag, retrieved a couple of sheets of paper she'd printed off earlier from the email Jess had sent her that morning, and handed one to Simon, telling herself she was doing the right thing. She and Simon really weren't compatible. What on earth could he have put when he'd written in to the paper – and if he hadn't made something up, what had Jess been thinking? Then again, what had *she* been thinking, expecting to meet the love of her life like this? Was she being stupid, hoping that fate might help her find her ideal partner, when it had hardly been kind to her so far?

She took a breath, and reminded herself how that kind of negativity wouldn't do her any favours. *Onwards and upwards*, like she'd just told Simon. After all, things surely couldn't get much worse.

She hoped.

'So why don't we just fill these in,' she said. 'I'll give them to Jess when I see her next, and that'll be the end of it.'

'What's this?'

Simon was frowning at the questionnaire, so Lisa smiled patiently. 'Our questions. For the interview. In the *Gazette*?' she added, noting Simon's blank expression.

'Right,' he said. 'Do you have a pen?'

She rooted around in her handbag and – despite three packets of tissues, four lipsticks, an unwrapped piece of chewing gum, and a half-empty strip of tablets so old she couldn't quite identify them – couldn't locate the pen she'd thought she had in there. 'Or we could just write the answers down on our phones like normal people?'

'Oh. Sure,' he said, fumbling for his phone in his pocket. 'So I'll just . . .'

'Me too.'

'Great.'

Lisa drained the remaining few drops of wine in her glass, then turned her attention to the questions in front of her. She glanced across the table at Simon as he did the same, and smiled. He looked like he was taking an exam at school, and she half expected him to be shielding his answers from her with a cupped hand, so she couldn't cheat.

The first question seemed an easy one: 'What were you hoping for from the date?' Or so Lisa thought, but the more she considered it, the more she wondered what they meant. Was it *physically* – as in was she expecting someone who looked like Harry Styles (her current crush, though she knew she was old enough to be his . . . She decided to go with 'much older sister') – or did it require a more general response, along the lines of 'A fun lunch', or perhaps simply 'Good food and good company'? All of these things were true, would have made her happy, but they also made her sound a little purposeless. But 'To meet the love of my life' might come across as . . . naive, perhaps. Stupid, even. Unrealistic, certainly. Though the truth was, that was exactly why she'd come – the hope she'd meet someone amazing, who might just feel the same way about her. Instead she'd ended up with . . .

Lisa caught herself. It wasn't about recriminations – not yet, anyway. She'd go for the 'love of my life' answer, and see where that took her. After all, as Jess had hinted, any man reading the piece would understand that was what she was about, and hopefully only men looking for the same would get in touch. If *anyone* got in touch.

As for the next section, 'First impressions?', well, that one was a little harder to answer. Yes, Simon had almost run her over, but she had to concede that was possibly a little bit her fault, and that had happened before she knew he was her date, so it couldn't really be her first impression. Then, when he'd turned up at the table, she'd been too busy trying to send him away that she hadn't really given him a *chance* to make a first impression, so by the time she'd realised who he was and he'd sat down, it had been a little bit late. And while he'd seemed nice enough . . .

Lisa tapped those last two words into her phone. That would do. Because Simon had. Or did. And that was surely something he – or they – could work on.

'What did you talk about?' she decided she'd leave until later, because 'A series of misunderstandings' probably wasn't a good answer, and 'The finer points of coffee' wouldn't send the best message about a tea drinker like her. But that led her on to 'Any awkward moments?' – and, to her mortification, Lisa realised she had more than a few to choose from, from stepping out in front of his car, not recognising him at the table and sending him away, getting confused when he'd told her what he did for a job . . .

She peered across the table to find Simon scratching his head. 'How are you getting on?' she asked, and he made a face.

'It's not as easy as it looks. And it seems a bit . . . stupid.'

'What are you suggesting? That we refuse to fill it in?'

'I'm not sure about you, but I'm not so keen on being in the paper. Or rather, this "date" being in the paper.'

Simon had used air quotes around the word, and while Lisa couldn't argue with his use of punctuation given that the past half-hour or so could hardly be called a date, when it came to it being in the paper that wasn't how she felt *at all*. She was desperate to at least salvage *something* from this mismatch, and between her and Jess they could surely make something up so Simon looked fine and she came off as some kind of catch.

'Maybe not,' she said, feeling a little guilty at having earlier lectured Simon on the need to tell the truth.

'Great.' Simon looked like the weight of the world had lifted from his shoulders. 'So you tell Jess, and I'll tell Will, and—'

'Sounds like a plan.'

'Doesn't it?' Simon was looking at his half-empty beer bottle as if considering finishing it, then he evidently thought better of it because he stood up instead, so Lisa did the same. 'Right, so . . .'

'So . . .'

'Nice to meet you.'

'And you.'

'Should we hug, or . . . ?'

Lisa thought for a moment. It would have been polite, she supposed, but the table was in the way, and she didn't want to risk another 'you go that way, I'll go this way' incident. 'I think a handshake will do.'

'Fine.' Simon held his hand out, so she shook it briefly. 'Well, good luck.'

'You too,' she said, thinking that if Simon continued his dates in this vein, he'd need it. And if things didn't pick up for her, then so, Lisa feared, would she.

'So . . .' Simon had begun walking towards the exit, as had she, and at this rate they'd be leaving together. As if sensing her reluctance, he stopped. 'You first,' he said. 'And I'll give you a minute or so before I go to my car. Don't want a repeat incident of . . .'

'Quite.'

She gave Simon the briefest of smiles, then headed back outside and began walking briskly towards the bottom of the High Street. There weren't that many people around – but, then again, there were *never* that many people around the old part of town nowadays, everyone preferring to shop at the new retail park a few miles away – and, for once, Lisa found herself grateful for the fact. Fewer people to notice she was on her own, she supposed. Miserably, she retrieved her phone from her bag and dialled Jess's number, responding to her friend's 'Babe?' with a loud sigh.

'That bad?'

Lisa almost laughed. 'Couldn't have gone worse, actually. I can't believe he's a friend of Will's.'

'He told you that?'

'Yup. Said Will had even encouraged him to write in.'

'Oh. Right. Yeah. And where's Simon now?'

'On his way home, probably.'

'Ah.'

'Yes, ah.'

'Lise. I'm *so* sorry.'

'Why on earth did you think we'd get on?'

'Well, um, *because* . . .'

Jess was drawing that last word out, and Lisa suddenly bristled. 'Jess!'

'Calm down. I'm just thinking how best to put it.'

'And?'

'Well . . . because Simon's not Chris.'

'That's *it*?'

'But he's *so* not Chris. In fact, he's the Anti-Chris. But in a good way.'

Lisa let out a short laugh, despite herself. 'Is that supposed to be funny?'

'A little.' Jess giggled down the phone. 'So it was a disaster. So what? I've been on worse first dates. Including . . .' She lowered her voice. 'This one guy I met on Tinder, he was really nervous, so he had a fair bit to drink, which seemed to relax him, then in the cab home he was getting so amorous I was thinking, *I'm in for a good time tonight*, but when we end up in bed and he's down under the duvet doing . . . well, you can imagine . . . the next thing I know, I hear this weird sound, and . . .'

'Do I really want to know?'

'It was him *snoring*!' said Jess, before bursting out laughing.

'Oh my god!'

'I *know*!'

'What happened the next morning?'

'Well, we're still together, so . . .'

'It was *Will*?'

'Maybe,' said Jess with a snigger.

'I thought you met at work?'

'We did. Thanks to Tinder, if you see what I mean. Anyway, don't you *dare* tell him I told you. Anyway. Enough about me. Where are you?'

'I don't know. Hang on.' Lisa found a tissue in her handbag, then blew her nose as she checked her surroundings. She'd been walking randomly since she left the restaurant, and now found herself standing in front of the pub halfway up the High Street. 'Outside The Old Cottage. Shortly to be *inside* The Old Cottage.'

'Right. Order a couple of large white wines, and I'll see you there in five.'

'Thanks, Jess.'

'One of those will be for me, by the way.'

'I guessed.'

'So don't drink it.'

'I get it, Jess!' she said, although – despite her friend's attempt to cheer her up – the way she was feeling, and with her hopes looking more like *nopes*, Lisa couldn't guarantee she wouldn't.

Chapter 11

Though he'd done his best to hide it earlier, Simon had been surprised he'd passed the 'emergency call' point. He and Lisa quite clearly hadn't been getting on, and, to be honest, after half an hour or so, he'd been wishing he'd arranged an emergency call of his own with Will.

He knew the strategy well – it had happened to him twice Before Alice. Once when a girl had told him her best friend had just been in an accident so she had to go, although when he'd offered to drive her, she'd told him that would have been inappropriate as her friend might have a phobia about cars now; and another time when a girl had simply picked up her phone and put it to her ear – *even though Simon hadn't heard it ring* – mumbled, 'I'll be there in five' into it, and then, in response to his raised eyebrows, had just grabbed her bag and left.

Still, this way was much better. No hard feelings – or hurt ones. He and Lisa had realised they were obviously looking for different things – in Lisa's case, a partner; in his case, not – so they'd agreed to disagree and gone their separate ways. And even though Jess would have to find something else to write about next week, he'd fulfilled his part of the bargain with Will too. Put himself 'out there', even though he'd been a little put out to find himself forced into that position.

The prospect of heading home to his empty flat hadn't been that appealing, and he'd needed some air (and perhaps a chance to vent) – and Will's place wasn't far. Now he found himself ringing Will's doorbell, and, as the door swung open, he hoped his friend wouldn't be too judgemental. Simon had had all the judgement he could handle for one day.

'Mate?'

Will's eyes had widened in surprise the moment he answered the door, and while Simon wasn't looking forward to what he could guess Will's response would be, he wanted to give his side of the story first. Just in case Lisa complained.

'Can I come in?'

'Lisa too shy to thank me herself?'

'What?'

'Don't tell me – she's waiting round the corner before you whisk her off for an afternoon of passion?'

Will was making a point of peering exaggeratedly over Simon's shoulder and up and down the street, so Simon pushed good-naturedly past him and into the flat. He made his way into Will's front room, pleased not to find Jess there. Since she and Will had got together a month or so ago, he'd managed to avoid meeting her. Not because he disapproved, but because the thought of being around the two of them made him feel a bit awkward. Like a third wheel. Lonely. Or, at least, made him remember that he'd once been part of a couple.

The television was on, showing some football match between two sides Simon didn't recognise, though that was no surprise. Simon didn't really 'do' football. Wasting hours every Saturday watching two teams of overpaid, over-tattooed, strange-haircut-sporting sportsmen chase a ball around wasn't his idea of fun. And nor was paying a small fortune for a replica shirt with one of their names printed on the back – like the one Will was currently wearing.

'Not interrupting anything, am I?'

Will followed him in from the hallway, picked up the remote from the arm of the sofa, and pressed Mute. 'Just watching the game.'

'Who's winning?'

'Not you, by the looks of things.' Will mimed a belly laugh at his own joke, then looked at his watch. 'That went . . . quickly.'

'Well, when you know, you know.'

Will frowned. 'It went okay, right?'

He nodded at the sofa, so Simon collapsed gratefully down on to it. 'Well, "okay" might be overstating things a bit.'

'Ah.'

'Yes. Ah.'

Will had walked across to the fridge, though when he produced a beer, Simon waved it away. 'Best not. I'm driving.'

'Suit yourself.' Will twisted the top off the bottle and took a glug. 'So?'

'So what?'

'Did you like her?'

Simon thought for a moment. 'Yeah,' he said, slightly surprising himself with his answer. 'She was nice enough. Attractive, obviously.'

Will gave a small bow. 'Obviously.'

'Though she seemed a bit . . . complicated.'

'Don't take this the wrong way, but you're hardly Captain Straightforward. Besides, isn't *everyone* complicated at our age?'

'Alice wasn't.'

Will scratched the top of his head. 'Si, you can't be comparing everyone to her,' he said softly. 'Otherwise you're never going to move on.'

'I know.' Simon leaned back on the sofa and stared hopelessly up at the ceiling. 'But what if I'm not *ready* to move on?'

'Why did you go out with Lisa, then?'

'Because you made me! Or, rather, tricked me into it.'

'For your own good.'

'Maybe.'

'You didn't tell her that, did you? That I had to . . .' Will frowned, as if trying to come up with just the right word. 'Coerce you into going.'

'Of course not! Well, not in so many words.'

'*Si?*'

'I think she could tell, though.'

'Tell what?'

'That I didn't want to be there.'

'Even though you were attracted to her?'

'That's not what I . . .' Simon sighed. 'I'm *not*. Well, maybe a bit. I don't know. It's just . . .' He stopped talking, trying to work out what that 'just' was. 'You're right, though.'

Will looked surprised. 'I am?'

'Yeah. There's something stopping me, and I can't decide whether it's that I'm afraid I'll never meet someone like Alice again, or whether I'm more worried I *might*.'

Will had perched on the arm of the chair opposite. 'Sorry, Si. You're going to have to explain that one.'

'Because if I do, it might mean Alice wasn't anything special. And that's not how I want to remember her.'

Will took a large slug of beer. 'Listen, Si. I know you probably don't want to hear this . . .'

'Don't say it, then.'

'And I'm not saying Alice wasn't special. Because she was. But you also have to accept the fact that Alice was a *freak* – and I mean that in a good way. A one-off. One of a kind.'

'I get it, Will.'

'Chances are you're never going to meet someone like her again.'

'Maybe.'

'But you can't let that stop you seeing what it might be like with someone different. You never know – it might even be better.'

Will held his beer bottle out, so Simon regarded it for a moment, then grabbed it, wiped the top with his sleeve and took a swig. 'Maybe,' he said. Though he doubted it.

'So, why not give Lisa another chance? You're single. She's single . . .'

Simon stared at his friend. 'I'm hoping you're going to add a few more observations to that.'

'And there's the obvious thing that Lisa has in spades, and it's something you could do with a bit of.'

'If you're being smutty again, I'm going to—'

'*Hope*, Si.'

'Huh?'

'After everything she's been through she still believes she'll meet someone. Be happy with someone.'

'What has she been through, exactly?'

'The way Jess tells it – her last boyfriend was a complete wanker.'

'As sad as that is, with all due respect, our situations aren't quite the same.'

'They're not a competition, either.'

'What do you mean by that, exactly?' said Simon, angrily.

Will made 'calm down' motions with his hands, as if playing an imaginary set of bongos. 'All I'm saying is, you've got to give these things a bit more time. Coming to terms with what happened to Alice is difficult.'

'I'm doing my best!'

'I know you are.'

Simon stared at the television, where a footballer with more visible ink than the tattooed ladies they used to feature at Victorian funfairs was rolling around on the grass as if he'd been shot. 'Maybe. Maybe I'm just not ready.'

'Maybe you are. Maybe Lisa's the one.'

'You're saying Alice wasn't?'

Will sighed. 'It's S-O-U-L-mate. Not S-O-L-E. You've got to put yourself back out there.'

'Yeah, but look what happens when I do,' said Simon, handing Will his beer back. 'Besides, I think it's a little too late where Lisa's concerned, given how she summarily dismissed me after half an hour. Don't you?'

'The day's still young.'

Simon made a face. *He* wasn't, and that was part of his problem.

He turned his attention back to the television. The footballer had made a miraculous recovery, and was now sprinting after the referee to complain about something.

'Oh well,' continued Will. 'At least you did it. And I'll tell Jess to go easy on you so when the paper comes out—'

'Yeah. About that.'

Will looked at him suspiciously. 'What about that?'

'Has Lisa been in touch with Jess?'

'Dunno. Why?'

'Well, because I – I mean, *Lisa* and I – thought it might be better if we weren't.'

'Weren't what?'

'Featured. In the paper.'

'Yeah. Good one, Si.'

'I'm serious. Let's face it, what went down between us doesn't exactly portray her or me in the best light, and it's not like I'm actively looking for a girlfriend anyway, so it wouldn't really be fair to . . .' Simon stopped talking. Will was staring at him, a look of horror on his face. 'What?'

'You have to!'

'Have to what?'

'Be in the paper.'

'Why?'

Will looked to his left, then his right, then leaned forward in his chair, as if about to impart some state secret. 'I'll level with you, Si. This wasn't all about you getting back out there.'

'It wasn't?'

'Well – mostly, yeah. But . . .' He lowered his voice, as if his flat might be bugged. 'Jess is in a bit of bother. At work.'

'And this has what to do with me, exactly?'

'I'm coming to that!' Will took another mouthful of beer, followed by an even bigger one. 'The "Blind Date" column. It's Jess's "special thing".'

'I thought that was you?'

Will smiled sarcastically. 'But they're thinking of cancelling it.'

'Why?'

'Well, because . . .' Will moved across to sit next to him. 'Because it doesn't have the best success rate.'

'What success rate does it have, exactly?'

'Including you and Lisa?' Will thought for a moment, as if totting something up in his head. 'Zero. And it's quite expensive, what with the *Gazette* picking up the tab for the dates. So our editor – Jess's boss – thinks that it's just people who want a free meal out, or fancy being in the paper, who write in. And he's told her if it doesn't work out for someone soon, then that'll be the end of it.'

'Right.'

'So Jess – well, *we* – thought if we got a couple of friends to go on one, then they'd, you know . . .' He looked at Simon the way a dog might look at someone holding a treat.

'I'm sorry. You want me and Lisa to lie, and say we've had a great time, and it's all happy ever after, just so Jess isn't out of a job?'

'Thanks, mate.' Will leaned over and clapped him on the knee. 'I knew you'd understand.'

'Hold on. I haven't said I'm going to! And why didn't you tell me beforehand? Or was Lisa in on this?'

'No way. We thought you might get on. That it might happen . . . naturally.'

'*Really?*'

Will shrugged dismissively. 'You never know. She's always been unlucky in love, gone out with losers, or wankers, and you—'

'Choose your next words carefully.'

'Well, you might just have been . . .'

'What? Desperate enough to think we had something?'

'Not desperate, exactly. Just . . . keen.'

Will nodded, as if happy with his choice of word, and Simon started at him incredulously. 'Even so. You were prepared to make me look like a loser in the local paper simply so your girlfriend didn't get in trouble?'

'I'd never make you look like a loser.'

'Don't tell me – because I do a good enough job of that by myself?'

Will laughed briefly. 'Listen, mate. You don't have to lie, exactly. Just pretend you had a good time, hint the two of you might have some sort of future, smile for the photographer, and—'

'Photographer? What photographer?'

'There's always a photo,' said Will, as if it was something Simon should know. 'You know, the happy couple, grinning at each other. Not that there's been many like that. Or any like that, come to think of it.'

'No chance!'

'Please. Do it for me. And if not for me, for Jess.'

Will was fluttering his eyelashes, and Simon didn't know whether to laugh or punch him. 'I don't know. And I'm pretty sure Lisa won't—'

As if on cue, Will's phone bleeped with a text. 'Jess,' he said, before he'd even read it, then he glanced down at the screen and smiled. 'The photographer's on her way. *She's* single, if you're—'

'Will!'

'Okay, okay. Just one photo. We can Photoshop the two of you so it looks like you're, you know, *together*. Then all you have to do is fill in that questionnaire.'

'*Will* . . .'

'I'll owe you. Big time.'

'You already do!'

'Please . . .'

Simon sighed. On the television, the game appeared to have finished, but he suspected he had no option but to play along with this one. With a final, heavy-eyed look at Will, he shook his head, in the manner of someone who knows they can't postpone the inevitable.

'Fine' he said, begrudgingly.

'That's my boy!' Will leapt off the sofa, and hauled Simon up from his seat. 'Now, come on. Pub!'

'I don't want to go to the pub.'

'It's not a case of "want", my friend,' said Will, putting an arm round his shoulders and steering him towards the door, and not for the first time that day Simon found himself being made to go somewhere he didn't want to be.

And for what he could only hope would be the last time, he went.

Chapter 12

Lisa was sitting at a window table in The Old Cottage, flicking idly through her Instagram feed, pointedly refusing to like any posts that featured hashtags like '#couplegoals'. Her #couplegoal was simply to *be* in a couple, and all these people grinning happily at the camera, their arms around each other, only served to remind her she'd got no closer to that particular end point today.

Maybe Simon was right, and they shouldn't be featured in the paper after all. Did she really expect that the potential love of her life would have written in to the *Gazette* in search of true love? A free lunch and the chance of a shag, maybe, but happy ever after? Lisa doubted it.

She considered checking out what her ex Chris had been up to, but stopped short of typing his name into the search box. She'd stopped following him (on Instagram – physically it had taken a week or so longer, when he'd almost caught her outside his house and she'd had to duck down behind a parked car) the day she'd come back from Cancún, telling herself she needed to move forward rather than keep looking back. But some days – today included – it was harder than others not to reminisce about what might have been; if, of course, things had been different. If *Chris* had been different. Though Lisa suspected if *she* had – if she'd been the person she was trying to be post-Cancún (i.e. herself) – she might not have been in this mess in the first place.

She double-checked the time on her phone against the clock above the bar. As usual, Jess's 'five minutes' was closer to ten, and she'd already finished her glass of wine (and was tempted to make a start on Jess's) by the time her friend finally appeared at the table.

'Sorry. I'm just . . .' Jess finished composing a text, then slipped her phone back into her bag as she waved a hand vaguely in the air. 'You doing okay?' she said, once she'd hugged Lisa hello.

Lisa glared at her, good-naturedly. 'I'm still trying to work out whether I'm mad at you or not.'

'Sorry, babe!' Jess made a guilty face, then nodded at Lisa's empty wine glass. 'Can I get you another?'

'Best not.'

'Suit yourself. So . . .' Jess sat down opposite her, clinked Lisa's empty glass, poured a good measure into it from hers, then patted Lisa's arm sympathetically. 'Want to tell me all about it – from the beginning?'

'Not really,' said Lisa.

'In my defence – *our* defence – Will and I thought this way was actually better.'

'I'm sorry?'

'Rather than set you up with someone random. Simon's actually Will's best friend. And Will's hardly going to be best friends with someone . . . dodgy.'

'Tell me again why you've never met your boyfriend's best friend?'

'Well, because Will and I are in that early stage of our relationship where we spend every spare moment—'

'Okay, okay.'

'I have suggested it. But Will's kind of skirted round the issue, now I come to think of it. But I can't believe he's dodgy. And even if he is, he can't be as dodgy as . . .'

'As Chris, you mean?'

'As Chris.'

'I don't think Simon's dodgy. He's just . . .' Lisa thought for a moment. 'He just didn't seem that interested.'

'In you?'

'In anyone. So why he wrote in asking to go on a blind date is a mystery to me.'

'Hmm,' said Jess, fishing a piece of cork out of her glass with her fingernail.

'As is why you put the two of us together.'

'Because I thought he'd take one look at you, and . . .' Jess mimed her heart pounding through her chest, and Lisa shook her head.

'Well, he didn't. So how's that supposed to make me feel?'

Jess smiled sympathetically. 'Never mind. You wait till you're featured in the paper. There'll be loads of men writing in to get your number. Stopping you in the street, probably. You'll be fighting them off.'

'That's not going to happen.'

'Of course it is!'

'No, I mean it's not going to happen, because I'm not going to be in the paper. Sorry, Jess, but the last thing I want is for everyone to see how desperate I am.'

'You're not desperate.'

'Or how badly the date went.'

'It didn't go badly. At least, that's how I'll write it up.'

'Jess!'

'I'm serious. Trust me – when the feature comes out, there won't be a single man in Margate who won't want to sweep you off your feet. And a few married ones too, probably!'

Lisa rolled her eyes at her friend's joke. 'Doubtful.'

'Especially when they see your photo.' Jess tapped the face of her watch. 'The photographer should be along soon. Then . . .'

'Jess . . .'

'Relax. All we need is one shot of you and Simon together, and—'

'The only way you're going to achieve that is via Photoshop! Though while you're at it, if you could do something about the bags under my eyes.'

'Deal!' said Jess, pouring the rest of her wine into Lisa's glass.

'That's not what I—'

'Tell you what. I'll just get us another round, and you can think about how you want to answer those interview questions I sent you, and—'

'I'm not doing any interview questions. Simon and I decided we wouldn't.'

'But . . . you *have* to!'

Lisa picked her glass up and emptied it back into Jess's. 'The only thing I have to do is go home, take a long hot shower, and put this . . . *debacle* behind me.'

'Whatever happened to "seize the day"?'

Lisa gave her friend a look. She'd like to seize the day – by the neck, and throttle the life out of it.

'Okay,' said Jess. 'But at least stay for another drink. Keep me company. That is, unless you've got somewhere else to be?'

Lisa gave Jess a different look. 'Fine,' she said, resignedly.

'Excellent!'

As Jess bounded off to the bar, Lisa slumped down on to the table, shut her eyes and rested her head on her folded arms. Idly, she wondered what Simon was up to right now – possibly having the same conversation with Will, in a different pub, and with another alcohol-free beer. Unless their meeting had sent him off in search of something stronger. It was a shame they hadn't connected. He *had* seemed like a nice guy. But you shouldn't worry about the things you can't change, as she knew. Or at least, as she often told herself.

The noise of a tray being set down on the table snapped Lisa back to reality, so she hauled herself back upright.

'Thanks, Jess,' she said, as her friend deposited a large glass of wine in front of her.

'Don't mention it.' Jess moved round to her side of the table and gave her a hug. 'Now budge up.'

Obediently, Lisa shimmied along the bench, just as she noticed a couple of bottles of beer sitting on the tray, then she frowned.

'Are we getting pissed?'

'No.' Jess let out her tinkling laugh again, and glanced over at the pub door. 'But *you* might be. With me.'

'Huh? I don't . . .' Lisa stopped talking. Over Jess's shoulder, she could see a man walking into the pub – a man who looked suspiciously like Will – closely followed by someone else.

Someone else she recognised.

Someone who she'd already had a drink with today – albeit a non-alcoholic one, in his case.

Someone she'd thought she might never see again.

As Jess waved both men over, Lisa gritted her teeth. 'What's going on?' she hissed, realising Jess had moved seats to ensure *she* couldn't.

'Will!' said Jess, louder than was perhaps strictly necessary, rising a little from the bench – just enough to give her boyfriend a kiss, but not enough to allow Lisa to make a break for it. 'And you must be Simon! What a nice surprise.'

'Jess,' said Will, then he flashed Lisa a sheepish grin. 'Hey Lise,' he said.

Jess was looking at the two of them in wonderment, as if this were some sort of special occasion. 'What a coincidence!'

'Isn't it,' said Simon, drily, causing Jess to laugh as if he'd just told the funniest joke in the world.

Jess sat back down and put an arm round Lisa's shoulders. A restraining one, Lisa couldn't help feeling. 'Lisa's been telling me about all the fun you two had. Haven't you?'

Lisa glared at her. 'Something like that,' she said, then she grimaced at Jess's response; that tinkling laugh was really starting to get on her nerves now.

'Join us?' said Jess, after several extremely uncomfortable seconds.

'Why not?' said Will, and as Simon tried to make eye contact with him, as if unsure what exactly it was they were doing, Lisa tried to nudge Jess along the bench so she could get out, but Jess had a firm grip on the underside of the table and she wasn't budging. Simon hadn't sat down – though Lisa realised that was probably just him being polite.

'At least till the photographer gets here?' suggested Jess.

'Whatever happened to "we can do it with Photoshop"?' said Simon.

'Well, we've still got to get a photo of each of you, and the photographer's on their way, so it's probably easier if we . . .' Will grabbed Simon by the shoulders and almost manhandled him down on to the bench, then nodded at the drinks, as if they were some sort of irresistible bribe, and though Lisa could certainly do with hers she left it where it was. 'Guys,' said Will. 'Please.'

'Just stay for one drink,' pleaded Jess. 'That's all we're asking. And if the photographer hasn't turned up by then, well . . .'

'One drink?' Simon was eyeing his beer thoughtfully, then he picked it up, so Lisa did the same with her glass of wine.

'Why not,' she said, then – as if of one mind – she and Simon raised their drinks, cheersed each other and both downed the contents in one.

'Right. Well then . . .' Simon stifled a burp. 'Lovely seeing you again, Lisa, but . . .'

'Hey!' Lisa was feeling a bit light-headed from necking her Chardonnay. 'Not so fast. What gives you the right to leave first?'

'I'm just leaving. I'm not leaving "first".'

'Too right you're not! Not before me, at least.'

She tried to push past Jess again, but Jess had wedged herself firmly in place, so Lisa slipped underneath the table, only to find her exit route blocked by the table's metal frame. In desperation, she grabbed one of the legs, trying to ignore whatever the sticky substance was that she could feel on the palm of her hand, and gave it a shove, but it was too heavy to move on her own.

She sat there for a moment, considering her options, hoping she wouldn't get splinters from the bare wooden floorboards. Staying where she was might work, but it wasn't the most comfortable place to wait it out, and, besides, she needed the toilet. Then she heard someone clearing their throat, so she looked up to see Simon, grinning at her from underneath the far end of the table.

'What?' she said, crossly.

'Need a hand?'

'No thank you! I'm quite capable of . . .' Lisa tried pushing on the leg again, but the table wouldn't budge. 'Actually, yes.'

'Okay. Hold on . . .'

Simon moved to one end of the table, Will to the other, and between them they managed to pull it out, revealing Lisa cross-legged on the floor. As Simon helped her up, Will and Jess were doing their best not to laugh, and Lisa had to try her hardest to stop a smile from creeping across her face.

'It's not funny!' she protested.

'It is. A bit,' said Simon, as he and Will shifted the table back to its original position. Then he sat down heavily on the opposite bench. 'Are you okay?'

'Downing that in one perhaps wasn't the smartest of ideas,' said Lisa, sitting herself back in her original seat, then she glared at Will. 'What's going on?'

'Nothing. Well, Jess thought . . . Ow!' Will said, then he leaned down to rub the spot on his shin where Jess had evidently just kicked him. 'I mean, *we* thought . . .' He reached across the table and took his girlfriend's hand, and Jess smiled.

'What Will's trying to say, Lise, is that I need you to complete the date. Or, at least, pretend you have. And that it's been the best date you've ever been on.'

Lisa frowned. 'And why is that, exactly?'

Simon cleared his throat. 'Because Jess might lose her job if we don't.'

'What?'

'He's right.' Jess had taken her hand. 'The pressure's on for this column of mine, if it doesn't produce a happy ending sooner rather than later.'

'In terms of the couple ending up in a relationship,' said Will. 'Rather than in a dodgy massage parlour sense . . . *Ow!*'

'Which is why they asked us to go,' explained Simon, as Will rubbed his other shin. 'Because if it had worked out between us, then great. If it hadn't, then it could still be great, because they could convince us to *say* it had.'

Will was nodding. 'In fact, don't worry about those questions Jess sent you. She'll – I mean, *we'll* – take care of those. So when the photographer arrives, if you two could just . . .' He grabbed Simon's hand this time, and placed it on top of hers on the table.

'I don't know,' said Lisa. 'I—'

'I'll make it worth your while,' said Jess, then she reached into her bag and retrieved a bank card. 'Or, at least, the *Gazette* will.'

'What's this?'

'My company credit card. Anything you want. Anything.' She handed it to Simon, then gestured around the pub. 'Within reason, of course. But seriously. Have another drink.'

'Have two!' suggested Will.

'On us.'

'Or rather, on the *Gazette*,' said Will.

Lisa sighed. Loudly. 'And all we have to do is pretend we've had a good time?'

'You don't even have to pretend that. Jess will make sure you did. Or that it looks like you did.' Will grinned exaggeratedly. 'All you have to do is smile for the camera.'

'One photo?' said Simon.

'One photo,' said Will. 'Though they may need to take a few. Just in case.'

'And you'll make it . . . flattering?' said Lisa.

Will nodded. 'Of course!' he said, as if the suggestion it would be anything else was outrageous. 'Though, obviously, where Simon's concerned that might be . . . *Ow!*'

'So you'll do it?' said Jess, as Will rubbed his other shin.

Lisa exchanged glances with Simon. 'I suppose so,' she said, eventually. 'If it's all right with . . .'

Simon was looking like a man asking to choose between being punched on the nose or in the mouth. 'S'pose,' he said, glumly.

'Great!' Will stood up abruptly. 'In that case, we'll leave you to it. Like I said, the photographer will be along at four-ish.'

'Here?' asked Lisa, and Jess shook her head.

'They'll meet you down by the harbour.'

'You know,' said Will, 'in case you're *harbouring* feelings for each other.'

He elbowed Simon in the ribs, and Jess laughed in her trademark way again. 'And listen,' she said, 'thanks. Seriously. I owe you one. Both of you. You're lifesavers. Well – job-savers . . .' Then she was on her feet too and was leading Will towards the door, as if worried staying any longer might mean Simon and Lisa would change their minds.

As their respective friends hurried out of the pub, Lisa sat there for a second or two, dumbfounded, then she gently but firmly removed Simon's hand from on top of hers. 'I'm sorry about that . . .' she said, at exactly the same time as Simon's 'I had no idea . . .' Then they both burst out laughing.

'Can you believe the two of them?'

Simon shook his head and peered towards the door, as if he were expecting Jess and Will to be watching them through the frosted glass. 'Not really, no.'

'She really might lose her job?'

'So Will said.'

'You don't think . . . ?'

'They're making it up? I would very much doubt it,' said Simon, and Lisa blew a raspberry with her lips.

'They left their drinks,' she said, after a pause.

'They did.'

'So should we . . . ?'

Simon slid Jess's wine glass towards her, then he picked up Will's bottle. 'Rude not to.' Then he made a face like a lightbulb had just appeared above his head. 'And how about some crisps?' he said, brandishing Jess's credit card like a referee sending someone off.

Lisa looked at him for a moment, then picked up Jess's glass and clinked it against Will's untouched beer.

'I like your style,' she said.

And, to her surprise, she realised that she meant it.

Chapter 13

Simon stifled a burp as he glanced back towards their table. They'd finished the drinks Will and Jess had left, along with two packets of crisps (cheese and onion – his favourite, as well as Lisa's, it had turned out), then decided they were still hungry, but the best the pub could do was more crisps, so – with an hour or so to go until the photographer was due – Lisa had suggested they take the short walk back to where they'd started this whole extravaganza, to try some of the street food they hadn't had the chance to sample earlier.

And though at first he'd been keen to get the photos over and done with, he'd been surprised by how glad he felt when Lisa had announced she was hungry. As time had gone on, Simon had begun to . . . well, not *enjoy himself*, exactly, but there was something about Lisa that was . . . 'intriguing' was perhaps too strong a word, but 'interesting' wasn't. Perhaps he'd been missing out on female company, he had to concede. Women were . . . vibrant. Animated. Chatty. Different. At least, this woman was.

She was pretty too – as he'd noticed when she'd stormed up to his car earlier – and (despite first appearances) had a good sense of humour, was quick to laugh at things (including herself) . . . Everything he might look for in a girlfriend, if he had been looking for one. Plus, she'd obviously had some bad luck on the dating front, and strangely, Simon was feeling a bit of a responsibility to prove to her that all men weren't bastards – something he understood was a common assumption.

It had even crossed his mind that it might be an opportunity to try out a bit of what he understood was 'banter', to see just how rusty he was, putting any faux pas he made (there had been several – and no doubt would be several more) down to rustiness, though given just how incompatible the two of them were, he'd decided not to bother. After all, what was the point of investing in lottery tickets if you didn't want to win the jackpot?

So they'd sat back down at their original table, got themselves the same drinks, and now he found himself in the queue for the burger van, relieved that Lisa had been very specific about her medium cheeseburger, extra onions, ketchup *and* mayo on the side, plus a side of fries *to share* – and he may have been clutching at straws, but Simon's jaw had almost hit the floor at the hint of intimacy that had implied, until he'd realised this may simply have been one of those tricks women sometimes used not to appear to be ordering something unhealthy, even though they'd then proceed to gannet down the majority of it. It had been one of Alice's tactics, and the memory made him smile and feel sad at the same time.

In truth, he'd had his eye on something Vietnamese, but a cheeseburger would do, and 'mirroring' was something apparently helpful when trying to get on with someone – and he and Lisa still had a way to go to make up for their original frostiness – so he'd decided he'd order the same. And while he felt a little bad that someone else was picking up the bill, he'd forked out for enough bad dates in his time. Besides, like she'd said, Jess (and the *Gazette* – seeing as Simon and Lisa were providing them with unpaid content) owed them.

'What can I get you, love?'

The woman in the burger booth was smiling at him, so Simon narrowed his eyes at the board to his left, even though he already knew what he wanted. 'Two cheeseburgers, extra onions, ketchup and mayo on the side, please. Plus one order of fries. To *share*,' he said, liking how the word sounded.

'How would you like the burgers?'

'Um, medium?' he said, more of a question than a statement, and the woman pressed a couple of keys on an iPad.

'Nineteen seventy-eight?'

It took him a second or two to realise she wasn't trying to guess his birth year, so he held the credit card up. 'Contactless?' she said, and he smiled grimly, thinking that would probably be a fitting description of how he and Lisa had ended the date earlier, and pressed the card against the monochromatic screen. After a moment, one that lasted so long Simon hoped Jess's card wouldn't be declined, the small machine buzzed and spewed out his receipt.

'Sorry about that,' said the woman. 'Connection problems.'

Tell me about it, thought Simon.

'Take a seat,' she said, presenting him with a metal spiked stand with a wooden block on the end with '13' written on it. 'Someone will bring them over when they're ready.'

He nodded his understanding. 'Great. We're . . .' He pointed to where Lisa was sitting, then frowned at the marker. 'You don't have a different one, do you? With a different number?'

The woman peered uncomprehendingly at him for a second or two, then she glanced at Lisa and smiled. 'First date, is it?'

'And the last one,' he said.

'Need all the help you can get?'

'More like she's a bit superstitious.'

He handed the marker back to her, and the woman rolled her eyes good-naturedly and exchanged his '13' for a '7' – something Simon was sure Lisa would be more than happy about – then he helped himself to two sets of cutlery and pushed his way back through the crowds to where she was sitting.

'They'll bring them over,' he said, setting the marker down between them on the table and sitting down.

'Great.'

'So.'

'So . . .'

He leaned back on the bench, forgetting it didn't *have* a back, and nearly toppled over, managing – just – to turn it into a comedy routine by picking up his non-alcoholic beer and staring at it accusingly in a 'how strong *is* this?' way, but when he looked at Lisa for acknowledgement, she seemed to be assessing more than just his comedic timing.

'Margate born and bred, eh?' he said, desperate to divert the focus away from his own awkwardness.

Lisa smiled politely. 'That's me.'

'And you work in . . . ?'

'Margate too.'

'No, what field?'

'I don't work in a field. That would make me a farmer.' She mimed a drum roll and cymbal hit, adding the *badum-tish* for good measure. 'Publishing.'

'Oh. Right. Doing what, exactly?'

'I design book covers.'

'Wow! So you're an artist?'

'I suppose I am, yes.'

Lisa was looking delighted at his observation, but Simon couldn't think how to follow it up. 'Great,' he said, before admitting, 'I don't know much about art.'

'But you know what you like?'

Simon recognised the line, but again drew a blank. 'Not really, no. I just never . . .' He shifted position on the bench, took another swig of beer and tried again. 'So, would I have read – or rather *seen* – any of your work?'

'Not unless you've a reading age of five to seven years. Or you've got a secret lovechild that Jess didn't mention.'

'Huh?'

'They're mainly for children's books.'

Simon acknowledged the comment with a smile, then he tried – unsuccessfully – to suppress a broader one as Lisa's stomach let out a loud rumble.

'Sorry.' She grinned sheepishly. 'I'm just a bit . . .'

'Hungry? Me too. Though evidently not quite as . . .'

'Audibly?'

'Exactly.' He drummed his fingers on the table, then glanced back over his shoulder at the burger booth. 'What on earth's keeping those burgers?' he said, wondering whether he should go over and check. 'It says they're organic. Maybe they have to kill the cow.' Lisa's face had morphed into a grimace, so Simon did the same. 'Humanely, I mean.' He sighed, picked his bottle back up, held it up to the light, then put it back down again, taking care to locate it exactly on the condensation ring it had left on the table. 'And no, I don't have any secret love-children,' he said, desperate to fill the lull in conversation. 'Not that I know about, anyway. So I suppose I could have. Which would be a shame. You know, to have one and not know about it, rather than have one . . .' He stopped talking, conscious he was tying himself in knots again. 'I just meant, you know, that I love kids – not in *that* way, obviously – and that I'd like to have them one day. Do you want kids?' He caught himself again. 'Sorry. A little early in the "date"' – he grinned as he air-quoted – 'for that kind of talk. Back to you. Or rather, your job.' He glanced around. 'Do you enjoy it?'

'I *love* it,' said Lisa. 'Working with authors, discussing their ideas, translating them into something the publisher thinks is commercial, then trying to convince the author . . . But the best bit is getting to present them with the finished article, when they finally see their germ of an idea – their months, and sometimes *years*, of typing – is actually a living and breathing *book* . . . And there's a lot of pressure not to let them down, you know? To make them proud of what they've created.'

It was the most animated he'd seen her, and Simon made a mental note to return the conversation to this particular subject if things began to flag.

'I can imagine. It sounds amazing!'

Lisa's face had lit up even more, so Simon congratulated himself with his successful repartee, then he realised it was simply because their burgers had arrived. He sat back as the waiter deposited a tray of condiments on the table, then watched, fascinated, as Lisa picked up the mayonnaise, removed the top of the bun from her burger, and squeezed a third of the bottle's contents on to its underside.

'Fancy some burger with your mayo?' he said, and Lisa gave him a look before she carefully placed the top of the bun back where it had come from and gave it a couple of swivels, as if to ensure the mayonnaise was evenly coating the burger.

'What are you doing that for?' he asked, as she took her phone out again and photographed her plate from several angles. 'Evidence?'

'Huh?'

'In case you get food poisoning?'

'Oh. Right. No. Instagram.'

'Isn't that a bit . . . weird? Posting pictures of what you eat?'

'Not at all! My feed's full of shots like this.'

'Hence the reason it's called a "feed"!' Simon waited for Lisa to respond to what he thought was a pretty good joke, but she was too busy finding the appropriate filter. 'Did you want to . . . ?' He slid his plate towards her. 'Or is mine not as photogenic?'

'No, that's fine,' said Lisa. 'Posting photos of your *own* food is fine, but someone else's . . .' She made a face, to suggest the concept was a little dodgy, and Simon nodded.

'Sure,' he said, though he wasn't.

'Right then.' Lisa unwrapped her knife from where it had been swaddled in a serviette with her fork, then began cutting her burger into tiny triangles. 'What?' she said, noticing Simon's horrified look.

'It's a burger. Not a Victoria sponge. Or are we going to be playing some form of food Trivial Pursuit?'

'Don't worry. I'm not going to *eat* it with my knife and fork.'

'Phew!' said Simon, exaggeratedly. 'Though that's as good as.'

'And what would be wrong with it if I did?'

'Because it's a *sandwich*.'

'No, it isn't.'

'Hello? Piece of bread, filling, another piece of bread . . . I think if you looked in the dictionary under "sandwich", that's possibly what you'd find.'

'And what if I looked in the dictionary under "pedant"?' Lisa picked up the ketchup bottle, deposited a dollop on her plate, then handed it to him. 'Anyway, there's a method to my madness.'

'Which you're going to have to explain.'

'I always like mayo on my burger. And sometimes a little ketchup. This way, I can control exactly how much.' She indicated her plate with a wave of her hand, like a game-show hostess showing off a prize, and launched into a demonstration, picking up one of the triangles, dipping the pointed end into the ketchup, then popping it into her mouth. 'See?' she said, once she'd swallowed it. 'Bite-size pieces, no mess, and if I want ketchup, all I have to do is dip.'

'Which you could have done by picking up the whole, undivided burger, and dipping the bit you were about to take a bite from.'

'But then you get ketchup on the outer circumference of the bun, rather than on the meat, which means it's harder to eat without making a mess around your mouth and ending up looking like the Joker.'

'It's a burger. It's *supposed* to be messy.'

'Two words,' she said, giving him a look. 'Coffee, tea!'

Simon watched her for a moment, trying to decide if Lisa was a control freak or if she was just plain weird and this kind of thing made perfect sense to her, then he decided that judging someone based on the way they ate a burger was probably a little shallow. Besides, Lisa was already on her second 'slice', so Simon picked his own burger up, suddenly extremely self-conscious about how to eat it.

'Fair enough,' he said. 'But don't you think you should perhaps . . . let yourself go a bit?'

'Look who's talking!'

'Pardon?'

'Jess told me the reason you haven't been on a date for the last two years was because you're . . . picky.'

Simon's heart had skipped a beat. But being called 'picky' was a lot better than having to talk about the *actual* reason.

'What's *that* supposed to mean?'

'That you're not open to new things. Or new people.'

'I am! Just not . . .' He indicated the two of them, then expanded the gesture to encompass the whole venue, worried Lisa might take it personally.

'Yes, well.' Lisa helped herself to a chip from the fake-newspaper-lined mini metal bucket everywhere seemed to insist on serving them in these days, and pointed at him with it. 'You've obviously never been in love.'

Simon had been about to take a bite of his burger, but at Lisa's comment he froze and put it back down, untouched, on his plate.

'Why would you say that?'

'Because if you had . . .' Lisa dunked the chip into her dollop of ketchup, then popped it into her mouth. '. . . you'd be keen to find it again,' she said, between chews. 'And the only way to do that is to . . .' She mimicked his earlier gesture, and Simon smiled wryly.

'Yes, well. There's love, and there's *love*.'

'It's *all* love.'

'I'm not so sure. I don't think you should generalise.'

'A statement which, in itself, is a generalisation.'

'What? No, I . . .' He sighed, and tried to ignore Lisa's victorious grin.

'So you *have* been in love?'

'Yup.' Simon did his best to keep his voice level. 'With my last girlfriend, actually.'

'And what happened?' Lisa was regarding her plate curiously, perhaps choosing which triangle of burger to eat next, then she finally selected a wedge and popped it into her mouth, evidently deciding to eat this one without ketchup. 'Didn't she feel the same way?' she asked through a mouthful of food, shielding her chewing with her hand.

'Oh no. We were in love all right. She was pretty much perfect, actually.'

Lisa indicated he should wait until she finished chewing. 'Bummer,' she said eventually, then she immediately looked like she felt awful at how insensitively trivial that sounded. 'Sorry. Do you mind talking about it?'

'In general? Or right now?'

'Both.'

'A bit, yes,' he said, aware that was possibly the understatement of the century.

'Right.' Lisa waited for a moment, took a sip of her white wine, then another one, and then said: 'But would you?'

'Fine.' Simon picked his beer bottle up, checked the level and took a swig. 'Where did you want me to start?' he said, hoping that answering specific questions might be easier than just blurting stuff out. And might get it over with quicker too.

'Did she have a name?' asked Lisa, then she facepalmed. 'Sorry, that was insensitive too,' she said, checking she hadn't smeared mayonnaise on her forehead as a result. 'What was her . . . I mean, *what's* her name?'

'Alice.'

'That's a lovely name,' said Lisa. 'Sorry, I sound like I'm addressing a toddler. And were you together for a long time?'

'Six months. And perhaps that doesn't sound like enough time to fall in love with someone . . .'

'*Of course* it does. After all, people fall in love at first sight. Not everyone, obviously. With some people it can take a while before . . . Sorry, I'll shut up.'

Simon tried not to look grateful at that. 'But when you know, you know. You know?'

Lisa nodded. 'You do,' she said, though it sounded a little like a question.

'And I think I *did* fall in love with Alice at first sight. She worked as a nurse at Guy's and St Thomas'. Used to come in for a coffee at the café I worked at on Bermondsey Street after her shifts. That's how we met.'

'What with you being a barista and all that,' Lisa said, then she briefly shook her head, possibly at the fact that currently she couldn't seem to open her mouth without saying something inane.

'Yeah. At first she'd order her coffee to go, then she started to hang around and we'd chat a little, then we'd chat some more, then one day . . .' He pressed his lips together in a wistful smile, though partly to stop his lower one from trembling. 'She asked me out. Can you believe that?'

Lisa shrugged. 'You're not *that* bad-looking.'

'I meant that it was something of a role reversal. But thanks. I think.'

'So what was it?' she asked, readying herself to take another piece of burger. 'You wanted different things? Couldn't decide whether to get a cat or a dog? No – don't tell me . . .' She selected another piece, dipped it into her rapidly diminishing dollop of ketchup, and smiled. 'You decided you didn't want anything serious,' she said, offering him a chip from the bucket.

'Nope.' Grateful for the distraction, Simon reached for a chip, studied it contemplatively for a moment or two, then put it into his mouth, chewed a few times and swallowed it. Now wasn't the time to tell the truth about Alice. What would be the point? He'd never see Lisa again after today – though perhaps *that* was the point.

'*So?*'

He helped himself to a serviette and wiped his fingers, aware of Lisa's eyes burning into him, knowing this was a test, desperate to keep it together, all too aware of the emotional tightrope he was walking. Then – and with the greatest of effort – he met her gaze. 'She . . . left,' he said simply. Keener to change the subject than he'd possibly ever been in his life – especially before Lisa asked the next, obvious question – he noticed she'd nearly finished her drink.

'Another?' he said, standing up and nodding towards the bar.

'I'd better not.'

'Are you driving too?'

'No,' said Lisa, and Simon frowned.

'Right, well . . .' He sat back down again, picked his beer up, realised the bottle was empty but decided to go for one last swig anyway, then sat there, with the bottle inverted over his open mouth, until he realised he probably looked a bit silly. Sheepishly, he put it back down again, smiled briefly at Lisa, and looked back over his shoulder.

'Are you sure you don't want another drink?'

'Oh, go on then,' Lisa said, and Simon leapt up out of his seat as if it were electrified.

He made his way across to the bar, then hesitated. Lisa had been drinking wine. White, he remembered – though perhaps she'd prefer red now? Maybe he should hedge his bets and get rosé, halfway between the two – or was it? Then again, if he got a red *and* a white, Lisa could either choose one of them, or mix them in her glass to *make* rosé . . . Perhaps he'd better check.

Embarrassed, he made his way back to the table, where Lisa was sitting, flicking through images on her phone – probably deciding which of the (what, to him, looked identical) photographs of her lunch to post – and waited politely until she noticed him.

'What would you like? To drink. I forgot to ask. Same again?'

She put her phone down and smiled up at him. 'Actually, no, I'll have something else.'

'And that something else would be?'

Lisa was looking at him like she was assessing him, and it was making Simon feel more than a little uncomfortable.

'Surprise me,' she said, so Simon nodded.

'Will do!' he said.

Though he didn't have the faintest idea how.

Chapter 14

Lisa was picking at the remnants of their lunch, shielding their plates from a passing restaurant employee who was circling the table collecting empties. The burger had been pretty good, and the chips (although cold now) still were. This would definitely be a place she'd come on future dates, *with* future dates. And while it was perhaps a bit noisy, she and Simon hadn't had too much of a problem communicating.

He'd been a bit tight-lipped about his last girlfriend, but Lisa had decided not to press him. After all, her own relationship history wasn't something she necessarily wanted to get into this afternoon, so she told herself it must just have ended badly. Most relationships did, otherwise they wouldn't end. And if he didn't want to talk about it, that was up to him. After all, Alice wasn't someone – or something – she had to deal with, just like he wouldn't have to deal with Chris.

She peered over towards the bar – Simon had been gone for a while – then did her best to keep her jaw from dropping open. He was on his way back to the table, carrying what looked like two goldfish-bowl-sized glasses of red wine. Carefully, he set one down in front of her, swivelled it round so the plastic straw protruding from it was facing her, did the same so his straw aimed at him, and slid back into his seat.

'Ta-da!'

'What on earth is *this*?'

'You said to surprise you.'

Lisa stared at her glass in disbelief. In her experience, men trying to get her drunk was more of a common tactic than a surprise; and besides, she and Simon weren't even on a date. Not a real one, at least. Not anymore.

'I said a drink. As in one glass. Not the whole bottle!'

Simon frowned, then he let out a short laugh. 'It's not red wine. Not all of it, anyway.'

'What is it?'

'Taste it, then I'll tell you.'

Lisa eyed him suspiciously. 'You first.'

'But I already know what it is.'

'That's not what I . . .' Lisa regarded the drinks for a moment, then she reached out and swapped them round. 'Sorry,' she said, clocking Simon's mystified expression. 'But you hear these stories of people having their drinks spiked, and I know you're Will's friend and everything, but I've never met you before today.'

'What reason could I possibly have for spiking your drink?' said Simon, aghast, and Lisa had to fight to stop the colour rising in her cheeks.

'Because you might want to, you know . . .'

'What?'

'Do I need to spell it out for you?' she asked, though from what she'd made of him so far, Lisa already knew the answer to that. 'Sleep with me!'

'That's a bit presumptuous, isn't it?'

'You're a *man*,' said Lisa, by way of an explanation, and Simon looked offended for a microsecond. Then – to his credit, Lisa thought – he let out a short laugh.

'I'd be pretty stupid to try something like that on a date that's going to be written about in the local paper, wouldn't I?'

'Like I said – you're a man.'

'Which means I'm likely to be stupid?'

'It means you tend to think with your . . . with a certain part of your anatomy.'

'Even so. It was a blind date. I had no idea what you looked like before we met. So do you really think I'm going to be bringing along some . . .' He thought for a moment. 'I don't even know what it's called . . . Just so I could slip it in your drink at the first available moment?'

'Just humour me, will you?'

Simon looked at her as if weighing something up, then he sighed. Loudly. 'Fair enough,' he said, in the manner of someone who didn't think it was fair at all. 'Though I could be double-bluffing you.'

'Pardon?'

He leaned across the table and lowered his voice conspiratorially. 'Maybe I suspected you might think that. Anticipated you'd swap them over. So I put the spiked one down in front of *me*.' He tapped the side of his nose. 'Clever, eh?' he said, sitting back up and folding his arms, evidently pleased with himself.

'Right.' Lisa slid her glass across the table so it was level with his, and angled both straws towards him. 'Taste them both.'

Simon regarded her incredulously for a moment, then he leaned in, took a sip from his glass, removed the straw, then dipped it into hers and did the same, following it with a satisfying lip-smack. 'Just so I don't have to go and get you a fresh straw,' he said, noting her confusion. 'Unless you're now worried that whatever I was planning to drug you with is in your *straw* . . .'

'No, that's fine.' Lisa understood she was being a little ridiculous, but she didn't care. Like she said, you heard the stories. Then again, it was possible Simon was knowingly drinking from the spiked glass because he already knew this would be a day he was going to want to forget . . . She caught herself, realised she was being a *lot* ridiculous, and shook her head.

'What?'

'I'm sorry. All this.' She indicated the drinks with a wave of her hand. 'I just . . . My ex-boyfriend, Chris . . . In fact, a lot of the men I've been out with have been a bit . . .' She fished around for the right word, then decided there were too many to choose from – and none of them complimentary. 'Not that I've been out with a lot of . . . Never mind. Let's just say it's not you, it's me, and start again, shall we?'

Simon was looking relieved, so Lisa picked 'her' glass up and clinked it against his. 'Cheers!' she said, then she regarded the deep red liquid for a second, swirled her straw around in it a couple of times and took a sip, widening her eyes as the fruity, fizzy and more-than-a-little alcoholic concoction hit her taste buds.

'This is *delicious*!' she admitted, grudgingly.

Simon was beaming across the table at her, as if he'd finally done something right today, and suddenly Lisa felt awful.

'It's sangria,' he said. 'Spanish for "bleeding", in fact, and—' Lisa made a face and he caught himself. 'Sorry, that doesn't make it sound quite as appetising, does it? But there's no, you know' – he mimed slitting his wrist and directing the flow of blood into his glass – 'in it. Ha ha. No, it's red wine and . . . actually, I'm not sure what else goes into it. But I had it on holiday in Spain a few years back, really liked it, and this is the first time I've seen it anywhere in Margate, so when you said "surprise me", I thought it might just surprise you. Because when I saw they had it at the bar, it, you know . . .' His voice was trailing off. '. . . surprised *me*.'

'Well, you thought correctly.' Lisa cheersed him again, silently this time, then she pulled her phone out, slid her glass to the middle of the table and took a picture of it.

'Instagram?'

'Of course!' Lisa snapped a few more photos, then she retrieved her drink, chased the straw round the rim of the glass with her mouth and took another sip.

'This is a bit awkward, isn't it?' she said, putting her glass back down.

'I'm sure you don't have to use the straw if you're finding it diff—' Simon facepalmed himself so hard that Lisa half expected him to develop a bruise on his forehead. 'You mean this whole "blind date" thing.'

'Duh,' she said, good-naturedly, and Simon grinned.

'Actually, I don't think there's any shame in the notion at all. After all, over a billion Indians can't be wrong.'

Lisa paused, mid-suck. 'I'm sorry, I don't . . .'

'Just that . . .' Simon had gone the same colour as his drink. '. . . they have, you know, arranged, um, *marriages*, and, well, this is, sort of, the same' – he picked his glass up, removed the straw and took a huge gulp – 'concept.'

'I suppose. But nowadays you kind of feel you should be able to meet people the normal way.'

Simon smirked. 'What is "normal" anymore, exactly?' he said. 'Logging on to some app where everyone lies about themselves, or uses a photo that's been taken on holiday years ago when they were much younger *and* thinner, pretending they're looking for "the one" when in reality they're just after the next one-night stand?'

'That might be your experience, but—'

'God no!' Simon had widened his eyes. 'You wouldn't catch me on the likes of Tinder. I had enough being the last one picked at games when I was at school, so repeating that as an adult is my idea of hell!' He stared wistfully into his glass for a moment. 'Besides, name one happy couple you know who met online?'

Lisa thought for a moment. Naming one happy couple she knew *at all* was proving difficult. 'Hang on,' she said, eventually, resisting the temptation to take her turn in the facepalm rota. 'Will and Jess. They seem to be getting on okay.'

'They met on *Tinder*?'

'That's right.'

'That's not how Will tells it.'

'No? Well, she told me this afternoon, so I'm pretty sure that—' Lisa stopped talking abruptly and clapped her hand over her mouth. 'Sorry. I think I might just have given something away there that I maybe wasn't supposed to.'

'Not to worry, I won't tell. But good to know for my speech. If, you know, they ever . . .'

Simon grinned shyly, and Lisa smiled broadly back at him across the table. Maybe it was the alcohol, or perhaps it was the way the conversation was flowing – it could even be the fact that Simon wasn't full of himself like so many other men she'd met – but to her surprise, she found herself enjoying his company. And while she'd initially thought she'd just stay and chat over a drink while they waited for the photographer, she was beginning to suspect there might be more to him than she could find out over one – admittedly large – glass of sangria.

She grabbed her straw purposefully to avoid a repeat of her earlier chasing-it-round-her-glass incident, took a long suck, then worried it was going down a little too easily – at this rate, her drink wouldn't *need* to have been spiked for her not to remember today.

And Lisa was beginning to think she might actually want to.

Chapter 15

Simon watched Lisa in awe as she picked at the crispy remnants at the bottom of the chip bucket – so keenly that he half expected her to peel out the greasy fake newspaper lining and lick it clean.

'Yum,' she said, sucking the salt from her fingers after she'd polished the last morsel off. 'Cold chips. They still taste good. Like cold pizza. Or . . .' She nodded towards her drink. 'What's that Spanish cold soup called?'

'Gazpacho?'

'That's the one,' she said, and Simon grimaced.

'What?'

'There are certain foods that *need* to be hot. Pizza and soup, to name two.'

'Interesting,' said Lisa, as if he'd just expounded his theory on life, the universe and everything in it. 'I *love* cold pizza.'

'And yet, if it was a cold calzone?'

'No way!'

'But that's pretty much a folded-in-half pizza . . .'

'Okay. You got me there. Mind you, I could never go out with anyone who eats the Italian equivalent of a Cornish pasty. Hot *or* cold.'

Simon nodded. 'Fair enough. Me either.'

'So where do you stand on iced coffee, Mister Barista?'

She'd angled her head, as if pleasantly surprised at the accidental poetry of those last two words, and Simon felt something inside him twinge at the cuteness of it. 'Nothing wrong with it if it's made correctly. But it's actually quite a different drink. Cold-brewed, rather than simply chilled hot coffee. The mistake people often make is just pouring a cortado into a glass with a few ice cubes. All that does is water it down, and . . .' Simon rolled his eyes at himself. 'There I go again.'

'Don't worry. It's nice to hear someone so passionate about their job.'

'Back atcha.'

'Sorry?'

'Like you were earlier.'

'Oh. *Back at you.* I thought you were getting all technical about coffee again.'

'Again.' Simon mimed shooting himself in the temple with an imaginary gun. 'Point taken.'

'No. It's fine. But all this "cold brew" and "cortado" . . .' Lisa made a confused face. 'I'm not sure I could tell the difference.'

'You could if I made you one,' said Simon, and when Lisa widened her eyes, he wondered whether he'd overstepped the mark a little. 'Speaking of which, did you want a cup of tea or something?'

'I've got a much better idea,' said Lisa, standing up abruptly and slipping her coat on. 'Dessert.'

'Dessert?' Simon felt a lump form in his throat. On his third date with Alice, they'd eaten dinner in a pub, and she'd looked at him with seductive eyes and asked if he wanted to come back to her place for 'dessert'. Simon, in his naivety, had peered at the menu and asked her if she had sticky toffee pudding at her place – and when, a little surprised, she'd said no, he'd suggested they stay where they were.

Alice had told him afterwards that had been the moment she'd fallen in love with him, and the memory seared through him like a lightning bolt. This time, though, he knew 'dessert' meant *dessert*, so he looked at Lisa for a moment, then he half smiled, half sighed.

'Fine,' he said, with a little less enthusiasm than she was perhaps hoping for.

'Great.' She beckoned him to follow her towards the door. 'Just to prove I can be a "sweet" person,' she said. 'We can get something down by the harbour. While we're waiting for the photographer. And while we eat it, you can tell me some more fascinating facts about coffee, and I'll . . .' She shrugged. '. . . well, pretend to be interested is the best I can promise.'

'Ha!' he said, then he followed Lisa out of the restaurant and on to the seafront. The afternoon sun was giving the golden sandy beach a warm glow, and the sight made him smile. The beach had always been a thing of beauty here in Margate, even if the town still had a way to go to catch up – and the two of them strolled in silence for a while, enjoying the view.

He checked his watch – half an hour to kill before the photographer was due to meet them down by the harbour – and supposed that Lisa's suggestion of finding somewhere for dessert wasn't a bad one. Then all they had to do was get their photo taken, and this whole experience – he'd been going to go with 'ordeal', but that certainly hadn't been true of the last hour or so – would be behind them. Something he was surprised to be feeling a little disappointed about.

'Not quite Playa Delfines, but not bad,' Lisa said suddenly, and Simon raised both eyebrows.

'Playa Delfines?'

'It's in Cancún. A really beautiful beach. Miles of golden sand. Turquoise water. Just . . . paradise.'

'You've been to Cancún? Actually, don't answer that. Of course you've been to Cancún, otherwise you wouldn't have said that. When did you go?'

'February,' said Lisa.

'On holiday?'

Lisa nodded. 'Kind of. I'd been through a bad break-up – *another* bad break-up – and I was feeling a little lost, then I read about this retreat where you were supposed to be able to go and . . . find yourself. So I went. To find myself.' She let out a short laugh. 'Sounds funny when I say it out loud.'

'And did you? Find yourself?'

Lisa thought for a moment. 'I did. Though I wasn't so keen on what – or rather who – it was I actually found. But Cancún was amazing. Lovely people. Amazing beaches. Fantastic food. I did a lot of yoga. A bit of meditation.'

'*Eat, Pray, Love?*'

'The first two, at least.'

'No, it's a book. About self-discovery . . .'

Lisa stopped walking suddenly, so she could dig Simon in the ribs. 'I *know* it's a book. I was making a joke.'

'Right.'

'Obviously not a very good one.'

'No. It was funny.'

'Sure it was,' said Lisa, sceptically. 'But Cancún kind of taught me I should be looking for the good in everything. Focus on the positive. Only worry about the things I can change, and not make myself a prisoner to those things in the past that I can't. Which has been quite a challenge for me, I can tell you.' She shuddered and made a face. 'When you've had the kind of relationship history I've had . . . it's kind of hard to see the positives in that.'

'It is,' concurred Simon, a part of him hoping she wouldn't go into detail. Because then *he* might have to. And that was the last thing he wanted.

'Though I suppose everything happens for a reason, so . . .'

'What?'

'It's fate. Our lives are actually predetermined . . .'

'I don't accept that,' said Simon, levelly.

'It's true!' insisted Lisa.

'You learned that in Cancún, did you?'

Lisa nodded. 'Along with a few other things. For example, we can't control what happens to us, or what other people say or do. The only thing we can *actually* control is what we think about those things. The judgements we make. They're the things that make us happy, or angry, or sad.'

'Right.'

'So once you accept that everything happens for a reason, you can rationalise . . .'

'Rationalise,' said Simon, doing his best to keep his voice level. 'You mean if you're, say, a smoker, and you're dying of lung cancer, then I suppose you could say that the reason you're dying from lung cancer is because you smoke. But say you' – his hands, in his pockets, balled into fists – 'have an accident—'

'It's not that kind of reason.'

'What kind of reason is it?'

'I don't mean it in a cause-and-effect sense,' continued Lisa. 'Rather that it's all part of a bigger, preordained—'

'Rubbish!'

Lisa's jaw dropped open. 'I'm sorry, Simon, that's just what I believe. And maybe you feel differently, but—'

'Too right I do! And as for all that "we can control what we think about these things" nonsense, there are some things you can't control!'

'Such as?'

'Emotions!' said Simon, his voice cracking. 'Feelings!'

She stared at him for a moment; then, as if taking her own advice, she said, simply: 'Well, let's just agree to disagree, shall we?'

Simon opened his mouth, keen to do some more disagreeing before he agreed to anything, then shut it just as quickly. There really was no point, and though he had the killer argument – if you excused the phrase – asking Lisa what part Alice's death could have possibly played in some bigger, preordained 'plan' would only upset him further. Besides, even though she might *think* she did, Simon wasn't convinced Lisa would have an answer to *that*.

'So . . .' Lisa was smiling, perhaps unaware – or oblivious to – the nerve she'd just touched. 'Dessert. On me. Well, on the *Gazette*. What do you fancy?'

Simon peered along the Harbour Arm, trying to make out the brightly coloured restaurants at the far end. 'How about we just get an ice cream?' he said, realising it was probably the quickest of the various options available to the two of them. 'We could eat it while we walk and talk. Or just eat it and walk. Without, you know, the talking.'

'Fair enough,' said Lisa, and Simon knew she'd got the inference. 'Sounds like a plan.'

He followed her to the ice cream shop opposite the town's art gallery, trying to settle his emotions after the reminder of Alice, wishing for a bit of alone time so he could calm himself down. But he liked ice cream. Especially when someone else was paying. And since they still had to wait for the photographer, two out of three wasn't bad.

'Right.' Lisa rubbed her hands together, marched up to the counter, and stood staring at the various flavours on offer, so Simon did the same. 'What'll you have?' she said, so he quickly made his selection.

'After Eight.'

'Even though it's the middle of the afternoon?'

Simon narrowed his eyes, then he caught sight of Lisa's expression. To her credit, she was trying to keep things light, and Simon decided he ought to at least try to do the same. 'Ha!' he said, politely, then he turned his attention to the woman behind the counter, her face suggesting she'd heard that joke a few too many times. 'One scoop. In a cup, not a cone. No sprinkles.' He looked at Lisa, for some reason feeling the need to involve her in the decision – or perhaps to get her permission – and he noticed she was looking at him strangely. 'What?'

'That was very . . . precise.'

'Says the woman who cuts her burger into identically sized wedges. Besides, when you know what you like, you know what you . . . What?'

'Like I said earlier, Mister Picky. You're playing it safe. Going for what you know. Whereas I . . .' Lisa was staring at the selection of flavours as if it was an intricate work of art. '. . . will go for coffee. And in a cone, please,' she added, as if announcing she'd like to sign up for a parachute jump.

'Coffee,' said Simon.

'Yup.'

'You're sure?'

Lisa nodded. 'As you said earlier, everyone likes coffee, so I might as well see if I can get a taste for it. There's plenty of things I used to dislike when I was younger, and now I love them. Like Brussels sprouts, and . . . well, that's the only one that leaps to mind, and to tell the truth, I don't *love* them . . . Anyway, my point is, sometimes your tastes change, maybe even without you realising, so you've got to keep trying new things. Approach life differently. Stop being so . . . intransigent.'

'Intransigent?'

'It means resistant to—'

'I know what it means. But asking for what you like doesn't necessarily mean you're being intransigent. It might just be you wanting something you're . . . familiar with. You discover you like something – *prefer* something – so you want to have it again. Repeat the positive experience.'

'But this way you might just discover a new thing. A *different* thing.'

As the woman behind the counter scooped up a huge ball of coffee ice cream, and balanced it precariously on top of a cone that hardly looked up to the job, Lisa gave him a look that suggested they both knew he'd lost this particular argument. 'Four pounds, love,' the woman said, and Simon produced Jess's card with a flourish that made Lisa smile.

'Thank you,' he said, and – once Lisa had taken the obligatory photograph – the two of them walked towards the harbour.

'It's like a sailing boat,' she said, gesturing with her cone at the nautical scene in front of them.

Simon peered at the assortment of boats in the harbour. The tide had gone out, leaving them balanced on the sand at various angles, like beached whales. 'Um, what is?'

'A sailing boat is perfectly safe in a harbour. But that's not what a sailing boat's for.'

'Right,' said Simon. It was becoming his go-to response where Lisa's observations were concerned, he realised. 'Learned that in Cancún too, did you?'

Lisa nodded. 'Like I said – that and some other stuff. Anyway . . .' She held her ice cream out towards him, and Simon was just about to lean in for a lick when she said 'Cheers' and tapped her cone against the side of his cup.

He watched, amused, as Lisa extricated the small, garishly coloured plastic spoon embedded in the side of her ice cream and waved it in the air in a 'here goes' kind of way.

'So?' he said when she'd had a taste.

Lisa looked like she was savouring her first mouthful, like someone might at a wine tasting. 'Not bad,' she said, eventually.

'But not good?'

'I wouldn't go that far.'

Simon gave her a look – not to prove that he was right, necessarily, but more to show that she perhaps wasn't.

'Besides,' she continued, taking another spoonful. 'Perhaps it's an acquired taste. A lot of things are. Some people too.'

Simon gave a wry smile. The thing about acquired tastes, he knew, was that you had to want to acquire them in the first place. It was all about the motivation. And his, right now, was slipping.

He glanced at his watch – almost four o'clock – and double-checked it against the time displayed on the clock tower. So far, their 'date' had felt like it had lasted *ages*, and yet it wasn't even three hours since they'd first met. Still, at least it would soon be over. They'd finish their ice creams, have their photos taken, he'd walk her to wherever their paths diverged – he'd already decided it was best not to offer Lisa a lift home, wherever that was – then they'd go their separate ways.

And while he knew he could get her number from Will (which spared him the embarrassment of having to politely ask for it later), realistically he couldn't ever see himself calling. They were just too different. Opposites. Despite that old maxim that 'opposites attract', Simon couldn't see it where Lisa was concerned. More importantly, Lisa just wasn't Alice, and though he wasn't realistically expecting her to be, wasn't expecting *anyone* to be, he had hoped that he might see *elements* of Alice in any other woman he dated.

He wanted to be in a relationship. Of course he did. To have someone to come home to, to share things with, to talk – *laugh* – about your day, to commiserate if you'd had a bad one, to feel close to, to love, to know you were loved by . . . who *wouldn't* want that?

But he and Alice had had a spark. Something really special. And lightning didn't strike twice. For many people – perhaps for Lisa – it didn't even strike once. And he should feel grateful it had, as his therapist had reminded him on more than one occasion. Not resentful that the spark had gone out. Or, rather, been *snuffed* out.

They'd walked as far as the end of the Harbour Arm by now, and a couple had just got up from the bench in front of them. Simon hadn't been here before, and the view was pretty spectacular: a panoramic spread of Margate's Victorian seafront. In other circumstances, and ignoring the slightly rotten whiff of seaweed drifting in on the light sea breeze, this might have been romantic. They'd have sat down, talked and talked, all the while edging closer to each other on the bench, until . . .

Simon almost laughed. Right now, he was quite happy standing.

He finished his ice cream, deposited the cup and plastic spoon in a nearby bin, and turned round. To his surprise, Lisa had taken a seat on one end of the vacant bench. What was more surprising was how she was patting the space next to her with her palm.

So – and only because he didn't know what else to do – Simon walked across to join her.

Chapter 16

Lisa waited until Simon was staring out to sea, then – with a disappointed 'Oh no!' – she 'accidentally' dropped her ice cream. Her choice of coffee hadn't turned out to be a good one, so she'd been surreptitiously holding the cone out in the hope that a hungry seagull might swoop down and relieve her of it like she'd seen in several YouTube clips, but, despite the dozens that were circling noisily overhead, none had taken the bait. Perhaps they'd tasted it before, Lisa thought, as she tried her best to ignore the weird aftertaste in her mouth.

'What's the matter?'

She nodded at the upturned cone – it had landed almost perfectly upside down, and she worried Simon would think she'd placed it there like that. 'My ice cream!' she said, not wanting to put the words 'I' and 'dropped' at the beginning of her sentence.

Simon was looking at her suspiciously, then he bent over and inspected the dropped cone, like someone might examine a discarded murder weapon on *CSI*.

'Aren't you going to photograph that?'

'Ha ha.'

'Would you like me to get you another?'

'No, thank you!' she said, a little too quickly. Perhaps sometimes this 'trying new things' philosophy wasn't all it was cracked up to be – although at least she'd learned something: that if coffee ice cream was any indication of how *actual* coffee tasted, then she'd probably be sticking to tea in the future. Which was a positive, she supposed. 'I mean no. Thank you.' She smiled, then turned her face back towards the view. 'You can put that down as our "Any embarrassing moments?" moment, if you like.'

'Pardon?'

'The questionnaire we've got to fill out for the *Gazette*.'

'I thought Jess said she'd take care of those?'

'Yes, well, I've been thinking about that. And I'm not sure it's such a good idea.'

Simon laughed. 'Was *any* of this a good idea?'

'You know what I mean! Isn't it better if we actually do them? Especially since we're going to be in the paper. Editorial control and all that?'

'Don't remind me.' Simon regarded her dropped ice cream, as if wondering whether it could be salvaged. 'And I suppose so. Although *that's* the embarrassing moment you want me to choose?'

Lisa gave him a look, then nodded. 'I've already picked mine.'

'Don't tell me – "he nearly ran me over before we even got to the restaurant"?'

Lisa made a face. 'How ever did you guess?' she said, then her phone pinged – a message from Jess. She read the text and her face fell.

'Oh no!'

'You already said that!'

'No.' Lisa showed Simon her phone. 'The photographer's been delayed. Something about a bus getting stuck under the railway bridge.'

'And that was more important than getting a picture of the two of us?'

Lisa gave him a look. 'Jess reckons they'll be here nearer six o'clock. Which gives us a couple of hours to kill. I guess we could go home, then reconvene here at . . .' She stopped talking as a thought occurred to her, and widened her eyes. 'Though here's an idea.'

'Where?' said Simon, without a lot of enthusiasm.

'Seeing how this date's being written up in the paper . . .'

'Unfortunately.'

'You have seen the feature, though?'

'Will shows them to me occasionally. Especially if there's some . . .' Simon thought for a moment. 'Comedy value.'

Lisa nudged him. 'And how do you feel about the people who take part?'

Simon rubbed his chin. 'A bit sorry for them if it doesn't work out. Especially if the girl seems nice and the guy comes across as a bit of a . . .'

'Knob?'

Simon laughed. 'Yeah.'

'Me too.' Lisa realised she'd folded her arms, so she uncrossed them. 'Or . . .'

'Or?'

'Well, sometimes, if the guy *doesn't* come across as a – you know . . .'

'Knob?'

'I think he seems nice, and what a shame it is that they're not going on a second date, and if I saw him out in a bar . . . You know, like I said, only if it hasn't worked out for the two of them . . .'

'And correct me if I'm wrong, but according to Will, it normally doesn't?'

Lisa ignored him. '. . . but the guy has come across as decent, I'd be tempted to go up to him and . . .'

'Commiserate?'

'Something like that.'

A seagull had landed in front of them, and was eyeing Lisa's dropped ice cream from a distance, so Simon rescued the cone, broke it into bits and threw it to the bird.

'I'm sorry, I'm just not following.'

'Don't you see? Even though our date's been a bit of a . . .'

'Disaster?'

'Well, "disaster" is perhaps a little strong. But even so, there's no need for anyone to know that, is there?'

'Huh?'

'In fact, there's no reason we can't come across as . . . well, fanciable. Dateable. In the eyes of someone else reading the article. Because the "fate" part of all of this might not be putting you and me together. It could possibly be putting us out there. So someone else can see us, think "they seem nice", and then, maybe they bump into me in town, or come into your coffee shop, and . . .'

The seagull had finished the pieces of cone and was edging closer to their bench. Simon was looking nervous, but Lisa suspected it wasn't the – admittedly huge – bird that was making him feel uncomfortable.

'What are you getting at, exactly?'

With a flourish, she pulled the "Blind Date" questionnaire out of her handbag, causing the seagull to fly off with an alarmed screech, and Simon looked like he wanted to do the same. 'Relax,' she said. 'All we need to do is make sure we come up with an amazing answer to each of these questions, so Jess has got no choice but to write something that makes us both look fabulous. Then . . . well, it'll be like an advert, won't it? As opposed to a . . .'

'Warning-off?'

'Exactly!' said Lisa, pleased with herself. 'But we'll have to be honest with each other too. If, you know, either of us puts something . . . inappropriate. Or thinks we're going in the wrong direction.'

With a barely disguised sigh, Simon took the questionnaire from her and studied it for a moment or two, perhaps debating whether to tell her they were already going in the wrong direction – or, in fact, that the right direction was probably a different one for each of them.

'So we're just going to . . .' He swivelled round to face her. 'Make it all up?'

'Why not? And over a drink or two.' She stood up from the bench and held out her hand. 'The *Gazette* are paying, remember?'

Simon was regarding her outstretched hand as if it were infected with some terrible disease, then he glanced across to the clock tower.

'Fine,' he said.

'Great!' said Lisa, enthusiastically, doing her best to offset Simon's obvious reluctance. 'It'll be fun!'

Trying her hardest to ignore the fact that Simon looked like he doubted that, she reached down, grabbed him by the hand and hauled him up off the bench.

And as she marched him back towards the seafront, Lisa tried – and failed – not to see the fact that she'd stepped in her dropped ice cream as an omen.

Chapter 17

Simon did his best to keep up with Lisa as she hurried the two of them back towards town. To be honest, he'd have been happy for them to have headed home to finish their questionnaires individually, then reappear at six to have their photos taken (though he couldn't guarantee he'd have turned up). And although, in a way, he could see her point – pretend they'd had a wonderful date, get a fantastic write-up in the *Gazette*, position them both as 'desirables' – the fatal flaw in her plan was this: if they'd had such a great time, then what possible reason could they come up with to explain why they weren't together?

Besides, Simon wasn't sure he wanted to be positioned as 'desirable'. The prospect of random women approaching him at the café or stopping him in the street to chat him up quite frankly horrified him – not that he thought there was any danger of it actually happening. No, this was all about Lisa, he suspected – though for some reason, he decided he'd go along with it. Something about her made him want to . . . well, *help*. She seemed like a lost soul, despite all her pronouncements and observations about preordained paths. And while he didn't believe any of them, maybe he could get her to see a little sense. See that life wasn't all rosy when you left things to fate, to the universe. Because, quite frankly, the universe could be an absolute bastard when it felt like it.

Still, he reminded himself, at least analysing their date in this way might be a good thing. So far it had been a pretty good dress rehearsal for when he eventually went out with someone he actually got on with and wanted to see again. And now, with Lisa saying she'd be honest with him at every step – and he'd already decided he wasn't going to pull any punches himself – surely this was the kind of insight that was worth its weight in gold?

'So, where do we start?' he puffed, the speed at which they were walking making them both a little breathless.

Lisa grinned. 'Well, if there's one thing working in publishing has taught me, it's that you've got to get the words right. Think about what people are going to be reading, and how they're going to interpret it. So . . .' She waved her copy of the questionnaire in the air. '. . . I'd suggest we go and find somewhere to sit, go through the questions one by one – *honestly* – and see where we're at. Then we can make sure we've got them right. Unless you've got any better ideas?'

She was looking intently at him, her expression suggesting she'd just laid out the most logical plan ever, but – given his lack of enthusiasm – Simon didn't have an alternative. And he supposed there was some sense in it, because the other option was to let each other make everything up individually – and what might *that* lead to?

'Sounds like a plan,' he said, even though he didn't think it was a very good one.

'Excellent!' Lisa punched him playfully on the upper arm, then peered across the road. 'Pub? The Lighthouse is nice.'

'Wherever,' said Simon, then he quickly added, '. . . you think', so as to at least sound keen, though in actual fact he could do with another drink if he was going to go through with Lisa's suggestion. And while he'd driven here earlier, the sangria had probably put him over the limit, plus the car would be safe enough until the morning. Whether *he* would be once he'd answered Lisa's questions truthfully was another matter entirely.

They strolled into the half-full pub, and Simon widened his eyes. He'd only ever seen it before from the outside, dismissing it as a bit 'spit and sawdust', but now he realised that had been a mistake. From the stripped wooden floorboards to the old black-and-white framed photographs up on the wall that depicted the town in its Victorian heyday, the place exuded a friendly vibe – as did the chalkboard by the bar advertising several 'guest' ales and ciders.

'Good choice!' he said, following Lisa to a table by the window, and, as she sat down, Simon stepped across to the bar. 'What would you like?'

Lisa was peering at the chalkboard. 'Whatever the guest cider is, please,' she said, and Simon raised both eyebrows.

'Guest cider, was that?' The landlord, a large-bellied, pink-faced man in his sixties with the whitest beard Simon had ever seen – put him in a red-and-white outfit and it'd be Christmas – was smiling at him from the other side of the bar.

'Two, please,' said Simon, backing it up with a Winston Churchill victory sign, though he didn't know why – it wasn't particularly loud in the pub, and he already knew the man spoke English.

'Pints?'

Simon glanced at Lisa, who simultaneously shrugged and nodded. 'Why not?' he said.

He stood there as the landlord poured their drinks, a little nervous about what he was letting himself in for, and trying to convince himself that Lisa's idea was a good one. But what was he worried about anyway? This way, they'd get to stage-manage everything. If he was going to get recognised from the local paper, it was better to know what he was going to be recognised for.

He paid for the drinks with the *Gazette*'s card, then carried them the short distance to where Lisa was waiting and sat down.

'Cheers,' he said.

'Cheers,' she replied, clinking her glass against his before taking a sip, nodding in approval as she swallowed. 'Delicious. Again.'

'Isn't it?' said Simon, taking a mouthful, and then another, relieved Lisa didn't seem to feel the need to be taking a photo of it.

'What happened to "I'm driving"?'

Simon laughed. 'You!' he said.

'So . . .' Lisa smoothed her copy of the questionnaire out on the table, and indicated that Simon should do the same with his. 'Let's start off by answering the questions now, as we see them – truthfully. Then we can compare responses and see what we need to do to, you know, make them *good*.'

'Right.'

'And be *honest*.'

'You're sure?'

'Best policy, and all that.'

Simon pursed his lips. Like he'd told Lisa earlier, he wasn't sure it always was. And given her evident emotional fragility, he worried that honesty might not even be the *second*-best policy where she was concerned.

'Okay. But don't get offended.'

'Why would I be offended?' Lisa took another gulp of cider. 'I'm old enough not to need things sugar-coated. And there's no point doing this if we can't be truthful with each other.'

Simon tugged anxiously on his earlobe. He didn't really think there was any point doing this at all. And as he scanned through some of the questions, he was more worried about offending Lisa than ever.

'So, should we do one at a time and compare our answers, or do the lot?'

'What do you think?'

He took another look at the sheet. 'The lot, I think. Otherwise I might say something that . . . upsets you, which might make you a bit more vindictive in your next answer, and so on, and before you know it you'll have emptied the rest of your cider over my head and stormed out through the . . .' He looked up to find Lisa staring at him, horrified. 'What?'

'Have I been *that* bad?'

'Apart from the road rage incident, scheduling a get-out call, and calling the date off after half an hour?'

'Fair point. Though I had already suffered a near-death experience.' She double-tapped the newspaper cutting with her index finger. 'Anyway. Shall we?'

Simon nodded, and turned his attention back to the questions. He'd answered most of them in his head earlier, but this time he felt under a bit more pressure – particularly because Lisa's future happiness might depend on what he put. Not to mention how he didn't want to come across as a laughing stock.

He worked steadily through them, tapping the answers into his phone, doing his best to be kind rather than honest, sipping his cider, until he realised Lisa was staring at him from the other side of the table.

'How far have you got?'

Simon rested his phone on the table, screen down, just in case Lisa saw something he'd written and took offence. 'Well, I've finished, but . . .'

'You've *finished*?'

'Yup.' Simon took a large gulp of cider. 'Though I'm not sure about a few of the answers.'

'How many?'

He picked his phone back up and frowned down at the screen. 'All of them! No, wait. I'm happy with the first one.'

'Go on, then.'

'Okay.' He looked nervously up at her for a second. 'Question one: "What were you hoping for?"'

'And what *were* you hoping for?' asked Lisa, when Simon didn't continue.

'That you'd turn up.'

Lisa burst out laughing, then she caught sight of Simon's expression and stopped abruptly. 'You're serious?'

'What's wrong with that?'

'Well, nothing, but . . .' She leaned forward, in the manner of a schoolteacher explaining something to a pupil. 'It doesn't make you sound particularly confident. And you've got to think about how you're going to come across.'

'It's question *one*. Early days.'

'And that leads us nicely on to question two. "First impressions?"'

'Hang on. What did you put for question one?'

'To meet the love of my life,' said Lisa, confidently.

'On a *blind date*?'

'Why not?'

'No pressure there, then.'

'Why else would anyone go on a date?'

'Well, because . . . I mean . . .' Simon scratched his head again. 'Okay. Fair enough. Even though it's a little different to my answer.'

'A *little*?' Lisa rolled her eyes. 'Let's move on, shall we?'

'Right,' said Simon, nervously. 'Next question.'

'You first.' Lisa sat back in her seat and folded her arms. 'And I'm assuming you've gone for when we first saw each other in the restaurant.'

Simon picked his phone back up, then hesitated. 'But that's not quite right, is it? We've got to go for when we first saw each other. Otherwise it's not a first impression. Unless it means when we first saw each other knowing the other one was our date.'

'Yes, well, then it's going to be "disappointed", isn't it? You because you assumed you'd blown it by nearly running me over; me because I thought we'd got off to a bad start.'

Simon put his phone back down on the table. 'Are you sure doing this is a good idea? Look, half of these questions . . .' He tapped a random one from the list with his index finger. '"Would you introduce them to your friends?" Our friends are the ones who introduced us in the first place, so that's a bit of a moot point. And "If you could change one thing about the date, what would it be?" Right now, you're probably thinking you wouldn't have come. Because – and don't take this the wrong way – I know *I* am.'

'What are you saying?'

Simon picked up his cider, drained the rest of it and then – worried Lisa would get the wrong impression – spat the last mouthful back out into the glass. Then he worried that was making an even worse impression – though so would re-drinking it (if that was even a word), but the thought was closely followed by the realisation that he didn't have to make an impression anymore, so he relaxed.

'It's just . . . this.' Simon slid the newspaper feature across the table towards her. 'It's . . . dishonest. We're trying to pretend we've had this amazing date, and I'm afraid people are going to see through it. See through *us*.'

Lisa was staring at him strangely, and Simon was seriously considering downing his regurgitated cider, then her eyes suddenly widened.

'Okay,' she said. 'Here's a thought. How about you and I start over?'

Simon rubbed his stomach. 'I'm not sure I could manage another burger. And judging by your little "accident" earlier, that coffee ice cream didn't go down so well.'

'Not like *that*.' She pulled her sleeve up to expose her watch, then shoved it right under his nose. 'We've got about two hours before we have to meet the photographer. Why don't we go and actually *have* the perfect date?'

'What?'

'I'm serious. I'll take you somewhere I think you might like, then you do the same with me. We'll really have fun. No pressure, no hidden agendas. And *that's* what we'll write up.'

Simon stared at her. Lisa was looking like she'd come up with the best idea ever, something on a par with achieving world peace or finding a cure for cancer, and though from where he was sitting it quite patently *wasn't*, try as he might it was hard to argue with her logic. Besides, as Will had reminded him earlier, the one thing she was full of was *hope* – something Simon had to admire. And who was he to crush that?

He drained the dregs in his glass, forgetting he'd already done that the once, and stood up. 'Why not?' he said, doing his best to phrase it in a 'what the hell' way.

Because, if pressed, he could probably think of *lots* of reasons why not.

Chapter 18

Lisa led Simon up the steep steps to the town's art gallery, feeling slightly nervous. She'd taken Chris here once, but only the once – fed up by his constant claims that he 'could do better than that rubbish' when confronted by some amazing piece of abstract art, or moaning that he'd seen similar drawings done by his five-year-old nephew and displayed on his sister's fridge. Such had been his level of complaining *he'd* begun to sound like a five-year-old, and while they'd eventually cut the visit short and headed to the pub (for Chris, the failsafe equivalent of sticking a child in front of a cartoon), she'd known better than to try to do it again.

She was pleased Simon had agreed to come to the Turner Contemporary – or the Turner Centre, as everyone local called it, perhaps because 'Contemporary' was a bit of a mouthful – mainly because it would help her to set her stall out. While she hoped he'd enjoy it, she wanted anyone reading about her in the paper to know this was her kind of thing. To see that she enjoyed a bit of culture. To understand that if they were going to take her out, she was more of a Canaletto girl than a can-of-lager one. More Picasso than pick 'n' mix. That she was turned on by Turner . . .

Lisa ran out of art analogies as she reached the top of the stairs, filing them away mentally in case they might look good in the paper, and turned round to take in the spectacular sight of the beach behind them.

'Come on,' she said. 'It's worth it just for the view.'

'You mean inside, or out?'

'Both!' Lisa smiled as Simon jogged up the last two steps then stuck his fists above his head and danced around like Rocky while he got his breath back. 'I can't believe you've never been!'

'I guess I just never thought it was my thing. And when you don't know much about something . . .'

'Well, prepare to be educated!'

'Can't wait,' he said, with perhaps a hint of sarcasm, as he followed her in through the heavy glass doors. 'Here,' he said, handing her the credit card, but Lisa waved it away.

'It's free!'

'Which means one of us is a cheap date!'

'Which one?'

'I'll let you know,' said Simon, and Lisa gave him a look.

They made their way through the gallery's reception and rode the lift up to the first floor, emerging into the building's main exhibition space, and Lisa gasped at the view. She'd been here a dozen times, and the way the huge picture window framed the sea never failed to take her breath away.

'So, who is this by?' Simon said, interrupting her reverie. He was pointing at a large seascape hanging on the wall in front of them, so Lisa switched into tour-guide mode.

'Turner.'

'Right.'

'Do you like it?'

'How could you not?'

'He's who the gallery was named after.'

'Really?'

'Yes. In fact . . .' Lisa noticed Simon was making a 'duh!' face, so she punched him lightly on the shoulder. 'He used to come here.'

'To the gallery?'

'To Margate! Around two hundred years ago. He really liked the light.'

'Which one?'

Simon was pointing at the lamps suspended from the ceiling, so Lisa shot him a look. 'The ambient light.'

'So I see,' said Simon, marvelling at a huge painting of a sunset on the adjacent wall. 'You studied this, did you? At uni?'

'Illustration. I wanted to do fine art, but wasn't quite good enough.'

'But you must be pretty good. Seeing as you do what you do for a living.'

'I guess.'

Simon nudged her. 'Have you got any of your work you could show me?'

'Not on me, no.'

'What about on your phone. On your Instagram?'

He voiced the name of the app like an old man might, which made Lisa smile. 'I might have a couple, but . . .'

'Let's see!'

'No!'

Simon had folded his arms, and looked like he was refusing to move until he got his way, so Lisa sighed exaggeratedly and retrieved her phone.

'Here,' she said, flicking through her feed until she found some of her recent cover designs, then angling the screen so he could see them.

'These are really good!'

Lisa was surprised to find herself blushing. 'You're just saying that.'

'What motivation would I have to . . .' Simon hesitated. 'Sorry. I didn't mean that to sound as harsh as it probably did.'

'No, that's okay. Serves me right. I was probably just fishing for compliments.'

'Well, I'm giving you them!' Simon peered around the gallery. 'Maybe you'll be in here one day.'

'I'm in here now!'

'I mean up *there*.'

'I think being here as a visitor is the closest I'll get.'

'You never know.'

'Oh, I think sometimes you do.' She met his gaze for a moment, then smiled. 'What about you?'

'What about me?'

'Have you always been a . . .' Lisa hesitated, wanting to pronounce it correctly. '. . . barista?'

'What, like was I *born* one?'

Lisa gave him a gentle shove. 'No, silly! For your job.'

'Nope,' said Simon as he moved on to the next painting, a large canvas depicting Margate beach, though from a time before the donkey rides and deckchairs that dominated it nowadays. 'I did a linguistics degree, then went travelling round Europe, where I just kind of fell into it, realised I loved coffee – or rather, everything to do with it – and . . .'

'Aha.'

'Where?'

'What?'

'The eighties Norwegian pop group. Are they *here*?'

'No.' She shoved him again, a little less gently this time. 'Your coffee story. Fate – you see?'

'What – my life's calling is to make other people coffee?'

'Why not? There's worse things to do. And like you said, people like coffee.'

'*Other* people, at least,' said Simon, and Lisa grinned.

'And where do you see it taking you?'

Simon thought for a moment. 'I'm not sure, really. I've always been more interested in the mechanics of it, rather than wanting to run my own café or anything like that. Plus coffee's the second-most traded commodity in the world, behind petrol, with around four hundred billion cups being drunk every . . .' Lisa's eyes glazed over, and he stopped talking. 'Anyway, so maybe I'd like my own roasters. Import beans from somewhere in South America, sell it here . . .' He nudged her. 'Hey – you could even design the packaging. I'd need a logo, and—'

'Whoa!' said Lisa. 'Steady on. I don't know a thing about coffee packaging.'

'And did you know anything about book covers when you designed your first one?'

'No. But I'd read a few books.'

'Well, maybe you ought to start drinking coffee. Just in case.'

Lisa nodded. Maybe she ought to. She glanced to her left and widened her eyes. 'Come on,' she said. 'They're just starting a demonstration.'

'Of?'

'Well, it's not going to be how to brew the perfect espresso,' she said, grabbing Simon by the arm and pulling him through into the next space, where a dozen or so people were stood in front of one of the gallery's staff. 'They often do these here. It's so people can connect with art.'

Simon hesitated in the doorway. 'It's some sort of drawing workshop,' he said.

'So?'

'I can't draw.'

'How do you know?'

'But—'

Lisa shushed him, picked up a couple of clipboards and pencils, and hauled him to the back of the group.

'Okay,' said the man at the front. 'In a moment, I want you to spend a minute just looking at the person next to you. Really study their face. Their features. Try to get a sense of them. Then I want you to put that down on paper.' He looked around the group, then said, 'Yes?'

Lisa glanced to her right. Simon had his hand up.

'What if you can't draw?' he said, and the man smiled.

'Everyone can draw. Some better than others, obviously, but there's no right or wrong here. It's not a competition.' He turned his attention back to the whole group. 'Just try to capture the essence of the person. Maybe incorporate something you know about them, something they do, or did. No one's going to be offended.'

'Want to bet?' whispered Simon, and Lisa smothered a laugh.

'Okay,' said the man. 'Write the name of the person you're drawing on the bottom of your sheet of paper and . . . everyone done that? Great. Your minute starts . . . *now!*

As Simon gulped audibly – an attempt at humour she appreciated – Lisa turned round to face him. It was the first time she'd really looked at his face, she realised, and she felt a bit mean after her 'Tesco Value Loki' description earlier. Yes, he had longish features, and his back-swept hair perhaps exaggerated them a little, but it suited him. Made him look somewhere between not trying too hard and not trying at all. The kind of man you wouldn't compete for bathroom time with, or who wouldn't be stealing your hair products. And his smile was . . . nervous? Like he wasn't too sure of himself. Not at all cocky.

As she studied him, trying her best to find his 'essence', she suddenly remembered he was doing the same to her, and for some reason Lisa found herself blushing. She couldn't remember the last time someone had looked at her so intently, and she felt a strange, unfamiliar sensation bubbling up inside her. Then, suddenly, and to her immense relief, she realised the man at the front had called 'Time!', so she turned her attention to her clipboard.

'You're a pro. This isn't fair,' Simon whispered, so she put her finger to her lips.

'Just get on with it,' she whispered back. 'Like he said, it isn't a competition.'

'Now remember,' said the man, from the front. 'Let your eye guide your hand.'

Simon had crossed his eyes, and Lisa had to try hard not to snigger. Instead, she did her best to concentrate on the task at hand and tried to reproduce on paper what she saw in front of her. In truth, Simon was easy to draw. Regular – if slightly exaggerated – features. Large eyes. A wide mouth. Hair that invited a sweep of a pencil.

This was what she loved. What she was good at. And what she could lose herself in. So much so that when the gallery worker eventually called time, she'd finished what had turned out to be a fairly detailed portrait.

'Okay,' said the man. 'Time to pass them all to the front, and we'll see what we have.'

He collected all the sheets and began calling the names out. 'Is there a Susan here?' he said, holding up a portrait of a middle-aged woman, only identifiable by the multitude of black squiggles where her hair should be. Sure enough, a woman sporting a huge perm in the middle of the group put her hand up.

'And what do we notice about the drawing?'

The group looked nervously at each other, no one wanting to be the one to speak, until Simon put his hand up.

'The, um, hair?' he suggested.

'That's right!' As a ripple of nervous laughter went round the group, the man at the front held his hand up. 'This is actually good,' he said. 'Because it captures something striking about Susan. A defining feature. The essence of her, as I said at the beginning. And that's what art is all about. A representation of what the artist sees. How he or she interprets what's in front of them. For example . . .' He sorted through the drawings, then squinted around the group. 'Where's Lisa?'

'Here,' said Lisa, nervously.

'Would you mind coming to the front?'

She exchanged a look with Simon, ignored his 'Teacher's pet' comment, then made her way through the group to stand next to the gallery worker.

'Right,' said the man. 'I'm going to show you Lisa's . . .' He squinted at the drawing Simon had produced. 'Portrait,' he said, as if unhappy with his choice of the word. 'And I want you to tell me what you see.'

'She's very . . . slim,' suggested a woman at the front.

'*Very* slim,' agreed another.

'And?'

'She's holding a megaphone,' said the first woman.

'Is she shouting?' asked a young girl at the back.

'It's an ice cream,' suggested a familiar voice. 'And she's dropping it.'

Lisa took a step forward and peered at Simon's drawing. 'A stick figure?' she said, trying to locate him in the group.

'I told you I couldn't draw.'

The man at the front laughed. 'Did you want to get your own back?' he asked, handing her the pile of drawings, so she leafed through and found the one she'd done of Simon.

'Now this is a little better,' said the man, showing it to the group, and, when there was a chorus of impressed gasps, Lisa blushed a little.

'That's amazing!' said an older woman at the back.

'And what's the first thing you notice about it?' asked the gallery worker.

'The eyes,' said someone else.

'What about them?'

The group had gone silent, and Lisa felt something flip in her stomach. She'd suddenly realised what it was – just as the woman at the front had put her hand up.

'Well, he's smiling,' she said. 'But for some reason, he looks . . .'

'Sad,' suggested someone else.

'Okay.' The gallery worker handed Lisa her drawing, then picked another one from the pile – and as he started to discuss that one, she made her way back through the group and retook her place next to Simon.

And though he *was* smiling, though perhaps not quite as broadly now, Lisa understood exactly what they meant.

Chapter 19

Simon sat on a bench and gazed out of the gallery window, his eyes drawn to the people milling about in the square outside. Mostly they were couples, off out for the afternoon – a visit to the gallery, followed by bit of shopping, perhaps, and maybe a coffee later. Much like he and Alice used to do at the weekends.

For a moment earlier, he'd almost struggled to keep it together. He and Lisa had been – though it would have pained him to have admitted it – having *fun* in the drawing class, but when he'd realised that was what that long-forgotten feeling was, he'd been stuck by a pang of guilt so sudden, so painful, that he'd had to fight to keep the smile on his face.

He hadn't looked at a woman's features so closely, so *intensely*, since the night Alice died, when he'd eventually plucked up the courage to go and see her body in the hospital, to say goodbye. Simon had been reluctant, worried about what he'd encounter, concerned that he didn't want that to be the last memory he had of her, but instead she'd looked . . . peaceful. Calm. In complete contrast to what he'd been expecting, given the nature of the accident that had ended her life and taken her away from him forever.

The accident. He hated the word. Calling it an 'accident' would suggest it was nobody's fault, and that absolutely wasn't the case. Lisa would probably disagree with that, of course. Tell him there was nothing he or anyone could have done to prevent it happening. That it was fate. But the only thing he knew for sure was that it had been fatal.

Then again, maybe Lisa's approach was the correct one. If there *was* nothing he could have done about it, then he shouldn't feel guilty. It would certainly make it easier to move on, if it had just been a bump in the road, rather than the complete dead end Simon had been treating it as.

He checked his watch. Lisa had been in the toilet for a while – perhaps not surprising, given the amount they'd had to drink earlier – so he'd taken the opportunity to collect his thoughts. Deep down, he knew that seeing this date through to the hopefully not-too bitter end was the right thing to do; not only because it was polite, or because Will needed them to – otherwise Jess would have nothing to write about (and it was surely better for Simon and Lisa to 'make up' the rest of the date themselves than to leave it to her imagination) – but also because the longer it went on, the more he had to admit that Will was right. He needed to 'get back in the saddle', as his best friend had so poetically described it – and far better to have a dry run with someone he had no prospect of ending up with, and to make any rusty or rookie mistakes on Lisa's time rather than potentially mess something up that had, well, *potential*.

The questionnaire had been tough too. He hadn't admitted to Lisa why he'd answered how he had for the first question, and, while he felt a little guilty, he'd had his reasons. The night Alice had died, he'd been due to meet her for dinner, so he'd sat there in the restaurant and waited, and waited, ignoring the looks from the other diners, the slightly sneering questions from the waiters as to whether he was ready to order. Then Alice's mother had called his mobile, sobbing, and though he'd found it hard to make out what she'd been saying, the word 'hospital' had sent him sprinting from the restaurant faster than he'd ever run in his life.

When he'd got there, a place where he'd met her after work dozens of times, the building where (ironically) Alice had helped save countless lives, he'd found her distraught family waiting in the corridor, with Alice's mother – normally a strong woman, and someone he'd always been a little scared of, if he was honest – a shadow of her former self, inconsolable, and her father pretty much the same. So he'd done his best to remain strong. Mainly because giving in to the alternative was something he might never have been able to recover from.

He hadn't even cried at the funeral. Still in shock – or, at least, that was what everyone assured him he must be. And while her family had been great – treating him like one of them, despite the fact that Alice and he had only been together for six months – he'd still felt like an outsider. An interloper. Gatecrashing their grief, like he didn't belong anywhere near it. And even though he'd promised them he'd stay in touch, it had been easier not to. Less painful, certainly. So when he'd moved down to the coast, he hadn't even given them his new address – something he still felt a little ashamed of, but not so ashamed that he wanted to do something about it.

But it was hard, when you lost 'the love of your life' – another phrase people would trot out on occasion, which was meant in some strange way to comfort him but instead had the opposite effect – although after a while, he'd begun to doubt if that had even been the case. How could he have *known* whether Alice was the love of his life or not? That was only something you'd be able to tell retrospectively – on your own deathbed, surely – so perhaps he shouldn't be putting her on such a high pedestal just yet? And, weirdly, that doubt had been the most comforting part.

What was worse was, Alice hadn't left a will. At twenty-nine, death hadn't been something that she'd thought she had to worry about, let alone plan for. They didn't live together, hadn't even been together for each other's birthdays, so Simon hadn't had – and therefore didn't have – anything of hers to remember her by, except for what he remembered *about* her.

And that had been – still *was* – his biggest fear about dating someone else; that by seeing somebody new, he'd forget all about Alice.

Because while that maybe wouldn't be a bad thing, in another sense it would be the worst thing in the world. But, even so, there were times when that was exactly what he wanted to do, because the pain was so great, the confusion over how he was supposed to feel so bewildering.

As time had passed, and he'd busied himself with his new life – his new job – there were occasions nowadays when it took him more than a moment to remember what Alice looked like. And that was the thing that made him the saddest of all.

'So, what's next?'

Lisa's voice snapped him out of his thoughts, and he leapt up from his seat like a schoolboy caught doing something he shouldn't.

'Next?'

'Your choice, remember. So, where are we going?'

'I don't mind.'

'Try to show a little enthusiasm, please!'

'Sorry. It's not that. I just . . . you're the local, and I don't really know . . .'

'Okay.' Lisa peered out through the gallery window and her face lit up. 'How about Dreamland?'

Simon frowned, wondering whether that was a euphemism, then he twigged. 'The *funfair*?'

'Why not? We've got to give the impression we've had the best date ever, done a ton of fun things, had some *excitement*!' She widened her eyes to emphasise that last word. 'And given that this is Margate, we don't actually have a lot of other options.'

'You wouldn't prefer something a bit more' – Simon performed the most exaggerated set of air quotes so far – '"romantic"?'

Lisa looked at him for a second or two, then she mimed a yawn; so, obediently, Simon allowed himself to be escorted out of the gallery.

'You've been before, I take it?' he asked.

'Once. When I was nine or ten. My mum and dad took me for my birthday.'

'But you've not been back?'

'Nope. Can't remember why. They never took me again for some reason, then it closed down, and they only reopened it a couple of years ago.'

'Are you sure it's open now?'

'One way to find out.' She grinned. 'Well, two really. I could phone
them, but . . .' She stopped walking and cupped a hand to her ear, indicating he should do the same. 'Listen.'

Simon strained his hearing, and sure enough, the sound of screaming could be heard, carried on the wind, from further along the seafront. And while he feared the sound of screaming was possibly a regular
thing in a faded seaside town like Margate, this time it was accompanied
by the unmistakable rumble of a rollercoaster.

'Great,' he said, with as much eagerness as he could muster.

'Come on!'

'Okay, okay.'

Lisa had tightened her grip on his arm, and was hurrying the two
of them past the clock tower. 'It'll be . . .'

'Please don't say "fun" again.'

'It *will!* It's a funfair – the clue's in the name!'

Simon gave himself a mental kick up the backside as they walked,
telling himself he owed it to her to be at least a little enthusiastic. Lisa
had seemed much more animated since she'd decided on this plan of
hers, and he envied her positivity. How could she still be so hopeful
when life had taught her that things – relationships, in particular –
didn't work out for her? Maybe he *could* learn something from her this
afternoon.

They made their way past the arcades that lined the seafront, ser-
enaded by the cacophony of bleeping and electronic music, illuminated by the gaudy flashing lights. Inside, people were playing the slot
machines as if their lives depended on it, feeding in coin after coin in the
hope of hitting the jackpot, and Simon tried to ignore the symbolism.
He'd loved arcades as a kid – the coin-balancing, sliding-ledge things

(he'd never known their actual name) had been his favourite, and he'd always believed *he'd* be the one who fed his two-pence piece in at just the right time, willing it on its jagged journey down to join the rest of the coins, where it would find just the right place to nudge a few unsuspecting coppers off the ledge and down to where his hands were eagerly waiting. Quite often he did win, through a combination of deft timing, a subtle spin on the coin as he fed it into the slot, an eye for the gap and a sense for the pile of coins that was the most likely to drop, as he'd tell himself. Nowadays he was wiser, knowing it was purely down to 'luck', whatever that was, and there was nothing he could do to influence the random way his money cascaded towards its destination – though Lisa might disagree with the word 'random', he realised with a half-smile. Her coins would be guided by fate, no doubt. Straight on top of the rest of them. Never to be seen again.

He'd always fed his winnings back in, of course, but that was never a tragedy. No one got rich playing with two-pence pieces (though he'd soon learned that no one got rich *at all* in these places). Then he reminded himself that wasn't the point. Wasn't why you played. You did it for 'fun'. The elusive thing he and Lisa were about to have.

Up ahead, just past the furthest of the arcades, a large, unshaven man in a poorly fitting tracksuit had been banging a fist against the side of the parking ticket machine. Now he was ambling towards them, and Simon instinctively stepped between him and Lisa.

'Got any change, mate?' the man said, and Simon shook his head.

'No,' he said. 'Sorry.' Then he noticed Lisa was reaching for her bag.

'Simon!' she admonished. 'What do you need?' she asked the man.

'Anything silver,' he said, as Lisa rooted around in her purse.

'Here,' she said, smiling sweetly as she passed the man a handful of coins. 'It's all the change I have. I hope it's enough.'

'Thanks, love,' he said, handing her a fistful of coppers, but Lisa waved it away.

'Don't be silly. Is there anything else I can get you? A hot drink?'

'Lisa, you shouldn't . . .' Simon stopped talking. Lisa was giving him a look – one he'd become quite familiar with, despite their short time together.

'Something to eat?' she continued, indicating the café next to the arcade, and the man peered at her strangely, as if struggling to focus.

'No, you're all right,' he said, sounding a little confused. Not that Simon could blame him.

'What are you doing?' hissed Simon as the man began counting out the coins.

'What am I doing?' She smiled sympathetically at the man, then took Simon to one side. 'I didn't have you down as one of those people,' she said, scolding him.

'One of *what* people?'

'Who doesn't believe in giving money to homeless people.'

'Pardon?'

'Okay, I know some people say you shouldn't, because it only perpetuates them being on the streets, but quite frankly I think we all need to show a little compassion from time to time – to brighten someone's otherwise-miserable day. Let's face it, it's just a handful of small change to you and me, but to them it might mean the difference between finding somewhere warm and safe to sleep this evening or spending another cold, uncomfortable night on the pavement. And if a hot cup of coffee and a sandwich—'

'He's not homeless.'

'What?'

'He just wanted some change for the parking meter.' Simon nodded towards the kerb, where the man was feeding Lisa's coins into the machine.

'What?' said Lisa, again.

As the machine spat out a ticket and the man stuck it on the windscreen of his car – his *expensive* car, Lisa gradually appeared to be appreciating – Simon started to laugh.

'Come on,' he said, but Lisa was already striding, red-faced, along the seafront.

He followed her at a safe distance, until she looked round for him, and Simon was pleased to see she was laughing too.

'Don't say a word.'

'Hey.' He held both hands up. 'I think that was . . . *admirable* of you.'

'Just drop it!' she said, struggling to keep the smile from her face.

'Okay, okay.'

He fell into step beside her, and the two of them followed the noise coming from the funfair. As they neared the entrance, Simon braced himself.

'So . . .' Lisa had stopped in front of the huge sign saying DREAM-LAND, and was preparing to address him as a tour guide might. 'This is for the "Did you go on somewhere?" section. I know normally they mean for a nightcap, or perhaps to a club, but I thought this would be a bit more original. Or perhaps highlight our sense of fu . . . um, adventure. Plus, it's only not even five, and clubbing and a nightcap are a long way off.'

'Right,' said Simon, neutrally, conscious that seemed to be his word of choice – and how he'd been saying it all day. 'And do we have to actually go in, or can we just *say* we went on something and be done with it?'

'Oh no, we have to go in! Keeping it real and all that.'

'But . . . there's nothing real about any of this!'

'Consider it research, then. You never know, Dreamland might be the perfect place to take a date in the future, so this can be like a dress rehearsal,' she said, grabbing him firmly by the arm and steering him through the amusement park's garishly lit entrance. 'I'm sure it's a great way to find out about someone, by seeing if they get scared on the rollercoaster, or how aggressive they are on the dodgems, or whether they try to take you into the tunnel of love.'

'Ooh-er!' said Simon, flatly, and Lisa gave him a look. 'This your kind of thing, is it?' he asked, peering up above their heads, to where the brightly lit Ferris wheel was – well, 'spinning' would suggest some kind of speed was involved, and from what Simon could see, the leisurely pace at which it was rotating wouldn't pose much of a problem to even the most nervous of riders.

Lisa let his arm go, then stood back to take a photo of the park's neon sign. 'I don't know yet,' she said. 'But sometimes you've got to seize the day. Be a bit more spontaneous. Say yes to things when they come up, rather than always saying no. Turn every negative into a positive. Otherwise you might be missing out on life.'

Though he just about managed to hide it from Lisa, Simon winced at that last sentence. *Alice* was missing out on life. And he was missing out too – missing out on a life with *her*. Instead – and the pang of guilt that had just seared through him almost made him want to throw up – he was about to go and spend a couple of frivolous hours at a funfair, with a *girl*. A girl who – as nice as Lisa was turning out to be – just wasn't Alice.

As Lisa made her way towards the ticket booth, he stayed where he was, rooted to the spot, wondering when – *if ever* – he'd stop feeling like this. For a while after Alice had died, even making coffee for female customers had felt like some sort of betrayal. Just chatting to them in that friendly-but-superficial way you did with the regulars had been about as much intimacy as he could cope with. As for *talking* to them, or the prospect of actually asking one of them out . . . This was what he'd struggled to communicate to Will – both because he didn't have the emotional strength and because he feared it would sound pathetic.

But this was grief, his therapist had told him. It was like a tsunami, thundering through your world, sweeping away everything you knew and loved, never to be seen again. And when you'd experienced that, dipping a toe back into the water was the last thing you wanted to do. In case it happened again.

'Lisa, I don't think I can do this . . .'

Lisa looked at him strangely, perhaps misinterpreting his reluctance to follow her as nervousness about going on the park's rides. 'Come on!' she said, grabbing his arm again and half dragging him towards the nearest of the brightly lit booths. 'You never know' – she fixed him with a smile – 'you might actually enjoy yourself.'

And though he nodded, and did his best to smile back at her, Simon doubted it.

Chapter 20

Lisa marched Simon towards the ticket booth, feeling a little guilty she'd forced him to come somewhere he so obviously didn't want to be, but also determined they'd have a good time – or, at least, *appear* to have a good time. After all, there was the small matter of appearing in next week's paper to think about, and while Simon didn't seem that bothered if he met someone as a result, Lisa was. Plus Margate was a small town, and she didn't want to scupper her chances of ever finding love again.

She'd spent serious time on the paper's website earlier in the week, reading through the previous fifty or so 'Blind Date' features, seeing what she could learn from each one. And while what she'd *actually* learned was how infrequently they worked out – at least, where the last few dozen or so were concerned – she'd taken heart from that. Like Russian roulette, where every time you pulled the trigger and didn't shoot yourself the likelihood that the next shot would blow your head off increased, she'd reasoned that each blind date that hadn't resulted in a happy-ever-after must surely increase the chance of hers being a success. And while she was now sure that being a success didn't mean that she and Simon would get together, she'd already resolved that both of them would be in a better position by the time the date ended.

'So,' she said, looking at the pricing board as they joined the short-ish queue. 'Do you want to get a wristband, or just pay for the rides we go on?'

'A *wristband*?'

'I suppose it's like those tags criminals wear around their ankles. Except you can go where you want, rather than nowhere.'

Simon ignored her joke as he consulted the board. 'Wristband's probably easier. Means we don't have to queue up to pay each time.'

'It's more expensive, though, especially if we only go on a few rides.'

'Your point is?' he said, retrieving Jess's credit card from his pocket, and Lisa smiled.

'Fair enough.'

They purchased their wristbands, Simon gallantly offering to 'pay', and headed on into the centre of the park. The place was busy – not surprisingly, perhaps, for a Saturday afternoon – with hundreds of over-excited children accompanied by exhausted-looking parents, and groups of too-cool-for-school teenagers gathered next to the more thrilling rides, the boys daring each other to prove their manliness by going on something that health-and-safety rules had probably sanitised beyond the slightest risk of anything dangerous happening, while the girls dared each other to talk to the boys. It was all so much simpler at that age, Lisa thought wistfully. Or perhaps it was simply that the stakes hadn't seemed so high.

'Where should we start?' she asked, and Simon peered around the park, taking in the various attractions.

'How about the Chair-O-Plane,' he suggested, pointing at the near-merry-go-round-level ride directly in front of them, where several small children were screaming at the tops of their voices despite the relative sedateness of the ride.

'That's for kids.'

Simon gave her a look as if to suggest it was *all* for kids. 'Okay. Why don't you choose?'

Lisa looked across at the rides on the opposite side of the park. 'Right,' she said, confidently picking one at random. 'Air Force it is.'

With Simon following half a pace behind, they made their way over to the ride, flashed their wristbands at the attendant and joined the queue of people waiting.

'So what does this one do?'

Lisa gazed up at the ride, where a number of tiny planes – which looked like they'd been designed by a five-year-old – were attached to a set of long metal arms, which allowed the planes to go up and down (as well as upside down, she noted nervously) as the ride rotated.

'I think it's kind of a flight-simulation thing.'

'Oh-kay,' said Simon.

'You could at least *look* as if you're enjoying yourself.'

Simon opened his mouth, perhaps about to say something, then shook his head. 'Sorry. You're right. I'm just . . .' He rapped a couple of times on the side of his head with his knuckles, as if to reset it. 'Flight simulation! Great! I had one of these when I was a kid. Not one of *these* these, but a flight simulator. On my computer. So this'll be . . .'

'A trip down memory lane?'

'Let's hope so. Though I always used to crash, so . . .' He made a face. 'Come on.'

The line was moving forward and the two of them shuffled towards the front, stopping agonisingly one place before getting on, so Lisa took the opportunity to scrutinise the ride. Each plane had room for two people, side by side: potentially perfect for future dating opportunities, she noted.

They'd stopped in front of the operator – an acned teenage boy with long hair – who was looking her up and down. Something Simon couldn't help but point out.

'He's checking you out!' he whispered, and Lisa reddened.

'Who is?'

'The ride operator.'

Lisa blushed even more as the kid looked away hurriedly. 'No, he isn't!'

'Well he *was*.'

'I'm old enough to be his . . .' She cleared her throat. 'Anyway. He was probably just making sure I'm the right height.'

'For?'

'The ride, dummy.' Lisa pointed at a notice by the safety gate. 'Look. "You have to be 1.25 metres tall to ride Air Force", it says.'

Simon let out a brief laugh. 'I very much doubt *that* was what he was checking.'

'Why?'

'You're clearly much taller than that.' He frowned. 'How tall are you, anyway? Or is that one of those things you're not supposed to ask a woman, along with how old they are or how much they weigh?'

'Too late now.' Lisa thought about asking him to guess, but she was sensitive about her height, and didn't want to risk him overestimating it (like men sometimes did when they guessed her age – something that never left her feeling particularly good about herself). 'I'm five-eight. You?'

'Six foot nothing,' said Simon, pulling himself smartly upright.

'Congratulations!' said Lisa, though she wasn't sure why, and Simon made a face.

'Tell me something . . . what is this fascination women have with men's heights?'

'We don't have a fascination.'

'No? Back before . . . I mean, in the days before Tinder, I signed up for this dating website, and it was always one of the first questions I'd get asked – one of the first ones that wasn't rude, anyway. So what's the big deal with being six foot tall? And if you're in a country that doesn't have the imperial system, what threshold do you choose? One-point-eight-three metres? Because that just sounds *weird*.'

Lisa thought for a moment. 'I don't know about the specifics,' she said. 'I suppose it's just that no woman wants to go out with a man who's shorter than her.'

'But most of us aren't. I mean, you're almost freakishly tall . . .' Simon winked at her outraged expression. '. . . so it might be a problem for you, but generally . . .' He threw his hands up in the air in an expressive shrug. 'And don't start on the "physical prowess" thing. It's not as if we have to be out hunting mammoths nowadays. Besides, most sex takes place in the dark, lying down, so height's hardly relevant, is it?'

'I suppose not.'

They stood there in awkward silence for a while, watching the ride go through a series of acrobatics, Lisa simultaneously wondering whether it was a wise choice as their first one and hoping her lunch would stay down. Then it was their turn, and as Simon helped her up into their 'plane' and ensured she was safely strapped in, she turned to him.

'Nervous?'

'Not as much as I was four hours ago!'

'Ha!' Lisa nudged him playfully, then she fixed her gaze in front. The ride had started moving, and she suddenly began to doubt the wisdom of coming on here after mixing her drinks all afternoon.

'Hold on tight,' said Simon as their plane picked up speed, but Lisa was already doing that, gripping the safety bar in a white-knuckled way.

'So do we control what we do, or . . . Jesus!'

With a lurch that made her want to throw up, they were suddenly lifted some twenty or so feet above the ground. Wild-eyed, she suddenly noticed Simon was grinning at her.

'This was your idea, remember?' he shouted, above the screaming that was coming from the other people on the ride. And, to her embarrassment, from Lisa herself.

'I didn't think . . .' She clamped her mouth shut as their plane suddenly spun violently upside down, wondering why on earth people *paid* for this. She shut her eyes, hoping it'd make the spinning seem less frantic, but it only seemed to make her dizzier. 'Oh god, oh god, oh god!' she squeaked, then she felt Simon reach for her hand and she squeezed his gratefully.

'Are you okay?'

'Make it stop!'

'I can't,' he said. 'You'll just have to see it through to the end. A bit like I'm doing as regards this date.'

Lisa would have shot him a withering look if she'd been brave enough to open her eyes. 'I want to get off!'

'Well, you can't. So think about something else.'

'That's helpful!' she said, doing her best to convey the exact opposite with her tone. 'And how, exactly, when I'm being thrown about like a boat in a storm?'

'Maybe we should have stayed in the harbour?'

Lisa detected a trace of irony in Simon's voice, so she squeezed his hand a little more tightly than perhaps was pleasant, for throwing her earlier 'sailing boat' analogy back in her face. His grip was firm, she noticed, and when she dared to sneak a quick peek at him, he looked like he was . . . well, 'enjoying the ride' would be over-egging it a bit. But for the first time since they'd met, he at least seemed to be a little less tense.

Eventually, mercifully, after another thirty seconds or so (even though it felt like a lifetime), the ride began to slow down, the planes returned to the horizontal and Lisa opened her eyes. Her breathing was just about normal again when she heard Simon clearing his throat beside her.

'What?'

'You're still, you know . . .'

Lisa followed his gaze and saw she still had a rather firm grip on his fingers. 'Oh. Right.' She let go of him, feeling a little guilty when he began massaging his knuckles. 'Sorry.'

'Not at all. That's a firm grip you've got. Perhaps not on reality, but . . . *Ow!*'

Lisa rubbed her elbow where it had just connected with Simon's ribs. 'Yes, well, terror does that to you.'

She sat back as the safety bar lifted, then – slightly jelly-legged – allowed Simon to help her back to ground level.

'Now *that* was fun!' he said, and she glared at him.

'If you mean seeing me like that, then that's not a very nice thing to say.'

'I meant the ride,' he said, jabbing a thumb back over his shoulder, then he clapped his hands together in anticipation. 'What's next?'

Lisa shook her head in disbelief. Not for the first time today, she didn't have a clue.

Chapter 21

Simon stared at Lisa as she marched across the park for the umpteenth time, though with a fair bit of admiration. She'd plainly hated that first ride, so he'd asked 'What's next?' – sure she'd say 'Home' or something similar. Instead she'd led him on a loop of the funfair to check out the rest of the attractions, then picked a ride called Pendulum, which looked even scarier than the one they'd just been on.

So he'd allowed himself to be strapped into the seat next to her, prepared for the bones in his other hand to be crushed, and braced himself as the ride gathered momentum, swinging – and eventually suspending – them some hundred or so feet above the ground. But while Lisa (along with the ride's other passengers) had screamed her head off again, this time she'd kept her eyes open, even when they were upside down. And, even though he'd offered it, she'd left his hand un-held – and therefore uncrushed.

They'd jumped off Pendulum and made straight for Pinball X, where the two of them were thrown around in a manner befitting the ride's name, and Lisa's screams of terror turned into ones of delight, so much so that as soon as they got off, she made them rejoin the queue and ride the thing again. From there, it had been Dreamland Drop, a ride that lived up to its name when Simon lost most of the loose change from his pockets (he'd wondered why a group of young boys had been hanging around underneath when they were plainly too small to go on it, but when he saw them scrabbling around on the ground for his coins as he sat, helpless, a hundred feet above them, he got it). Lisa's whoop of combined terror and excitement as they were catapulted upwards had made him laugh, though, and he'd had to remind himself he wasn't supposed to be enjoying himself.

Then he'd suggested they ride the Scenic Railway, which Lisa had complained was too sedate but Simon had insisted. It was a classic, he'd reminded her. The only original thing left in the park. They couldn't possibly miss out on it. Though in reality, he didn't really care about that. He just needed a break from being thrown around.

'Slow down!' he called after her, but Lisa just beckoned for him to keep up.

'The park closes at six!'

Simon checked his watch as he jogged after her: half past five. 'Thank god!' he muttered under his breath.

'I heard that!'

'Sorry.'

'No, you're not.'

'I am! Sorry you heard it, that is,' he said, falling into step alongside her. 'Okay. Onwards and upwards – for the next thirty minutes, at least, then photos. Then . . .' Simon stopped talking. They both knew what 'then' meant, and he found himself strangely saddened by the prospect of saying goodbye.

'Fine.' Lisa narrowed her eyes and nodded at their destination. 'Dreamcatcher.'

'What on earth is *that*?'

'Hard to describe, really.' The ride was next to the first one they'd been on, and consisted of a large metal structure that reminded Simon of an umbrella that had been stripped of its waterproof material. Around the outside – in pairs, and set one behind the other – was a series of chairs. Ones that – given the large hinges and heavy-duty restraints – looked like they were built for punishment.

'Okay. But I'm sitting in front.' He nudged her. 'Just in case you're sick. The last thing I want is a face full.'

'Whereas down the back of your neck is fine?' Lisa mimed feeling ill. 'Suit yourself,' she said, grabbing him by the hand and half dragging him towards the ride, and Simon laughed.

'What's so funny?'

'You are!' He lengthened his stride as he struggled to keep up with her. 'You quite obviously didn't enjoy anything about that first ride. Then you forced yourself to go on the second, and the third, and so on, and now you can't wait for the next one.'

'May I refer you to my earlier point about intransigence?'

'Yeah, yeah, yeah. Blah, blah, blah, Cancún, blah, blah, blah!' he said, a smile on his face.

'Don't knock it. There's a reason it's called *Canc*ún, and not Can't-cún.'

'They have that as their slogan, do they?'

Lisa ignored his sarcasm. 'Saying yes to everything gives you a belief that you can do new things. It's *transformative*.'

'Sure it is,' said Simon. 'But the thing is . . .'

'What?'

'You've got to want to like whatever it is you're trying to make yourself like.'

'I'll try not to take that personally!'

'Oh god, Lisa, I'm so sorry! I didn't mean . . .' Worried he'd offended her, Simon looked up guiltily, but Lisa had begun reeling him in with an imaginary fishing rod, so he smiled. 'I just don't think you should try *everything* simply for the sake of trying it.'

'But that's half the fun, surely?' said Lisa. And try as he might, Simon couldn't think of an appropriate response.

They'd reached the start of the line for Dreamcatcher, so – grateful for a change of focus – Simon stared up at the imposing skeletal structure.

'Are you sure you want to go on this one?'

'Why wouldn't I?'

'It looks a bit like something Skynet might control. You know, from *Terminator*.'

'I have absolutely no idea what you just said.'

'Plus, there's no one in the queue.'

'You're saying that like it's a bad thing.'

'If no one wants to ride it, it can't be all that good.'

'Says the man who's been single for two years!' said Lisa quickly, then she clapped a hand over her mouth. 'Simon, I'm so sorry,' she said guiltily. 'In all the excitement, I'd forgotten about you and . . . you know . . . . that she left you.'

'Don't worry,' said Simon, though he felt a little guilty too. Because for the last hour or so, or at least since they'd entered the park, he'd done exactly the same.

And, though he felt a little ashamed of the fact, it had actually been a bit of a relief.

Chapter 22

Lisa glanced at her watch as she led a slightly queasy-looking Simon away from Dreamcatcher. The park was due to close in fifteen minutes, and then they had to go and find the photographer down by the harbour, so they probably only had time for one more ride. But which one? She widened her eyes at Simon – and, as if reading her mind, he smiled.

'You choose.'

'How are you with heights?' she said.

'It's a bit late to ask *that*, isn't it?'

'I mean *real* heights.'

'Do they involve drops?'

She grinned. 'Not this time,' she said, and Simon nodded.

'In that case, I can do heights.'

'Great.'

Lisa grabbed his arm and hustled him towards the Ferris wheel. While she might have preferred one last adrenaline-filled experience, she could tell Simon had probably had enough and was only going through the motions for her. Besides, they'd been thrown around, spun, turned upside down, lost their loose change (and nearly their lunch) more than enough times, and finishing off their date with a slow, made-for-Instagram, bird's-eye view of the town was a lot more romantic. Or that's how it would seem in print, at least.

The attendant was just closing the doors on one of the gondolas, so Lisa shouted to him to wait, then she and Simon jogged across and jumped inside. Another couple were in there already – mid-snog, she was embarrassed to see – so Lisa averted her eyes as she and Simon took the seat opposite. Though as the attendant locked the doors behind them and the wheel began its slow, circular journey up into the sky, Lisa suddenly found herself wishing she hadn't been so hasty. The kissing pair had unclamped their faces and turned round to see who'd just joined them for the ride, and the male half of the couple was the last person she wanted to acknowledge. Let alone spend fifteen minutes trapped on a Ferris wheel with.

'*Chris?*'

'All right, Lise?'

At the sound of his gruff, Margate accent, Lisa shuddered. Chris Wilson. The guy she'd been seeing up until two months ago. The one who'd sent her tearfully scurrying off to Cancún to do some soul-searching, to work out what exactly it was she'd been doing wrong. Or – as Jess was fond of pointing out – the wrong *who* she'd been 'doing'.

Lisa glanced nervously across at Simon. She and Chris had gone out for the best part of a year – though the *actual* 'best' part had turned out to be the first few weeks, when he'd been on his best behaviour while doing his utmost to get her into bed. Once he'd got what he wanted (and, to be fair, it was what Lisa had wanted too – right up until they actually slept together and Lisa realised the phrase 'all mouth and no trousers' pretty much summed up Chris's seduction technique) then the majority of their relationship had fallen into the same old routine, with Lisa trying her best to be what she thought Chris wanted her to be (and, on occasion, what Chris specifically *told* her to be) and putting her own interests, her own passions, on the back burner as she did her best to turn the heat up on their relationship.

She'd assumed if she did this, then it would only be a matter of time before he realised she was ideal marriage material and got down on one knee. And, just when she'd been hoping it might happen, he did get down on one knee – in the 'set' position – then as if someone had fired a starting pistol, he'd made a run for the door and, she suspected, into someone else's bed. When she'd confronted him, feeling cheated (even though he insisted he hadn't), he'd told her this was just how he was, and that she was being ridiculous; that he didn't want anything serious. So she'd told him the only ridiculous thing was their relationship and stormed out, and Lisa had never heard from him again. Never even seen him again, which in a town the size of Margate was quite a feat. He hadn't answered her texts, or her phone calls – so much so that Lisa had realised she'd been well and truly ghosted. And yet now here he was, with another girl, the two of them looking like a 'normal' couple. And like they'd been one for a suspiciously long time.

'This is a . . . surprise,' was the best she could manage.

'Yeah,' said Chris, his arm looped tightly around the waist of the woman whose face he'd just been devouring. 'How have you been?' he said, as if none of the above had happened, and Lisa stared at him. It took a lot to make her speechless, but right now she couldn't think of an appropriate response.

'*How have I been?*' she said, eventually.

'Yeah.'

Fighting the impulse to reply with 'Where have *you* been?' Lisa cast her eyes around the interior of the gondola, desperate to get off. Maybe it had an emergency stop button like an elevator, or a handle like the one you pulled when you were on the Tube to alert the driver that some sweaty old pervert was groping you. Failing that, she could maybe make a jump for it – they weren't that high yet – but the door looked like it was locked from the outside, and the bars that ran like a cage round the top of the gondola were a bit too closely spaced for her to squeeze through, and a little too high to climb.

'Hi.' Simon's voice made her jump. 'I'm Simon.'

'Chris,' said Chris as they shook hands.

'Lisa said. And you are?'

Interesting to see how you answer that, thought Lisa, then she realised Simon had addressed the question to Chris's (literal) squeeze. The girl was looking at her – she could tell something wasn't quite right, Lisa knew. Though why *she* was feeling embarrassed, Lisa didn't have the faintest idea.

'I'm Cat,' said the girl, finally switching her gaze back to Simon, so he shook her by the hand too.

'Short for "Catherine",' said Chris, and Cat nodded.

'He doesn't like "Catherine",' she said.

'You could have fooled me!' said Lisa, following it up with a little-too-loud laugh.

Simon was looking obliviously at the three of them, and Lisa knew what was surely coming next. *Please don't say it, please don't say it*, she willed him, even though she suspected it was inevitable, and when Simon's, 'So, Chris, how do you and Lisa know each other?' broke the uncomfortable silence, Chris hesitated.

'We, um, used to . . .'

He looked at Lisa, evidently hoping she'd be able to supply an appropriate definition. And, while she could think of several, she decided to go with something tame.

'See each other. That's about right, wouldn't you say, Chris?'

Chris let out a nervous laugh. 'See each other. Yeah.'

'Oh. Right,' said Simon. 'You're *that* Chris.'

'Yeah,' said Chris, then his smile faltered a little, perhaps because he was wondering what 'that Chris' actually meant.

Simon had a look on his face that suggested he immediately regretted asking, and Lisa was staring at him, hoping that might mean his enquiries would stop. But whether it was the awkwardness of the confined space, or the fact that he was trying to make polite conversation, he couldn't seem to help himself.

'And you two are . . .' Simon seemed to be searching for an appropriate term. '. . . going out now?'

'Well . . .' Chris swallowed so hard that Lisa could hear it even above the noise of the funfair beneath them. 'Actually . . .' He was sounding increasingly uncomfortable. Though so was Simon. And Cat wasn't looking like this was her favourite fairground ride either.

'We're not "going out",' she said. 'Not anymore, at least.'

Lisa paled. Cat was gripping Chris's arm tightly with her left hand – and on the third finger she could quite clearly see what appeared to be an engagement ring. Before she could help herself, she felt the tears spring to her eyes.

'You're kidding!'

Chris shook his head. 'I just asked her. And she said yes.'

'You *just asked her?*'

Chris changed his headshake to a rapid nodding. 'Right before you two got in. I was going to wait until we got to the top, but then I saw someone else was about to join us, and thought it might be a little awkward.'

'Unlike it is now?' said Simon, and Chris chuckled nervously.

'I don't believe it!' was the best Lisa could manage, though she'd meant to keep that to herself.

'It's true!' Cat was grinning like her Cheshire namesake. She wiggled her ring almost under Lisa's nose, and it was all Lisa could do not to grab her finger and snap it off.

'And how long have the two of you been together, exactly?'

'Since you and I, you know . . .' mumbled Chris, and Lisa had to stop her jaw from hitting the floor.

'Since you dumped me, you mean?'

Chris laughed nervously. 'Uh . . . yeah!'

'That's . . . two months!'

'Yeah. It's been a bit of a whirlwind, to be honest.'

Lisa stared at her ex-boyfriend in disbelief. The man who 'didn't want anything serious' had gone out and done the most serious thing you could do, and *right after he'd dumped her*. What was worse was that he'd done it with someone half her age, *and* half her weight. At a loss for what to say next, she put her head in her hands, not sure whether she wanted to punch something or scream.

Dimly, she became aware that Simon had edged a little closer to her, so she took a couple of breaths to centre herself and looked up. Cat was admiring the diamond on her ring, while Chris seemed to be eyeing the gondola's bars, as if considering making a break for it.

'Are you okay?' said Simon, quietly, and Lisa took a few shallow breaths.

'Yes,' she said. 'It's just . . .' She waved a hand vaguely in the air. 'I just remembered I'm not that good with heights.'

'Phew!' said Chris. 'For a moment I thought it might be . . .' He glanced at Cat. 'You know.'

'Not at all!' Lisa said. Then, with an effort she didn't think she'd be able to make, and although it went against what every fibre in her body was telling her to do, she forced a smile. 'I'm sorry. Where are my manners? Congratulations!'

'Really?' Chris was looking like a death-row prisoner who'd just won a last-minute reprieve. 'Thanks, Lise!'

'Really. I hope you'll be very happy together.'

'Thank you!' Cat had leaned across to give Lisa a hug, and she did her best not to pull away in horror.

'So, are you two . . . ?' Chris was looking at her and Simon, wobbling his head from side to side as if to indicate some kind of sexual activity, but before Lisa could respond Simon laughed.

'Us? Well, we're . . .' He glanced across at her, as if looking for confirmation, but right now Lisa would struggle with her definition of their relationship. 'First date, actually!'

'Is that right?' said Chris.

'Yup!' said Simon. 'Obviously I'm hoping it won't be the last!'

'Yeah,' said Chris. 'She's special, that one.'

Lisa stared at him, wondering whether to point out that she evidently wasn't *that* special. Then she reached across and grabbed Simon's arm, both for support and to keep the charade going. After all, the last thing she wanted was for Chris to think he'd moved on and she hadn't.

'Early days,' she said. 'But I'd say he has . . . potential.'

'So,' said Simon. 'Any tips?'

Chris frowned. 'Tips?'

'You know.' Simon was patting her thigh, and for a moment Lisa couldn't work out why. 'Me and her.'

Lisa glared at him. 'What are you *doing*?' she hissed.

'The exit interview we discussed,' he whispered back.

'What about it?'

'Remember how I suggested it might be a good idea to administer one after every failed relationship?' He nodded at Chris. 'Well, now's your chance. And in real time.'

'*What?*'

Simon raised his voice slightly. 'I said, now's your chance to find out—'

'I heard, you, Simon. I just can't believe you'd—'

'Why ever not?' Simon was looking like the idea made perfect sense to him. 'You've said you're happy for him, which would suggest you're over him. If I make someone a coffee, and they don't like it, isn't it a good idea to find out *why* they don't like it, so I don't make the same mistake again?'

'This is hardly the same thing!' Her eyes met Cat's. 'Or the time or the place to . . .'

'Oh, don't worry about me,' said Cat, pleasantly. 'I'm not the jealous type.'

Simon nodded. 'You and Chris dated. Then you didn't. Now he's *engaged*, and you're . . . well, *not*.'

'Hey! I've been single by *choice*!' snapped Lisa.

Cat had tentatively raised a hand. 'If you don't mind me interrupting, from what Chris told me, it wasn't *your* choice.'

'Yes, well,' spluttered Lisa, then she glared accusingly at Chris. 'He told me he didn't want anything serious.'

'With *you*,' said Cat, reaching over to pat the back of her hand, her engagement ring clearly visible, and Lisa had never felt closer to committing murder. Though out of everyone in the gondola, she didn't know who she wanted to kill first. And that maybe even included herself.

'And shouldn't we at least try to establish why that is?' Simon's reasonable tone seemed at complete odds with the words that were coming out of his mouth. What was worse was that Chris seemed to be actively considering the idea.

'You sure?' Chris said, after a moment, and Simon nodded encouragingly.

'And be honest,' he said, 'because this might be the best chance Lisa gets to get some . . .'

'Closure?' suggested Cat.

'I was thinking more along the lines of feedback,' said Simon, then he chuckled. 'Though depending on what you say, she might get that too.'

Lisa was balling her fists, and was about to tell Simon what he might get if he continued this line of questioning, but before she could say – or do – anything, Chris shrugged.

'All right, then. But only because Cat doesn't mind.'

Cat was apparently too busy admiring her new engagement ring to mind. *Lisa* minded, though her opinion didn't seem to matter much, and by now she was almost too stunned to object. Right now she felt trapped in her own worst nightmare, though, like when she'd surveyed the gondola earlier, she couldn't see a way out.

But maybe there *was* a positive here. Perhaps, as she'd learned in Cancún, she should be Zen about this, hear what Chris had to say and learn from it. Grow as a person.

With a sigh, she made herself comfortable on the bench, then forced herself to smile.

'Do your worst,' she said.

Then, to her horror, Chris did exactly that.

Chapter 23

Simon was beginning to suspect he'd made an awful mistake. Okay, so he was a little rusty when it came to knowing what women were thinking or feeling, and today's events prior to his trip to the funfair had certainly reinforced that, but, judging by the way Lisa's grip on his knee during Chris's 'analysis' had tightened to a degree where he'd got pins and needles in his foot, he'd misread her 'okay-ness' with her ex's new situation by quite some degree.

Right now, he was feeling terrible – and on Lisa's behalf too. He didn't know too much about her history, but he suspected she'd been devastated when Chris dumped her (though he was mystified as to why – Chris was, to use Lisa's earlier description of the various loser men in previous 'Blind Date' articles, a 'knob'). And now, to see him engaged to someone else when Lisa had probably once thought he'd been about to ask *her* . . .

Lisa, to her credit, had congratulated the two of them, and Simon had assumed – post-Cancún – she was being genuine, which was why he'd suggested she take the opportunity to find out where she'd been going wrong. But as she'd sat patiently through the remainder of the ride while Chris had seemingly taken her instruction to 'do your worst' literally (not that she had a lot of choice, given her inability to get off), even with his limited experience of women, Simon could tell she was torn up inside at the things Chris was saying.

He'd pretended to be interested too – in both her *and* Chris's obser-vations – acting like the attentive boyfriend, just so Lisa wouldn't feel miserable. But while she'd responded in kind – or, at least, not shoved him away when he'd put an arm round her shoulders to marvel at the view from the top – he'd felt how tense she'd been. Then, when the ride finished – after ten or so minutes that had felt at least twice that long – they said their goodbyes, and she even wished Cat good luck (and Simon suspected she'd need a *lot* of it). Although, to his surprise, as they stepped out of the gondola, Chris was doing the same to him.

'I'm sorry?' he said. 'Why would I need . . . ?'

'Because Lisa can be a bit . . . full on at times. Doesn't believe in taking it slow. And not just in the bedroom . . .' He gave Simon a covert wink. 'Sorry – too much information. But you know when you go for a dip in the sea, and it's a bit cold, so you jump in and swim really fast at first to try to warm up? That's her in relationships.'

By the muted gasp that had just come from behind him, Simon was sure that Lisa was listening. Though, even if she hadn't been, he'd still have felt compelled to defend her. Particularly because Chris had just turned his 'knob' knob up to eleven.

'I'm sure she was only like that because she was keen. Not . . .'

'Desperate?'

'Right,' said Simon. 'Though why she would have been like that in your case is a bit of a mystery, I have to say. Then again, from what she says, you were really mean to her, and if "treat 'em mean, keep 'em keen" is true, then you can't really blame her.'

'Yeah!' Chris let out a short laugh, which in Simon's mind was accompanied by the *whoosh* of what he'd just said shooting over Chris's head. 'Thing is, they all want the same thing,' he said, in a stage whisper louder than his normal speaking voice.

'By "they", you mean your girlfriends, or . . . ?'

'*Women!*'

'Which is?' asked Simon, though against his better judgement.

'This.' Chris did a thing with his hands that at first Simon assumed was rude, before realising he was miming slipping a ring on a finger. 'Or, at least, they seem to with *me*.'

'Right. God knows why, eh? But thanks. I'll bear that in mind. Anyway . . .' Cat had taken Chris's hand and – with a face like a bored teenager – had started to pull him away from their awkward foursome, so Simon draped his arm around an equally sulky-looking Lisa. 'Still, your loss is my gain, I think. And on that note, it looks like we're all off, so thanks for that. Especially the advice. Good to hear it from the horse's mouth, I think . . .'

He let the sentence trail off, mainly because Lisa had grabbed him even more tightly round his waist and begun marching him in the opposite direction to the one Chris and Cat were headed in. A little breathlessly, he did his best to keep up with her as she all but race-walked them out of the amusement park.

'Horse's *arse*, I meant,' he said, adding, 'You're welcome,' partly in jest, once she'd checked over her shoulder to see whether they were still in visual range of Chris and Cat and then let him go, though the look on her face when she stopped abruptly and whirled around didn't suggest she'd found his attempt at humour funny.

'Enjoyed that, did you?'

'What?'

'Seeing me humiliated like that. For *ages*!'

'By that loser? You were hardly humiliated. And it was more like ten min—'

'That was the most embarrassing thing that's ever happened to me!'

Simon swallowed hard. 'I only put my arm around you because—'

'Not *that*!' Lisa was wild-eyed. 'I meant Chris, parading some fit young thing in front of me who he's known for *five minutes*, and – and here's the cherry on top of the icing on top of the cake – even though, knowing Chris, they'll probably only *last* for five minutes, he's gone and asked her to marry him, whereas he couldn't *wait* to be rid of me!'

'I'm sure it's not like—'

'Then you have the' – Lisa looked like she was struggling to find an appropriate word, but Simon didn't dare suggest one – '*audacity* to suggest I might want to hear from him all about just what was wrong with our relationship. Or rather, what was wrong with *me*.'

'That wasn't what I—'

'When Chris dumped me, I cried so much that I actually, *physically*, became dehydrated. I only stopped when Jess managed to convince me that it was *him* who had the problem, not me – and trust me, I took a *lot* of convincing. So thanks, Simon. Thanks a lot. That's really made me feel great.'

'Hey.' Simon reached for her arm, but Lisa batted his hand away angrily. 'I just thought, you know, post-Cancún, you might not be holding anything against him. That you might genuinely feel happy for them. Because that was what you *said* . . .'

'Are you *completely* stupid?'

'No,' said Simon, though he suspected he might be at least partially. 'But surely you can see you're better off out of there?'

'Which means I was the stupid one for being "in" there in the first place?'

'No, that's not what I meant.'

'Well, what *did* you mean, exactly?'

'Just that . . .' Simon was beginning to regret starting this particular conversation. Then again, he'd been regretting pretty much everything that had happened so far today. 'He did you a favour by dump . . . I mean, by ending things with you, if you ask me.'

'I didn't ask you!'

'At least now you can see where you've been going wrong and—'

'Where *I've* been going wrong?'

'Well, yes.'

'So you think his behaviour was acceptable, do you?'

'No, although I'm hardly the best person to judge . . .'

'No, Simon, you're not! So don't. Okay?'

Simon looked at her, wondering what on earth to say next. He'd genuinely thought that hearing Chris's opinion might be valuable, could even make Lisa feel better – yet now, he could see it wasn't, and that he'd achieved the exact opposite.

'I'm . . . sorry?'

'You made that sound like a question.'

'I *am*. I didn't realise you . . . I mean . . .' He sighed. 'Listen. Would it make you feel better if you did the same to me?'

'Slept with you for the best part of a year, then dumped you out of the blue and never called you again?'

Lisa was staring at him expectantly, and Simon could feel himself going red. 'No! I meant tell me where *I'm* going wrong.'

'What?'

'Just to prove that it's a useful exercise.' He stuffed his hands into his pockets. 'We've already established that you and me won't . . . I mean, aren't . . .'

'Too right we have!'

Simon tried not to let the sudden – and surprising – pang of hurt he felt in his chest at Lisa's all-too-quick dismissal of the possibility of the two of them show on his face. 'So perhaps you could give me a few tips. An assessment of how I've done so far. Leaving out the bit when I nearly ran you over, obviously.' He forced himself to grin at that, though if Lisa found it funny she didn't let on.

'You're serious?'

Simon nodded. 'Only seems fair.'

'Right.' Lisa took a step backwards, folded her arms and looked him up and down. 'Okay. For a start, you turned up to lunch looking like you were going anywhere but a date. And a girl needs to see you've at least made more of an effort than if you're just popping down to the shop to pick up a pint of milk.'

'That's . . .' Simon wondered whether now was an appropriate time to tell Lisa he hadn't actually known he was going on a date. But this particular exercise was about making *her* feel better, he reminded himself. Not him. 'Fair enough.'

'And then talk about *nervous*. You seemed like you wanted to be anywhere but sitting in front of me. And that can give off the wrong vibe. As can expecting me to make a run for it the whole time.'

'But you *did*! Or at least, you cut it short after—'

'*Before* that.'

'Right. Sorry. Carry on.'

'And you didn't really seem that interested in me.'

Simon decided against telling Lisa that was because he wasn't interested in *anyone*. Mainly because he suspected she'd had all the feedback she wanted for one day.

'And . . .' she continued, and Simon blanched.

'There's more?'

'There is. And it's a biggie.'

Simon tensed a little. He could guess what was coming. 'The "Alice" thing?'

Lisa nodded. 'Telling any girl that your ex was to all intents and purposes *perfect* . . . You need to think a bit about how you introduce that in the future. *And* when. It's not exactly first-date material.'

'Uh-huh.' Simon did his best to keep his voice level. 'Which date material is it, exactly?'

'I don't know. But keep mentioning it on the first and you'll probably never get a chance to find out.'

'Oh-kay. Anything else?'

Lisa thought for a moment. 'No. That's about it.' She smiled grimly. 'You're right. I do feel better for that.'

'Great,' said Simon, as enthusiastically as he could muster. 'I'll be sure to take that all on board.'

'Just like I should take everything on board that Chris said, you mean?'

Lisa's eyes flashed with anger again, so Simon knew he had to tread carefully. 'Here's the thing,' he said. 'It was plainly Chris's fault that you and he, you know . . .' He cut the sentence off there, pretty sure spelling it out wouldn't do him any favours. 'But perhaps you can still learn something from it.'

'What?'

'I said, perhaps you can still—'

'No – what can I possibly learn from that . . . ?' Lisa let out a small scream. 'I'm so angry I can't even think of the right word to describe him. And trust me, I've come up with a *lot* since he dumped me.'

Lisa had taken a step closer to him, and her face wasn't that far from his, and while Simon suspected that – proximity-wise, at least, and on another occasion entirely, and perhaps with another *person* entirely – this might be a good opportunity to lean in for a kiss like they did in the movies, where locking lips seemed to miraculously turn murderous intent into high passion, right now he just hoped he'd get out of this situation alive.

'I don't know.' Simon threw his hands in the air in an exaggerated shrug. 'Not to go out with someone like Chris again, for one thing.'

'Oh. Right. Of course. Thank you so much for pointing that out.' Lisa slapped herself exaggeratedly on the forehead. 'How stupid of me. Well, that's all my dating problems solved now. All I need to do is find someone – *anyone* – who's *not* Chris, and . . .'

'You're being sarcastic.'

'Me? No. Why would you think that?' Lisa glared at him. 'And yes, that was me being sarcastic. *Again!*'

Lisa spun round and stormed out through the park's exit, so Simon hurried after her. 'Obviously I'm not suggesting it's as simple as that,' he said. 'But why did you stay with him for so long if he was so . . .'

'Manipulative?'

'Exactly.'

'Hello? *Because* he was so manipulative.' Lisa was looking like one of those cartoon characters who was about to blow steam out of their ears. 'Please, Simon, spare me any more of your insights, which quite frankly . . .'

Lisa stopped talking mid-sentence, then let out a brief, high-pitched scream, which Simon guessed was his cue to shut up. While he wasn't a fan of awkward silences, he consoled himself with the fact that – given how far out of his depth he was, and how relationships *so* weren't his specialist subject – this one would surely be less awkward than anything he might say. But as she stomped angrily back along the seafront, his desire to make Lisa feel better got the better of him.

'All I'm saying is . . .' Simon took a deep breath. '. . . and, like I mentioned, I'm hardly an expert, so feel free to disregard anything I say, which I imagine you'll probably do anyway, but don't you think you just need to find someone who appreciates you? Chris clearly didn't. And maybe going out with a man who seems to like to upgrade his girl-friends as often as he upgrades his phone isn't the smartest . . .' Simon had walked on a few steps more, then he noticed Lisa hadn't, so he wheeled around smartly and walked back to where she was standing.

'*Upgrade?*'

Simon winced, pretty sure the almost-pleasant tone Lisa had adopted was a complete contrast to how she felt inside. 'That's not what I meant, and you know it.'

'It's not that easy,' she said, quietly.

'Why not?'

'Because men are liars!' spat Lisa, angrily. 'They say one thing and then do something completely different. Or they tell you what you want to hear, but all the while they're thinking the complete opposite. Or they promise you the world, then let you down. And so how are you supposed to tell the good ones – if there are any – by what they say, because . . .'

'What about by what they *do*? "Action is character", and all that?'

'You're quoting literary stuff to *me*?'

'I didn't know it was, um, literary stuff.' Simon was about to attempt air quotes, but he quickly pulled them back in. Lisa was looking like she wanted to break his fingers.

'Yes, well. You'll excuse me if I take your advice with more than a pinch of salt. Because for one thing, *you're* a man. And if it was that easy . . .' Lisa glared at him for a moment, and Simon instinctively braced himself. 'I wouldn't have found myself having to go out on a stupid blind date with someone like you!'

As she began walking, Simon started to apologise again – on behalf of all males of the species – but her 'Don't!' made him clamp his mouth shut.

'Where are you going?'

'Hello? The photographs?'

'You still want to . . . ?'

'It's not a case of "want", Simon,' she said, angrily. 'So let's just go and get them done, smile for the camera, then we can put an end to this charade and we'll never have to see each other again.'

'You're angry . . .'

'*Yes*, I'm angry, Simon! Well spotted! And I'm afraid that's not something you can just turn off.'

'Lisa!' he said, then he repeated her name, a little louder this time, but she seemed to be making a point of pretending not to hear him. Almost as though she was giving him the same treatment Chris had obviously meted out to her after they'd split up.

And as he thought about it – remembering what she'd been through, then trying to put himself in her shoes – Simon decided he couldn't blame her.

Chapter 24

Lisa stormed along the seafront, Simon following obediently a few yards behind like a scolded puppy. *Yes*, she was angry: angry with Simon, angry with Chris, angry with Jess, angry with Will – but more importantly, angry with herself. And the worst thing was, Simon was right. She did know how to pick them.

She checked her watch, unable to believe how the day was turning out. They were due to meet the photographer in five minutes, and although she'd rather not have to endure a photo shoot where she had to pretend to be all lovey-dovey with Simon – or anyone, for that matter – she'd promised Jess she'd go through with it. Plus she had a vested interest in the feature getting published. Once it was out, she'd be 'fighting them off' – or, at least, fielding interest from men as a result. And, more importantly, men who were her type. The Anti-Chris, as Jess had put it earlier. Men who wanted to date an attractive, arty, thrill-seeking, independent woman. Men who wanted to *commit* to one.

A man was down by the harbour, taking photographs of the boats, a large camera with a lens the size of a bucket slung round his neck, so Lisa gave Simon a 'hurry up' gesture, and walked over to where he was standing. She hesitated before stepping gingerly on to the beach: the tide was out, but the sand was still a little damp and her shoes were expensive. Still, she reminded herself, what was a little wet sand when the end prize was such a big one? It would brush off. Just like she'd be giving Simon the brush-off in a few minutes.

'Hi,' she said, and the man lowered his camera and turned around. 'Lisa? And Simon?'

The man gave her the once-over, then he glanced at Simon. 'Right,' he said. 'And?'

Lisa pointedly glanced at her watch. 'Well, seeing as we're all finally here, perhaps you could take our photos now? Unless something more important comes up? A cat stuck up a tree, for example?'

'Take . . . your photos?'

'That's right. I'm sure we're all keen to get this over and done with, plus it looks like the tide's coming in, so . . .' Lisa peered around their area of the harbour, then rubbed her hands together. 'Where do you want us?'

'Pardon?'

The man was frowning at her, so Lisa pointed towards the beach. 'Down there might be good?'

'For?'

'Our photo. You could use the harbour as a backdrop. Not that I want to tell you how to do your job.' Lisa caught Simon's eye, and realised that was exactly what she was doing. Still, the quicker they got these shots done, the quicker they could be on their way. 'So, shall we?'

'Shall we what?'

'Pose.'

'What?' The man looked down at his camera and did a double take, almost as if he'd forgotten it was round his neck. 'You want to pose for me?'

'I think that's the general idea,' said Lisa, sarcastically.

'Well . . .' The man stared at her for second or two, then he glanced across to where Simon was standing, and when Simon simply shrugged, he nodded. 'Fine,' he said, reaching down to fiddle with a couple of buttons on his camera.

Lisa grabbed Simon's arm and hurried him towards the harbour wall. 'Come on,' she said, and Simon frowned.

'Are you sure this is . . . ?'

'Don't tell me you're getting cold feet?'

'What?' Simon peered down at his trainers. 'Oh, no. It's just . . . the photographer's supposed to—'

'I'm sorry if you think I'm being bossy, but by the looks of him he's a bit dopey, so I'm just giving him a friendly kick up the—'

'But . . .'

'Do you want to be in this photograph or not?'

Simon was looking like he'd rather not, and Lisa couldn't be bothered to argue with him. 'Photoshop it is, then,' she said to the photographer. 'So maybe take a few shots of me first? You can always add him in later.'

'Right,' said the man. 'So, if you could just . . . ?' He nodded towards the sea wall, so Lisa went and positioned herself in front of it. The stone was wet and covered in seaweed, so she didn't particularly want to lean against it.

'How do you want me?'

'That's fine,' said the man. 'I'll just take a couple of test shots.'

'So should I smile, or what?'

'If you like.'

Lisa stood there, feeling a little self-conscious as the man zoomed in on her and fired off a few shots. 'Right,' he said, checking the results on the screen on the back of his camera, and Lisa frowned.

'Is that it?' she said, marching across the short expanse of wet sand between them.

'Well . . .'

'Only I've – I mean, *we've* – been hanging around for hours for these. The least you could do is take a couple more.'

'What for?'

'So we've got a selection!' Lisa said, in an 'obviously' way.

'Well, I kind of wanted to . . .' The man indicated the boats he'd been photographing earlier, and Lisa widened her eyes.

'Can I at least see what you've taken?' Without waiting for an answer, she grabbed the camera and peered at the screen on the back. 'How do I . . . ?'

'This button here,' said the man, in something of a strangled voice, though perhaps because Lisa's tugging on the camera had tightened the strap around his neck.

'Sorry,' she said, relaxing her grip on it as she reviewed the pictures, then her face fell. 'These aren't very flattering.'

'Excuse me!' The man was looking a little put out, but Lisa was determined not to let it drop. After all, no matter what she and Jess could concoct between them regarding the date, if her photo let her down, then the only invites she'd be getting would be to Halloween parties.

'Can we just try a few more?' she pleaded, then she jabbed a thumb at Simon. 'Then you can get a couple of him, and that'll be it.'

'Fine,' said the photographer.

'And maybe try to find my best side?'

'Which is?' he said, and Lisa gritted her teeth. Chris had said it was her *back*side, but there was no way she was going to . . .

She caught herself. If she wanted this to pay off, then maybe she did have to go the distance. Take one for the team – photographically, at least. Even though the team didn't include Simon.

'How about this?' said Lisa, looking coquettishly back over her shoulder at him, then sticking her bum out a little. 'Or is that a bit too much?'

'No, that's—'

'Or this?' she said, maintaining the bum-out position and doing the same thing with her chest, much like she'd done for some of the more adventurous yoga poses in Cancún.

Matt Dunn

The man seemed a little more animated now, and seemed to be taking a few more photos than perhaps strictly necessary, and Lisa felt a bit awkward. She wanted to look good in the paper, but maybe she'd taken things a bit too far. And shouldn't Simon be in some of these shots too?

She glanced to her left, where he was standing next to one of the boats, and noticed he was trying to attract her attention. He'd been joined by a woman carrying a metal equipment case, and the two of them seemed to be discussing something. The woman laughed, and Lisa was surprised to feel a pang of jealousy.

'Can you stop that? You're putting me off.'

'Stop what?'

'Whatever it is you're doing,' said Lisa, crossly.

'You might want to do the same,' suggested Simon.

'Why?'

'Because this is Alex.'

'Who's Alex?' she said, hoping she didn't sound jealous.

'The photographer. From the *Gazette*.'

Lisa's jaw dropped open. 'But . . .' She turned to stare at the man who'd been photographing her. 'Who are you?'

'Me? I'm Dave,' said the man.

'You're not from the *Gazette*?'

'Should I be?'

'Yes!' Lisa glared at him as she quickly straightened up. 'What are you doing, taking photographs here?'

Dave looked shiftily at her. 'It's a free country,' he said.

Lisa could hear a laugh, and didn't need to look across to know that it had come from Simon. 'Well, if you could please delete those ones of me!'

'But you *asked* me to take them.'

'And now I'm telling you to do the opposite!'

'Suit yourself,' he said, stabbing at the buttons on the back of his camera, and Lisa was about to berate him, tell him he was a pervert, then she remembered she *was* the one who'd asked him to take her photo. Instead, she harrumphed as haughtily as she could, and strode over to where Simon and Alex were standing.

'So,' said Simon, doing his best to smother a grin. 'Alex. This is Lisa. I'd say she's probably warmed up by now, so where did you want us?'

Alex smiled at her, then peered up at the sky. 'Down by one of the boats might be nice, so we can get a bit of authentic seaside atmosphere in. The tide's out, so we can hopefully get a few photos on the sand before it comes back in.'

'Fine,' said Lisa, glaring at Simon, though he responded with a 'not my fault' gesture, and she supposed she couldn't blame him.

'How's it gone so far?' said Alex. 'Will our readers be hearing wedding bells, or alarm ones?'

Simon and Lisa exchanged glances, and she was surprised to see him blushing. 'It's been . . . fine,' she said.

'Only I have to ask. Whether you want a photo with you both looking all romantic, or . . .' Her eyes flicked between the two of them. 'Not.'

'Why don't you take a selection,' said Lisa. 'Just in case.'

'Early days, eh?' suggested Alex.

'Something like that.'

'Right, well, let's . . .'

Alex was indicating the nearest fishing boat, currently marooned on the sand, so Lisa went and stood in front of it, careful to avoid the pool of seawater around the hull. 'Okay,' she said, as Simon came over to join her. 'What would you like us to do?'

Alex smiled. 'Just relax, and talk to each other. Or pretend you're talking, if that's easier. I just want to get a few natural shots, then we'll go in for some poses.'

'Right. So . . .' Lisa looked up at Simon, who, to his credit, looked like he was enjoying himself, and Lisa hoped that wasn't because their 'date' was almost over. As he seemed to be struggling to suppress a laugh, she reached across and dug him in the ribs.

'What's so funny?'

'Sorry. Just . . .' He nodded over to the far side of the harbour, where Dave was doing his best not to watch the proceedings. 'Do you suppose he's going to put those photos of you on *his* Instagram?'

'As long as that's all he does with them,' said Lisa. Then, when Simon grimaced, she let out a long *eew!* and added, 'I didn't mean *that*.'

'No. Of course. Sorry.' Simon grinned and, conscious Alex was still taking photographs, smoothed down the front of his sweatshirt. 'So, should we . . . ?' He made to put his arm round Lisa's shoulders, but she moved to block it, as if the two of them were choreographing a fight scene.

'Best not. Don't want to give people the wrong impression.'

'Oh. Sure. Sorry.' Simon thrust his hands into his pockets. 'And what would the right impression be, exactly?'

'Just that, you know, we've had a nice time, but . . .' Lisa looked down at her feet, ostensibly to avoid standing in a pile of seaweed. 'This is where it ends. That we got on, fancied each other, had a great day, but for reasons that shall remain a mystery, decided we weren't right for each other. Just didn't . . .' She paused as Alex fired off another shot. '. . . click. Something like that, anyway.'

Simon puffed air out of his cheeks. 'That's rather lot to try to convey in a photograph, don't you think?'

Lisa shrugged. Maybe it was. But what was the alternative?

'Okay,' said Alex, nodding towards the sea. The tide was coming in rapidly, and waves had begun lapping round the fishing boat. 'We better move up off the beach. Just in case.'

Lisa followed the two of them across to where a low concrete jetty, covered in green seaweed and with black barnacles clinging to one side, jutted out into the harbour. Simon offered her his hand, but with a terse 'I can manage' she batted it away and climbed up beside him. The wind was getting up a little, and she shivered.

'Did you want my sweatshirt?' said Simon.

'Please. Then I can have my photo in the paper looking like a pathetic female.'

'Suit yourself,' he said, and Lisa realised she'd possibly been a little rude. Besides, by going on this blind date in the first place, she probably *already* looked like one.

'Okay,' said Alex. 'This is great. I'm just going to take a couple of longer shots for atmosphere, so if you two could just lark around a bit.'

'"Lark around"?' said Lisa.

'Yes. Perhaps Simon tries to kiss you, you look horrified, you put an arm around him, he looks awkward, that sort of thing. Then we'll do a couple where you look like you actually like each other.'

Lisa nodded, but Simon was glancing at his watch, and she couldn't blame him.

'Bored?'

'Pretending to be. It's called "larking around".'

'That's hardly—'

'No – that's good!' said Alex, then she moved a few paces back and began taking photos, so the two of them went through the various poses as instructed. 'Right,' she said, eventually. 'A couple more, then we're done. Lisa, if you could reach up and pretend to strangle Simon, then we'll do it the other way round.'

'Really?'

Lisa and Simon had said this simultaneously, which made all three of them laugh, so Alex nodded. 'It's for comedy value,' she said. 'You know, in case it turns out you two end up hating each other.'

Simon was looking horrified. 'I don't think I could . . .'

'Aww,' said Lisa. 'That's sweet of you.'

'Strangle you, I meant.'

'Give it a go,' said Lisa, reaching for his neck, so Simon pretended he was being throttled.

'Perfect!' said Alex. 'Now if you could just square up to each other, like you're in a boxing match.'

Lisa assumed the position. 'These dates really don't work out that often, do they?' she said.

Alex looked like she was doing a quick bit of mental arithmetic. 'Not *that* often,' she said, hastily taking a few more photographs. 'Okay. Now, Lisa, if you could fold your arms and look angry?'

'What do I do?' said Simon.

'You should . . . Wave!' said Alex, so Simon raised his hand.

'Like this?'

'No!' Alex was back-pedalling along the jetty as quickly as she could, though, to her credit, still taking pictures as she went. 'Wave!'

Lisa looked round and froze. A freak wave had just broken over the far end of the jetty, and a wall of water a foot or so high was heading towards them. And while she feared for her shoes she was more worried she might be swept off the jetty and into the sea below.

'Simon . . .' she said desperately, figuring it was probably too late for her to run, wondering what the appropriate action was in a situation like this. She'd seen *Titanic* about a hundred times, but nothing prepared you for when it happened to you in real life. With no other option, she braced herself, mentally bid her heels and her dignity goodbye, and prepared for the onslaught of what was sure to be cold, sandy, seaweed-ridden water.

Then, and before she knew what was happening, Simon had gently swept her off her feet and lifted her up and out of danger. Now he was holding her in his arms as the sea lapped around his ankles.

She stayed there, her arms linked around his neck, waiting for the water to recede, marvelling at the feeling of being held. If she'd been here with Chris, he'd probably have made a run for it – or, even worse, tried to jump into *her* arms.

'That's perfect!' said Alex, still snapping away from the other end of the jetty.

And Lisa realised she couldn't argue with that.

Chapter 25

For the second time that afternoon, Simon did his best to stifle a burp. He'd never been particularly keen on champagne (and hadn't had many occasions to drink it since Alice), but as Lisa had reminded him, the *Gazette* was paying, and although he felt slightly guilty that Jess might have some explaining to do to her editor when she submitted her expenses, she and Will owed him. Big time. Especially since he might be adding 'new trainers' to the list.

He hadn't thought too much about what he'd done – when the photographer had shouted 'Wave!' Simon had remembered the tide was coming in, put two and two together, and looked round just in time to see what Lisa had described rather melodramatically afterwards as a 'mini-tsunami' rushing in towards them. In the absence of any other ideas, he'd swept Lisa off her feet – ironically, the only time he'd done that all day – braced himself, and stood there as the wave crashed around his ankles, soaking his trousers from the knees down, and filling his trainers with icy seawater.

It had made the perfect photograph, according to Alex – and the picture had certainly looked both dramatic *and* romantic when she'd shown it to the two of them: him stood there stoically with Lisa in his arms, her gazing adoringly up at him, in (what looked like) the middle of the sea. It was just a shame that wouldn't be the photograph they'd be using to illustrate the piece. It wouldn't be appropriate. Not if they wanted people to think they weren't going to end up together, or didn't have any 'spark'.

Embarrassed, he'd waited until he was sure the wave had receded, carried Lisa the few paces to the end of the jetty and gently lowered her to the sand, and she'd looked at him with an expression of . . . well, Simon hadn't been sure what on earth it had been. Gratitude, maybe. He at least felt he'd atoned for the Chris incident earlier. And hoped that they wouldn't be parting on such bad terms.

But when they'd said goodbye to Alex, Lisa had suggested they find the nearest pub with an open fire so Simon could dry off; then (as compensation for everything they'd been through, and as a thank you for saving her – though Simon suspected it was more for saving her shoes) he and Lisa had ordered a bottle of the pub's finest bubbly, which – although it had turned out to be the pub's *only* bubbly, *and* had only been twenty-five pounds, *and* had tasted a little more 'moat' than 'Moët' – had gone down rather well. Simon did fear it might come up again later, but at least he was feeling better about how the day (he couldn't really call it a 'date') was ending.

They'd done their duty as far as Will and Jess were concerned, and Simon was pretty sure Lisa had forgiven him for the Chris-on-the-Ferris-wheel incident – or maybe the excitement of her 'near-drowning' (as she'd begun referring to what he'd saved her from, after her second glass of champagne) had meant she'd temporarily forgotten about it. But since arriving at the pub, Lisa and he had talked – *really* talked. Like friends, even. And if that was what they became after today, Simon decided it wouldn't be a bad outcome.

'So?'

Lisa had climbed – a little unsteadily, perhaps not surprisingly – to her feet, and he looked up at her. Maybe it was the champagne, maybe it was even that she was growing on him, but he suddenly remembered just how attractive she was. Nothing like Alice, perhaps, but . . . not in a different league – more like a different sport entirely. A redhead, as opposed to Alice's brunette, with long hair, in contrast to Alice's crop. A fuller figure too. Not fat; but not thin, like Alice had been. And with a completely different sense of style too – more expressive, whereas Alice's dress sense was . . . He thought for a moment, struggling to remember what his ex had been like . . . Converse – no, that wasn't it. Conservationist . . . ? He shook his head to try to clear it. *Conservative.* That was it. Then he remembered Lisa's 'So?' was probably a question, so he did his best to focus on her.

'So?'

'How are your shoes?'

Simon wiggled his toes around in his trainers, and tried not to grimace at the combination of soaked sock and wet sand he could feel. 'Getting there.'

'Great.' Lisa smiled down at him. 'Well, I'm not sure I can have any more to drink, so did you want to go on somewhere, or . . . ?'

Confused, Simon frowned. Going on somewhere would surely mean more to drink, and he'd had enough too. Going on somewhere might also mean a club, and he hadn't been to a club since . . . well, he couldn't remember when. A fact that was more down to how long it had been, he realised shamefully, rather than the amount of alcohol he'd consumed so far today. But at the same time, he didn't want the evening to end either.

He checked his watch. Nine o'clock. Since Alice – and since Will had met Jess, and therefore been too busy to drag him down to the pub – his Saturday nights had mostly been spent on his own in front of Netflix, trawling through series after series. But now, being out in Margate, and after dark . . . He almost laughed at how uneasy that made him feel. A night-time stroll through Margate was hardly like venturing on to *The Walking Dead* set. Despite appearances to the contrary.

'I don't think I *can* go on somewhere,' he said, then he wondered if he'd imagined the look of disappointment that flashed – albeit briefly

– across Lisa's face. 'I'd offer you a lift home, but . . .' He mimed being drunk, then frowned. 'Where *is* home?'

Lisa hesitated, and Simon feared he'd overstepped the mark, then he realised she was just trying to focus. 'Addington Street,' she said. 'It's not that far. So no need. For a lift. Home.'

Simon hid a smile. Lisa was having trouble constructing sentences – or at least, ones longer than three or four words. Then he began to worry. Addington Street *wasn't* that far, but it was getting late, and it *was* dark, and Lisa was a little tipsy. Perhaps it wouldn't be safe for her to walk home on her own.

'Let me call you a taxi, at least.'

'Don't worry. I'd rather walk. I could do with the fresh air.'

'Let me walk you home, then.' He saw Lisa's eyes widen, and held both hands up. 'No funny business. I just want to make sure . . . What?'

Lisa had begun to snigger, and Simon wondered why. Was his dating technique really so bad that she'd think that was some clumsy attempt at a chat-up line?

'*Funny business!*'

'What about it?'

'The phrase! "Funny business" . . . How old are you?'

'Thirty-one. Didn't Jess tell . . . Ah. Yes, I suppose it does sound a little old-fashioned.' He tried, and failed, to prevent the redness spreading across his cheeks, but to his surprise Lisa had reached down to place a palm against the side of his face.

'You're sweet,' she said, patting his cheek as he hauled himself to his feet. 'But I'll be fine. Honestly.'

'You're sure?'

'I'm sure.'

'Great,' he said, though he wasn't convinced it was.

Lisa had picked her bag up and was walking towards the door of the pub, so Simon hurried to get in front of her, opened the door and ushered her through. The rush of cold night air hit him instantly, and he realised a walk might do him good too.

'Where are you parked?' she said, and Simon thought for a moment. Where *had* he parked? It seemed like so long ago now.

'Top of the High Street.'

'In that case, let me walk you to your car.' She smiled. 'Seeing as it's on my way.'

'What? Oh. Okay. Sure.'

Obediently, Simon fell into step alongside her. He had no intention of driving – he'd drunk way too much for that – but he could do with a little longer in Lisa's company, if only to convince her to let him walk her home. And even though the taxi rank was in the opposite direction – and Simon didn't think Margate had smartened itself up so much that he needn't worry about walking around the town centre alone late at night – he didn't have the heart to tell her.

'Listen,' he said, after an uneasy couple of minutes of what had felt like perhaps the most heavily loaded silence he'd ever experienced. 'Thanks again for – you know . . .'

'Sure,' said Lisa. 'Back atcha.'

'It's been . . .'

'Interesting!'

Lisa was smiling – Simon could see her out of the corner of his eye as he walked – but she was right. It *had* been an interesting experience. Not at all what he'd expected. But while perhaps the romance wasn't there, would they be ending it as friends, or just on friendly terms? Because 'friends' would suggest they'd be seeing each other again, even just on a non-romantic basis, whereas the alternative was – probably – to never see Lisa again. And Simon wasn't quite sure how he felt about that.

He walked on for a moment or two, trying to tread as lightly as possible to minimise the squelching sounds his trainers were making, hoping Lisa wouldn't notice the trail of wet footprints he was leaving, then he had an idea, and while it was perhaps a bit shameful, he was quite proud of himself. His car was just up ahead, but on the opposite side of the road. If he remembered his geography, Addington Street wasn't that far away. So all he had to do was distract Lisa, get her to keep walking, maybe by getting her to start talking – and in a few minutes, he'd have achieved his goal of walking her home.

But what to talk about? He and Lisa had covered a lot this evening, and for someone who wasn't skilled at making small talk with women, he'd pretty much run out of conversational gambits. Lisa had been the one who'd been doing most of the talking – probably because Simon had been content to just sit there and listen – and he couldn't think of a thing to tell her. Unless . . . finally, some of Will's advice might actually prove to be useful.

'I imagine Cancún was quite a change from Margate?' he said. And when Lisa's face lit up, he knew he'd hit the jackpot.

'It was *amazing*.'

'I've never been. And, to be honest, I'm not exactly sure where it is.'

'Mexico,' said Lisa. 'Facing Cuba. It's like paradise. Follow me on Instagram and you can see all the photos . . .'

'I'm, um, not on Instagram.'

Lisa stopped walking abruptly, and Simon worried his plan had been scuppered. 'Why ever not?' she said, as if Simon had just admitted he didn't breathe oxygen.

'Well, because it's kind of a platform for people to show off their perfect lives, isn't it? And there isn't that much about mine that's worth sharing.'

'Don't sell yourself short.'

'You'd be surprised,' he said, then thought she probably wouldn't. 'Besides, there's only so many photos of cups of coffee I could post on there before people got bored and stopped . . . what was it?'

'*Following* you.'

'Thank you.'

'You never know. If you're as into coffee as you sound, you could end up being an influencer. You could call yourself "Mister Bean" and . . . No, hang on.'

Simon laughed. 'Better that than "Has Bean".' He nudged her playfully, hoping he hadn't just steered their evening towards ending on a downer. 'So . . . you were saying?'

'Eh?'

'Cancún?'

'Oh, yes!' Lisa brightened up suddenly again, and Simon mentally patted himself on the back. 'I was feeling a bit . . . lost, to be honest. Chris and I had just . . . well, you know the story. And, like I said earlier, I'm a Virgo. And Virgos are constantly analysing and thinking, which I think I'd been doing a little too much . . .' She let out a short laugh. 'And there I go again! Anyway, then I read this quote about how most people tiptoe quietly through life, and for what? Hoping they make it safely to the end of it? Where's the fun in that? So I thought, if I wanted to change, I had to take a few risks. Then one of the influencers I follow . . .'

'On Instagram?'

'That's *right*!' Lisa gave him a quick round of applause, evidently pleased he'd been paying attention. 'So she was posting all these amazing photos and inspirational quotes from this retreat, and before I knew it I'd booked my ticket.'

'And it changed your life?'

Lisa puffed air out of her cheeks as they turned the corner. 'It's a bit early to tell, to be honest. It changed *me*, though, so I'm expecting it to. Eventually.'

'So how long have you been trying this new approach of yours?'

Lisa looked at her watch. 'Since I agreed to go on a certain blind date,' she admitted, sheepishly, and though the next, obvious question to ask was 'And how is it working out for you?', Simon didn't dare.

'Well, I think that's . . . admirable,' he said, and Lisa punched him lightly on the shoulder.

'Are you taking the piss?'

'Not at all! I just wish I – I mean, *more people* could be that brave.'

'Well, *you* obviously are.'

'Me?'

'Hello! It wasn't just me on this blind date! And by the sound of things, you've made some big changes too. Moving here from London, for example. That's quite a dramatic step. Takes some guts.'

'Margate's not *that* bad.'

'That wasn't what I meant.'

Simon ever-so-gently returned her shoulder punch. 'Maybe,' he conceded, then a thought occurred to him. 'Hey – maybe you could be one of those "influencers" you mentioned?'

'Doubtful,' said Lisa as they turned into Addington Street. 'Who could possibly be influenced by *me*?'

Simon smiled. Because, right now, he could think of at least one person.

Chapter 26

'Oh!' said Lisa, suddenly recognising that the house they were standing in front of was hers. 'Where's your car?'

'Where I parked it.' Simon rocked nervously from foot to foot. 'At the top of the High Street.'

'But that's . . .'

'Where it's staying, given how much I've had to drink. And I told you I wanted to see you home. It's not safe to be out around here at night. There's all sorts of strange men . . .'

'So I see,' she said, and Simon half smiled.

'Anyway . . .' He looked at his watch, then glanced towards her door, and Lisa wondered if he was angling for an invitation. Then she caught herself. One thing she'd realised about Simon over the course of the day – and especially when he'd saved her so heroically from the incoming tide – was that he was the perfect gentleman, so he was probably just making sure he'd accomplished what he'd set out to do. Though what exactly that was, Lisa wasn't quite sure.

'So, should we catch up some time next week?' he said, though he quickly followed it with: 'Just so we can touch base about our answers. Get our stories straight. Otherwise Jess is going to be writing I-don't-know-what.'

'I guess,' said Lisa, suddenly disappointed. Before they'd met, she'd assumed today would be hers to lose: Jess had told her once that the fundamental difference between men and women was that if a woman went out for the evening, she was pretty much *guaranteed* sex – after all, how many men would turn it down if offered? And while she hadn't offered – it hadn't been that kind of date – the least she'd have expected was for whoever she'd met to be asking for her number, or at least to ask her on a second date. Nobody had *ever* rejected her before – or, at least, not shown any interest of *that* kind (or 'tried it on', as her parents might say), especially not after spending what had turned out to be the best part of nine hours with her. And suddenly, Lisa realised, she needed to find out why.

Of course, Simon's lack of interest might simply be because Lisa had indicated – several times – that she wasn't interested in him. But they'd been getting on so well this evening, so much so that Lisa had been convinced that – the 'Alice' legacy aside – Simon *was* interested. And standing there, a little drunk, and very, very lonely, Lisa decided she needed to know if she was right.

'Did you want my number?' she said. When Simon looked a little confused, she continued: 'So we can, like you said, touch base.'

'Oh. Right. Yes, please.' Simon fished his phone out of his pocket and handed it to her, so she punched her digits in and handed it back.

'Call me,' she said, and when Simon's eyes widened she added, '*Now*, I mean. So I can save yours.'

'Sorry. Of course.'

Simon pressed the dial button, waited until he heard Lisa's phone ring from inside her bag, then cancelled the call. 'Okay then.'

'Right.'

'So . . .'

'Well . . .' Lisa put one hand on her front gate. 'I'd ask you in for a coffee, but, as you know, I don't like coffee.'

'That's fine,' Simon said. 'It's late, anyway. For coffee, I mean. Because of the caffeine. Not because I wouldn't want to . . .'

'Tea?'

'It's got caffeine in it too,' said Simon. 'Depending on the kind of tea, of course.'

'Well, did you want to come in and wait for a cab?' Lisa said, curtly.

'What?' Simon narrowed his eyes at her for a moment, then he looked aghast. 'Oh my god, I'm sorry! I thought when you said "tea" you were asking me *about* tea. Not asking me *for* tea. Well, not *for* tea, exactly. I'd be several hours too late. But if I wanted to come in for a *cup* . . .' He glanced up at the heavens, then folded his arms. 'As you can see, my smoothness hasn't improved at all since lunchtime.'

'Do you want one or not?' said Lisa, mock angrily, as she fished her keys out from her handbag.

'I could force one down,' said Simon with a grin, and Lisa felt her heart leap a little – stupid of her, she knew – and she hurried down her garden path and fumbled to get her key in the front door, surprised by her sudden nervousness.

'Only thing is . . .'

Simon was hovering on the doorstep, so Lisa frowned at him. 'What's wrong?'

'I don't want to make a mess on your carpet.'

'Hello?!' Lisa stared at him, then burst out laughing. 'Euphemism alert!' Then, when Simon went red so quickly it would put a traffic light to shame, she laughed even more raucously, and realised she was a little drunk.

'My trainers,' he said patiently, once she'd calmed down. 'They're still a bit wet from the sea. I don't want to ruin your . . .' He nodded at the hallway carpet, and Lisa smiled.

'Take them off, then. We can put them in the tumble dryer.'

'Right.'

He did as instructed, then hesitated on the mat, so Lisa said, 'Yes?'

'And my socks are a little damp.'

'Fine,' she said. 'Anything else?'

'Well, now you mention it . . .' Simon pointed down at his calves, the lower halves of each one a darker blue than the rest of his jeans.

'Well, take them off too!'

'I would. But . . .'

Lisa suddenly twigged what was wrong. 'Hold on,' she said, shutting the door behind him, nipping into her bedroom and retrieving a sarong – one of her Cancún beach purchases – that was hanging over the chair in the corner. 'Put this on and I'll just . . .' She nodded at the bathroom door and Simon stared at her, dumbfounded. Lisa wondered whether she had to explain everything to him, then she remembered he had no way of knowing that her bathroom was behind that particular door. 'Ladies' room,' she said, by way of an explanation, then wondered why she'd called it *that*. Then again, it *had* been a while since any man had set foot in there.

'Are you sure?'

Lisa made a face. 'I'm sure I can resist you. The kitchen's through there,' she said, pointing to the other end of the hallway. 'You go in and put your wet things in the tumble dryer, stick the kettle on and I'll just , . . like I said . . .'

'Go to the toilet.'

'Exactly.'

As Simon headed dutifully along the hallway, she popped into the bathroom, locking the door behind her (then – rolling her eyes at her own behaviour – unlocking it again almost immediately), reapplied her lipstick and stared at her reflection in the mirror above the sink. This had really turned into the strangest of days. She'd started out hoping – no, *believing* – she was going to meet someone amazing; and in a way, she had, yet she'd ended up . . . Lisa frowned at herself. She wasn't sure where she'd ended up. Then again, the evening wasn't over yet, so perhaps she hadn't *reached* the end.

She flushed the toilet for good measure, then wondered why she'd felt the need to pretend she'd just disposed of her own bodily waste, and made her way back out and into the kitchen. The kettle clicked itself off – just the right amount of water for two cups too, according to the display on the side – and Simon had laid all the required tea-making implements out on the kitchen worktop: two mugs, two teaspoons, a carton of milk from the fridge and a bag of sugar. Now he was standing in front of the open cupboard next to the oven, dressed in the unlikely combination of his sweatshirt and her sarong, staring in awe at the contents of her top shelf.

'That look suits you.'

'Thanks.' He did a little shimmy, grabbing frantically at the sarong as it threatened to fall off as a result, then returned his gaze to the interior of the cupboard.

'Everything okay?'

He spun round to face her, a look of bewilderment on his face. 'You've got the biggest collection of tea I've ever seen!'

Lisa beamed at him, then wondered whether that was, in fact, something to be proud of. 'Choose one.'

'I'm not sure I can!' Simon was picking up boxes, peering at the labels, sniffing them and putting them back where he'd found them. 'What do you recommend?'

Lisa walked over to stand next to him, then regarded the various options. 'Depends what you like.'

'Well, I like coffee, but I can't see a coffee-flavoured one, so . . .'

She elbowed him gently in the ribs. 'In that case, you might as well just shut your eyes and pick one at random.'

'I'm blind-dating *tea* now, am I?'

'Just do it, smart-arse.'

Simon side-eyed her for a moment, then he closed his eyes and did as instructed. 'Ah,' he said, showing her the box, where BEDTIME was written in large white letters. 'Maybe I'd better choose another.'

'No, that's fine,' said Lisa, then she blushed. 'I didn't . . . I mean, that's a good one. It's supposed to help you – you know, *relax*.'

Simon handed Lisa the box. 'I could have done with one of those earlier.'

'You and me both!' she said, retrieving two teabags and dropping them into the mugs on the counter.

'Sugar?' he asked, handing her the bag.

'Yes, honey?'

'No, I . . .' He shook his head. 'Sorry.'

Lisa did an exaggerated fist pump at catching him out. 'You don't need it.'

'Because I'm sweet enough already?'

'Because it's herbal tea.'

'Good to know,' said Simon. 'Milk?'

'And you're not really supposed to add milk.'

'Because I'm not . . .' He frowned. 'Sorry. Can't think of anything appropriate except for something to do with cows,' he said, then he picked the carton up and sniffed it apprehensively. 'It's off.'

'As you'll be, if you keep those jokes up!' she said, mock sternly. 'But like I said – not really the done thing.'

'Good to know.'

Lisa smiled to herself as she made the tea. Simon seemed to have relaxed, at least – though perhaps that was because he didn't feel any more pressure regarding the 'date' part of the day, and the thought made her feel a little disappointed. Okay, she'd already decided the two of them probably weren't compatible, but she'd also wanted him to at least show a little interest – or rather, disappointment – when she turned him down. Then it occurred to her that wasn't actually a very nice thing to think, especially given her new positivity, and she immediately felt bad.

She found a packet of Jaffa Cakes in the fridge, considered putting them on a plate, then remembered she didn't have the Queen round for tea, so instead handed the box to Simon, picked up the mugs and indicated he should follow her through to the front room.

'Nice house,' said Simon, giving the room a quick once-over before sitting down on the far end of the sofa. 'Do you live here alone, or . . .' He stopped talking again, and adjusted the sarong to protect his modesty. 'Sorry. That's the kind of thing a murderer would say. And, despite what you might have thought when we first met, I'm not. Honest.'

Lisa sat down in the armchair opposite him. 'Hey. I seem to remember I went on to accuse you of being a potential date rapist too, so I've got a lot of apologising to do myself.'

'Don't mention it.'

Simon picked his mug up, and Lisa nodded at it. 'It'll be hot.'

He gave her a 'ya think?' look, sniffed his tea tentatively, blew across the top, then took a sip. 'Not bad,' he said, fanning his mouth with his hand. 'The temperature of molten lava, mind you, but not bad.'

Lisa smiled smugly. 'I knew I could convert you.'

'How is "not bad" a conversion?'

'Just you wait.' She pushed the box of Jaffa Cakes across the coffee table towards him. 'Biscuit?'

'What?'

'*Biscuit*. As in "would you like one".'

'Oh-kay. Well, that was a "what" as in "but they're Jaffa Cakes".'

Lisa stared blankly at the box for a moment or two. 'So?'

'So they're not biscuits.'

'What are they then?'

'Well . . .' Simon took another sip of his tea. 'They're *cakes*, obviously.'

'Cakes?'

He tapped the side of the box. 'The clue's in the name.'

'Right.'

'No problem. Easy mistake to make.'

Lisa sipped her tea and regarded Simon over the top of her mug. 'Cakes.'

'That's right.'

She put her mug down, picked up a Jaffa Cake, and regarded it like an antiques expert might if checking out a potential fake. 'What makes them cakes, exactly? Apart from the name.'

Simon thought for a moment. 'They're made of sponge,' he said, as if delivering the killer blow in an argument.

'But they're the *size* of biscuits.'

'Size isn't important,' said Simon, meeting her gaze across the coffee table. 'It's what they're made of that counts.'

Lisa glared good-naturedly at him, then something occurred to her. 'What about sponge fingers?' she said, triumphantly. 'They're biscuits.'

'Hardly.'

'Well, they're not cakes.'

'They're fingers.'

'Like Cadbury's Fingers. Which I think you'll find are most definitely biscuits.'

'But they're *made* of biscuit!'

'If you don't want one, you just had to say . . .'

'No, I'd love one,' said Simon, quickly helping himself to a Jaffa Cake. 'Might help take the taste of this disgusting tea away!'

Lisa's eyes flashed at him, then she saw he was joking and she smiled. 'I bet you never thought this evening's conversation would be so . . .'

'Stimulating?' Simon laughed. 'I suppose it beats "What's your favourite colour?"'

Lisa turned red again, remembering that had been one of the questions he'd teased her about earlier. She sighed and, as if to make a point (though she wasn't quite sure *what* point), she popped the whole Jaffa Cake in her mouth.

'So, listen,' she said, once she'd chewed and swallowed it. 'Should we do our review of the date now, seeing as we're here?'

'Why not? Seeing as it's going to be a good five or six hours before this tea has cooled down enough to drink.'

'Excellent. We should make sure we get our stories straight. That way, when Jess . . . you know . . . So we look . . .' Lisa found herself faltering a little. Somehow, it seemed a little disingenuous to talk about this now, after everything that had happened between them today. And a lot *had* happened, so unless they agreed between themselves what exactly they were going to report . . . 'For example, this Jaffa Cake debate would make an amusing "Any awkward moments?" alternative to our *actual* awkward moment earlier.'

'Which one?'

'It hasn't been *that* bad, has it?'

Simon took another tentative sip from his mug. 'I suppose not,' he said with a smile.

'What was the highlight?' Lisa said, before catching herself. '*Was* there a highlight?'

'Actually, this last couple of hours has been pretty good.' He indicated the two of them. 'Just talking. Getting to know each other. Without any . . .'

'Pressure?'

'I was going to say "agenda", but you're right too.' He grinned again. 'And actually finding we do have stuff in common.'

'We do?' said Lisa, then she looked guiltily across at Simon. 'Sorry. I didn't mean that to sound so much like a question.'

He smiled. 'We do,' he said, dipping his Jaffa Cake into his tea, holding it there for a moment, then a moment longer. 'Although there is one, possibly insurmountable, difference.'

'Which is?'

Simon removed the Jaffa Cake to find the chocolate had melted clean off the dipped part, like the dirt from a half-dunked dish on a television washing-up liquid advert might.

'This is *definitely* not a biscuit,' he said.

Chapter 27

Simon watched Lisa suck absentmindedly on the end of her pen as she pored over the *Gazette*'s questions, the *thump-thump* of his trainers in the tumble dryer providing them with an almost-hypnotic drumbeat soundtrack. He wanted to help her look her best when the article came out – *of course* he did – but that meant putting himself out there as some sort of 'catch' too. And that was the last thing he wanted to do.

Will was always telling him he needed to 'get back in the saddle'. That dating was 'like riding a bike'. And while he knew Will meant that it was something you didn't forget, you surely had to have been good at it in the first place, and Simon wasn't sure he had been: before Alice, that kind of 'riding a bike' had never been something he'd felt completely comfortable about, as if he'd had his stabilisers removed a little too early in the learning process and was still a bit wobbly as a consequence.

Besides, if his experience over the last nine or so hours with Lisa was anything to go by, it was a miracle he'd even managed to get Alice to go out with him in the first place. It had been the weirdest day – and evening – of his life (well, second-weirdest, if you counted the night Alice died), and he supposed he'd be pleased when it was finally over. Though while he could see the logic in Lisa's plan, he wasn't actually sure he wanted to be a part of it – though he was worried that reluctance was purely for selfish reasons.

Lisa was alternating between frowning at the questionnaire and him now, so he drained the last of his tea and put his mug down, careful to locate it on the coaster rather than the polished wooden surface of the coffee table. A joke Will had made once about 'putting a ring on it' sprang to mind, and he thought about telling it to Lisa, but given her reaction to Chris and Cat's engagement, he quickly decided against it.

'Problem?'

'The last-but-one question.'

'What about it?'

'See for yourself.'

She slid the paper across the table towards him, so he picked it up and scanned down to near the bottom of the page.

'Ah.'

'Yes. *Ah.*'

'Shouldn't we just put "no"?'

'Well . . .'

'It says "And did you kiss?"'

Lisa nodded, in that way people did when someone else was stating the blooming obvious. 'I know.'

'But we didn't. Kiss.'

'Ri-ight.'

Simon raised both eyebrows at Lisa's elongation of the word. 'What's *that* supposed to mean.'

'Well, here we are, giving each other a glowing review, having had a fabulously fun and romantic date, supposedly fancying the pants off each other, and we haven't even kissed?'

'So?'

'Don't you think that's a little weird?'

Simon made a face, because what about today *hadn't* been? 'Don't you think people are going to think it's weird that we've had such a nice time and we aren't together at the end of it?'

'We'll just tell them it didn't work out.'

Simon scrunched his face up. '*Tell* them?'

'When they ask.'

He scrunched his face up even more, not sure who 'they' were. 'Oh-kay.'

'What does *that* mean?'

'I suppose you're making a valid point.' He realised he was still making a face, so he relaxed his features. 'We're constructing this fabulous date, and people are supposed to believe it's come to nothing. Why wouldn't it work out?'

'Maybe you're a lousy kisser?'

She'd obviously meant it as a joke – or, at least, he hoped she had – but Simon bristled a little. Particularly because Alice had always assured him of the opposite. 'Maybe *you* are.'

'I've never had any complaints!'

'Neither have I!'

'Perhaps it's not the kind of thing people complain about. Did you think about that?"

'I think I'd be able to tell if I was doing it wrong.'

'How?'

'Trust me. I haven't been.'

'And neither have *I*.'

'You do realise we're arguing about a fictional event here?' Simon rolled his eyes. 'So let's just put "yes".'

'Really?' Lisa indicated the questionnaire's various sections with her pen. 'All I'm saying is, we *did* go on the Ferris wheel, have champagne in the pub, enjoy a romantic stroll with an ice cream on the Harbour Arm . . . We're not lying about any of that.'

'So, do you *want* to kiss?'

'It's not really a case of "want", is it?'

'So, we *should*?'

'Don't you think?'

'Fine!' said Simon, then he realised he sounded a little petulant. 'So should we stand up, or just . . .'

He indicated the sofa, though he worried it might come across as suggesting they lie down on it. In any case, before he could correct himself, Lisa nodded.

'Standing is good, I think.'

'Right.' He got to his feet, slid his mug away from the edge of the coffee table just in case, moved round to where Lisa was standing, then found himself doing that weird neck-rolling-loosening thing people did in films before attempting a particularly difficult rifle shot or fighting move. 'Ready?'

'And they say romance is dead . . .'

He stuck his tongue out at her, then gently took her by the shoulders. 'Ready,' he said, a little more softly this time, then he leaned in and kissed Lisa briefly on the lips. 'There,' he said, awkwardly taking a step back, nearly tripping over the coffee table in the process. 'That wasn't so bad, was it?'

'Is that the best you can do?'

'Huh?'

'I'm not your grandmother.'

'I don't kiss my grandmother on the lips!'

'That's not exactly what I meant, Simon.'

'Sorry. And got you. I just thought . . .'

Lisa took a half-step closer to him. 'Maybe the secret is *not* to think.'

'Okay. Don't think. Got it. Mmph!'

Lisa had placed a hand on the back of his neck and gently pulled his head down so their lips met, and Simon allowed himself to enjoy the sensation for a few seconds. Then he broke away, a startled look on his face.

'There,' said Lisa, as if she'd just administered a measles inoculation to a nervous child. 'Now *that* wasn't so bad, was it?'

'No, it was . . .' Simon gazed down at her, his eyes darting alternately to each of hers, and for the first time he noticed how beautiful they were – such a deep green, slightly brown around the pupils, as if they'd just begun to change colour, like a leaf at the beginning of autumn. 'Nice.'

Lisa smiled coyly. 'Nice?'

'But . . .'

Her smile suddenly faded, as if a switch had been flicked. 'But what?'

She hadn't moved – her body was still only inches from his – and Simon didn't know what came over him, but before he could stop himself, he'd taken her hands in his. 'I can do better.'

'Pardon?'

'I can do better. So we really have something to write about.'

'Okay.'

He frowned down at her. 'Sorry – was that an "okay" giving me permission, or an "okay" just acknowledging . . . ?' When Lisa didn't answer, he gently pulled her closer. 'Never mind,' he said, then he angled his head down, placed his mouth lightly on hers and closed his eyes, responding in kind when he felt her tongue softly probing his lips. Letting go of her hands, he took her in his arms and pressed his body against hers, revelling in the sensation of having someone so close, realising he'd missed this *so much*. Lisa had been right. She was a good kisser. At least, she certainly wouldn't be getting any complaints from *him*.

When, finally, he tentatively opened his eyes again, he found Lisa looking up at him. 'Wow,' he said, and by the sudden look of delight on her face, he knew it was exactly the right response.

'"Wow" is right!' she said, then she stood up on tiptoe and kissed him again, more insistently this time, the kiss lasting . . . Simon couldn't tell if it was a minute or an hour, he was so lost in the moment.

She eventually broke away, and Simon had to remind himself to breathe. Her lips had been so warm, and so moist, and so soft, and so pliant, and had tasted of oranges, and chocolate, and alcohol, and . . . what was that tea called again?

'Bedtime,' he whispered, pleased he'd remembered the name, but then – and to his amazement – Lisa took him by the hand.

'My thoughts exactly,' she said, leading him along the hall.

Chapter 28

Lisa didn't know what had come over her, but one thing was for sure: Simon was a *great* kisser. And while she knew that kissing was like the tango – insomuch as it took two people to do it, rather than that it involved exaggerated leg movements performed to the sound of an accordion – she'd never been kissed like *that*. So much so, and despite what she'd said a few moments ago about not having had any complaints, that she'd even been a little concerned she wasn't giving as good as she was getting.

The funny thing was, she hadn't *meant* to provoke him into kissing her, unless she'd done it subconsciously. But when they'd started pushing each other's buttons about it, Lisa had suddenly taken the challenge on, and, to her surprise, he'd caved pretty quickly. Then, when they'd kissed, he'd begun pushing her buttons in a different way – a way she hadn't ever felt before.

Maybe it had been aided by the champagne, or the memory of him whisking her off her feet on the beach earlier, or it could simply have been the moment – and as Lisa had learned in Cancún, in life you had to grab the moment. 'Seize the day' – it was what the Latin tattoo on her hip meant (though it also meant she shouldn't drink five margaritas at a Mexican beach bar, then stagger on a drunken whim into the nearest tattoo parlour). So when Simon had suggested they go to bed, she hadn't given it a second thought, but instead had just grabbed his hand and led him along the hallway and into her bedroom, grateful it was dark enough that he couldn't see the mess she'd left it in while she'd been panic-choosing her outfit earlier.

Now they were standing in the middle of the room, kissing passionately . . . No, not passionately. Tenderly. Softly. Insistently. And yet it was one of the sexiest things she'd ever experienced. Most of the other men who'd made it this far couldn't wait to get her into bed, and foreplay had been something they'd thought they'd accomplished simply by buying her drinks at the pub. Once they were naked . . . well, Lisa had often worried they'd assumed they were in an episode of *Countdown*, as if determined to finish before some imaginary timer went off. But Simon? He seemed content with the kissing part, as if it were something he'd just remembered he loved doing, so he was in no rush to move on. And right now that suited Lisa just fine.

Eventually, reluctantly, she broke off, partly because – given the difference in their heights – her neck was getting stiff. Then she remembered Simon's earlier comment about everyone being the same height lying down, so she cleared her throat in what she hoped was a sexy way.

'Shall we?' she said huskily. Then, without waiting for an answer, Lisa manoeuvred him down on to the bed and straddled his lap. 'Now, where were we? Oh yes. Right about . . .'

She touched a finger to his lips, then put her lips where her finger had been and kissed him again, harder this time, running her hands through his hair, telling herself to slow down – but right now Lisa was very turned on. And, judging by what she could feel as her body pressed against his, she was sure Simon was too.

Her lips still locked with his, she reached down and began unbuttoning her shirt, then she grabbed Simon's hands, placing them where she'd left off so he could finish the job. But when he moved them round behind his back, she repositioned them.

'It's okay,' she whispered into his ear, giving the lobe a gentle bite for good measure, though her words seemed to have the opposite effect, as Simon suddenly pulled away from her.

'No, it isn't,' he said, softly.

'What?'

'I can't do this.'

Lisa fumbled for the bedside light and switched it on, resisting the temptation to shine it in Simon's face like an interrogator might.

'What do you mean?'

'This,' he said, hovering his hands over her half-uncovered breasts, then pulling them away, as if Lisa's bra was radioactive.

'You mean *generally*?' she said, suddenly a little fearful of where this conversation might be going.

'No!' Simon said, perhaps a little loudly, then he softened his voice. 'I mean, I can *do* this. Of course I can. I just can't do it *now*.'

'Is it the champagne? Because if you're worried about *things* working – from where I'm sitting I can reassure you that they are!'

Lisa was hoping for a 'yes', but Simon was already shaking his head. 'No, it's . . .' Gently, he wriggled out from underneath her and leaned back on the bed. 'You and me.'

'*What*?'

'Well, mostly me, if I'm honest.'

'I don't . . .'

'I just . . .' Simon had taken her hand, and Lisa had to resist the temptation to snatch it back. 'After Alice, I've always promised myself that this – sex – had to mean something. Needed to be something done by two people who . . .' He seemed to be searching for the right word, but Lisa didn't dare suggest one. '*Cared* about each other. Not just something that you *do*, like having another drink, or . . .' He frowned. 'Going for a jog. And if you'd asked me ten minutes ago, or an hour ago, or even before we met, whether I thought *this* was on the cards, I'd have laughed – and not just because I'm maybe a little out of practice, but because it wasn't something I expected at all, so much so that when you seemed to think it was such a natural thing to do . . .'

'It *is* a natural thing,' said Lisa – a little petulantly, she realised. 'It's the *most* natural thing.'

'I meant, given the run of play this evening. Everything from when we had an ice cream – when *I* had an ice cream, at least – was based on you wanting to construct this perfect date to show you in a good enough light so you could meet someone else. Someone who *wasn't* me. So you'll excuse me if I'm feeling a little confused.'

Simon was looking as uncomfortable as she'd seen him all day, and Lisa knew that of course she *should* excuse him. But right now her dismay at being rejected was outweighing her sense of fairness.

'But that was . . .' She felt herself colour. 'Until we kissed.'

'And suddenly one kiss changes everything?'

Lisa bit off her 'yes!' and stared at him. The truth was, one kiss *had* changed everything. Though not in the same way for both of them, it was becoming apparent.

'Simon, I . . .' She moved to sit next to him on the bed, careful to leave a distance between the two of them – though not one that was as wide as the apparent emotional one, which appeared to be growing in size by the second. 'I thought you . . . I mean, you walked me *home*. Or rather, tricked me into letting you.'

'Because I was worried about you walking home on your own.'

'And then you came in. For tea.'

'Because you asked me. And because I was thirsty. And because . . .'

He stopped talking, so Lisa took his hand, pulled it into her lap and gave it a squeeze. 'What?'

'Well, because you seemed . . . lonely.'

Lisa almost threw his hand back at him. 'Fuck off!'

'I didn't mean it like *that*.'

She was surprised to find that tears had sprung to her eyes. 'How exactly *did* you mean it?' she said, angrily.

'I just . . .' Simon stood up, adjusted the sarong and began pacing round the bedroom, picking his way through the clutter of discarded pairs of shoes and – Lisa was ashamed to see – not-so-new pairs of knickers scattered across the floor. 'Well, we're both lonely. Aren't we? Otherwise we'd hardly have ended up on a blind date in the first place. And there's no shame in admitting that. A lot of people are lonely. Some of them are lonely and they're *in* relationships. But when you're single, especially when you don't want to be . . .' Simon stopped pacing, then he perched on the edge of the chair opposite and rested his head in his hands. 'All I'm saying is, I don't want this to be some sort of . . . *comfort shag*. Something you're doing because you feel sorry for me, or something you're doing because you feel sorry for *you*. We'd just wake up in the morning and feel lousy.'

'Well, I'm certainly going to be doing that *now*!'

He looked across the room at her. 'Come on, Lisa. Up until about five minutes ago, you had absolutely no intention of ever seeing me again. And the rest of the "date"' – Simon put an exaggerated set of air quotes around the word, and Lisa's position on the 'feeling awful' scale worsened by a notch or two – 'has been all about you pretending you want to do something for the two of us when, in reality, it's all been about you. You've been using me. Just like you were about to again. And I'm sorry, but all this "say yes to everything" stuff you learned in Cancún, all this "living in the moment"? It sounds good in theory, but life isn't just a moment. It's made up of a past. A future. It's forever. And I'm sorry to have to be the one who breaks this to you, but there's no certainty about that either.'

Lisa stared at her feet, unable to meet Simon's eyes. Part of her suspected he might be right – although a bigger part of her didn't want to admit it. But a part of him – a *big* part of him, if you excused the phrase – had responded when they'd kissed, so she *knew* he fancied her. If that had been all she'd set out to prove, then surely she'd done that, and yet – yet again – Simon had surprised her. Though, this time, not in a good way.

She sniffed, then began fastening the buttons on her shirt, not wanting him to go but not wanting him to stay either, trying desperately to stop the tears from coming. Balling her fists, she scrunched her eyes shut and rubbed them until her vision swam, then she took a deep breath.

'I think you'd better leave,' she said.

But when she opened her eyes again she saw that Simon had already gone.

Chapter 29

Simon grabbed his jeans and socks from the tumble dryer and pulled them on, wincing as the hot metal rivets in his Levi's touched his skin, then slipped the warm-but-still-damp trainers on to his feet and let himself out of Lisa's front door. After a moment's hesitation, he pulled it softly shut behind him and made for the relative safety of the pavement. How on earth had today ended up like *this*?

Okay, so kissing Lisa had felt . . . well, rather wonderful, now he thought about it. And Will would probably call him an idiot for turning down what was probably a 'sure thing', in his friend's words. But that was the problem. *Simon* wasn't 'sure'. He began a series of slow, controlled breaths, a technique he'd learned in therapy, and willed the competing knots of grief and guilt that had been building up inside him to dissipate. Deep down, he'd known he shouldn't be looking to replace Alice like-for-like – though to tell the truth (not that he could bring himself to tell Lisa), he hadn't been looking to replace Alice *full stop*. And while he'd initially been sure he and Lisa weren't at all compatible, and eventually decided to treat the date as an exercise, she'd . . . well, like he'd thought earlier, 'grown on him' was probably how he'd describe it.

Of course, he should have just told her the truth about what had happened to Alice, and not just taken his anger at his feelings of guilt out on her, or tried to fob her off with some story about how sex had to 'mean' something. Simon wasn't stupid, nor was he a prude – sometimes all sex meant was that you felt horny, and that was fine. And while it had been *two years* – Simon added the emphasis in his head just like Will would do out loud every time it came up – well, that was another issue too.

No, all things considered, it would have just been too complicated. He was best out of there. Even though it didn't quite feel like it.

Besides, telling Lisa that Alice had died was a pretty big bombshell to drop, and a pretty big 'ask' for anyone. Especially someone who – as Simon had found out over the course of the day – was quite plainly trying to deal with a number of issues herself. Plus, he hadn't been sure Lisa was genuinely attracted to him – or even that interested, to be honest. She'd been a little drunk, and so had he, and Simon didn't want that to be the reason anything might happen between the two of them, especially if that was all it was. Plus he'd wanted to spare them both the awkwardness – the guilt – that was sure to come afterwards. In any case, one-night stands had never been his thing – not that he'd had that many opportunities to *have* a one-night stand. He and Alice hadn't slept together until their fourth date (though it should have been their third, no thanks to his 'dessert' faux-pas) – a fact he'd regretted when they were lying in bed after their first time, and then after she'd died, when he realised he'd never be able to sleep with her again.

He blinked a few times, trying to get rid of the film of tears that had suddenly misted his vision, and peered up at the night sky, the stars just about visible through the light cloud cover, wondering if Alice was looking down on him. Would she be amused by what she'd seen this evening? Or horrified that he was 'saving' himself for . . . he didn't know what.

If he were like Lisa, he'd no doubt be looking for a sign. Perhaps the clouds *were* one, obscuring Alice's view of the goings-on. Maybe he *should* have read his horoscope this morning, just in case. And then just stayed at home.

He made his way back to the main road, pulled his phone out to check his quickest route back to the car (not that he was planning to drive, but his coat was in there, and he didn't want to wake up tomorrow having caught a chill on top of the hangover he was sure to have), and almost dropped it in shock when it rang at exactly that moment. Will, no doubt keeping tabs on him again. Simon considered not answering, but that would only delay the inevitable. And unlike sex with Lisa, a dressing-down from Will was something he was keen to get over and done with.

'Mate?'

Will was sounding less confident this time. Perhaps Jess had received a call from the bank telling her someone had been abusing her credit card. Or maybe – and Simon really hoped not – Lisa had called Jess the second he'd left, then she'd shared what she'd heard with Will, and Will was calling him to tell him exactly what he thought of him.

'Hey, Will,' he said, as neutrally as possible. 'What's up?'

'Just checking in.'

'Checking up, more like!'

Will laughed. 'Okay, okay. Guilty as charged. So . . . ?'

'So what?'

'Just wanted to make sure that you and Lisa, you know, *did it*?'

Simon's jaw almost hit the floor. Either Will was psychic or he'd been tailing him, or – and he wouldn't put it past her – Lisa had phoned Jess from the bathroom to tell her Simon was back at her house for 'coffee' (even though, of course, it had been tea). But it was one thing for Will to try to get him back dating; another for him to check up on whether he'd had sex or not. And after the day he'd had Simon's patience was pretty much at an end.

'Not that it's any of your business, but, no, we didn't!'

'Maaate! Why ever not?'

Will sounded disappointed, which only served to make Simon even more angry. 'It just . . . I mean, I . . .'

'Maybe we can get the two of you together tomorrow. Have another go.'

Simon couldn't believe his ears. Or 'ear', to be strictly accurate, since he had the phone pressed up against his left one. 'Another *go*?!'

'Yeah,' said Will, then his voice adopted a more sympathetic tone. 'What was it? The Alice thing again?'

'The *Alice thing*?' said Simon, exasperatedly. 'No, I . . . I couldn't go through with it. And then, when I explained why, she asked me to go.'

'Shit, mate. Maybe you shouldn't have told her. I did warn you that—'

'Jesus, Will! What do you want me to do here? Carry this big secret around inside me, not tell anyone, or just refer to it like some minor event in my past – like, I don't know, having my tonsils out when I was twelve, and how even two years later I can't even comprehend the thought of trying to meet someone else so I have to be conned into it by my so-called friend who seems to thinks he knows what's best for me, despite not having the *faintest idea* how I feel because nothing remotely like what happened to me has ever happened to him? Oh, and while I'm on the subject, thanks for setting me up with someone so emotionally fragile that the minute I try to tell her why I feel how I feel without going into what actually happened, *and* without sensationalising it or collapsing into a teary mess because that's exactly what my therapist told me I should do, should be *able* to do, she's virtually shoving me out through the bedroom door.'

Simon paused for a much-needed breath, and, after a moment, perhaps because he was waiting to make sure Simon had finished, Will's voice came back on the line.

'The *bedroom* door?'

'That's right.'

'Si, when I asked you if you "did it", I meant did you get the photos done? Not had you *slept together*.'

'Ah. Right. Well, don't worry. We got your precious photos.'

'Excellent!' Will's tone had changed to one of relief. 'But now you've brought it up . . . what were you doing in her *bedroom*?'

'We, um, well, it's a long story involving a wave and a cup of tea, and no trousers . . .' Simon realised he'd gone the wrong way at the previous junction, so he turned back on himself, aiming for the High Street. 'Suffice it to say, I couldn't . . .'

'Take it to the next level?'

'Yeah. And yes, that was partly because of Alice. But also partly because of . . .' Embarrassed, he lowered his voice a little. 'Performance anxiety.'

'That's not surprising, after *two years*.'

Will had put even more emphasis than usual on those last couple of words, which only served to heighten Simon's feeling that he'd done the right thing.

'And when I told her I wanted sex to mean something . . .'

'It *should* mean something. You're right. Though sometimes all it means is that you fancy each other and want to . . . demonstrate that. And that's fine.'

'I know, but . . .' Simon sighed. 'It wasn't just that, Will. I was worried Lisa wanted something I couldn't give her.'

'Maybe she only wanted the one thing you *could* give her. Did you think about that?'

'Will . . .'

His friend chuckled. 'Sorry, mate. I didn't know she'd react like that.'

'Didn't Jess warn you what she was like?'

'Well, yeah. She said she used to be a bit . . .'

'A bit *what*, exactly?'

Will let out a short laugh instead of an answer. 'But apparently she's on this new "see the good in everyone" Buddhist positivity kick.'

'Yeah, well, perhaps she's putting on a front. Some sort of defence mechanism. It'd be understandable. After all, she's been hurt too. You can't just decide you're over someone. So maybe Jess should have filled her in beforehand. Checked she was okay meeting someone like me. Someone who'd lost . . .' Simon swallowed hard, feeling all the fight go out of him. He'd done his best to hold it together over Alice so many times, had even practised on numerous occasions how to tell people if – or when, he now knew – the subject came up, so he wouldn't get too choked up, wouldn't have to force the story out between bouts of uncontrollable sobbing, as had happened the first dozen or so times. Now, his restraint seemed to have had the opposite effect – and was making him feel pretty lousy to boot. 'I just wish . . . I mean, if I'd suggested we meet at a different restaurant, or even at a different time, maybe even just five minutes later, Alice wouldn't have . . .'

'Hey!' said Will, the sharpness of his tone making Simon jump. 'What happened to Alice wasn't your fault.'

'Well, why does it feel like it was?'

'It's called *grief*, Si. It does strange things to people.'

'How would you know?' said Simon, dismissively.

'Because I read up on it. After she died. In case you ever needed to talk about it. Not that you ever seem to want to.'

'I . . . but . . . that's . . .'

'Yeah, well,' said Will, sounding a little embarrassed. 'Anyway. What are you up to now?'

'Heading home. Finally!'

'Do you want me to come and get you?'

Simon shook his head, then remembered he was on the phone. 'I'll be fine. I just . . .' He sighed. 'I know you're right, Will. And I need to do this. But maybe I'm not ready yet – you know?'

'Si, it's been *two years* . . . Sorry. You don't need me to tell you that again. But Alice . . .'

'If you're about to say "would have wanted you to see other people", I'm going to come straight round to your flat and . . .'

'Okay, okay.' Will laughed nervously. 'But she would have.'

'*Will* . . .' Simon rolled his eyes. He knew his friend was only trying to help. Though there were times like now that he really wished he wouldn't. 'Listen, I'm at my car now,' he lied, 'So . . .'

'Right. Sorry, mate. That it didn't work out. And I'm here, if you want to, you know . . .'

'I know. Thanks.'

'Oh, and Jess says there are plenty more girls who've written in, so—'

'Bye, Will!'

Simon took a few breaths, the tightness in his throat as much from his friend's compassionate admission as any guilt about Alice. He'd read up on it too – how grief was like walking through an alpine pass, where mountain after mountain loomed in front of you, and the only way to get through it was to climb up and over each one that appeared in your path. The trouble was, every time he got over a peak, another appeared, and it was often higher than the last. One day, he knew, he'd reach the final one. He just hoped that he'd have the strength left to climb it.

He checked his phone for messages, then strode towards the top of the High Street, where he'd parked his car. He was definitely over the limit, he reckoned, so there was no way he'd be driving it home, even if the alternative was a long and (given the late hour) slightly chilly walk back home. He could try to call a taxi – Margate didn't do black cabs, or Uber – but it was Saturday night, and by the time it arrived he could probably be at his front door anyway. Besides, the walk – and the fresh air – would do him good. Help him sleep. After everything that had happened today, he'd probably need it.

Rounding the corner, he spotted his car, pleased to see it was still where he'd left it (this was Margate, not Mogadishu, and it was a Ford Focus and not a Ferrari, but you never knew), and patted his pockets to locate his keys, then his face fell. They'd been in his front pocket, right up until . . . well, up until he'd taken them out of there to put his jeans in the tumble dryer, and in his rush to get out of Lisa's house he'd forgotten to pick them up.

He groaned, then leaned against the nearest lamp post, banging his head steadily against it, wondering what on earth to do, only stopping when an old lady walking her dog gave him a funny look from across the street. He could hardly march back to Lisa's house, knock on the door and sweetly ask her to hand them over, but, equally, he wouldn't be able to get back into his flat or collect his car in the morning if he didn't. And while he could text her, perhaps ask her to leave them on the doormat for him to collect, he didn't want to risk her throwing them at him when he appeared. Or flushing them down the toilet. Those remote fobs were expensive to replace.

He pulled out his phone, began dialling Lisa's number, then cancelled the call just as quickly. Some things needed to be sorted out face to face. Besides, he couldn't – and shouldn't – leave things between the two of them like this.

With a sigh, followed by another, more pitiful one, Simon turned around and began retracing his steps.

Chapter 30

Lisa had polished off the rest of the Jaffa Cakes, and now she was standing in her kitchen, peering into her fridge, wondering whether it was too late to open the 'emergency' bottle of Chardonnay she kept in there for incidents like this. Well, for incidents full stop. Because, when she thought about it, she realised there hadn't been many incidents like *this*.

And though she'd thought about it *a lot* since Simon had hightailed it out of her bedroom, Lisa still wasn't sure exactly what had happened. Okay, maybe getting him to kiss her hadn't been strictly necessary (and had perhaps been a bit mischievous), but she'd just felt like it, and Cancún had taught her that life was all about going with your feelings, acting on impulse.

And then, when they'd kissed . . . It hadn't been a spark that she'd felt, but more of a heat. A warmth. There had been something quite intoxicating, and yet – strangely – quite comforting about that.

So when Simon suggested they move to the bedroom, Lisa had thought *Why not?* – and so she'd led him along the hallway, and he'd allowed himself to be led (and he wasn't the type to be easily led), then they'd kissed some more, and then . . . She had felt he wasn't faking it. So why on earth had he stopped?

Lisa rested her forehead against the top of the fridge, appreciating the cool flow of air. All that 'after Alice' stuff, about wanting the fact that they'd slept together to mean something . . . Simon was a man, after all, and all men only wanted one thing, despite whatever backstory they might give you. Surely no dumping could be so severe that it would put someone off sex for two years? No . . . in her experience, no one – *especially* not a man – turned down sex. Unless the prospect of who you were about to have sex with was the reason.

She breathed into her cupped hand and smelled it, then laughed at herself. A bit of tea breath was hardly going to put someone off, even if they *were* a self-avowed coffee drinker. Besides, the tea wouldn't have been called 'Bedtime' if it wasn't supposed to . . .

Lisa didn't need to see her reflection in a mirror to know she'd just gone pale. Simon hadn't been suggesting they moved to the bedroom. He'd simply been telling her what her kisses tasted of. And – not for the first time – Lisa had misinterpreted, jumped the gun, jumped on *him*, and (to continue the gun metaphor) it had all backfired spectacularly.

She grabbed the bottle of wine from where it was lying on the fridge shelf, twisted the top off and took a large swig, not even bothering with a glass. *This* was why she was still single – or, rather, why she couldn't find anyone prepared to commit to her. Because she was too gullible. Too eager to give men what they wanted – or what she thought they wanted.

What about what *she* wanted? Then again, she had wanted it. Wanted *him* . . .

A brief, tentative ring on the doorbell interrupted her thoughts, and Lisa's heart leapt. Simon had come back! But *of course* he had. Understood what he'd been missing, probably. A bit of fresh air must have cleared his head, and he'd realised he'd made a mistake. Well, she wasn't going to forgive him *that* easily. No – he'd have to work for it. She'd need some serious sweet-talking before she let him back in. Though Lisa already knew she'd sleep with him if he wanted to. It was unfinished business now.

She carefully set the bottle down on the kitchen table, wiped her mouth on a paper towel in case she'd been a little too overenthusiastic with the Jaffa Cakes, and rushed to the front door, then remembered she shouldn't perhaps be *too* keen. She waited until the doorbell rang again, counted to ten, fixed a half-smile on her face and fastened the chain across the door. But when she opened it, and saw who was standing on the path, her face fell.

'*Chris?*'

'All right, Lise?'

Lisa stared at her ex, wondering if her eyes were playing tricks on her, then she shook her head in an attempt to clear it.

'What are you doing here?'

Chris took a drag on the cigarette he was holding, and glanced nervously back over his shoulder, as if worried he'd been followed. 'Can I come in?'

Dumbstruck, Lisa slid the chain off the door, then stood to one side to let him by, before she realised he hadn't answered her question. 'Hang on,' she said. 'Do you have any idea what the time is?'

Chris looked at his watch. 'Half ten,' he said, flicking his cigarette out on to her lawn through the doorway, then he hesitated. 'Is he here?'

'Who?'

'Your bloke.'

'My . . . ?' Lisa suddenly remembered the circumstances of their earlier meeting. 'He's not . . .' Lisa stopped short of saying 'my bloke'. 'Why?'

Chris seemed visibly relieved. 'Is it serious?'

'Are *you?*'

'Sorry. It's just that . . . Stephen?'

'Simon,' said Lisa, shutting the front door.

'Sorry. I'm not very good with names.'

'Yeah, you seemed to forget mine soon enough!'

'Ha! Good one,' said Chris, then he realised Lisa hadn't been joking. 'Sorry about that. But that's kind of why I'm here.' He glanced along the hallway. 'You don't have anything to drink, do you?'

Lisa looked at him for a moment, then she sighed. 'In the kitchen. You remember where *that* is, I take it?'

'Yeah. Cheers.'

She followed Chris through into the kitchen, still none the wiser as to what he could be doing at her house at this time of night. Though when he spotted the open bottle of wine on the kitchen table, he grinned.

'Started without me?'

'I had to do *lots* of things without you.'

'Yeah. Well, like I said, that's why I'm here. Glass?'

'I wasn't bothering, actually.'

'For *me*?'

'Oh.' Lisa indicated vaguely towards the far wall. 'In the cupboard.'

As Chris found himself a wine glass, she picked the Chardonnay up and took another swig directly from the bottle, to his evident horror.

'You want some or not?' she said.

'Yeah. Please.'

Lisa splashed some wine into his glass, then took another swig, ignoring Chris's widened eyes. 'It's been a long night,' she said, suspecting it was about to get even longer.

'Right. Cheers.' Chris clinked his glass against the bottle, and took a deep breath. 'So . . .'

'So?'

'So your Simon seems like a decent bloke. And he made me think that, maybe, when we were seeing each other, I wasn't. Decent. And I know this might not sound like something you want to hear, but I felt like I owed you . . .'

'An apology?'

'An explanation. As to why, you know . . .'

'You dumped me, and then five minutes later got engaged to someone who's barely left school?'

Chris grinned, then seemed to realise perhaps he shouldn't have. 'Yeah,' he said, gulping down a large mouthful of wine. 'I mean, it's not like there's anything wrong with you.'

'Thanks very much!' said Lisa, pulling out a chair and collapsing heavily on to it.

'It's just, sometimes you need to go through something with someone to make you realise you're looking for the exact opposite. Not in a bad way . . .'

Lisa glared at him. How could that *not* be in a bad way?

'And sometimes . . .' continued Chris, '. . . something like that helps make your mind up. When we split up I knew I wanted a . . . well, a Cat.'

Lisa tried not to laugh at the irony. That was almost exactly what she'd done. She'd even gone as far as visiting an animal rescue centre before realising it was *her* that needed rescuing.

'And where is Cat? In bed already? It's not a school night, is it?'

'Ha ha. Yeah. Another good one!' Chris let out a brief, forty-a-day rumble of a laugh. 'But seriously, then I met her, and I knew I didn't want to lose her.' He was beaming widely, and Lisa felt pangs of both jealousy and resentment at how happy he seemed. 'But I felt bad because it was so soon after me and you, plus I didn't know how to tell you, didn't know how you'd feel about it, so I thought not telling you made the most sense, and because I didn't want to lie to you, I thought it was best if we didn't speak at all. And I know that doesn't sound like it makes much sense, but it made sense to me at the time.'

'And does it now?'

He gazed off into the near distance, evidently replaying what he'd just said in his head. 'Not a lot, no. But there you go.'

Lisa was conscious it was probably her turn to say something, but for the life of her she couldn't think what. Eventually, 'Am I supposed to feel better now?' was the best she could manage.

Chris shrugged. 'I hope so. And it's good that you've moved on. Great, even. I'm happy for you.'

'Huh?'

'With Simon. He's obviously really into you.'

'Huh?' said Lisa, again, even more confused this time.

'Course he is. I saw the way he was looking at you earlier. Made me feel a little jealous, to be honest. Just . . .'

Lisa narrowed her eyes. 'Just *what*?'

'Well, I'm probably the last person to give you advice. Or, at least, the last person you want to hear it from. But . . .' He put his glass down and looked earnestly at her. 'Just take it slowly, will you? Men can be a bit put off if the girl's too full on.'

'I'm not full on. And besides, and not that it's any of your business, but I don't think I'll be seeing Simon again.'

'I wouldn't bet on that,' said Chris, then he checked the time on the clock on the oven, and looked anxiously across the kitchen at her. 'So. We good?'

Lisa stared back at him for a moment, surprised to find she didn't actually care that much. '*Good?*'

'Great,' said Chris, either not even waiting for her to answer, or mistakenly thinking she already had. 'In that case, c'mere.'

'What?'

He was standing there, his arms wide open and a puppy-dog look on his face, so Lisa thought: *What the hell.* The quicker she got shot of him, the quicker she could get shot of the rest of that Chardonnay. Reluctantly, she stood up, strode across the kitchen and allowed herself to be hugged. And hugged. Because, for some reason, Chris wasn't letting go.

'Chris, what are you . . . ?'

'You smell good.'

'Thank you, but—'

'I missed you, you know?'

'You could have fooled me.'

'I did. Still do, actually.'

Chris leaned down and kissed her briefly on the forehead, and when Lisa looked up, more in surprise than anything else, he planted a kiss on her lips.

'What are you doing?'

'Come on, babe. You and me were good together.'

'Evidently not *that* good.'

'No, I meant . . .' He indicated the way to the bedroom. 'In *there*.'

'Speak for yourself. No, hang on, that didn't come out right.'

'So how about it? One last time. For old times' sake?'

Chris still hadn't let her go, and Lisa's jaw had dropped open in amazement, though he seemed to see it as an opportunity, as a split second later he'd clamped his mouth to hers, stuck his tongue in and was moving it around like someone trying to find something in a lucky dip.

She stood there for a second or two, trying not to gag at the taste of Chardonnay and stale tobacco, wondering how best to respond. A knee in the groin might do the trick, though clamping her jaws shut would probably produce a similar effect. Eventually, a swift shove to his chest gave her the space she needed to duck down and out of his grasp.

'What on earth was *that*?'

Chris was looking surprised, in a 'how on earth could you turn me down?' kind of way. 'I thought you wanted it.'

'Why on earth would you—'

'It's Saturday night. You're lonely. I'm . . .'

Lisa held a hand out to stop him. 'You really don't want me to complete that sentence.'

'Oh well. Worth a try.' He winked at her. 'You're sure now?'

Lisa stared incredulously back at him. 'Yes, I'm sure! And what about Cat?'

Chris stared at her, seemingly genuinely puzzled. 'Oh. Right,' he said, after a second or two. 'What she doesn't know won't hurt her.'

'It *will*, Chris. Eventually.'

'She's getting what she wants.'

'Maybe not what she deserves, though.'

Chris shrugged again, though a little less confidently this time. 'Anyway,' he said, after a pause, 'I've said what I came here to say. Sorry for coming round so late and all that, but I just thought you needed telling.'

'Which bit?'

'All of it, Lise.'

Lisa felt the tears build in her eyes. Maybe she *had* needed telling, but tonight wasn't the best time for her to hear such a thing. She eyed the bottle of wine thirstily, but decided she'd wait until Chris had gone before she finished it off.

'I don't know why you're looking so upset,' he continued. 'You should be flattered.'

'*Flattered?*'

'Yeah,' said Chris, strutting out of the kitchen and into the hallway. 'Anyway. No harm done. I'll see myself out. You take care now, Lise. And don't fuck it up with Stephen!'

He raised both eyebrows in rapid succession as he said the wrong name, and Lisa knew it was probably meant as a joke, but it took all her willpower not to pick the wine bottle up and chuck it at his head. And 'flattered' was . . . actually, the opposite was true. That he'd think she'd have gone for his offer . . . It said a lot about him. Though perhaps it said a little about her, too.

She sat back down at the kitchen table, wondering whether the day could get any weirder. There were positives she could take from this, she knew, not least that Chris was a shit, and she *was* best out of there. Also, she reminded herself, he'd wanted to sleep with her despite his twenty-one-year-old girlfriend, so she couldn't be that bad at sex, despite Simon's earlier rejection. And lastly – and most importantly – she hadn't caved. She'd been drunk, emotional, lonely and feeling rejected, and someone had come along who might have made her feel better about all of those things – even if she'd have ended up feeling worse in the long term. And that – strangely enough – *was* worth celebrating.

She blew her nose noisily on a piece of paper towel, reached across the table and purposefully picked up the wine bottle. She shouldn't keep drinking straight from it, she knew, but she didn't want to use Chris's glass and she couldn't be bothered to walk across to the cupboard and get a fresh one.

Lisa looked around the kitchen. Her glass measuring jug was on the draining board next to the sink, within reach, and it had a handle. More importantly, it held a decent amount. Not really appropriate, but it would do for now.

A phrase, Lisa suspected as she emptied the bottle into the jug, that had probably applied to most of the men in her life.

Chapter 31

Simon stood and stared at Lisa's house, steeling himself to go and knock on the door. The lights were still on, which he supposed was a good sign – at least he wouldn't be waking her up. He'd spent the short walk back planning what to say. A simple 'I think I left my car keys on the dryer' should do the trick – though, then again, that might remind Lisa he'd had his trousers off earlier (and consequently how he'd been so keen to put them back on again), and out of spite she might decide not to let him in.

Perhaps it would be better to make a joke of it. Keep things light. After all, they still had to get together to make sure their answers for the *Gazette* tallied up, and . . . actually, perhaps not. Lisa hadn't looked particularly amused earlier, so any attempt at humour might not go down all that well. Simon suspected she might not see the funny side yet. If ever. He was having a hard enough time doing that himself.

No, a simple in-and-out, bolstered by the reminder about getting their stories straight, made the most sense. Perhaps he should suggest *that* was why he'd come back. Deal with that tonight, then he'd be out of her life for good, she'd never have to see him again . . . Yes, he *should* lead with that. Tell her he'd come back so they could finish what they'd started – though not the *other* thing they'd started – and try to make peace with her, tell her they needed to make sure they were singing from the same hymn sheet, work through the last bits of the questionnaire (though he was already nervous about revisiting the 'Did you kiss?' section), and at some point she was bound to need the toilet. Then all he had to do was sneak into the kitchen, retrieve his keys and job done.

Simon caught himself. Why was he being so disingenuous? Sneaking around wasn't him. Never had been, in fact. Surely it was better to just knock on the door, and then, when she answered, he'd smile apologetically, pat his pockets, wonder where his keys were, he and Lisa would hunt round the house for them, and – *ha ha!* – they'd find them on the dryer. Although that might involve going back into the bedroom, of course – and Simon wasn't sure that was such a good idea, in case Lisa got the wrong idea, because he didn't think Lisa could take being turned down a second time. And – given how their kiss was playing on his mind – he was worried he might not be as resolute as he'd been earlier.

He walked along the garden path and readied himself at the front door, but just as he was about to press the bell, the door opened and – though it was a toss-up as to who was the more surprised – Simon was shocked to find himself face to face with Chris.

'It ain't what you think!'

Simon frowned. 'What isn't?'

'Me being here now. With Lisa,' he said, jerking a thumb back over his shoulder, in case Simon was in any doubt where she was.

'And what do I think, exactly?'

'You know.' Chris looked sheepish. 'That there's been anything weird going on.'

Simon almost laughed. He'd had enough weirdness today to last him a lifetime.

'In fact,' continued Chris, 'I've just been telling her not to fuck it up with you. Excuse my French.'

'Right. Thanks,' said Simon. 'Or rather, *merci beaucoup*. If you excuse mine!'

Chris looked a little confused. 'Listen, I'll be off. Can't keep Cat waiting. Told her I was only heading out to the garage to get some fags, and I've been gone so long she'll be wondering what I'm up to!'

Simon made a neutral face, even though Cat wasn't the only one.

'Anyway. I'll leave you two to it!' Chris winked, then – giving him a wide berth on the path – hurried off out through the garden gate, so Simon made his way inside and closed Lisa's front door softly behind him.

He crept along the hall, then saw the kitchen light was on, so he quietly pushed the door open. Lisa was sitting at the kitchen table, a determined expression on her face, emptying the contents of a bottle of wine into a glass measuring jug. As she raised it to her mouth, he knocked lightly on the door frame, and she nearly dropped the jug in surprise.

'What the . . . ?'

'I could ask you the same question.'

Lisa glanced guiltily at the jug of wine. 'I was, um, measuring how much was left,' she said, half-heartedly attempting to pour it back from the jug into the bottle.

'Um . . . why?'

'Why not?' Lisa said, sharply.

'Oh-kay.' Simon walked over to stand behind the chair opposite her. 'Chris let me in.'

'No shit, Sherlock.'

He flinched at the venom in Lisa's reply. Still, he realised, he couldn't blame her for being angry. 'Can I ask what he was doing here?'

'No, you can't!' Lisa huffed impatiently, then gave up on trying to refill the wine bottle. 'He came round to apologise. For being such a shit. Then demonstrated exactly what a shit he was by trying to sleep with me.'

Simon was surprised to feel a mix of anger and jealousy bubbling up inside him. 'Oh-kay,' he said again, and Lisa's eyes flashed angrily.

'Will you cut that out?'

'Cut what out?'

'That sanctimonious "oh-kay" of yours.'

'Sorry.' Simon nodded at the chair in front of him. 'May I?'

'It's a free country.'

He took that as a yes, albeit hardly an enthusiastic one, and sat down.

'So what did you want?'

'Me?'

Lisa gave him a look, and Simon made a face.

'What Chris wanted. Well, not *exactly* what Chris wanted.' He grinned, but when Lisa didn't return as much as a flicker of a smile, he understood that may have been a little insensitive. 'Firstly, to apologise. And because I didn't want to leave things like that. Especially since we still have to finish that questionnaire. You know, to make each other look good.'

'And having "Lisa's a slut because she tried to force me to sleep with her" in the paper might not be the best way to achieve that?'

'You're not . . . I mean, I don't think . . .' Simon sighed. 'It . . . *Events* just took me a little by surprise, that's all. As you know, I'm not that experienced in what happens on dates nowadays. And you know how they say "it's not you, it's me"? That's actually true.'

'Yeah, right.' Lisa was eyeing the wine-filled measuring jug as if she was considering downing the whole thing, and Simon was keen to make sure she didn't –though she might pass out, meaning his route to retrieving his keys would be easier, he couldn't leave her like that if that was the case.

He reached across the table gingerly, and slowly and carefully removed it from in front of her, as if disarming a trigger-happy gunman.

'It's true. I . . . freaked out, okay?'

'Thanks very much!'

'Why do you keep making this about you?'

Lisa was staring at him, and Simon wondered what he'd said wrong now. Though fortunately – or unfortunately, depending on your point of view – she had no issue in telling him.

'How can it not be?'

'Because not everything is!'

He'd almost shouted that last sentence – not meaning to raise his voice, but somehow the evening's events had got to him. And, for some reason, he wanted – no, *needed* – Lisa to understand. She deserved to know.

Now was as good a time as any. And, Simon suspected, quite possibly his last chance.

'Listen, Lisa. Alice and I didn't split up, or finish with each other, or anything like that,' he said quietly.

'I don't—'

'She died.'

'What?'

'Alice died. Unexpectedly. In the middle of what I hoped was going to be the last relationship I'd ever have.'

'Oh, *Simon.*'

'Yup.'

He put his head in his hands, unable to meet Lisa's eyes. It was the first time he'd admitted that to anyone, despite his therapist advising him to do the opposite, since he'd run away (because that *was* what he'd done, he now knew) from London and moved to Margate. But somehow, this evening, perhaps due to a combination of everything that had happened, the emotions Lisa had stirred up, and not an inconsiderable amount of alcohol, everything had fallen into place. Become clear.

Why he'd felt the need to tell Lisa, of all people, was beyond him. Maybe it was just because she was *here*. But, right now, he was really glad she was. Glad *he* was. And then, like a thunderbolt, Simon realised something. That sometimes, the purpose of your pain was that it might help you connect with someone else. And that Lisa might be that person.

'How did she . . . ?' Lisa's expression was hard to read, but Simon could only imagine what *his* face looked like. 'I mean, what . . . ?'

'Happened?' He puffed air out of his cheeks. 'A road accident. The other driver was on their phone. Sending a text. He was going way more than twenty miles per hour, and . . . well, he didn't see her. She didn't stand a chance. The ambulance crew did their best, but . . .' He hesitated, aware his voice was cracking, and Lisa reached across to give his hand a brief supportive squeeze.

'And when exactly did this . . . ? I mean, how long ago did she . . . ? I'm sorry, I don't seem to be able to finish my . . .'

Simon looked at his watch, which Lisa evidently found strange, until she realised he was checking the date. 'Two years ago,' he said.

'*Today?*'

Simon let out a short laugh. 'That would be a bit weird, wouldn't it, me coming out on a date on the anniversary? If "anniversary" is the right word?'

'I suppose,' said Lisa. 'Gosh,' she said, looking like she was doing her best to take it all in. 'And the driver?'

'He was okay, unfortunately. Denied he'd been texting. Even tried to blame her for the accident, so he didn't have to lose his no-claims bonus.'

'But that's . . .'

'Isn't it.' Simon shook his head slowly. 'He said she'd run a red light. Pulled out in front of him.' He paused again, and Lisa blushed, perhaps at her earlier road-crossing faux pas. 'But Alice was a good driver. And wasn't the type to take risks. She was a nurse, and she always said she'd seen enough accidents during her time working in A&E to make her *extremely* aware of her surroundings. But sometimes, despite your best efforts . . .' He pressed his lips together and took a moment to compose himself. 'Anyway, his phone records proved he was lying. Which was something, I suppose.'

'Is he in prison?'

'Yeah. Six years for dangerous driving. Out in three. Hardly seems fair, if you ask me.'

Lisa put her hand over her mouth in shock. 'That's . . . ridiculous.'

'Isn't it? But it's also the law. Unfortunately.'

'Christ. I bet you wished you *were* a barrister. Maybe you could have done something about that.'

'Good one,' said Simon, flatly, and Lisa suddenly looked horrified at herself.

'I'm so sorry,' she said, though if she meant for his loss or the stupid thing she'd just blurted out, Simon wasn't sure. She reached out across the table again, but drew her hand back without touching his, perhaps worried it might be inappropriate, then looked at him earnestly. 'How on earth do you get over something like *that*?'

Simon reached for a piece of kitchen towel from the roll on the table and blew his nose. 'I'm not sure you do. But you can move on. According to my therapist. Though I'm still trying, to be honest. As Will keeps reminding me. Which is why . . .' He indicated the two of them, then he blushed furiously. 'I'm sorry. That didn't come out right at all. What I mean is, life goes on – for the rest of us, at least – and when something like that happens, you've got two choices: either carry on with things, or curl up into a ball and hide away from the rest of the world.' He gave her a humourless smile. 'Which is kind of what I did for a while. For almost two years, actually.'

Lisa had gone silent, and was currently staring at a spot on the table in between the two of them, so Simon reached for the wine jug and took a swig. Maybe telling her about Alice *was* a mistake, but the evening's events seemed to require an 'all cards on the table', full-disclosure policy, so why not? It wasn't a secret, and it wasn't as if Simon had murdered her, so why on earth shouldn't he mention it? Plus his therapist had *told* him to talk about it. As much as possible. Made him promise he wouldn't skirt around the subject if asked. The fact that for the past two years he'd avoided putting himself in a position where he would be asked was neither here nor there. And while constantly referring to something had seemed to him a rather strange way to achieve what was apparently called 'closure', perhaps it had been good advice – though, like all good advice, it had been difficult to hear, and was even more uncomfortable to act on. And although he'd worried telling any woman he met might put them off, he reminded himself that putting *Lisa* off wasn't actually a problem, seeing as he'd already managed to achieve that. Plus, finding out how she reacted might just be useful in the future. If and when he decided to start dating again.

He took another large gulp of wine and stared at the same spot on the table that Lisa had found so fascinating, then became conscious she'd moved round to sit next to him.

'Oh, *Simon*,' she said again, before tentatively putting an arm round his shoulders and hugging him, her act of compassion making him well up inside.

'And there's something else,' he said, wiping away the solitary tear that was rolling down his cheek.

'Tell me.'

'Because we didn't split up, or finish with each other, or anything like that, any time I might absentmindedly look at another woman, or Will tells me I should seriously think about going out with someone – or even just sleeping with them – I feel like I'm being unfaithful.'

'But that's . . .'

'Stupid? I know! And I don't believe in heaven or hell or anything like that, but I do feel like Alice is watching me sometimes. And yes, before you say anything, everyone tells me that she'd be happy for me to meet someone else. Want *me* to be happy. But I was happy with her. I didn't *want* to meet anyone else. Never ever thought I'd have to. And when you've had that ripped forcibly away from you, you just can't help feeling that way.' Simon eyed the jug of wine again. Finishing it was becoming more and more tempting by the minute. 'And then I meet someone like you, and you're beautiful, and smart, and sexy, and funny, and caring and with so much going for you, but for some reason you've been picking the wrong men – maybe because you think you're not worth what you so obviously are, or that you're damaged . . . and you are, but we *all* are, so it's nothing to be ashamed of, and we've had such a rollercoaster of a day – no pun intended – but by some miracle we still ended up in a position where we were about to . . .' He nodded awkwardly in the direction of the bedroom. 'And instead of being able to go with it, to enjoy the moment like I wanted to – and believe me, I wanted to – I'm still suffering from a . . . *hangover* from Alice, too full of what might have been with her to respond like I should.'

Lisa removed her arm from his shoulders, and swivelled round to face him. 'Why didn't you tell me earlier?'

'Because I don't tell anyone,' he said, doing his best to keep it together.

'Why not?'

'Because I don't want it to define me. You know . . . *there goes Simon, the poor bloke whose girlfriend died.*' He'd put on a funny voice, for some reason, but, perhaps not surprisingly, Lisa wasn't smiling. 'And I know this might sound crazy,' he continued, 'and this is proof it wasn't about you' – he looked up at her, his eyes red-rimmed – 'but I haven't had sex for two years, and the last time was with Alice. So I was petrified that either I wouldn't have been able to, you know' – he cleared his throat awkwardly – '*do it*. Or I'd have done it too quickly. And I worried you'd have thought even more badly of me if either of those things were the case.'

'I'm sure it wouldn't have been like that.'

'*I'm* not. Will keeps telling me it's just like riding a bike, but I haven't ridden one for so long that I . . .' He smiled grimly. 'Well, I'm not sure I've got enough air in my tyres to get me to the end of the road.

And I know that's something I'm going to have to face the first time, but the longer I leave it, the more I worry about it, the more pressure I'm going to feel . . .'

His voice trailed off, and he stared miserably back at the table. Then, to his surprise, he felt Lisa taking his hand, and heard the scrape of her chair on the kitchen floor as she stood up.

'Come on,' she said, helping him from his seat.

'I know, I know. You want me to leave.'

'Quite the opposite, actually.'

'What? I don't . . . ?'

'All that stuff you said.' Lisa smiled. 'I understand. Really, I do. And thank you for saying it, and for choosing me to be the one you said it to. I know it must have been hard. But . . .'

'But?'

'Something else I learned in Cancún is that you've got to confront your fears. Head on.'

Simon wiped his eyes on his sleeve. 'And how on earth do I do *that*?'

Lisa stood up on tiptoe, planted a brief kiss on his cheek, then took his hand. 'I have an idea,' she said, leading him back towards the bedroom.

Chapter 32

Lisa was staring at her bedroom ceiling, squinting against the rays of dawn sunshine forcing their way in past the edges of the blinds, wondering what on earth had happened last night. She knew *what* had happened, of course, and understood *how* it had happened. She just wasn't sure *why* it had happened – and she was even more unsure of what was going to happen *next*.

She carefully angled her head to one side, checking Simon was still asleep. By the deep, regular sound of his breathing, he was dead to the world. And why shouldn't he be? Especially after last night's exertions.

In the end, he needn't have worried. He'd been fine. More than fine, in fact. Mindful of his fears, Lisa had taken things slowly – which, to her surprise, had made things better for her. And the end, when it eventually came, when *they* eventually came, had been . . . well, she'd almost felt like crying herself. She hadn't had sex like that since . . . Lisa thought for a moment, then wondered who she was trying to kid. She hadn't had sex like that *full stop*. And then, as if keen to prove it hadn't been a fluke, and once they'd both got their breath back, they'd gone in for a repeat performance, which had been just as good as the first time.

She fought to keep the smile from her face as she recalled the previous night. She'd been a little nervous too. Worried that she wouldn't be able to live up to the memory of Simon's perfect ex. Scared that she'd overreact if he cried Alice's name out – but he hadn't, so she hadn't. And then, afterwards, they'd held each other until they drifted off, and Lisa had got the best night's sleep she'd had in a long, long time, involving a dream about going fishing – which she knew probably meant something, but right now she couldn't be bothered to try to work out what that was.

Gently, she lifted Simon's arm from where it was draped across her chest (on top of the duvet, though – even asleep, Simon was still a gentleman), wriggled to her left and cautiously hauled herself upright. She could feel the beginnings of a hangover – not a surprise, she knew, given how much she'd ended up drinking yesterday – though that wasn't the only reason her head was spinning.

She still didn't know what had led to this. His reappearance had hardly been a 'you had me at hello' moment, although his apology *had* tugged at her heartstrings (unlike Chris's earlier, somewhat cruder attempt). But as to why she'd taken him to bed – was it simply that she'd felt sorry for him? Lisa doubted it. And as for helping him over his 'hump' (if you excused the word) – well, Lisa wasn't a charity worker. And Simon wasn't a charity case.

No, she decided, they had a genuine connection. Last night had proved that. And she had to admit that fate seemed to be doing a good job of keeping them together – as it had over the whole date, now she thought about it: from their first, dramatic meeting on the pelican crossing, to Will and Jess ensuring they gave each other a second chance by insisting they stuck it out until the photographer arrived, to the freak wave that meant she'd ended up in his arms, then back at her place, then them *not* having sex, him leaving under a cloud and feeling guilty and coming back to apologise. . .

She swung her feet down to the floor and gingerly stood up, then she padded out through the bedroom door and into the kitchen to get herself a glass of water. The jug of wine was still sitting on the table, so she thought about pouring it down the sink, but the lurch in her stomach as she neared it meant she thought she'd better leave it for later.

Surely she hadn't had *that* much to drink yesterday? Lisa knew she hadn't taken Simon to bed because she'd been drunk. It had been because she'd wanted to. And, she suspected, given how Simon had come back last night, he'd wanted to too.

A set of car keys was sitting on the kitchen work surface above the tumble dryer – not hers, obviously, and given the lack of anyone else in her house right now, probably Simon's. He must have removed them before he'd put his jeans in there last night . . . The thought of him parading round the house in her sarong – along with the memory of the events leading up to it – made Lisa smile as she crept back into the bedroom and slipped them back into his jeans pocket.

She peered at the bed. Simon still hadn't moved, so she tiptoed into the hall, retrieved her phone from where she'd plugged it in to charge last night, quietly made her way into the bathroom and shut the door softly behind her.

She studied her reflection in the mirror above the sink, doing her best to ignore the odd grey hair, pulling her skin taut and watching it move back into place with a little less 'snap' than it used to, and wondering whether the bags under her eyes were going to be a permanent fixture or simply a result of her hangover. She'd seen better days, she knew. But, then again, she hadn't had that many better nights.

She sat down to pee, wondering what her and Simon's next steps might be. Worst-case scenario, they had a slightly awkward breakfast, he pecked her on the cheek in a chaste 'goodbye and thanks' kind of way, and they never saw each other again. Best-case? They made plans to do it all – well, maybe not *all* – again another night. And another. And another . . .

Lisa smiled at the prospect as she flushed the toilet, then she sniffed her left armpit, wrinkled her nose in disgust, and padded across to the bathtub. A shower was definitely required. She listened out, half wondering whether Simon might like to join her, but when she heard no signs of movement from the bedroom, she quietly locked the bathroom door, ran the water as hot as she could stand and climbed under the purifying jets.

Chapter 33

Simon waited until he heard the shower running; then – as if reacting to a starting pistol – he leapt out of bed. He'd been awake for hours, ever since Lisa's contented snoring had woken him, though he'd considered it rude to just get up and leave. Besides, lying there, pretending to be asleep as Lisa snuggled contentedly against him, had given him valuable thinking time. Not that he'd come to any conclusions yet.

He tiptoed along the hallway, crept into the kitchen and made his way across to the tumble dryer, surprised not to see his keys on the surface where he'd remembered leaving them. Confused, he pulled open the dryer door and rooted around in there, checking the filter in case they'd somehow found their way into the system – but no joy.

Simon scratched his head, then he checked the rest of the kitchen surfaces, then the tea cupboard, even pulling open a couple of drawers for good measure. Where could they be? Unless Chris had taken them by mistake yesterday, or Lisa had thrown them away in a fit of anger after he'd left the first time . . .

He checked the bin, then the fridge, then headed back the way he'd come and began hunting frantically around Lisa's bedroom, but there was no sign of them on the floor, or on the bedside table, or on the dresser, or even under the bed (though he didn't want to think about what *was*). Panicking, he pulled the duvet and pillows off the bed, shaking them out in case his keyring had somehow wound up inside the covers during last night's exertions, but without any luck.

Desperately, he mentally ran through the events of the previous evening, remembering how he'd been careful not to put them in the tumble dryer, how he'd purposefully put them on the wooden surface so he wouldn't forget them – *ha ha!* – but if that was the case, where were they now?

Suddenly conscious he was naked, and fearing Lisa might emerge from the shower at any moment, he hurriedly pulled his clothes back on and – to his surprise – found his keys in his jeans pocket. Confused, he held them up and peered at them, double-checking they were actually his. That was the *last* place he'd expected them to be.

Then again, Lisa's bedroom had been the last place he'd expected to find *himself* in. Last night had been . . . Unexpected. Amazing. Surprising. Confusing, too – he wasn't sure whether Lisa had taken him to her bed because she'd felt sorry for him, or had wanted to 'help' him get over his fears, or had fancied him, or had just been drunk, or horny, or any combination of the above. But when they'd got there, none of that had seemed to matter. Because the sex had seemed natural. Spontaneous. Not at all awkward. And – Simon felt the heat rush to his face as he thought about it – he'd actually acquitted himself pretty well.

Twice!

He thought back to Will's 'riding a bike' comment, and smiled to himself. Will had been right! Though with Lisa, it was as if he'd been on one of those full-suspension, carbon-framed, top-of-the-range bicycles, rather than the rather functional fixie he had sitting in his hallway at home (he made a mental note not to use that analogy if he ever talked to her about it).

He felt a little guilty too – not because of Alice directly, but because he hadn't thought of her once during the whole time he and Lisa had been intimate. Being in bed with her had been . . . overwhelming. And it was only early this morning, with the torture of insomnia and the pressure of a full bladder that he hadn't dared respond to in fear of waking Lisa up and her deciding to do it a *third* time, that it had occurred to him that maybe he'd not behaved that well. Had perhaps allowed himself to be led into something he wasn't – shouldn't be – quite ready for. After all, he didn't do one-night stands, so as for what came next . . . maybe he should let Lisa take the lead. Much like she had last night.

He crept along the hall and into the kitchen, his stomach lurching slightly at the sight of Lisa's unfinished jugful of white wine, wondering whether he should empty it down the sink or attempt to save it – eventually deciding on the latter, though as he poured it back into the bottle and put the cork back in, he suspected doing the same with his and Lisa's relationship wouldn't be quite so easy.

Then again, maybe this was what he'd needed. A 'kick up the arse', as Will would no doubt describe it. A reason to start dating again. He'd always promised himself that he wouldn't sleep with anyone unless he was in a relationship with them, and there was no reason why this couldn't work the other way round. And, besides, wasn't that what people did nowadays? Sleep with someone first, and decide to go out with them later? Be 'exclusive', as he'd heard Will refer to it – rather than reclusive, as he'd been since Alice.

Since Alice.

Simon sat down heavily on the nearest chair, wondering what his ex-girlfriend would make of all this, then did his best to dismiss the thought. He couldn't – *shouldn't* – live the rest of his life desperate for her approval. Besides, she *would* want him to be happy, surely? To move on, as long as he didn't forget her – and Simon was pretty sure that would never happen.

In therapy, he'd learned that bereavement left a hole in your life – a hole you hoped would eventually get smaller, maybe even disappear, but, over time, you realised would always be there. You just had to build a life *around* it. And if he and Lisa were going to build something together, after last night – after *yesterday* – he suspected they had good foundations. The sex had been good, and they had already gone through a lot in a short space of time (including a significant number of arguments, and arguments were evidence of strong feelings, weren't they?). So maybe the two of them *could* work. At the very least, it was worth a go. If she'd have him.

Besides, as much as he'd tried to deny it, fate did seem to keep pushing the two of them together. That thing with his keys – he'd been positive he didn't have them when he reached his car last night, and yet here they were, in his pocket . . . Maybe he'd imagined the whole key-removal-for-the-tumble-dryer incident, so who was he to argue with a higher power? He already knew Lisa probably wouldn't.

He filed that thought away as he padded around the kitchen, softly opening and closing a few random cupboards in search of something to eat, intending to make them both breakfast. They could go out, but they'd probably need to talk, and talking was something Simon much preferred to do in private. Besides, he spent most of his life in a café, so the chance of an intimate breakfast, sitting round the kitchen table, just the two of them, was – unlike more of Lisa's tea – something he was keen to sample.

He stole back along the hall and put his ear to the bathroom door. The shower had stopped but seemed to have started again – and Simon hoped it wasn't because Lisa felt dirty after last night. He could wait for her to come out, check how she was feeling, check *what* she was feeling – but surely it was better if he slipped out now to pick something up from the shops? They'd both feel better after a decent cup of coffee (or perhaps tea, in Lisa's case. He'd seen a box with 'PG' written on it which might suit her this morning – though those two letters hardly applied to what they'd done last night!) and something to eat.

He stood there for a second or two, his hand poised to knock on the door, wondering whether to tell her what he was up to, then he thought better of it. He'd be back before she knew it, and, even if he wasn't, Lisa might want a bit of space. A bit of thinking time. God knows *he* did.

Quickly, Simon nipped back into the bedroom, straightened out the duvet, plumped up the pillows, and stood back to admire his bed-making skills. Then he took a deep breath, tiptoed back along the hall, and let himself quietly out the front door.

Chapter 34

Lisa carefully towelled herself dry, then she wiped the steam from the bathroom mirror, checked her reflection again and readied herself to go and face Simon. She knew there was a chance he might not ever want to see her again, realised he was probably feeling guilty after last night, and understood the best she might get out of him this morning was an embarrassed mumble, but that was fine. They'd talk about this another time, if that was the case, when they'd both had time to process what had happened. Perhaps even on a second, less frantic, less pressurised date. Or even just as friends.

She'd already decided she'd leave the ball in his court. He had a lot to deal with, after all. Much more than her. It was no wonder he'd been behaving how he had, given what he was carrying around with him – if that had happened to Lisa, she wasn't sure she'd be able to get out of bed, let alone go on a date with someone. And if he needed a little time . . . well, that was fine. Though she suspected that what had happened between them last night wasn't just a one-night stand. When things were that good (and she'd been pretty sure Simon hadn't been faking it – *she* certainly hadn't been, and surely neither of them had it in them to fake it *twice*) you wanted to repeat them another time. And, hopefully, more than once! Then again, Simon might be the kind of person who'd prefer to put it down to being 'one of those things', or who felt that the circumstances that made it special couldn't be repeated.

Perhaps that was how he felt about him and Alice. And, if that was the case, he and Lisa had no hope.

She glanced down at her phone and noticed the message light was flashing – Jess, no doubt, texting her to see how things had gone – and when Lisa checked it, the one-word message from her friend simply read: *Well?* Hurriedly, she began composing a text in response, then she remembered a technique she'd seen in some spy film she'd watched on Netflix the other night, turned the shower back on to muffle the sound of her voice, and dialled Jess's number.

'He's still here!' she said, when Jess answered with her customary 'Babe?'

'What?'

'Simon,' whispered Lisa. 'He's asleep.'

'On your sofa?' said Jess, in a tone that suggested she already knew that wasn't the case.

'Not exactly . . .'

Jess let out a scream so loud that Lisa feared Simon could hear it despite the running water.

'Long story short, he and I—'

'I want the long version,' interrupted Jess. 'All the details, and in glorious technicolour!'

Lisa laughed. 'I can't right now. Suffice it to say, he stayed the night.'

'And?'

'It was *amazing*!'

Jess screamed again, louder this time, so Lisa moved her phone away from her ear and reduced the volume a few notches.

'Can I be your maid of honour? Then Will can be Simon's best man and . . . No, scratch that. We can do a double wedding. It might give Will a kick up the backside to—'

'Steady on, Jess. It was only one night. You're being a bit premature.'

'I take it *he* wasn't?'

'Jess!' Lisa was surprised to feel herself blushing. 'And no, he wasn't, if you must know.'

'Are you going to see each other again?'

'In about two minutes. I'm in the bathroom.'

'I mean *romantically*.'

'I . . .' Lisa hesitated. 'I'm not sure. I suppose we could go on another date, if he wants to, just to see if anything might happen between us.'

'From what you've just told me, it's *already* happened.'

'Yes, but . . .' Lisa paused, trying to put her thoughts into words. 'A lot happened yesterday. I kind of feel everything's been . . . accelerated, so far.'

'So take your foot off the gas,' said Jess.

Lisa thought back to Chris's comment. 'I'm not sure I know how. Which is possibly why we ended up in bed last night.'

'Even so. You might want to take it slow where Simon's concerned.'

'What's that supposed to mean?'

'It's just . . . Simon . . .' Jess cleared her throat. 'The reason he hasn't been out with anyone for a couple of years is . . . Well, the reason he moved down here, actually, is because . . .'

'Jess . . .'

'He used to go out with this girl. Alice. And . . .'

'He told me.'

There was a pause, and such a long one that Lisa began to think Jess had hung up. 'He did?' she said, eventually.

'He did. Though why didn't *you* tell me?'

'Will told me not to. That sort of thing really needs to come from Simon, don't you think?'

'I suppose.'

'But you're okay with it?' said Jess, tentatively.

'We've all got exes, Jess. We were probably in love with some of them. They leave us for a variety of reasons, a lot of times beyond our control. There's not a lot I can do about it anyway, so as long as he's over her . . .'

'That's good. Because Will was worried he wasn't.'

'Well, he certainly seemed to be last night!'

'Even so. Imagine. You were in love with someone and they *died*.'

Lisa felt the first fingers of nervousness clutching at her stomach. 'Can we change the subject, please?'

'Of course!' Jess laughed again. 'I just think it's *amazing*. Yesterday Simon didn't even know he was going on a date, and today . . .'

'*I know*. We . . . wait. *What?*'

'Simon didn't know he was going on a date yesterday.'

'He didn't?'

Jess laughed a third time, though a little nervously. 'Will sort of . . . tricked him into it.'

Lisa began pacing around the bathroom – something made a little tricky by the fact the room was only a couple of paces wide.

'Explain, Jess.'

'Well, Simon hadn't been on a date for a couple of years, since you-know-what happened, and Will was getting more and more worried about him, so he arranged to meet him for lunch yesterday, except . . .'

Lisa felt a knot form in her stomach. You didn't have to be Sherlock Holmes to work out what was coming next. 'Simon was actually meeting me.'

'Yeah!' Jess had pronounced the word in a 'great plan' kind of way, then evidently realised perhaps she shouldn't have. 'Although he did *actually* tell him. About five minutes beforehand. And Simon obviously decided to go through with it, and then what happened happened, so . . .'

'*Go through with it?*' Lisa lowered the toilet lid and sat down heavily on it, wincing a little at the feel of the cold plastic against her bare backside.

Jess sighed. 'I didn't mean it like that.'

'How did you mean it, exactly?' hissed Lisa, conscious she'd been 'in' the shower rather a long time now, and Simon might be wondering what was going on.

'But it kind of proves that Simon's over Alice, doesn't it?'

'Does it?'

'Yeah. If I hadn't wanted to go on a date with someone, and ended up spending the next . . . what's the time?'

'Five to eleven.'

'*Almost twenty-two hours* with them, then it would suggest I was rather keen. Don't you think?'

'So he takes one look at me, and suddenly all his . . .' Lisa struggled to find an appropriate word. 'Issues are gone.' She clicked her fingers. 'Just like that?'

'Why not?'

'You're suggesting I . . . *fixed him*?' Lisa reached across to turn the shower off, then lowered her voice. 'I'm not sure it's that simple.'

'Well, it should be!' Jess went back to her trademark tinkling laugh. 'Now, stop wasting time on the phone with me, and go back to him. And Lise?'

'What?'

'Don't let this one go! And more importantly . . .'

'Yes?'

'Don't scare him off!'

Lisa opened her mouth to protest, but Jess had already ended the call. Surely she didn't scare men off? She hadn't with Chris . . . Or had she, being too keen? She felt her earlier confidence starting to evaporate. This needed thinking about. *You're in love with someone, they die, then you start dating again* . . . How could any new partner possibly live up to the tragi-romantic idea of what life could have been with the old one? Especially because it was sudden, Simon never getting a chance to say goodbye, left with a vision of . . . Lisa didn't want to think of what. It had happened to someone from one of the group therapy sessions in Cancún, his girlfriend meeting her end courtesy of a bungee jump that went wrong, a fact Lisa had only discovered after she'd made some comment about him being 'on the rebound', which had sent the poor guy into floods of tears and meant Lisa had spent the rest of the week avoiding him.

She took a series of slow breaths – a technique she'd learned at the retreat – and tried to centre herself. She couldn't imagine how Simon had coped. *If* he had coped. Because this kind of thing damaged you, didn't it? And Lisa wasn't sure she'd have been strong enough to pick up the pieces if it had happened to her, let alone anyone else. But Simon didn't look all that damaged. Hadn't sounded too distraught. Maybe he *was* 'over' Alice. Perhaps spending the day – and the night – with Lisa had made him realise that.

In any case, there was only one way to find out, so with a final check of her reflection in the bathroom mirror, Lisa pulled on her dressing gown, took a few breaths to ready herself, unlocked the door and made her way back to the bedroom.

'Simon?' she said, knocking lightly on the door as if it wasn't her room, then smiling at her own ridiculousness. But when there was no sign of him there, she checked the rest of the house – finding nothing – then returned to the bedroom. *Perhaps he's hiding,* she thought, peering into the wardrobe and even under the bed (finding, to her horror, what looked like a pair of Chris's discarded boxer shorts) – then she noticed the bed had been made.

'Simon?' she said again, looking suspiciously around the room, as if this might be one of those pranks she'd watched on YouTube and there was a hidden camera somewhere.

Her gaze returned to the freshly made bed. Perhaps it was Simon's attempt to atone for the previous evening, or a way of pretending it hadn't happened. Either that, or he suffered from OCD. Whichever it was, Lisa feared it wasn't good.

She retrieved her phone, sat down on the chair in the corner of the room and hesitantly unlocked the screen, trying to work up the courage to call him – but what would she say? 'Where are you?' might sound a little judgemental, assuming he even answered. And as for 'Are you okay?' – Lisa already suspected she knew the answer to that particular question.

She *knew* she'd been too forward. Simon *hadn't* been ready, and she'd virtually frog-marched him into bed and forced him to have sex with her. He'd just been too much of a gentleman to say no.

Twice.

All of a sudden, she felt cheap. Used. And pretty unloved, now she thought about it. *Of course* Simon had done a runner. Who'd want to go out with *her*? Chris hadn't – though he'd been perfectly happy to come round and try to sleep with her. Now it looked like Simon had done exactly the same – and Lisa almost marvelled at how clever he'd been to turn her down in the first place, giving him the perfect 'out' this morning.

And yet he *had* come back last night, desperate to explain, to make her understand. That wasn't the action of a man who was simply after a shag. One he'd already been on the verge of getting, before he'd made a bolt for the door. So why had he . . . ?

Lisa froze.

His car keys. She'd found them by the dryer – which meant he'd come back for them, not her. And in all the confusion with Chris, and then Simon's sob story – *cover* story, more like – she hadn't put two and two together. Instead, she'd fallen for it, just like she'd promised herself she wouldn't with anyone ever again . . .

Lisa felt her throat tighten as a creeping feeling of despair began to spread through her. She thought the way she'd responded to Chris last night had been progress, and yet now she could see that history had repeated itself. And despite Cancún, despite all the changes she thought she'd made, it would probably *always* repeat itself . . .

She set her phone down beside her, put her head in her hands, burst into tears, and sobbed until she had nothing left inside. This couldn't be happening *again*. Simon hadn't wanted to be there in the first place. He quite evidently wasn't ready for a relationship. Everything he'd done had been . . . Well, because he'd been *forced* to, not because he wanted to. And as to whether he was over Alice – well, hot-footing it out of the house while Lisa was in the shower, even making the bed to cover his tracks, as if he'd never even been there . . .

Suddenly angry, Lisa snatched a tissue from a box on the dresser and blew her nose loudly. The weeks of uncertainty after she'd split up with Chris had been a nightmare (once she'd eventually understood that they *had* split up), and that wasn't something she wanted to go through again. No, this time she wanted closure right away. To 'get her retaliation in first', as she'd once heard someone say. She wasn't prepared to wait for Simon to be ready. Simply because there appeared to be a big chance he might never be.

With a steely determination she didn't know she had, she picked her phone back up, scrolled through to Simon's number and began composing a text.

Chapter 35

Simon made his way back to Lisa's house, with something of a spring in his step. It certainly felt different to when he'd walked there the previous night, and although that might simply be the fact that his trainers had dried out, he doubted it. No, he'd unburdened himself last night, and it had felt – well, not good exactly, but a relief, at least. He certainly felt – what – lighter? Freer? And he had Lisa to thank for that.

Instead of doing what Simon had feared every woman would do when he told them about Alice – running a mile – she'd done the exact opposite; which was a credit to her, he knew, especially after what she'd been through. No, if he was going to move on – and by that he meant move on *with* someone – Lisa might just be the one. She wasn't Alice, but *no one* was. No one would be. And comparing was a futile task – therapy had taught him that. But yesterday – or, rather, *Lisa* yesterday – had made him *believe* it.

The petrol station on the corner of the next street had provided him with fresh milk, a packet of Lavazza ground coffee, some freshly squeezed orange juice and some just-baked *pains au chocolat*. (Or was it *pain au chocolats*? Simon couldn't remember. Despite his doorstep exchange with Chris the previous evening, French had never been his best subject. And, besides, his degree had been a long time ago.) Now he was heading back to Lisa's, sure she must have an appetite – *he* certainly did, especially after last night.

There'd been a bucketful of bouquets of cut flowers by the till, and he'd considered getting one of those too, but in the end he'd thought better of it. Breakfast, in particular a good cup of coffee (he'd noticed a moka pot – still in its box – in Lisa's kitchen cupboard when he was looking at the tea last night, and if he was going to start educating her as to how good coffee could taste, a cup made in the traditional stovetop way wasn't a bad place to start) accompanied by the sweetness of a French pastry, would do. Flowers were a bit presumptuous. And Simon didn't dare to presume anything where Lisa was concerned.

He had paid an extra five pence for a plastic bag, though. He didn't want Lisa to think he was cheap. Which was why he'd nipped out to get breakfast, so he could impress upon her he wasn't the type to do a runner after . . . well, after what had happened.

But what *had* happened? Had it just been one amazing night between two lonely people, or was there more to it than that? Simon suspected there was only one way to tell – and that was a second date. As to whether he had the nerve to ask Lisa for one . . . He needed a coffee first. Maybe even two.

For a moment, he wondered if he should run it by Will first – after all, if he hadn't set yesterday's events in motion, then none of this would have happened. Then again, what was there to run by? He and Lisa had obviously taken things to – as Will would call it – the 'next level' last night. Simon could surely handle things from here on in. Plus Will would get even more of a surprise when Simon and Lisa turned in their interviews – and it would make a nice change to be able to get one over on his friend.

He strolled down Lisa's road, swinging his plastic bag, realised he was whistling, and almost burst out laughing. He hadn't felt this happy since he didn't know when . . . Actually, strike that. He knew *exactly* when. He pulled out his phone and composed a quick text to Lisa, typing – then deleting just as quickly – *breakfast in bed?* and replacing it with a slightly more reserved *on my way back with breakfast!*, though almost the moment he pressed 'Send', his phone beeped with a reply.

Simon grinned – so she *was* keen – and clicked on the message, then his face fell. He knew a fault with text messages was that they were open to different interpretations (and don't get him started on emojis) and the meanings weren't always that clear, though even with his lack of experience he suspected that Lisa's final sentence – *I think we should just be friends* – was, as the characters in Alice's favourite soap *EastEnders* might say, 'crystal'.

He hurriedly ran through the events of last night in his head, wondering how he'd got it so wrong. Perhaps it *had* simply been a sympathy shag, along the lines of what Will had told him he might get if he trotted out the Alice story, but *twice*?

Then again, maybe the second time they'd had sex wasn't because he was that good, but instead because Lisa couldn't believe the first time had been that *bad*. Or perhaps, after her experience with Chris, the text was her defence mechanism springing into action. A test, to see whether he really was keen. Push him away and see how he responded. After all, she might have listened to Chris's advice the previous afternoon – especially that bit about her diving in and swimming frantically – then woken up this morning and realised she was doing exactly that, and this was her way of slowing down to a leisurely breaststroke. If you excused the phrase.

That was fine, though, Simon decided. He could go along with that. After all, he didn't want to scare her off. So he'd go round, make Lisa breakfast, they'd finish their questionnaire for the paper, and over the course of the rest of the morning, he'd slowly and steadily convince her that they should go out on a second date. Or, at least, he'd try to.

Feeling a little less confident than five minutes previously, he located Lisa's house, walked up the garden path and rang the bell. After a moment or two, a red-eyed, angry-faced Lisa threw it open.

'Forget your car keys again?'

'No, I just went out to get . . .' Simon lifted up the shopping bag. 'Breakfast?' he said, then he paled. Lisa had said 'again'. 'Didn't you, um, read my text?'

'Didn't you read mine?'

'Well, yes, but . . .' Simon remembered his resolve of a few moments ago. 'We still have that questionnaire to finish. And seeing as you didn't have any food in the house. Or milk. Or coffee. I thought I'd . . .'

Lisa had raised one eyebrow in a 'that was presumptuous of you' way, so Simon held the bag out as a peace offering, but Lisa was inspecting the contents like someone might look at the half a dead mouse their cat had just brought in.

'I'm not hungry.'

'Is something wrong?' he asked tentatively, probably already knowing the answer to that particular question.

'What do you think?'

'If it's about me coming back to get my car keys last night, then . . .'

'Duh!'

'I can explain.'

'You should have. Last night. Before we . . .'

'I tried. But you didn't give me a chance to . . .'

Lisa's eyes flashed angrily, then she widened them. 'I'm sorry. It's *my* fault?'

'That's not what I meant. And I was a bit thrown, seeing as Chris was here.'

Lisa widened her eyes even more. 'And *that's* my fault?'

'No, that's not—'

'You should have told me, Simon.'

'Told you what?' he said, though again he already knew the answer to that.

'That our date yesterday was a set-up.'

'But that's what a blind date *is* . . .'

'That *you'd* been set up.'

Simon stared at her for a moment. 'You *know*?'

'Yeah.' Lisa folded her arms. 'But I would have preferred to hear it from you.'

'I wanted to tell you. Even though Will told me not to. But I didn't know how. Or when.'

'You should have found a way. Or a time. You lied to me about the date, you lied to me about why you came back last night . . .'

'I wasn't lying so much as—'

'If you say "postponing the truth" I'll—'

'Right. Sorry. Of course.' Simon took a deep breath, then another. Lisa was looking like she wasn't going to let him get away with not giving her an explanation. And after yesterday – or more specifically, last night – Simon probably owed her one.

A couple walking a pug along the pavement were doing a bad job of pretending not to listen to them, and seemed to be taking an inordinately long time to pick up after the dog, so Simon gave them a look before turning back to Lisa.

'Can we perhaps do this inside?' he asked. 'Like I said, I've got breakfast.'

'And like *I* said, I'm not hungry,' said Lisa, approximately half a second before her stomach rumbled so loudly Simon was sure the dog walkers could hear it.

'Okay, okay,' he said, suddenly desperate to grab some more time with her. 'Well, let's at least finish off our questionnaires, like we promised we'd do. Then we can just say goodbye, and . . .'

He retrieved the *pains au chocolat* (or *pain au chocolats* – he still didn't know) from the shopping bag and waved them enticingly under Lisa's nose, hoping the just-baked smell would do the trick.

And whether it was that, or whether she felt sorry for him, or even pitied him, Simon wasn't sure. But with a sigh, she opened the door wide and beckoned him inside.

Chapter 36

Lisa sat at the kitchen table and sipped her coffee – *not bad*, she had to admit, and certainly better than anything she'd had in the past (she tried to ignore the fact that might just be the weekend's biggest metaphor so far). But that was just the way things were: the whole blind date idea had been built on a lie; Simon hadn't been looking for, wasn't *ready* for a relationship – and Lisa didn't think they had a way back from that.

In truth, she was – what – devastated? No . . . too strong. Disappointed, perhaps. Both with Simon for being disingenuous and with herself for leaping in with both feet – and leaping *on* him – when she didn't have all the facts. Then she recalled how it was Simon's fault she didn't have all the facts, and remembered she should be angry with him, though as to *why* he hadn't told her . . . Lisa knew she couldn't be angry with him for that.

Simon was watching her intently, so she looked at her mug, nodded a couple of times with her head at a slight angle and her lower lip sticking out – the universal 'surprisingly good' gesture – then did her best to ignore Simon's look of genuine relief.

'Right,' she said, setting her coffee down on the table. 'Shall we?'

Simon stared vacantly at her, so she brushed pastry flakes from the sheet of paper in front of her on the table, then tapped it with a fingernail. 'Our *questions*.'

'What? Oh. Right.' He picked up the copy she'd printed out for him and quickly scanned through it. 'So, should we perhaps discuss our answers *before* we put them this time?'

'Good idea. That way we can make sure we come across just as we're intending.'

'Sure,' said Simon. 'So . . . "What were you hoping for?" What do you think?'

'We did this one yesterday. When you said, "That you'd turn up".'

'Which you said was a pathetic answer, because I didn't sound very confident.'

'And which I now know was a lie, because you were probably hoping for the exact opposite. Besides, I'm not sure I used the word "pathetic" . . .' Simon was giving her a look, so she shifted uncomfortably in her seat. 'All I'm saying is, your answer isn't particularly inspiring. It suggests you've been stood up before, for example. And that says something about you.'

'You don't think it's funny?'

'No.'

'Makes me sound humble?'

'It makes you sound desperate.'

Simon was giving her a worse look than before, so Lisa picked her coffee up and took another sip. She was really quite enjoying it, and under different circumstances might have asked him to make her another one. But if another coffee was as far as it was ever going to go, what was the point? And – while she thought about it – what was the point of *this*, if Simon wasn't ready for a relationship anyway?

'What should I put, then?'

Lisa downed the rest of her coffee, then put her mug to one side and mulled the question over. Suggesting 'To get the date over and done with as quickly as possible' had been her first thought, but she didn't want to keep calling Simon out on what she'd just found out about yesterday, otherwise they'd never get this done. Plus, he might walk out. And like it or not, *she* needed to get this part right.

'What about, "A fun time with someone I was attracted to"?'

Simon grimaced. 'What are *you* going to put?'

'I told you yesterday: "To meet the love of my life".'

'You still want to go with that?'

'Why shouldn't I?' said Lisa, folding her arms defiantly.

'Well, because it suggests you . . .' He swallowed audibly. 'No, actually, that's fine. It makes you sound optimistic. And it means you'll hopefully attract—'

'Serious daters?' Lisa fixed him with a glare, but Simon kept his gaze firmly on the questionnaire.

'Exactly.'

'Fine,' she said. 'Question two. First impressions.'

'I thought I'd go with "Pretty . . ."'

'Aah. Thank you!'

'". . . angry".'

Lisa smiled flatly. 'Is that supposed to be funny?'

'Isn't it?'

'Remember, we're trying to make *each other* look good here. Not just big ourselves up.'

'Right. Sorry.' Simon looked a little crushed, and Lisa felt a twinge of guilt. 'I'll just go with "Pretty", then.'

'Fine.' She watched him as he exaggeratedly crossed out the word 'angry'. 'Aren't you going to ask me what I put?'

'Do I really want to know?'

'Why would you say that?'

'Because this is all just a bit . . . dishonest, isn't it?'

'Only if we don't tell the truth.'

'But we're not!' Simon picked up the pot, poured some more coffee into Lisa's mug without asking her first, then slid it slyly across the table towards her, almost like a dealer encouraging a new addict.

'Where aren't we?'

'Anywhere.' Simon pointed at the sheet of paper in front of him. '"What did you talk about?" Do you mean the first time, when you hated me on sight, or afterwards? And "Any awkward moments?" How about you accusing me of spiking your drink, or us bumping into your newly engaged ex-boyfriend at the funfair? Because that's what actually happened. And none of those seems to have made it on to here.'

'Yes, well, they'll hardly portray us in the best of lights.'

'Portray *you*, you mean . . .'

'That's rubbish!' spluttered Lisa. 'I've said some nice things about you.'

'Such as?'

'That you've got good table manners, for example. And how you're a good listener.'

Simon sighed exasperatedly. 'I'm sure to be fighting the women off when *that* appears in the paper.'

'Excuse me, but you don't actually seem like you want to.'

'Want to what?'

'Fight them off. Or even be in a position where you have to.'

'I don't even know what that means.'

Lisa stared at him uncomprehendingly. 'What are you so worked up about?'

'I just . . . this whole thing. I wish . . .'

'That we'd never met?'

Simon opened his mouth, then quickly clamped it shut again, as if worried he might regret what he was about to say. 'No,' he said, eventually. 'It just wasn't what I was expecting. That's all.'

'You and me both.' Lisa exhaled slowly. 'Tell you what. Let's just finish this on our own, if that makes you feel better. Put what you like, I don't care. And I promise I'll be . . . kind.'

'Kind.'

'Sympathetic. Mindful of your . . . circumstances.'

'Thank you,' said Simon, though he didn't sound like he meant it. 'And you're not worried that I'll . . . ?'

Lisa shrugged. 'I was prepared to put this whole thing down to fate. So that's what I'm doing, aren't I?'

'Oh-kay. Well then . . .' As Simon picked up his questionnaire, folded it into quarters and slipped it into his pocket, Lisa felt a sudden sense of dread. Was this really it? Surely now was the time for him to say something. That was, if he *wanted* to say anything. For all Lisa knew, he could simply be desperate to get out of here and never see her again. And yet, whether it was simply to collect his car keys, or to bring her breakfast, he'd kept coming back . . .

And, as hard as the weekend had been for her, Lisa couldn't begin to think about how tough it must have been for him. Simon had been head over heels in love, then he'd had that savagely, prematurely and unfairly ripped away from him, and he'd only recently plucked up the courage to re-emerge into the light – if in a roundabout way. And – of all places – on a blind date with *her*.

All of a sudden, her head began to swim. She remembered watching some dating programme on television recently where the date had seemed to have gone fine, then, when they'd paid the bill, one half of the couple (because that was what they surely were going to become) had announced they had some terminal disease, and – if you excused the phrase – that had been the end of *that*. And Lisa had sided with the 'well' one, because that wasn't how love was supposed to be: it was hard enough meeting someone and hoping they wouldn't leave you. Knowing it was only a matter of time before they would, and that there was nothing you could do about it, was a lot more than she – and probably most people – could bear.

Though this perhaps wasn't quite the same, and while Lisa *was* looking for something – that thing wasn't to be Simon's therapist, especially since she was sure her head needed a lot of sorting out too. Something else she'd learned in Cancún was that it wasn't her job to heal everyone she met – especially because, in the words of her instructor, 'you can't pour from an empty cup'.

Say they did start dating, then Lisa decided Simon wasn't for her, how could she ever leave him after what he'd been through? The pressure would be too great. *Was* too great. Look what had happened the previous evening, when he'd admitted the truth about Alice and his insecurities: Lisa had felt so sorry for him that she'd taken him to her bed. Was it always going to be like this, her doing everything out of *pity*? The realisation made her feel sick to her stomach, and it was all she could do not to start hyperventilating. She looked up to find Simon watching her, a concerned look on his face.

'Are you okay?' he asked, and Lisa felt her insides flip.

'Fine,' she said curtly, summoning all her reserves to keep her face from betraying her true feelings.

'Right, well . . .' He stood up awkwardly, so Lisa did the same. 'So, should we shake hands, or hug, or . . . ?'

Lisa nodded quickly. 'A hug would be . . .' She spread her arms wide and took a pace towards him just as he did the same, but they mistimed their embrace and she headbutted him lightly on the chin. 'Sorry.'

'Don't worry.'

'Should we try that again?'

'I think we're good.'

'Okay then.' Lisa nodded, reluctant to see him go, but reminding herself he wasn't looking for a relationship and she was. Which was possibly the most important difference between them. 'And good luck with meeting someone else,' she said, escorting him along the hallway. 'When . . . *If* you eventually decide you want to.'

'Thanks,' said Simon, though he didn't sound all that much like he meant it. 'Though, um, I don't want to.'

Lisa had reached the front door, and she froze. 'What?'

'Meet someone else. *Anyone* else . . .'

'Simon, I'm so sorry,' she said, though as he nodded in acknowledgement of what he must have assumed was sympathy, she hurried to correct him. 'No, I mean, I'm sorry, but I can't . . . I won't . . . I thought I could. But this is all too . . .'

'Lisa—'

Simon didn't get a chance to finish his sentence. The doorbell rang, accompanied by a loud 'Woo-hoo!' and Lisa clasped a hand to her mouth.

'Oh *no*!'

'Whatever's the matter?'

'You have to get out of here. Now!'

'What?'

'Or hide! Quickly!'

'Why?'

'Trust me. It'll be better for everyone if you just—'

'You're not *married*, are you?'

'What? No!' Lisa glanced worriedly towards the front door, where someone was attempting to peer through the letterbox. 'It's worse than that!'

'What could be worse than—'

Simon stopped talking again, though this time because of the sound of a key in the lock, accompanied by a woman's voice.

'Lisa, darling?' the voice said, anxiously. 'Are you there?'

As the front door slowly opened, Lisa paled. 'Hello, Mum,' she said.

Chapter 37

Simon was standing in the hallway, doing his best to keep completely still, hoping he wouldn't be noticed, the way he remembered people were always advised to in *Jurassic Park* whenever the T-Rex was on the loose. Although judging by Lisa's terrified expression, the woman who'd just marched in through her front door, and who he understood to be Lisa's mother, was scarier than any dinosaur – computer-generated, or not.

'Let yourself in, why don't you?'

'Nice to see you too, dear!'

Lisa's mother was holding a front door key, and Lisa glared at it. 'I gave you that for emergencies,' she scolded.

Her mother tutted loudly. 'I thought it *was* an emergency when you didn't answer your door.'

'You gave me about ten seconds. I might have been on the toilet.'

'Well, you weren't, were you?'

'Even so.' Lisa folded her arms. 'I'm not Usain Bolt. You could leave it a bit longer before you barge in and . . .'

'Oh, I'm sorry,' said Lisa's mother, pushing the door shut behind her and striding into the hallway. 'I didn't realise I was interrupting something. And you are?'

Lisa's mother was staring at him, so Simon attempted a feeble smile.

'Just leaving,' said Lisa, quickly, and he couldn't help his face from falling. 'So, Simon, I'll . . .'

'You'll call me?' he said, more of a question than a statement.

'Sure.' Lisa had a hand on the front door lock, and Simon realised he should be feeling better. Lisa had said she'd call. Or rather, *he'd* said she'd call. Though judging by the tone of her 'sure', he wasn't convinced she would.

'Not so fast!' Somehow, and with an agility belying her age, Lisa's mother had managed to position herself between the two of them and the front door, and Lisa would have had to barge her out of the way to open it – something Simon could tell from the look on her face she was actually considering. 'I'm Sonia. Lisa's mother. In case you hadn't gathered,' she said, extending a hand out towards him, so, without knowing what else to do, Simon shook it. 'Simon, was it?'

'That's right.'

'Are you Lisa's boyfriend?' she asked, though before Simon could answer, Lisa's aghast 'Mum!' made him clamp his mouth shut.

'Or should I say *latest* boyfriend?' continued Lisa's mum. 'Only she does seem to rather go through them. No fault of her own, I'm sure. Although her father and I were already married at her age. *And* pregnant with her.'

Simon stared at the two women, knowing he was expected to say something, though a hesitant 'Congratulations?' was all he could come up with.

'Simon and I have been out on *one* date,' huffed Lisa.

'Last night,' said Simon, helpfully, before realising it was quite possibly the worst thing he could say given the way Lisa's mother raised both eyebrows.

'And you're still here?' she said, consulting her watch exaggeratedly.

'It was . . . I . . .' He thought about saying 'slept on the couch', but even as he tried the thought on for size, he realised no one was likely to believe that. 'We just . . . chatted. All night.'

'Your jaws must be positively *aching*.'

'Mum, please stop giving Simon the third degree. What I get up to in my private life is nothing to do with you.'

'I know it isn't, sweetheart.' Lisa's mother sighed exaggeratedly. 'Your father and I just want you to be happy. That's all.'

'I *am* happy.'

'That's good.' She reached over and caressed her daughter's cheek. 'Because you weren't happy with that Christopher character. Or the one before him. Or the one before *him*, come to think of it.'

'How would you possibly . . . ?'

'A mother *knows*, darling.' Lisa's mother smiled. 'You'll realise that when you have children.'

'*If* I have children.'

'When. You'll be a wonderful mother. As long as you don't leave it too late,' she said, flicking her eyes at Simon. 'And your father and I would make excellent grandparents. So it's the least you could do.' She smiled again. 'That's not too much to ask. Is it, Simon?'

Simon shook his head rapidly, like a guilty teenager denying something to a policeman, though he wasn't sure *what* it was that Lisa's mother was asking wasn't too much.

'Anyway,' said Lisa, after a pause so uncomfortably long Simon was sure he was about to say something stupid just to break the silence. 'What are you doing here?'

'Lunch, remember? Your father's waiting in the car. We had a . . .' Lisa's mother gave Simon a lingering look. '. . . date.'

'Oh, god, I completely forgot. Simon, I'm sorry, but I have to . . .'

Simon stood there, feeling more than a little self-conscious. Maybe Lisa was finding her mother's visit embarrassing too, but at least it was cutting short their awkward goodbye. And perhaps this way was best. He'd say a cheerful 'cheerio', leave Lisa to head on out for what was sure to be a Spanish inquisition of a Sunday lunch with her parents, and that would be it. Last night would be chalked down to experience. He'd have to accept that – as pleasant as it had been – it had been a one-off (or, technically speaking, a two-off). They could both go their separate ways, and . . .

'Though here's an idea,' said Lisa's mother, addressing him directly. 'Why doesn't Simon join us for lunch?'

Lisa's eyes had suddenly gone all deer-in-the-headlights, and while Simon felt the same way, for some reason he found himself nodding.

'That would be lovely, Sonia,' he said.

Chapter 38

Lisa escorted her mother and Simon out through the front door, her head spinning. While it occurred to her to let them go through, slam it behind them and lock it from the inside to spare her from what was sure to be an excruciating couple of hours, that would be rude. Besides, as her mother had demonstrated a few minutes ago, she had a key.

No, better to get lunch over with – plus it might give her a chance to see another side to Simon, which might help her (or rather, help her to help him) with her write-up. He'd already proved he could be thoughtful, and now she'd get to see what he was like with other people (though those 'other people' were her parents, and hardly representative of 'normal').

As to why he'd agreed to join them, Lisa could only guess. He'd been about to say something when her mother had barged in, and, though she didn't like to admit it to herself, Lisa was intrigued to find out what that had been. Perhaps he *was* genuinely interested, and this was a good way to spend more time with her? Maybe he wanted to check her out some more before he decided if he wanted to see her again – you could tell a lot about a person by meeting their parents, seeing what they were like in a family environment. Then again, he hadn't wanted to go on their date in the first place, she reminded herself.

She crammed her feet into the bright-red Adidas trainers she kept by the door and followed the two of them down the garden path, then along the pavement to where her parents' Toyota was parked, gleam-ing from its usual Sunday-morning trip to the car wash. As her mum headed round to the other side of the car, Lisa ignored her dad's look of surprise from the driver's seat, and grabbed Simon gently but firmly by the arm.

'What are you playing at?' she hissed.

'I was a little hungry, so . . .'

'We've just had breakfast!'

'Yes, but when you consider yesterday's dinner only consisted of one Jaffa Cake . . .'

'Simon!'

He grinned sheepishly. 'Maybe I'm taking a lesson out of your book?'

'I don't have a book! And, even if I did, who said you could read it?'

'How does it go?' he said. '"Seize the day"? Like it says on your tattoo?'

'When did you . . . ?' Lisa found herself blushing. She knew exactly when Simon had seen her tattoo. And had forgotten that he could probably translate it.

'Or, at least, I imagine it's *supposed* to say that.'

'What do you mean?'

Simon lowered his voice. 'There's no "t" on the end of "carpe".'

Lisa turned a shade of red that matched her trainers. 'I *knew* I shouldn't have had those margaritas!' she said, more to herself than anyone else, and Simon grinned.

'As I was saying: be a bit more spontaneous, you said. Say yes to things when they come up, rather than always saying no – like I've been doing for the last couple of years. Turn every negative into a positive. It's called *Can*-cún, rather than Can't-cún.' He counted Lisa's earlier pronouncements off on his fingers, then fortunately stopped before he ran out of digits. 'That kind of thing.'

'But . . .'

'And what was it you said? About a ship being safe in the harbour?'

Lisa stared at him for a moment. That hadn't been the answer she'd expected. But Simon was watching her intently, and while it occurred to her to tell him that particular ship had sailed, she had to concede he'd won that round. She allowed him the briefest of smiles in return, then she stood back as he opened the car door for her.

'Hello, love!'

'Hi, Dad.'

Lisa leaned over the seat-back and kissed her father on his cheek. He always had a way of making her feel like a little girl around him. Something she didn't particularly want to let Simon see.

'Peter, this is Simon,' announced Lisa's mum, as Simon got into the car.

'Nice to meet you, Simon.' Her dad swivelled awkwardly round in his seat to shake Simon's hand, then arched an eyebrow at his daughter. 'Simon's, um . . .'

'A *friend* of Lisa's,' interrupted her mother.

Her mum had added a clear 'don't ask any more' emphasis to the word 'friend', so her dad just nodded. 'Great,' he said, fastening his seat belt before starting the car. 'Any friend of Lisa's, and all that.'

'Especially a *boy* friend,' said her mum. 'Don't you agree, Simon?'

Simon looked round sharply from where he'd been staring out of the car window, like a convict taking a last look at freedom. 'Um . . .'

'Mum!' said Lisa, for the second – and what she suspected wouldn't be the last – time today.

'Are you joining us for lunch, Simon?' said her dad.

'He is!' interrupted Lisa's mum, as if announcing a win on the lottery. 'Isn't that right, Lisa?'

'I suppose so,' said Lisa, though as if she'd just found out the lottery win was a ten-pound one.

Her dad let out a short chuckle as he put the car in gear, and Lisa tried to ignore the fact that he seemed to be watching her in his rear-view mirror, doing that thing with his eyebrows that reminded her of a ventriloquist's dummy.

'Can you just drive, please, Dad?'

'Will do!'

'We've booked a table at The Hussar,' announced Lisa's mum, as the car pulled away slowly from the kerb. 'Do you know it, Simon?'

Simon nodded. 'It's my local,' he said. 'As in, it's near where I live, rather than me going there all the time.'

'Isn't that a coincidence? And it's nice to know you're not an alcoholic!'

'Mum!' Lisa shook her head at her mum's latest insensitive observation. 'Do you have no filter at all?'

'I'm just saying.'

'He could still be an alcoholic. Just because he doesn't drink himself silly in his local pub doesn't mean . . .' She stopped talking. Somehow her mum made her lead herself up these kinds of conversational dead ends, and Lisa often wondered how on earth she'd got there.

'Calm down, dear. I was making a joke. I didn't really think Simon was . . .' She paused, and mimed someone all over the place while holding a glass of something, and Lisa felt herself shrink into her seat. 'You're not an alcoholic, are you, Simon?' she said.

'No, Mrs . . .' Simon had paled, and Lisa realised it was because he couldn't remember her surname. How did that look, given the fact her mum assumed he'd spent the night? Though, fortunately, her mum saved the day.

'Please. Call me Sonia.'

'Okay. Sonia it is. And no, I'm not an alcoholic.' He lowered his voice, and said, so only Lisa could hear, 'Not yet, anyway.'

And to her surprise, and though she did her best to hide it from him, Lisa found herself feeling glad Simon was there.

Chapter 39

Simon laid his knife and fork carefully on the plate, pushed them together to indicate he was finished, then slid the plate an inch or two away for good measure. He'd never eaten such a huge serving of roast chicken in his life, hadn't even known his local pub put on such a spread every Sunday, or that it was such a nice place to while away a few hours at the weekend. If being out was like this, then he really *did* need to get out more.

Lisa's parents had been great hosts, insisting lunch was on them as soon as the menus had arrived so Simon could 'have what he wanted', and while initially what he'd actually wanted was to do a runner given the way Lisa had been glaring icily at him when they'd first arrived (and when Lisa's mother had insisted the two of them sit side by side on the small sofa she'd delightedly said was called a 'love seat'), she'd defrosted a little once the starters had arrived – or rather, when the second bottle of wine had. She'd even spent two minutes photographing everyone's roast dinners in order to make an Instagram collage (something her mother had said sounded like a posh photography school – an observation that'd had the entire table in hysterics).

Surreptitiously, he checked no one was watching him and sneaked a glance at his watch. Half past two! So far, yesterday's 'date' had lasted almost twenty-five and a half hours, and, judging by the way Lisa's dad was eyeing the dessert menu written on the chalkboard next to the bar, it wasn't over yet. How had what was supposed to have been a routine lunch with Will turned into *this*?

The pub was warm, so he pushed up the sleeves of his sweatshirt, hoping he didn't smell. After all, he was still in yesterday's clothes, and he – unlike Lisa – hadn't had a chance to take a shower (or two, as he'd heard her apparently do earlier). But, if anything, Lisa's mother had taken every opportunity on her frequent trips to the loo to give him a hug as she passed, so he doubted that was the case. Even so, it hadn't stopped him disappearing off to the bathroom earlier to surreptitiously sniff his armpits.

'So, Simon. How come you're still single?' Lisa's mum was on her fifth glass of wine, and though he doubted it was possible, her questions were becoming even more personal. 'I would have thought a catch like you would have been snapped up by now?'

'I'm hardly a catch.'

'Of course you are!' Lisa's mum reached over and squeezed his hand – for a little too long, Simon felt. 'Stop being so modest. As I always used to tell Lisa, you believed in Santa Claus for the first eight years of your life, so you can at least believe in yourself for five minutes!'

Lisa's mum threw her head back and laughed so loudly the people at the neighbouring table looked round, and Simon had to stop himself from cringing.

'Never met the right girl, eh?' Lisa's dad winked at him across the table, then pointedly looked at his daughter, but when Simon caught Lisa's eye, she appeared to be mortified.

'Dad, *please* . . .'

'I'm just making conversation. Or "banter", as I think you'd call it.'

'Well, whatever it is, Simon doesn't need to be subjected to your grilling.'

'It's hardly a grilling,' Lisa's dad protested. 'More of a light toasting.'

'There's nothing light about it! So please just drop it.'

'No, that's okay,' Simon said neutrally. 'Actually, the truth is, I did meet the right girl. A while back, when I lived in London. Her name was Alice.'

'Oh.'

Lisa's mum and dad were exchanging disappointed glances, and while he was pleased he'd finally managed to silence them – temporarily, at least – he knew what was coming next. And while Lisa was giving him a look that inferred both 'please' and 'no', Simon was past covering this up. Alice dying was as much a part of his story as this weekend might turn out to be. And it was nothing to be ashamed of.

'So, what happened?'

'Dad!' said Lisa, though with the resigned tone of someone who realised any further protestations were futile.

'She . . . well . . .' Simon looked at the three of them in turn, then realised something. While his therapist had told him he needed to talk about it, not everyone needed to know. It shouldn't define him. And, although he was glad he'd told Lisa, right now there was no upside to telling her mum and dad. It would mean lunch finishing on a massive downer, they'd end up feeling sorry for him and somehow he knew they'd then make Lisa feel bad about it if – well, *when* – he couldn't convince her to go out with him.

'It just didn't work out,' he said, just catching Lisa's sigh of relief.

'Why not?'

Lisa's mum, like a terrier with a bone, was staring at him intently from across the table. Or, at least, as intently as someone who'd already consumed the best part of a bottle of rosé could.

Simon smiled at Lisa, then he took a breath, and as he exhaled he felt the weight of the world slip from his shoulders. 'Fate, I guess,' he said.

Lisa's mum stared at him for a moment longer, as if disappointed she'd been denied a juicier story, then she picked her glass up and clinked it against his.

'Well, lucky for Lisa it didn't,' she said.

Suddenly embarrassed, Simon glanced across at Lisa, wondering what she'd made of the exchange. And although she was looking at him strangely, he decided not to take it personally.

Chapter 40

Lisa followed Simon out of the pub, rolled her eyes as her mum and dad hugged him goodbye, and rolled them again when her mum made him promise he'd see them again 'soon'. Then she quickly kissed her parents before setting off along the pavement, Simon keeping pace obediently by her side.

As lunch had progressed, she'd simultaneously found herself having a good time and feeling *awful*. Simon had been great company: funny, well mannered, laughing politely at her dad's terrible 'dad' jokes and humouring her mum's inquisition, and all the while being attentive to Lisa regarding everything from checking her wine glass was topped up to offering her the last of the gravy. Jess had been right – he was the Anti-Chris. Which is why she was feeling awful about dismissing him so soon.

She'd realised she might have been using his 'disappearance' this morning as an excuse – as proof that he wasn't ready for a relationship, backing up what she'd heard from Jess about him having to be tricked into turning up yesterday. And she was beginning to suspect she'd actually been worried about 'taking him on', given the Alice thing. So it was possibly more of her problem than his. Which made her feel ashamed.

She'd suggested they walk home, batting off her parents' protestations – quite frankly, she'd had enough insinuations and questions for one day – and, since they were near where he lived, insisted she walk *him* home. So now they found themselves heading towards Simon's street.

'I'm sorry about those two,' she said, fixing a smile on her face as she waved her parents' car away. 'They can be a bit full on.'

'Hey. It was . . .' Simon narrowed his eyes. 'I'm going to go with "fun".'

'I won't ask you what you *didn't* go with,' she said. Then, after a moment: 'Why didn't you tell them?'

'What?'

'About Alice.'

'I did.'

'Yes, but . . . not the whole story.'

'Like I said last night, I don't tell *anyone* – at least, not *just* anyone. And what purpose would it have served? We were all having a nice lunch. The last thing we needed was for me to put a damper on the whole thing. Especially if I might never . . .'

He'd stopped talking, and seemed to be staring off into the distance, so Lisa rested a supportive hand on his shoulder. 'What?'

'See them again.'

'Oh.' She hastily withdrew her hand. 'Right.'

'Not because *we* won't . . . I mean, we might . . .' He smiled flatly. 'I don't know what to say. It's been a rather . . . crazy last twenty-four or so hours, that's all.'

'Hey. At the very worst, you'll be on my Christmas card list. Not that I tend to send cards nowadays. Apart from e-cards. For charity. Sometimes.' Lisa shuddered. 'Anyway. I hate Christmas, so . . .'

'You *hate* Christmas?'

'Yeah. Is that bad of me?'

'Depends why.'

Lisa thought about it for a moment. 'It always makes me feel like a failure.'

'You're going to have to explain that one.'

Lisa glanced back over her shoulder: A car was driving slowly along the road behind them, and she half suspected it might be her parents, having circled the block to keep tabs on them at her mum's behest – and she didn't want to launch into an explanation if that were the case.

'Okay. Here goes,' she said, as the car – a Toyota, but not her parents' model – reversed into a parking space. 'Every year, I spend Christmas with my mum and dad.'

'They weren't *that* bad.'

Lisa punched him playfully on the shoulder. 'That's not what I meant. It's just . . . *every* year. I generally have far too much to drink, so I end up staying over, then I wake up on Boxing Day morning in my single bed in my old room and realise . . .' Her voice caught a little in her throat. 'Well, that I'm no further on in my life. After another year. Nothing's changed.' She forced a smile. 'Which is partly why I decided *I* had to.'

'So it's more what it represents, and not that you don't like Christmas per se?'

'I'm not sure what that means.'

'Itself.'

'What?'

'*Per se*. It's Latin. It means—'

'No, I got that, Mister Linguist. I meant the other bit. About representing something.'

Simon laughed. 'Sorry. That's an overspill from my time in therapy. People tend to associate an event with something they don't like, so they transfer the dislike to the event itself. I had a lot of that after Alice. Things I wouldn't dare do, or allow myself to enjoy, simply because I used to do and enjoy them with her. And then, eventually, you realise the only person you're being untrue to is yourself.'

'So what's the cure?'

'I'm still working on that one.' They'd stopped to wait for a car to pass before crossing the road, and Simon smiled wistfully. 'Alice used to love Christmas.'

Lisa turned to face him. 'I'm sorry, Simon. I really don't know what to say whenever you mention her. I've never lost someone close to me, so I can't think of an appropriate . . . I mean, what *would* be appropriate?'

Simon checked right, left, then right again, and indicated it was safe to cross the street. 'I dunno. I've never really thought about it. How did it – *does* it – make you feel?'

Lisa felt her insides lurch. This was her opening, her opportunity to tell him exactly that. But what good would explaining actually do? It might make her feel better, but to tell him she didn't want to – or rather, *couldn't* – be the one who helped him get over such a tragedy felt . . . well, 'mean' was the best word she could think of to describe it. She took a couple of deep breaths to settle herself, and forced a smile.

'Simon, I . . . it . . . I don't . . .'

'Hey,' he said, soothingly, both hands held out and palms down as if to calm some distressed animal, and Lisa feared the gesture was a little too appropriate. 'Jess should have said something. *Warned* you.' He stuffed his hands into his pockets. 'Or maybe I shouldn't have told you.'

'No, you should have. *Of course* you should. I'm sorry. It's me. It's just something I wasn't . . .'

'Expecting?'

'Well, no. Wasn't prepared for, either.' Her mouth suddenly felt dry, and Lisa wondered whether it was too late to head back to the pub. 'Right. Well. Here goes. It's just . . . this morning. My text. After what you told me last night had sunk in, and what Jess had said . . . It's pretty unforgiveable, I know. But I wanted to explain. To tell you that . . .'

'You don't have to—'

'No, I do. Because I'm not proud of myself, and I need you to understand.' Lisa took a deep breath, wondering how to explain exactly what she was scared of. If he and Alice had split up because of – if you excused the phrase – natural causes, then she wouldn't have worried. They'd have finished because something was wrong, i.e. Alice – or

Simon – might have done something, something tangible, something *avoidable* that Lisa would be aware of. But this way, Alice was always going to be perfect. Simon's 'what might have been'. And how could you – how could *she* – compete with an angel?

She'd seen *Ghost* – it was one of her favourite films. It had even inspired her to take up pottery in the hope it might lead to the odd sexy clay-covered encounter, though the reality had been a dry brown residue under her fingernails for a week, and a boxful of misshapen pots she kept in a cardboard box in her shed. But to want to go through something like that, to follow Alice – like the supporting act for a legendary band, but going on stage *afterwards*? Lisa wasn't sure she had it in her.

'My relationship history is . . . well, suffice it to say, and, as you quite rightly pointed out, I don't exactly have twenty-twenty vision when it comes to picking men, so I've been lied to or cheated on more times than I care to remember, and this is going to sound terrible, but when you told me about what happened to Alice I thought it was almost . . . romantic.' Lisa hesitated, feeling terrible about the look that had just flashed across Simon's face. 'And I know that sounds bad, but I've always felt like *I* was the damaged one, so last night it was almost a relief that I . . .' She swallowed hard, not sure where she was going with this. 'I started to realise that I'd *so* been seeing the wrong kind of men, and even though they were quite obviously the wrong kind of men, they still all ended up dumping *me*, and . . .' She clenched her hands into fists, determined to finish what she wanted to say. 'So when you think about that, it doesn't give you a lot of confidence in yourself, or the choices you make, which is why I left this whole "choice" thing to fate . . .'

'In the guise of the *Gazette*.'

'Exactly.' Lisa nodded. 'Which sounds even more of a recipe for disaster, now I think about it. Anyway, to cut a long story short, which I'm conscious I haven't, then *you* come along, with everything that's happened to you, and I realise that you deserve someone pretty special after what's happened, and "special" is the last thing I think I am, and that's why I, you know . . .'

'I think you're pretty special.'

'Please, Simon. Don't. Because if you're going to start dating again, you need someone . . . better than me. More sorted. Less of a car crash . . .' Horrified, Lisa clamped her hand to her mouth, but Simon smiled forgivingly.

'That's not how you come across.'

'But it's how I obviously am!' Lisa shook her head in disbelief – not at herself, but at how Simon didn't seem to be agreeing with her. 'I berate you for nearly running me over when it was probably my fault, then I accuse you of trying to spike my drink so you could sleep with me, which must have made me seem really . . .'

'Full of yourself?'

'I was going to go with "suspicious", though that's a good one too.' Lisa forced a smile. 'But, either way, it's not good. And then, when you open your heart to me, when you've got no reason to do that, I take you to bed, then get cold feet and make a bolt of "Usain" proportions for the door.' She stared off into the distance, then a thought occurred to her. 'Why did you tell me, by the way?'

'Tell you what?'

'About Alice. Something so personal. So early on. After all, you hardly know me.'

Simon angled his head and stuck his lower lip out a little, as if it were the first time he'd ever been asked this question and he wanted to get his answer just right. 'I told you about Alice because . . . well, because you deserved to know why I was behaving like *I* was. Why I was worried I wouldn't be able to . . .' He'd turned a shade of red, and Lisa nodded supportively. 'Like I told your dad, I *did* meet the right girl, but it didn't work out, perhaps not for the usual reason these things don't work out, but even so. Even though it wasn't my fault. Even though I didn't do anything wrong.'

Lisa nodded. 'It's possible to do everything right and still lose. That's not a weakness. It's life. I learned that recently.'

'Tell me about it!' Simon made a face. 'And I'm sorry for not telling you earlier.'

'Earlier?'

'Before the first time we . . . or rather, we *didn't*, but to be honest, since, you know . . .'

'The accident?' suggested Lisa, and Simon flinched.

'Since Alice was *killed*, I was going to say . . . well, I've tended to, what's the phrase . . . ?'

'Bury it?' suggested Lisa, before quickly facepalming herself, but Simon forced a smile.

'Yeah. That's the only way I've been able to deal with what happened, even though I realise now that I *haven't* been dealing with it.' He shook his head. 'Alice was a very positive person – you had to be, when you did what she did for a living – and she always used to say that this kind of incident in your life could either make or break you, and I'm sure – mainly because it's what Will keeps telling me – that the last thing she'd have wanted was for me to let what happened to her, and therefore to *me*, ruin any chance of future happiness I had. And I realise now I've been letting her down. Though it occurs to me I owe you an apology too.'

'An apology? For what?'

'I've spent the last two years so worried about how to tell people what happened without *me* collapsing into a tearful mess that I never stopped to think how *they* might react. It's not the kind of thing you should just put out there, I suppose. I've had two years to deal with it. I know what's coming when I start the story. No one else does – and my therapist warned me I could expect all sorts of reactions.'

'Including women taking you to bed?' asked Lisa, shame-faced.

'I wish they'd warned me about that one. I might have told more people!' He smiled. 'Hey. You tried to make me feel better, and believe me you did. Twice! And . . .'

Simon had stopped talking, so Lisa reached out a hand and rested it on his arm. 'And what?' she said, but Simon just grinned sheepishly.

'And nothing. I just assumed that was a good place for an "and", but then I realised I'd said all I wanted to say. So, I stopped. And now it's my turn to listen,' he said, half jumping off the kerb to avoid a puddle, then offering his hand to Lisa as she did the same.

'Are you . . . over her?'

Simon stuck his lower lip out as he thought about it. 'Possibly not. There's a chance I never will be. But I also know there's a chance that I might be mourning something that I think might have been, when in reality things might not have worked out between us anyway. So am I going to look at you . . .' He blushed. 'I mean, am I always going to be looking at any potential new partner and comparing them with Alice every time? Maybe, for a while. But that'll change. I'm sure of that.'

Lisa realised she was still holding his hand, so she gave it a brief squeeze before letting it go. 'You'll probably end up with someone completely different to Alice, who you'll love just the same, if not even more.'

'Maybe,' said Simon, jamming his hands into his pockets like a miserable teenager, and Lisa let out a short laugh.

'What's so funny?' he said.

'Listen to us!' said Lisa. 'We're supposed to have had this perfect date, and yet we're here trying to outdo each other with our tales of misery and hopelessness. Which is hardly going to look good in the write-up in next week's *Gazette*.'

Simon pulled his hands out of his pockets, but only to bury his face in them. 'I'd forgotten all about that.'

They walked on in silence for a while, then Lisa cleared her throat. 'Do you think you'll ever, you know . . .' She readied her fingers for a set of air quotes, then thought better of it. 'Love again?'

'Oh yes,' said Simon, quickly. 'I guess everyone does, no matter who they've lost, or how they've lost them. Otherwise what would be the point of going on—'

'Don't talk like that!'

'What?'

'There's always a point to life.'

'I wasn't talking about *killing myself.*' Simon looked aghast. 'I meant, what would be the point of going on dates?'

Lisa narrowed her eyes at him. For someone who hadn't wanted to come on *theirs*, that was a strange thing to say.

'Will said something to me yesterday,' he continued. 'About there being more than just one person out there for everybody.'

'Do you believe that?'

'I suppose it's the kind of thing you need to have proved to you.'

'I suppose.'

Simon let out a short laugh, and Lisa frowned. 'What's so funny?'

'Something else Will told me. A while back, about falling in love being like losing your virginity.'

Lisa made a face. She'd lost hers in a brief, uncomfortable encounter on the back seat of a Ford Focus, an experience so awful she hadn't wanted to repeat it for the best part of a year, although she was pretty sure he didn't mean it like that.

'In, um, what way?'

'It's easier the second time. But the first time is such a big deal that, afterwards, you think it'll never happen again. Or at least, I did.'

'You're still talking about the virginity thing, right?'

'And then you realise it *will* happen again, and it's not such a big deal . . .'

Lisa made another face, and Simon stopped talking. 'What?'

'I'm beginning to think I haven't. Ever.'

'I'm guessing you're talking about being in love, rather than the other thing, otherwise last night . . .'

She laughed. 'Yeah. I mean, I thought I was in love with Chris, but now I think about it, about *him*, and how he treated me so badly, how he was – *is* – such a . . .' She ran through a selection of words in her head, but couldn't find one rude enough to sum her ex up. 'Anyway. Suffice it to say, I can't have been in love with him, because being "in" love suggests it's a two-way thing, and I don't think someone like Chris has it in him to love anyone except for himself.'

'Well, that's his loss.'

'Isn't it just?' Lisa nudged him. 'You *are* easy to talk to, you know.'

'Hey.' He nudged her back. 'Are we becoming friends now?'

Lisa's eyes widened. '*When Harry Met Sally*!'

'What?'

'That's a line from the film.'

'I'll take your word on that.'

Lisa stopped dead in her tracks. 'You've never seen *When Harry Met Sally*?'

'Er . . . no? Have you?'

'No – my superpower is being able to quote lines from films I've never seen!' Lisa gave him a playful shove. 'Only about a hundred times!' she said, though she feared even that was an underestimate.

'What's it about? Apart from someone called Harry meeting someone called Sally, of course?'

'You *have* seen it.'

Simon acknowledged her joke with a tilt of his head. 'What's so good about it?'

Lisa stared at him, open-mouthed, doing a good impression of Meg Ryan from the film. 'Do you have Netflix?'

'Of course! I'm not completely unsophisticated.'

'Says the man who's never seen *When Harry Met Sally*.' She grabbed him by the arm and marched him along the pavement. 'Well, prepare to be blown away! Which is your street?'

'We, um, passed it a couple of minutes ago.'

'Why didn't you . . . ?'

'I was enjoying the walk.'

Lisa mock-glared at him, then spun him round and they headed back in the opposite direction. And, to her surprise, she realised she'd been enjoying the walk too.

Chapter 41

Simon stared at his television screen as the closing credits to *When Harry Met Sally* rolled. He'd not sat through a rom-com for ages – most of his televisual entertainment nowadays was the kind you didn't have to concentrate on too hard to follow, and quite often involved ridiculously muscled men dressed in ridiculous costumes and doing ridiculous things, thanks to a ridiculous amount of CGI. But even though this particular film was almost as old as he was, and starred only one person he recognised (courtesy of the *Star Wars* franchise), he already knew it was possibly one of the greatest movies about relationships he'd ever seen.

As much as he'd enjoyed the film, he'd enjoyed sitting next to Lisa too, just 'chilling', relishing her closeness, appreciating having someone else in the flat, remembering what it was like to have company on a lazy Sunday afternoon doing nothing in particular except vegging out in front of the TV. And, most importantly, Simon realised just how much he'd missed it.

'What did you think?'

Lisa was watching him intently, and not for the first time. On several occasions, during what he recognised were the key moments in the film, he'd been aware of her eyes on him, trying to gauge his reaction, but he'd been careful not to give too much away. And if he'd managed to maintain a poker face during Meg Ryan's fake-orgasm-in-the-diner scene, he was pretty sure he could do that now.

'Not bad.'

'*Not bad?* It's a classic! Maybe even *the* classic.'

'I suppose.'

'You *suppose?*'

He could hear the italics in Lisa's words, and Simon suspected he wasn't going to get away with things quite that easily. And while he'd initially thought she just wanted to get him to see one of her favourite films, now he was a little suspicious as to her motives. After all, the movie raised a few questions, didn't it? And given what had happened between them, one rather obvious one.

'It was funny, obviously. But it made you think, didn't it?'

Lisa was giving him a look that suggested she didn't believe he was capable of thought. 'Did it?' she said, sweetly. 'About what?'

He hauled himself up from the sofa – the two of them had been sitting there for a little over an hour and a half, maintaining a respectable distance – and headed into his kitchenette. Coming back to his flat had been the obvious option – they'd found themselves just around the corner when Lisa had made her *When Harry Met Sally* suggestion – and, suddenly, he was a little embarrassed about the state of the place. It was a rental, and since he'd moved in Simon hadn't bothered to do much to it. Do anything to it, to be honest, mainly because he never brought anyone back here except for Will, and as long as there was a beer with his name on it in the fridge, Will didn't care if the place didn't exactly look like an *Interiors* magazine photoshoot.

'Coffee?' he said, performing an exaggerated stretch.

'Please,' said Lisa, and Simon was pleased she hadn't asked for tea. 'And don't avoid the question.'

'I'm thinking about it,' he said, opening the cupboard where he kept his coffee-making paraphernalia. 'How do you like it?'

Lisa shrugged. 'Until this morning, I didn't know I did. So . . .'

'Surprise you?'

She beamed at him, then nodded, and Simon felt a swelling in his chest that he hadn't felt for a long time. 'Okay,' he said, removing two smallish glasses from the cupboard, followed by his AeroPress coffee maker. 'This is that cortado I mentioned yesterday. Spanish for "short".'

'The one I shouldn't just drop a couple of ice cubes into.'

'You *were* paying attention!' said Simon proudly, filling the kettle with just the right amount of water and clicking it on. 'Half warm milk, half espresso.'

'With an "s", not an "x".'

'Exactly!'

'Shouldn't that be "esactly"?'

Simon gave her a look as he poured an appropriate amount of semi-skimmed into his milk frother. Then, as per his usual routine, he added a filter paper to the AeroPress's cap, inserted the plunger into the end of the device, turned it upside down and spooned coffee into the cylinder. With an unnecessary flourish, he switched the frother to 'warm', and waited for the kettle to boil, enjoying the process. He'd loved making coffee for Alice, turning the steps almost into a show, like a croupier might with a few fancy card-shuffles. This time, though, with Lisa studying him closely, for some reason he felt under a bit of pressure.

Once the kettle had boiled, and with the AeroPress still upside down (his preferred method, and the one the real aficionados used, if you subscribed to the forums like Simon did), he counted to ten, added the appropriate amount of just-off-the-boil water, gave it a stir, screwed the cap on and let the coffee brew for just the right amount of time. Then he upended the device, placed it over one glass and slowly depressed the plunger, repeating the procedure with the other, then topping them both up with the warmed milk.

'Should I applaud now?' said Lisa, and Simon performed a curt bow. The last time he'd made one of these for anyone outside of the café had been for Alice, and, though it seemed silly when he thought about it, the fact that he'd managed to get through this unscathed felt like he'd passed some sort of test.

'Sugar?'

'Yes, honey?'

Simon couldn't stop himself from reddening, and did his best to ignore Lisa's gloating look at having caught him out like that again.

'Not really,' she said, so he handed her one of the glasses, then watched as she carefully blew over the top of the drink and took a sip.

'Well?'

Lisa nodded appreciatively. 'Not bad,' she said.

'Touché.'

'Though . . .' She took another sip of coffee, then put the glass down. 'There's not a lot to it, is there?'

'Hence the name. But it's all about quality, not quantity, as in if you get the *quality* right . . .'

'Then surely you'd want more?'

'Now *that's* a metaphor.'

'Is that a different type of coffee?'

'Ha!' Simon mimed applause in appreciation of Lisa's joke. 'Seriously, though . . . did you *want* more?' He averted his eyes, wondering if Lisa had picked up on the inference, then sat back down next to her and smiled. 'Which brings us back to the film.'

'And?'

He gestured towards the TV. 'That's the movies. Not real life. Real life doesn't happen so . . . neatly. There's not always just the one question to answer.' He took a sip of coffee, then swivelled round on the sofa to face her and steeled himself. If ever there were a time to talk about the two of them, where they went from here, it was now. 'For example, that central premise, that men and women can't be friends because the sex gets in the way . . . What's so funny?'

'You said "the sex"!'

'And?'

'That just sounds weird.'

'Huh?'

'Sex. It's just "sex".'

Simon hesitated. Was Lisa referring to his grammar, or making an observation about the previous evening? If so, maybe she was trying to let him down gently. And if *that* was the case . . .

Lisa's expression had suddenly become hard to read, so Simon decided to change tack a little. While big declarations always seemed to work at the end of any romantic comedy he'd ever sat through, so far his and Lisa's relationship – if you could call it that – had had precious little that had been romantic *or* funny about it. Besides, he wasn't sure he had it in him to make one.

'Anyway,' he continued. 'It doesn't mean *we* can't be friends.'

Lisa stared at him for a moment, then she put her coffee down on the table next to the sofa and clasped her hands in her lap. 'You want to be *friends* with me?'

'Well, *yes*.'

'Why?'

Simon considered reminding her how that had actually been her suggestion in her earlier text, but something about Lisa's tone of voice made him quickly decide against it. 'Well, um, because, you know, eventually, I think we might realise that we're good . . .' Simon stopped short of adding 'together'.

'Good *friends*? Or do you mean *just* good friends?'

Not for the first time, Simon wasn't sure what point Lisa was making, so he decided soldiering on was the best strategy. Or rather his only strategy. 'Either. Or both. Because we've already got "the sex"' – Simon added air quotes around the last two words for what was, he hoped, comedic emphasis – 'out of the way.'

'*Out of the way?*'

'That's right.' Simon grinned, pleased she'd got it, though his smile faded almost as quickly because Lisa was looking *horrified*.

'I'm sorry you feel it was something you wanted to "get out of the way",' she said, leaping to her feet. 'And they say romance is dead!'

'I didn't mean it like that,' said Simon, quickly. 'I was talking in terms of timeline.'

'We don't *have* a timeline!'

Lisa was looking angrier than Simon had seen her all weekend: Certainly more so than when he'd nearly run her over, and even angrier than when she'd stormed off after the funfair.

'Lisa. Please. Sit down. I . . . I got that wrong.'

'Well, *there's* a first!'

She was striding towards the door, and Simon realised his window of opportunity was closing rapidly. Not in the least because his flat wasn't that big, and she didn't have all that far to go.

'What are you going to do?' he asked, desperately. 'Storm off again? Because that would be the second time in a little over twenty-four hours.'

'Yeah, well, maybe you're the kind of man women storm off from. Did you ever think about that?'

Lisa was already halfway out of the front door, and Simon sat and watched her pull it shut angrily behind her, the resounding slam knocking the one photo he had of him and Alice off the top of his bookshelf and on to the floor.

And though he didn't believe in signs, or omens, or anything like that, Simon knew he'd be a fool if he didn't recognise how that had been an almighty one.

Chapter 42

Lisa hurried towards the bus stop on the Canterbury Road, cursing under her breath when she saw the number 8 bus that would take her virtually to her front door had just left, then began walking after it. This weekend couldn't have been any weirder. Still, at least it was over now. Or it would be when she eventually got home.

She strode along the pavement, watching out for dog mess, grateful she had a pair of 'sensible' shoes on given the potentially long walk she had in front of her. Putting them on when she'd left the house had been the only sensible thing she'd done all weekend – and surely what had just happened had been one of the stupidest.

She spotted a poster advertising Dreamland on the side of a bus going in the opposite direction, and allowed herself a wry smile. The date had been a rollercoaster of its own, without them needing to go to the funfair. And yet . . . it hadn't all been a disaster.

They'd had a nice lunch, and her parents' approval had been so obvious she could have pulled up a chair and asked it to join them at the table – the one time she'd taken Chris home and presented him to her mum and dad, their faces had fallen so quickly it had been like the 'after' and 'before' of a plastic surgery advert. Perhaps, as a result, as the four of them had demolished their roasts today, she'd found herself warming to Simon, so much so that she'd began to think that Jess had been wrong: he *did* want a relationship. Or, at least, he wanted one with her. But then – and even after a film guaranteed to put even the most cold-hearted man in the mood for love – he'd told her he just wanted to be friends.

She shook her head and muttered to herself, then noticed a couple of old ladies walking their miniature more-hair-than-body dogs in the opposite direction giving her a funny look.

'I'm not mad. Honest,' she said, though they looked as if they didn't believe her. And yet Lisa *was* mad. Mad with herself for letting Simon get to her just now. Angry that she cared about what he thought. Annoyed that she couldn't deal with things like an adult. And pissed off that she'd probably have to go through all of this again with someone else.

She strode on purposefully, sighting the next bus stop four hundred or so yards in the distance – hoping she might reach it just as the next bus turned up – just as a second number 8 roared past her. Hurriedly, Lisa sized up the distance between her and the stop, considering putting in a sprint, then decided at this rate she'd probably miss *every* bus. She could only hope *that* wasn't a metaphor.

Lisa heard a noise behind her – running footsteps – and told herself not to look round, just in case it was Simon, chasing after her to apologise, just like they'd watched Billy Crystal sprint across New York on New Year's Eve to make *his* declaration of love. Then she realised this was Margate, not Manhattan, and she was a bit worried it might be a mugger, so she stepped to one side of the pavement and spun round, only to see a middle-aged man jog past, a phone wedged into the waistband of his shorts and a pair of Apple earbuds sticking out from either side of his head as if his ears were new and someone had forgotten to cut the tags off them.

She swallowed her disappointment that it hadn't been Simon, continued on to the bus shelter in front of The Hussar and slumped down heavily on the bench, ignoring the rude graffiti scrawled on the glass partition by her head. The last thing she wanted to do was play bus-stop tag, especially the way her luck was going. No, she'd just sit here and wait until the next one came along, and . . .

Lisa sat up with a start. *This* was her problem. Always waiting for something to come along, rather than being in control of her own destiny. Why hadn't *she* taken the lead, asked Simon out, told him she'd like to be more than friends . . . ? But Lisa knew the answer to that. She was fed up of rejection. And surely that was what she was going to get. After all, she'd just spent the best part of the weekend with someone who might well be perfect for her, and at almost every step of the way she'd managed to mess things up. It wasn't a surprise, then, that Simon had only wanted to be friends . . . No, scratch that, it *was* a surprise. After the way she'd treated him, she should be surprised he wanted anything to do with her at all.

A flash of red in the distance made Lisa look up. The number 52 this time – not quite her bus, but it would take her to the bottom of the High Street rather than to the top of her road, so Lisa waved it down, then, for some strange reason, found herself waving it on again. After all, unless you were on the bus that took you exactly where you wanted to be, surely there was no point getting on just for the sake of it?

The bus had stopped anyway, and, as the doors hissed open, the driver, a friendly-looking woman a decade or so older than Lisa, smiled at her from behind the wheel.

'You getting on, love?' she said, and Lisa smiled back and shook her head, even though the opposite was true. She *was* getting on. And she couldn't afford to hang about.

As the bus pulled quickly back out into the road, Lisa hauled herself up off the bench and began walking home again. She needed time to think about what her next move should be – after all, the cosmos didn't work to anyone's timetable but its own.

Still, she remembered, after Jess wrote up the 'Blind Date' piece in the *Gazette* she'd be fighting them off. And while none of 'them' would be Simon, at least they'd come without an impossibly perfect dead girl-friend for Lisa to try to live up to.

No, she told herself, she'd actually just had a lucky escape.

So why did she feel so miserable?

Chapter 43

Simon was on the top deck of the bus, on his way to collect his car. He'd thought about going after Lisa, but she seemed to be a fan of dramatic exits, and while so far this weekend he'd chased the others down, he'd quickly decided he'd let her have this one. Mainly because he didn't have the faintest idea what to say.

So, instead, he'd given it ten minutes and then – half expecting to see her loitering outside, and *more*-than-half disappointed to see that she wasn't – headed out of his flat and made for the bus stop on the Canterbury Road. The number 52 was just pulling in, so he'd hopped on board, nodded at the cheery hello from the female driver, and made his way up to the top deck. Now he was sitting next to a teenage boy playing music so loudly through his headphones that Simon could almost feel the seat vibrate.

He sighed, surreptitiously stuck a finger into his ear in an attempt to block out the *tsk-tsk* of the music, then looked out of the window, marvelling at the view of the sea to his left. The sun was glinting off the water, and the sky was a cloud-free powder blue – the kind of day that made you glad to be alive. Even though he'd had the kind of weekend that made you almost wish you weren't.

Still, Will had told him he shouldn't expect the date to be plain sailing. He'd be 'rusty', plus Lisa might be on edge, or have expectations he couldn't possibly expect to meet, and not forgetting the fact that attraction – and blind dates – was all about chemistry. As he knew from his barista training, you had to have the right combination of ingredients – and at the right temperature – to produce something good. And while he suspected he and Lisa *had* all that, somehow it had gone off the boil.

He glanced up and noticed the left-hand front seat was empty, so Simon jumped smartly up and made his way towards it, though he nearly tumbled down the stairs when the bus slammed its brakes on, pulled in towards the shelter in front of The Hussar, stopped briefly, then accelerated out again. He used to love riding the buses in London – Alice had too, preferring them to the Tube. On buses, you got a view, and quite often a seat, rather than standing up on a miserable underground train where no one ever spoke to each other or you had to spend the majority of the journey with your face wedged into someone's armpit. And like nudist beaches, which were never populated with the finer-figured of people, you could always guarantee the people you found yourself pressed against didn't exactly smell like a walking advert for deodorant.

He sat down, all too aware of the empty space next to him. Once in a while, he and Alice would ride a London bus for fun, picking a number almost at random, seeing where it took them, like some sort of poor man's mystery tour. Sometimes they'd manage to secure the front seat on the top deck, where they'd sit, giggling childishly to each other, pointing out sights you'd never be able to see from the ground level, from interesting architectural features to peoples' gardens, and – surprisingly often – naked occupants of first-floor flats who'd forgotten to – or didn't care to – close their curtains.

One time they'd ended up in Walthamstow, a slightly dodgy part of town then, and when the bus had reached its final stop they'd almost cowered under the shelter, wondering how they were going to get home – *if* they were going to get home, given the menacing-looking groups of youths hanging around – until the bus driver had simply changed the display on the front of the bus and beckoned them back on board. And that had been the other good thing about the buses: there was always one going in the opposite direction. And, on occasion, the one you were on might even do a loop and take you all the way back home again.

He'd missed that, he realised. Not just riding the bus, but letting it take you somewhere – *anywhere* – without necessarily being sure of (or caring) where you were headed. Just seeing where the journey went, going with it . . . But it had been easier when you had someone to do that with, which was why he hadn't been on a bus since Alice. Hadn't done a *lot* of things since Alice. Maybe now *was* the time to start.

He felt the familiar sensation of someone sitting down next to him, so he swivelled round, then reminded himself not to be so stupid. *Of course* it wasn't Alice. It couldn't be. And the chances of it being Lisa were almost as remote – even if she had got on this bus, there was probably no way she'd want to sit next to him.

'Do you mind?'

An older man – seventy, give or take, Simon guessed – wearing a woollen hat and dressed in a similar puffer jacket to the one Simon had allegedly been about to steal yesterday – had just sat down next to him and was addressing him, so Simon quickly regained his composure.

'Not at all.'

The man peered back over his shoulder. 'I know there's other seats free, but I just fancied the front. Can't beat the view.'

'No,' said Simon. 'You can't.'

'Funny, though. When you're a kid, you convince yourself the back seat's the place to be, then eventually you realise you've got it completely wrong, because the *actual* place to be is where you get to experience everything!' He grinned. 'You off to the festival?'

'Festival?'

The man laughed. 'I'll take that as a no. The arts thing. At the gallery.'

Simon shook his head. 'Just going to pick up my car.'

'Ah.' The man tapped the side of his nose. 'Heavy night last night?'

'You could say that.'

'Well, good on you. You don't want to be drinking and driving. That's how accidents happen.'

'I know,' said Simon. 'And people using their phones at the wheel.'

The man nodded. 'It's not safe out there. Which is why I like the bus.' He nudged Simon. 'Plus, it's free.'

'Huh?'

The man reached into his pocket and showed Simon his photo card. 'People always use the phrase "getting your bus pass" as a bad thing,' he said, slipping it away again. 'It's *amazing*. You can go anywhere you want. You just have to pick a destination. Takes a while, sometimes – a few changes on occasion – but you always get where you want to be in the end.'

Simon smiled flatly. He wasn't so sure about that. 'What's the festival about?'

'No idea.' The man made a face. 'But my girlfriend fancied going so I'm meeting her . . . What?'

Simon realised he must have been looking strangely at the man, so he smiled. 'It's just . . . you said "girlfriend".'

'Well, she's not my wife. Not that I'm, you know . . .' He gave Simon another nudge and a wink. 'My wife passed away. Last year.'

'I'm sorry.'

'Don't be. Wasn't your fault.' The man reached up to adjust his hat, then he turned and looked out of the window.

'Even so.'

'What can you do? We had a good time while it lasted. And life goes on.'

'Does it?'

The man regarded him with wise old eyes, then he reached out and rested a hand on Simon's arm. 'It does. It may be a different life, and

314

not the one you'd been expecting, but you've got to play the cards you're dealt, haven't you?' He let out a short chuckle. 'You married, are you?'

'No, not . . .' Simon stopped just short of saying 'yet'. After Alice, and certainly after this weekend, he knew he couldn't be sure of it ever happening. 'Married,' he said.

'Looking for someone?'

Simon thought for a moment. 'Yes. I suppose I am.'

'Good for you. After all, as the song says, one is *definitely* the loneliest number.'

'Right,' said Simon. Though he didn't know the song, the sentiment was a little too familiar.

The man suddenly caught sight of something out the window, then reached a hand up and stabbed at the bell. 'Whoops! Almost missed my stop,' he said, hauling himself out of his seat. 'You make sure you don't miss yours, now.'

'I won't,' said Simon, though he couldn't help but wonder if he already had.

He glanced out of the bus window and spotted the dramatic outline of the gallery, the clean white lines of the modern building a striking contrast to the churning blue-grey sea behind it. The memory of his time there yesterday came flooding back: the class with Lisa, the way they'd really looked at each other, how she'd captured his sadness yet still put a smile on his face, and suddenly Simon knew what he had to do. After all, he was *tired* of feeling sad.

With a whispered '*Carpet diem*' followed by a barely contained laugh, he leapt to his feet, stabbed at the 'Stop' button and quickly descended the stairs.

Chapter 44

Lisa was exhausted. She'd been walking for the best part of twenty minutes, needed the toilet, her hangover had caught up with her with a vengeance, plus she'd had a late night . . . The cause of the last of those things made her smile, then she realised she shouldn't be so pleased about it given how things had turned out.

Without looking where she was going, she stepped out into the road, only to hear an urgent beeping, accompanied by a loud screech of tyres. Her heart hammering, she turned and scowled at the driver, then rolled her eyes in disbelief.

'You're kidding me!'

Simon had wound his window down and he was glaring back at her. 'Do you have a death wish or something?'

'Me?' Lisa marched up to the car. 'More likely you've been cruising the streets looking out for me so you can run me over.'

'The thought had occurred to me. Though, technically, most people are run *under* rather than over.'

'What?'

'When they're, you know . . .' Simon performed a little puppet show with his hands to demonstrate his point. 'Then again, you're so good at running out on me I doubt I'd be able to!'

Lisa stared at him, open-mouthed. 'The only reason I – to use your delightful phrase – "ran out on you" is because you keep driving me away.'

Simon angrily put the car into gear. 'Yes, well, now it's my turn to do some driving away!' he said, though he was showing no sign of wanting to go anywhere.

'What are you doing here anyway?'

'I came to find . . .' He hesitated. '. . . my car.'

'And my street was on your way home, was it?'

'This isn't your street.'

'It's the street that *leads* to it.'

'Yes, well, it's the way the car was pointed, so . . .'

'You couldn't have done a three-point turn?'

'I . . . um . . . well . . .'

Lisa listened to him stammer, suspecting he was about to launch into a not-dissimilar manoeuvre.

A honking from the car behind made Simon look anxious, so Lisa waved a 'sorry' at them, then she marched round to the passenger side of his car and – before she really knew what she was doing – jumped in.

'What are you doing?'

'It's the safest place. In fact, the *only* place where you can't run me over.'

Simon widened his eyes, then he pulled the car over to the side of the road and started to laugh.

'What's so funny?'

'This fate thing of yours. It's doing its damnedest to keep us meeting.'

'This isn't fate!'

'What is it, then?'

'Coincidence.'

Simon side-eyed her. 'Isn't that sort of the same thing?'

'Not at all. Maybe. I don't know.' Lisa ran both hands through her hair. Her house was just round the corner. A minute, maybe, if she walked quickly. Sixty seconds, and she'd never have to see Simon again. And yet the last thing she wanted to do was get out of the car.

There was a warmth in here that . . . well, it was nothing to do with the heater being on.

'All we do is argue,' she said.

'That's not *all* we do.' Simon smiled. 'Besides, this isn't an argument.'

'Yes, it is.'

'No, it isn't. It's a *conversation*.'

'What's the difference?'

Simon nodded patiently. 'An argument is two people trying to decide *who* is right. A conversation is when you're trying to work out *what* is right.'

'No, it isn't.'

'Now *that's* an argument. Just not a very good one.'

'Besides, I'm not sure I know what *is* right. *Who* is right. Which is probably why I'm always the one who gets left . . .' She forced a smile at her own joke. 'Maybe fate's just got it in for me. Perhaps I did something wrong in a past life, and karma is—'

'Hey!' The sharpness of Simon's tone made her jump. 'The way Chris treated you is nothing to do with you – and everything to do with *him*. He didn't deserve you, and you *certainly* didn't deserve him.'

'Maybe,' said Lisa, hesitantly.

'Any man would be lucky to have you. *I'd* be lucky to have you.'

'As a friend?'

Simon was staring out through the windscreen. 'As more than a friend.'

'I'm sorry – are you asking me out?'

He swivelled round to face her. 'What would you say if I was?'

'I don't know, Simon . . .'

'As in, you don't know what you'd say? Or you don't know if you'd go out with me?'

Lisa sighed. 'We're just so different. And we want different things.'

'Which means we want each other, if you think about it!'

Lisa fought to keep the smile from her face. 'I can sort of see how that makes sense. But . . .'

Simon puffed air out of his cheeks. 'A "but" . . .'

'It's just . . .' Lisa thought for a moment. 'Yesterday, you didn't know you were going on a date, weren't even ready for a relationship, and now you are. What happened? What suddenly made all the difference?'

'You're right. I didn't. Wasn't. Then . . .'

'Then?'

'Then I met you,' said Simon, quietly.

'Well that's . . . I mean . . .' Lisa felt a lump forming in her throat. 'Simon, I'm not . . .'

Simon made a face. '*Uh-oh*.'

'What's "uh-oh"?'

'That didn't sound that good. Especially after your earlier "but".'

'This time yesterday, I was wishing I'd never met you. And right now I feel exactly the same way, but for a different reason. Because you had to lose Alice for it to happen.'

'But I *have* lost Alice,' he said. 'Though it was two years ago. And a wise person told me yesterday that you shouldn't be a prisoner to those things in the past you can't change.'

'Which is true,' said Lisa.

'For both of us.'

'I know. But you have to realise I'll never be . . .' She hesitated. '. . . her.'

'I don't expect you to be. And, what's more, I don't want you to be. In fact, I don't want you to be *anyone* else. Except for *you*.'

'Simon, I . . .' Lisa was gripping the edge of her seat so hard her hands were hurting. 'What reassurance do I have that you won't make a run for it at the first sign of trouble?'

'That's rich, coming from Margate's answer to Usain Bolt!' He leaned across and nudged her playfully. 'In case you hadn't noticed, we've already had several signs of trouble. And yet . . .' He indicated 'Here I am!' with his hands, and Lisa couldn't help but smile.

'Even so. You don't think something's trying to tell us . . .'

'That's exactly what I think!' Simon threw his hands up in the air in desperation. 'This whole weekend, something's been doing its best to get us together – and *keep* us together – whether it's Will and Jess, or your ignorance of the Highway Code . . .'

'You mean your driving!'

'. . . or your mum inviting me to lunch, or the photographer being late, or me forgetting my car keys, or us having to do those stupid questions for the *Gazette*, or even your knob of an ex-boyfriend.' He shook his head slowly. 'I've always been the last person to believe in fate, and all that "it was meant to be" rubbish or "everything happens for a reason" nonsense, because then I'd have had to try to work out what the reason was for Alice being taken from me like that. But say it *is* true, and that there really wasn't anything anyone could have done to prevent what happened.' He reached down and fiddled nervously with the handbrake. 'In a way, that's actually comforting. And it's made me think . . .'

He had gone quiet, so Lisa took his hand and held it tightly. 'What?'

'Well, that . . .' Simon swallowed so hard Lisa could hear it. '. . . that you never know what's coming.'

'Like a silver Ford Focus, for example?'

'Lisa, I'm giving you my best speech here!'

'Sorry.'

'Right.' He took a moment, perhaps to calm himself. 'So, as I was saying . . . *because*, you know, you never know what's coming, when "it" comes . . .' Not for the first time that weekend, the air quotes were out, though this time they took Lisa's breath away. 'You kind of have to . . .'

'Just say it.'

'Go *with* it.'

Lisa locked eyes with him for a moment – one that seemed to last forever – then she reached up over her shoulder, grabbed hold of her seat belt and fastened it with a loud click.

Simon smiled, then he slipped the car into gear, checked the rear-view mirror, flicked the indicator and pulled away from the kerb.

'Where are we going?' he asked, so Lisa shrugged.

'Surprise me!' she said.

After all, if she *was* leaving things to fate, then perhaps she ought to start trusting it.

ACKNOWLEDGMENTS

Thanks:

To Sammia Hamer and the amazing (and too-many-to-mention-individually) Amazon Publishing team. Without you, I might have to get what my mother-in-law refers to as a 'proper' job.

To super-editor Sophie 'harsh-but-fair' Wilson, for turning my typing into something pretty much book-shaped.

To the fastidious (but not furious) Gemma Wain, for spoting all my misstakes.

To the lovely Zizi, for coming up with such a great title.

To the usual suspects (my lawyer advises me not to name names), for the continued supply of material/not suing me.

To the Board, for the regular, necessary sanity checks, and for being just the nicest, most supportive bunch *evah*.

To Tina, for everything else, and more.

And lastly (but by no means leastly), to everyone who's ever read, recommended or (nicely) reviewed one of my books. I (and my newly acquired expensive mountain biking habit – thanks, Joan!) am – and will continue to be – eternally grateful.

ABOUT THE AUTHOR

Photo © 2014, Cassandra Nelson

British writer Matt Dunn is the author of thirteen (and counting) romantic comedy novels, including *A Day at the Office* and *At the Wedding* (both Kindle bestsellers), *The Ex-Boyfriend's Handbook* (shortlisted for both the Romantic Novel of the Year Award and the Melissa Nathan Award for Comedy Romance) and *13 Dates* (shortlisted for the Romantic Comedy of the Year Award). He's also written about life, love and relationships for various publications including *The Times*, the *Guardian*, *Glamour*, *Cosmopolitan*, *Company*, *Elle* and the *Sun*. Before becoming a full-time writer, Matt worked as a lifeguard, a fitness-equipment salesman and an IT headhunter.